New W

An Antho

Michael Moorcock was editor of *New Worlds* from 1964 until 1971, and again in 1978. Born in London in 1939, he was contributing to and editing juvenile magazines such as *Tarzan Adventures* while still in his teens. As a writer of science fiction and fantasy he has acheived an international reputation: *Behold the Man*, the Jerry Cornelius tetralogy (*The Final Programme*, *A Cure for Cancer*, *The English Assassin* and *The Condition of Muzak*) and the novels in the Elric, Dancers at the End of Time, Hawkmoon and Corum series are classics of their kind. In recent years he has moved steadily away from this field and is now recognised as a major contemporary novelist, through such novels as *Gloriana*, *The Brothel in Rosenstrasse* and *Byzantium Endures*, the first volume of a long and ambitious work entitled *Between the Wars*.

Available in Fontana by Michael Moorcock

Byzantium Endures

New Worlds
An Anthology

Edited by
Michael Moorcock

FLAMINGO

Published by Fontana Paperbacks

Acknowledgements

With the exception of *Traveller's Rest* by David I. Masson, which is
reprinted by permission of Messrs Faber and Faber, who control the
rights to Masson's collection *The Caltraps of Time* (currently out of print),
all stories are published here by permission of the authors, who hold the
copyright on their work.

Gravity copyright © Giles Gordon 1968
Concentrate 3 copyright © Michael Butterworth 1970
Dr Gelabius copyright © Hilary Bailey 1968
The Four-Colour Problem copyright © Barrington Bayley 1971
Running Down copyright © M. John Harrison 1975
The Eye of the Lens copyright © Langdon Jones 1968
The Assassination Weapon copyright © J. G. Ballard 1966
The Heat Death of the Universe copyright © Pamela Zoline 1967
The Valve Transcript copyright © Joel Zoss 1968
The Tank Trapeze copyright © Michael Moorcock 1969
Angouleme copyright © Thomas M. Disch 1971
Scream copyright © Giles Gordon 1968
Masterson and the Clerks copyright © John T. Sladek 1967
Multi-Value Motorway copyright © Brian W. Aldiss 1967
Traveller's Rest copyright © David I. Masson 1965
A Landscape of Shallows copyright © Christopher Finch 1968
The Disaster Story copyright © Charles Platt 1966
Conversations at Ma Maia Metron copyright © Robert Meadley 1975
No Direction Home copyright © Norman Spinrad 1971
Mr Black's Poems of Innocence copyright © D. M. Thomas 1969
The Soft World Sequence copyright © George MacBeth 1967
Space Hopping With Captain God copyright © John T. Sladek 1969
Scholia, Seasoned With Crabs, Blish Is copyright © John Clute 1973
Sweet Analytics copyright © M. John Harrison 1975
A Literature of Acceptance copyright © Michael Moorcock 1968
Alphabets of Unreason copyright © J. G. Ballard 1969
Language Mechanisms copyright © Christopher Finch 1967
The Languages of Science copyright © David Harvey 1967
The Circle of the White Horse copyright © Francis Arnold 1952
A version of the Introduction appeared in *Foundation*
  copyright © Michael Moorcock 1979

Contents

Dedicated to all those enthusiasts, readers, writers, editors and publishers, who kept *New Worlds* alive for over the years, and especially to E. J. 'Ted' Carnell whose good sense and kindness is remembered with affection by everyone who worked with him.

Foreword

I have tried to include stories in this anthology which are not as frequently reprinted as some. The reader will therefore see that some 'quintessential' *New Worlds* stories are missing. I have also left out all the recipients of Nebula and Hugo Awards because these exist in volumes almost always in print. 'Behold the Man', 'A Boy and his Dog' by Harlan Ellison, 'Time Considered as a Helix of Semi-Precious Stones' by Delany and others are therefore excluded. I regret that I have not been able to include the longer material which we serialised, such as Disch's *Camp Concentration* or Ballard's *Crystal World*. With the exception of Frank Arnold's reminiscences I have excluded material from the eighteen years during which E. J. Carnell was editor. Again, most of the best of this exists in book form (see the Anthologies section at the end of the Appendix). I have had to exclude, because of length and because it is currently in print, the work of writers like Keith Roberts and Roger Zelazny who contributed a good deal of their most ambitious work to *New Worlds*. I must also admit that a fairly large proportion of the contents represents my personal choice of what I think was best in *New Worlds*, and in this I think I have indulged myself rather more than I did when I was editing the magazine. I have tried to reproduce, through my choice, some of the atmosphere of the magazine. Without graphics, editorials, letters and display type (the things which help give any magazine its special character) this has been difficult. A magazine has one thing which makes it attractive to readers and writers alike: a sense of freshness and immediacy. This anthology can only function as a retrospective look at *New Worlds* when the material you find here was printed for the first time. I should like to thank John Eggeling, Michael Ashley, Brian R. Tawn, Les Flood, Ken Slater and Linda Steele for their invaluable help in assembling the material for the introduction and appendix. Especial thanks to Francis – Frank – Arnold who played such a central part in starting *New Worlds* and keeping it going during its early years.

Introduction

I don't think it's safe to say that *New Worlds* is dead. It's true that, as I write, we have not seen an issue for a couple of years, but I am assured that two editors (R.G. Meadley and Richard Glyn Jones) are currently at work on the 217th issue, and it could have appeared before this introduction is published.

New Worlds has its origins in a cyclostyled fan magazine produced before the Second World War by a group of young sf enthusiasts which included Arthur C. Clarke, John Christopher, Charles Eric Maine, Jonathan Burke, William F. Temple and E.J. Carnell. It was then called *Nova Terrae*. A professional version almost appeared in 1939/40 but was shelved because of the War. In 1946, as various members of the original group were demobbed, the idea of *New Worlds* became a possibility again. Frank Arnold, whose reminiscences of those early days are reprinted in this collection, encouraged E.J. Carnell to take his plans for the magazine to Arnold's own publisher:

> There were many realistic arguments against such a visit but Frank convinced me that there was no harm in trying, so we walked along Chancery Lane into Lincoln's Inn and up to the top floor of No. 10 Old Square, where the name-plate read *Pendulum Publications Ltd*. There I was introduced to one Stephen D. Frances, a mercurial young man full of enthusiasm for science fiction (and later to become universally famed as thriller writer 'Hank Janson'). Steve Frances was convinced that sf would rapidly become a universally popular form of fiction – were we not already in the throes of a technological explosion brought on through the exigencies of war? He could see no end to the advancement of science or to the possibilities of science fiction going hand in hand with it. He was also a very astute young publisher . . . I finally left the office having been given carte blanche to edit and produce the first two issues of *New Worlds* on a quarterly basis. A flat fee was to be paid to myself out of which I would pay the authors.
>
> (John Carnell in *Visions of Tomorrow*, 1970)

Carnell wanted a magazine which would publish a distinctive kind of

British science fiction being produced by the increasing number of writers who had no home-based market. *New Worlds* became the first digest-sized (like *Lilliput*) sf magazine and was characteristically more sedate than its US counterparts in its choice of illustrations and captions. Through a number of ups and downs, supported often by nothing but the enthusiasm of Leslie Flood, G. Ken Chapman, Walter Gillings, Frank Arnold, Carnell himself and other members of the original consortium, it ran for eighteen years. During Carnell's editorship it published the work of most of the best British writers as well as stories by Americans which could not find markets in the more cautious and prudish US pulps. *New Worlds* soon came to be considered, in Britain and America, as the most 'literary' of the sf magazines. It received a Hugo Award (the only non-US magazine ever to do so); it published for a while a separate American edition; its influence became considerable. The Anthologies section of the Appendix (see p. 495) speaks for itself. Nova Publications, which had by this time been taken over by the larger firm of MacLaren, published a number of of novels in paperback which were, for their time, remarkable for the quality of their production. Two companion magazines were added: *Science Fantasy* (again developed from an amateur magazine, Gillings's *Science Fantasy Review*) and *SF Adventures* (originally a reprint US magazine which outlived its parent). By the 1950s *New Worlds* had begun to publish the early work of writers who, encouraged by Carnell, were breaking away from American sf models and rediscovering their own tradition, a Wellsian tradition coupling naturalistic narrative and characters with romantic imagery and idealism. These writers included Brian W. Aldiss, James White, Bob Shaw, John Brunner and Arthur Sellings, all of whom believed that popular writing should be well-written and have ambitious themes. In 1956 the lyrical and exotic stories of J. G. Ballard began to appear with 'Prima Belladona' (*SF*, December) and 'Escapement' (*NW*, December). Ballard's stories were received with considerable enthusiasm by Carnell. He privately preferred the romantic language and imagery he published in *Science Fantasy*. It was here that the first work of the so-called 'new wave' was to appear, far more frequently than in *New Worlds* itself.

In 1963 magazine circulations were declining badly and Nova Publications' parent company decided to close down *New Worlds* and *Science Fantasy*. *SF Adventures* (which had published Ballard's *The Drowned World*) was already dead. Carnell gave up any further attempts to nurse the magazines along and made arrangements with the publishing houses of Corgi and Dennis Dobson to edit an sf paperback series of original stories to be called *New Writings in SF*.

Although writers like Ballard and myself had the option of being published in American magazines, it seemed that a period of experimentation have been nipped in the bud. We had gradually been introducing more unconventional themes into our work. Ballard in particular had recently sold the reluctant but always open-minded Carnell his superb *The Terminal Beach*, and I had sold stories which at that time would have been unsaleable elsewhere. We knew there was little chance of more conservative magazines taking our work. The only short-story outlets of the time included *Argosy*, *Encounter*, *Paris Review* and *Playboy*, none of which would find our stories either comprehensible or, as often as not, of a suitable length. We considered the possibility of publishing a new magazine, and I prepared a dummy issue. It would be on art paper, to take good quality illustrations; it would be the size of, say, *Playboy* so that it would get good display space on the news-stands; it would specialise in experimental work by writers like Burroughs and artists like Paolozzi, but it would be 'popular', it would seek to publicise such experimenters; it would publish all those writers who had become demoralised by a lack of sympathetic publishers and by baffled critics; it would attempt a cross-fertilisation of popular sf, science and the work of the literary and artistic avant garde.

Meanwhile, a chance conversation between the *New Worlds* printer (who was looking for replacement work) and David Warburton (of the publishing firm of Roberts and Vinter) caused Warburton to decide to buy the magazines from Nova Publications. His firm had hitherto specialised in girlie magazines and, by coincidence, the paperback adventures of Hank Janson (no longer written by Frances). They needed an entré into a more respectable millieu. The sf magazines were already distributed by the powerful W.H. Smith and John Menzies chains. These chains, with virtually a monopoly of wholesale and retail outlets, could make or break a publication. The directors of Roberts and Vinter and its various parent companies thought they could follow behind the magazines with other publications which Smith's and Menzies had hitherto refused to handle. *New Worlds* and *Science Fantasy* were to become, of all things, a posh 'front'. David Warburton's ambition was to 'upmarket' his firm and begin publishing fiction of a reasonable quality. When he heard of Warburton's intention, Kyril Bonfiglioli, then an Oxford art-dealer and bookseller, now a successful comic novelist, asked if he could edit the magazines. Bonfiglioli was an sf reader, a friend of Brian Aldiss, and he shared many of Aldiss's views about the need to improve the quality of writing in sf. In the meantime, unknown to me, Carnell had put my name forward as editor. Although I was only 23, I had had a great deal of practical editorial experience and Carnell obviously saw me as someone who would promote and extend his editorial policies. Sensibly, Warburton decided to split the magazines between myself and Bonfiglioli. I was asked which I wanted. I said *New Worlds*. I showed him the dummy I had made and told him what I had in mind. He showed me a paperback printed on cheap paper. That was to be the format because it fitted in with their other publications. It would initially be bi-monthly, alternating with *Science Fantasy*. I accepted his decision. We agreed that we would re-think the format if the magazine increased its sales. My first issue (no. 142) was for May–June 1964. It contained a new serial commissioned from Ballard (*The Crystal World*); an article on William Burroughs by Ballard; an editorial by me ('A New Literature for the Space Age') and work by Aldiss, Brunner and Barrington Bayley, almost none of which would have previously been acceptable to the magazines of the day but which now seems very ordinary (Brunner's 'The Last Lonely Man' was successfully televised and remains one of his very best short stories).

Although much more sophisticated in its ideas and intentions, it retained the old messianic tone of most sf magazines (and writers) but now it attacked the 'literary establishment' as well as social institutions and scientific orthodoxy. 'Certain British writers,' I wrote in my first editorial, 'are producing a kind of sf which is unconventional in every sense and which must soon be recognised as an important revitalisation of the literary mainstream. More and more people are turning away from the fast-stagnating pool of the conventional novel – and they are turning to science fiction (or speculative fantasy). This is a sign, among others, that a *popular* literary renaissance is around the corner. Together, we can accelerate that renaissance.' Elsewhere, Ballard was to say of Burroughs: 'His three novels are the first definite portrait of the inner landscape of our mid-century, using its own language and manipulative techniques, its own fantasies and nightmares ... The almost complete inability of English critics to understand Burroughs is as much a social failure as a literary one, a refusal to recognise the materials of the present decade as acceptable for literary purposes until a lapse of a generation or so has given to a few brand names an appropriately discreet nostalgia. One result is the detachment of the English social novel from everyday life to a point where it is fast becoming a minor genre as unrelated to common experience as the country house detective story (by contrast the great merit of science fiction has been its ability to assimilate rapidly the materials of the immediate present and future, although it is now failing in precisely those areas where the future has already become the past). Whatever his reservations about some aspects of the mid-twentieth century, Burroughs accepts that it can be fully described only in terms of its own language, its own idioms and verbal lore.'

This approach was not to every reader's taste, and although we gained circulation, we also lost a number of regular subscribers. No one had been prepared, it seemed, for what we intended to try to do. Although I had written a number of critical articles and 'guest editorials' for the Carnell magazines, my reputation with regular readers was for the Elric stories and other fantastic romances in the tradition of Haggard, Merritt and Howard, which I had published regularly in *Science Fantasy* since 1961. I had had a few stories in *New Worlds*, but none of these was remarkable. Therefore it was expected that I would choose *Science Fantasy*. I chose *New Worlds* because the title was open to a number of potential interpretations and I felt that if the magazine was worth taking over (I had been reluctant to edit a purely sf magazine; I had little relish for most sf) then it should become the vehicle for various ideas I had had for some time. These ideas had been given encouragement and clearer shape by my friendship with J.G. Ballard, whose enthusiasm vindicated many of my half-hearted attempts to find out what was 'wrong' with the sf genre and most modern literature in general. In this, at that time, I was somewhat at odds with the other group, who were also critical of the state of sf writing but seemed to believe that it could 'rise' to the level of contemporary fiction exemplified by Anthony Powell or Lawrence Durrell. This was the group which came to publish two issues of its critical journal *SF Horizons*. They were equally vociferous in their condemnation of bad writing and bad thinking in sf. Comprised primarily of Brian Aldiss, Harry Harrison and Tom Boardman (the publisher), the group's opinions differed from mine only in degree. My views were more radical. I did not share, for instance, its enthusiasm for the work and opinions of writers whom I regarded as mediocre. I believed that a different kind of fiction, perhaps developing different kinds of narrative technique, could come out of a marriage between existing 'experimental' forms and old-style genre sf. I believed that we needed more rigorous criticism to seek definitions of the forms we were working in, since we were all somewhat confused. I found, for instance, the sf criticism of Amis, Crispin and Conquest condescending, fatuous and weary. Characterised by a kind of hearty complacency and defiant philistinism, it had a blowsy air to it. It was no better than the pieties of Sunday newspaper lead-reviewers which had in common the atmosphere of the social club, the saloon bar, the locker room. I was far too puritanical to respond either to the pieties or the philistinism. I had a relish for contemporary forms of fiction as well as a passion for the classics. I found most English fiction of the fifties and sixties worn-out, cliché-ridden, laborious, seemingly the tail-end of a literary movement which had begun in the twenties and petered out by the forties. This 'modern' fiction was unadventurous; it was cautious of criticism; its aspirations were safe and they were low. The lush romantic generalisations of writers like Colin Wilson seemed specious and equally dull. I had been bored by most Osborne plays. I had no idea what 'Damn you, England' meant. I had suffered no traumas from the A-Bomb or the Suez Crisis. Most modern poetry seemed mean and self-conscious. I enjoyed the work of Burgess and Angus Wilson (perhaps because they contained stronger imaginative elements and a genuine passion for literature) and I liked the early books of Iris Murdoch and William Golding, but most of those who received high praise in the fifties I found unoriginal and uninteresting. One could find better popular writing in *Sexton Blake Library* (which I had edited as a teenager) than in the work, say, of Ian Fleming. I saw Cyril Connolly refer to Ian Fleming as 'a master craftsman' and was genuinely astonished. Fleming's style, structure and imagination would have shamed any regular contributor to *Detective Weekly* or *Black Mask*. I was bewildered when, on occasions, I expressed a liking for Ronald Firbank or Henry Green, whom I 'discovered' in my teens, and was jeered at! Few of my highly praised contemporaries seemed capable of constructing a simple narrative, let alone a story on several levels of interpretation. Few showed any passion for language or relish for the world. Many claimed to identify themselves with the working class and yet were afraid to betray any sort of vulgar taste. Vulgar writing, like Fleming's, had to be dignified, justified, explained. An appalling hypocrisy seemed to exist everywhere. A conspiracy of self-deceit.

By the early 1960s it seemed to me that the very writers whose opinions we had rejected had reappeared and were trying to advise us on how to produce a form of fiction which I and a few others had begun to develop on our own account! It was shocking to be condescended to by Robert Conquest; to be taken aside by Edmund Crispin and told, over some gin or other, that all our ideas had been tried and found wanting in the 1920s, that the appeal of the sf genre was that it *was* a genre, fulfilling like the mystery story, certain acceptable genre expectations.

Those first editorials and articles, almost entirely written by Ballard and myself, were therefore often fiercely opinionated and probably over-stated, largely in reaction to these new conservatives who had appeared (with *New Maps of Hell*, the *Spectrum* anthologies, reviewing spots in the *Observer* and *Sunday Times* and so on) to advise sf writers (and anyone else) against anything but the most gentle of ambitions. Amis, with his lazy paradoxes, reviewed the first issue of *New Worlds* we produced by referring to Burroughs as not the far more interesting and imaginative Edgar Rice but the boring William. The fruity ghost of Chesterton, never far away, was wagging the finger it had once waved at Wells. We celebrated the work of William Burroughs and invoked the names of surrealists, romantics, imagists, allegorists. Borges, Hesse, Peake, Calvino, Kafka, Wyndham Lewis, Vian (then hardly any of them available to an English public) were called upon as examples not necessarily because they were admired but because their techniques, their angles of attack, were different. *New Worlds* evolved into an avant garde magazine through necessity, not through any abstract ambition to be different,* *and it retained a popular audience.* A disgruntled audience, sometimes, or a confused one, but a fascinated one which continued to buy the issues. The writers had few enthusiasms in common. I had no interest in Dali, whom Ballard frequently mentioned, nor in Nabokov, who was much admired by Langdon Jones; they did not share my liking for, say, Brecht. My view of writers like Pynchon or Barth was that they were clumsily, by means of long-winded parody, trying to achieve results already achieved in *New Worlds.* We published Pynchon's *Entropy* for the first time in England, however. Being easily bored ourselves, I think we stimulated readers who were equally bored with most of what was offered to them.

The fifties had been a demoralising time for anyone not interested in jazz or party politics. I was ten in 1950. By 1955 I was completely confused by the opinions and prejudices of those only slightly older than me. Although my reading had been wide I had had a boyhood enthusiasm for Edgar Rice Burroughs and by 1955 was publishing a Burroughs fanzine, which gradually evolved into a general magazine as my interest in E.R.B. waned. By 1956 I was a professional commercial writer. By 1957 I had become editor of the juvenile magazine *Tarzan Adventures* and had already altered its format and contents radically to include far more text and far less strip. Contemporary literary and artistic life was pretty dull. Only in the sf magazines did one occasionally come across imaginative work. Bester's remarkable *The Demolished Man* and *The Stars My Destination* appeared in *Galaxy* in 1952 and 1956. Ballard published his first stories in 1956 and had begun to appear regularly in *New Worlds* and *Science Fantasy* by 1957. Borges was yet to be published by New Directions in the USA (I first had his work *recounted* to me – along with that of Calvino – by a multi-lingual Swede in Uppsala) and it would be some years before Calder published him here. William Burroughs had not begun his ambitious work. The best we had were the rather sentimental declarations of the beats – of Ginsberg and Kerouac; the declamations of Cowper Powys and Wyndham Lewis; the self-involved work of post-Dylan Thomas poets. Of living English writers only Mervyn Peake seemed to have an interest in contemporary life as well as a romantic relish for rich language and strong imagery, for characterisation which was neither fey nor misanthropic. He dared to use words and images and was neither plummy nor vaguely metaphysical. He had the wit of Maurice Richardson (whose superb *Exploits of Engelbrecht* had had limited publication in 1950 but was not reprinted until 1977), a Dickensian enjoyment of human eccentricity, an

*See a letter in *New Worlds* from Moorcock (March 1963). Also Guest Editorial, April 1963.

artist's original eye (for the angle at which a character sat, as well as for bizarre landscape). Peake described a world which equated with my experience. Peake appeared to *accept* the world, which was what made him so different from his contemporaries, most of whom were producing at best 'satires' on the level of Boulting Brothers comedies and who seemed to express a conventional distaste for the modern world. In the sf magazines, too, there regularly appeared writers who also accepted the world and who celebrated its wonders – Aldiss, Ballard, Bester, Harness, Cordwainer Smith, Sheckley. With little else in common, they shared a vigorous idealism and an ironic enjoyment of contemporary society. Their minds were not protected by cynicism, like those whose ideas had been formed by too much university and literary in-fighting, who fought an 'establishment' of which they were spiritually a part, who denied their innocence. The sf writers ignored that establishment, either because they didn't know better or because they simply couldn't understand its assumptions. Sf was attractive because it was overlooked by the critics and it could be written unselfconsciously, just as, in the early days, it was possible to do interesting work in popular music as a rock and roll performer. There was no sense of having someone looking over your shoulder.

By 1960 most sf was messianic and naive (as in *Astounding*) or becoming cautiously literary (as in *Fantasy and Science Fiction*). The healthier pulps, *Planet, Super Science, Famous Fantastic Mysteries, Startling* had folded. *Galaxy* was past its prime. Most of the short-lived magazines had collapsed – *Fantastic Universe, Infinity,* and so on, were gone. *Amazing Stories* and *Fantastic Stories,* two of the longest running, were showing some signs of revived life under the editorship of Cele Goldsmith, who later ran Fritz Leiber's excellent fantasies, as well as work by Ballard, Zelazny and Disch. All these magazines, of course, were American. The other British magazines (*Nebula* and *Authentic*) had folded. The most interesting and humane sf had begun to appear in Carnell's *New Worlds* and *Science Fantasy*. What Ballard and I had in common was that our knowledge of sf was not profound. Neither of us had read most of the well-known writers or stories. We had no particular taste for them. Ballard enjoyed Bradbury. I enjoyed Bester. We imposed our own imagination on the rest of sf, thinking most of it was better than it actually was; when we had to read it (say, for reviews) we were therefore disappointed. We had turned to sf magazines because we had been unable to find much that we liked elsewhere. By the early 1960s a few of the less obscure imaginative writers were available, and we were delighted, though the dominating styles were not particularly attractive. The ecstatic prose of *The Journal of Albion Moonlight,* for instance, had no more appeal than the well-bred ironies of the Polish and Czech fabulists. However, as Burroughs (whom we did admire, of course) and Calvino and Borges and the others began to be published, we used their names at every opportunity, in articles and letters to the sf magazines. We were surprised by the lack of response from old-guard sf fans, who, we had assumed, were as hungry for real imagination as we had been. Naively, we had honestly expected that these readers would be more open to new kinds of writing. It took me some years to learn that a certain kind of sf fan is about the most conservative reader of all!

By 1964, I had already made several speeches at sf conventions, written a great deal of valedictory criticism of the writers I admired, scathingly attacked the sf and literary establishments for their complacency, and taken part in a long recriminatory correspondence in the *TLS* over William Burroughs's work (the 'UGH' controversy) in which I had defended Burroughs at length after a silly review, and Edith Sitwell had said that she didn't want to spend the rest of her life with her nose nailed to a lavatory seat, and Victor Gollancz, as I recall, bemoaned declining moral standards. As was usual, few of the writers who complained about Burroughs had actually read his books. I was an admirer of Burroughs's use of modern imagery and idiom, for his *metaphorical* use of sf ideas, for his ear for the language and ironies of the drug underworld and of the streets. He seemed the first writer to celebrate the present as well as to lampoon it. His work was ironic but it was not the obvious satire of *That Was The Week That Was* or *Private Eye* (both of which seemed, as the Angry Young Men had seemed, merely the other side of the Oxbridge middle-class coin). *The Naked Lunch*. *The Ticket that Exploded* and *The Soft Machine* in their Olympia Press editions fired us with fresh enthusiasm for our own work. It was not that we were actually influenced by Burroughs, but we were very much heartened by him. It could be significant that our enthusiasms were never reflected by the likes of *Private Eye*, whose philistinism extended to attacks on almost every attempted innovation in the arts and whose conservatism and implicit authoritarianism was as entrenched as that of its ostensible targets.

By the end of 1964, when we returned to a monthly schedule, *New Worlds* was encountering prejudice from the sf old guard, from the *SFH* group, from Amis, Crispin and so on, from the ordinary literary establishment, from American sf critics. Most of our criticism was moderate in tone. We had yet to publish much in the way of 'typical' work. And yet we received more letters of complaint than letters of praise. My experience on popular magazines, however, had shown that it did not take long for people to get used to changes. The circulation had gone up (doubtless due to improved distribution) and a new generation of writers was beginning to appear. The early work of these young writers was not particularly polished, of course, but it had that enthusiasm we sought. Soon, alongside good conventional sf by the likes of Roger Zelazny, Keith Roberts, Barrington Bayley, George Collyn, Daphne Castell, Arthur Sellings, John Brunner and Harry Harrison, we ran the early 'experimental' work of Thomas M. Disch, Langdon Jones, Peter Tate, Michael Butterworth, Graham Hall, Charles Platt and others, who also contributed more or less familiar kinds of fiction as well. Ballard remained the backbone of *New Worlds*'s policy. His influence was seminal and it was profound. We were soon publishing his first 'concentrated novels' (of which 'The Assassination Weapon' was one). By 1966, when we increased our pages, we had achieved what many people still think was an admirable balance between the old-style sf and the new fiction which had no generic name but which Americans were beginning to call 'the British new wave'. Some of those who had initially felt a certain reservation about what we were doing began to contribute. We began to receive stories from Brian Aldiss, hitting one of his finest and most creative veins, which culminated with his Charteris stories – later expanded to book-length as *Barefoot in the Head*. David I. Masson became a regular contributor, beginning with the superb 'Traveller's Rest'. Masson was to contribute a handful of brilliant short stories before he appeared to stop writing fiction completely (all his *New Worlds* stories were collected in *The Caltraps of Time*, 1968). Keith Roberts – who wrote primarily for Bonfiglioli's *Science Fantasy* (of which he was to become assistant editor) – contributed some of his best stories. We were receiving work from Disch which became more and more adventurous while retaining that sound, disciplined feeling for prose which marks all his writing (and which, I like to think, marks that of the typical *New Worlds* contributor). John Sladek became a regular. We published some of Roger Zelazny's best stories (notably 'For A Breath I Tarry') and Americans such as Kit Reed, Robert Silverberg, Kris Neville, J.J. Mundis and Samuel R. Delany. We began to publish George MacBeth and other poets fascinated with contemporary life. We published the long and most complex poems of D.M. Thomas. Our criticism began to find its own vocabulary and came gradually to define what we were trying to do.

In the meantime *Science Fantasy* had changed its name to *SF Impulse* but continued to show a penchant for publishing rather whimsical 'English' stories. It had certainly published some good material by Aldiss and Roberts (his *Pavane* mainly appeared there), but its ambition to improve standards of writing in the genre hadn't much shape, and Bonfiglioli, although a charming man, was not a hard-working editor. In 1966 he resigned, and for a few days J.G. Ballard was editor, before failing to be reconciled either with the publisher or with his assistant editor, the patient Keith Roberts. Roberts refused the editorship out of loyalty to Bonfiglioli – although Roberts was chiefly responsible for publishing most of the best work to appear in the magazine. Harry Harrison took over and turned *Impulse* into a pretty good version of a US-style sf magazine. By the end of 1966 the bankruptcy of Roberts and Vinter's distributors caused them to re-think their policy and to abandon their 'posh' books and magazines in order to retrench. They returned to soft pornography and we were told that *New Worlds* and *SF Impulse* were to fold. By this time we had developed an excellent team, with Keith Roberts doing most of the covers for both magazines, Charles Platt designing *New Worlds* typographically (his designs were to be much imitated) and Langdon Jones playing an increasingly important part as assistant editor. Once again it seemed we were to fold just before we could begin a new stage. I started to fight to keep *New Worlds* alive. We survived a little longer than *Impulse* by incorporating it into our magazine. Expecting to go down, we fired off all the guns we had left. In March 1967 we published a novel which had found no publisher anywhere but which I had enjoyed a great deal, Brian Aldiss's *Report on Probability A*. One of the other stories in that issue was Ballard's 'The Assassination of John Fitzgerald Kennedy Considered as a Downhill Motor Race' (after Jarry), which his American agent had thought too unpleasant to send on to Harlan Ellison's new anthology *Dangerous Visions*.

The April issue (confusingly mis-dated March) was the last paperback issue and something of a rag-bag of the material I did not particularly want to use in the next issue. This was to run Disch's outstanding *Camp Concentration* (announced tentatively in the April issue, when we hoped 'to be seen in an entirely new format'). At this stage we had very little hope that we would find a publisher.

Brian Aldiss, who had begun by being extremely sceptical of *New Worlds*'s policies, now worked energetically on the magazine's behalf. David Warburton and I discussed forming a company just to publish the *New Worlds* I had originally had in mind. In the meantime, Brian Aldiss contacted various well-known writers and critics and asked them to approach, with him, the Arts Council. He hoped that a grant would save both magazines.

I had no belief whatsoever that the Arts Council would look twice at the application. I was grateful to Brian for his enthusiasm, but I neither expected nor wanted a grant. I had, in fact, a prejudice against Arts Council patronage which I believe to be deterimental to the arts supported. When the grant was given to *New Worlds* (thanks, it emerged, primarily to Angus Wilson, who was familiar with the magazine and who was then Chairman of the Arts Council Literature Panel) I was astonished. We were to receive £150 an issue. The cash was in itself not enough to keep us going, but the attendant prestige gave David Warburton the confidence to agree to publish 'my' *New Worlds*.

He accepted responsibility for the printing while I undertook to pay contributors and editorial expenses. The large-size *New Worlds* (173) was launched in July 1967. That issue was the first English-language magazine to publish the graphic work of M.C. Escher. Our serial was Disch's *Camp Concentration*. The other contributors were J.G. Ballard, John Sladek, Dr Christopher Evans, Pamela Zoline ('The Heat Death of the Universe', her first story), David I. Masson, Charles Platt, George MacBeth, Roger Zelazny and Brian W. Aldiss. The next issue was to include Langdon Jones's 'The Time Machine', but the printer refused to print it ('too dirty') and it subsequently appeared, in edited form, in Damon Knight's *Orbit* collection. In its place we published the first stories of Gene Wolfe and James Sallis, both talented Americans. The same issue contained Christopher Finch's first art article, on Eduardo Paolozzi (Paolozzi himself was now on the masthead as 'Aeronautics Advisor'), Peter Tate, Michael Butterworth and Brian Aldiss ('Multi-Value Motorway'). The cover was a collage of Paolozzi's *Moonstrips Empire News*. The first five issues did not sell the numbers needed to make the venture attractive to David Warburton. By November 1967, when 177 appeared, it seemed yet again that *New Worlds* was to fold. While I had been in America, David Warburton had decided to end his involvement with the magazine and had gone to Scotland, leaving a note to tell me that the magazine was now mine to do with as I pleased.

Publicity in, as I remember, *The Times* Diary, led to Silvester Stein of Stonehart Publications appearing on the scene, offering to publish the magazine. I never did understand his motives. I think they were amiable enough. The firm specialized in financial newsletters and property advice, although Stein himself had been associated with *Drum* in South Africa. He was full of enthusiasm, although our communications were always poor. We missed a couple of weeks in our schedule, but were out again with a December–January issue, which was the first to run Norman Spinrad's serial about political corruption in a near future United States. *Bug Jack Barron* was another book which had been unable to find a publisher before we took it.

By this time I was slightly crazy, due, I suppose, to the worries involved in publishing the magazine. None of the writers was supported by the Arts Council grant, which David Warburton and subsequently Silvester Stein had put towards printing costs, and I was having to write books to pay them, as well as staff wages, running expenses, and so on. *New Worlds* 178 had a rather more manic visual style than before. The title of Thomas M. Disch's short story 'Linda and Daniel and Spike' had been lettered onto the bare back of our Advertising Manager, Diane Lambert, and was featured on the cover with a TV set (Spinrad's story was about the uses of television), a car (for Aldiss's 'Auto-Ancestral Fracture') and a movie projector (for Ed Emshwiller's visual feature *Movies*). In the next issue we began an attack on what we regarded as undisciplined and directionless romanticism in popular art. 'Barbarella and the Anxious Frenchman' was a visual feature attacking the contemporary enthusiasm for comic strips and technology and bizarre sexual imagery which had come with the Swinging Sixties. It was puritanical, sardonic and asked 'Has the Fad for the Bad Gone Too Far?' It attacked, needless to say, many of those things most associated in some people's minds with *New Worlds*: sensationalism for its own sake, fashionable crazes, a superficial understanding of scientific developments and so on. Films like *Barbarella*, books like *The Penguin Book of Comics*, the vogue for old Batman serials and *The Lord of the Rings*, for bad rock-and-roll and James Bond were all condemned as substitutes for genuine exercises of the imagination. In 180 we continued this theme with an attack on, among others, the Maharishi, degenerating popular music, fashionable sadism and so on. We also ran a long story by Langdon Jones, 'The Eye of the Lens,' and the second part of Spinrad's bitter attack on corrupt politics (anticipating much of the mood and detail of the Watergate scandal), as well as Carol Emshwiller's 'Lib' and D.M. Thomas's 'The Head Rape'.

It was with this issue that we learned that W.H. Smith and Sons, in collaboration with John Menzies, had refused to distribute *New Worlds* on grounds of 'obscenity and libel' (we never did find out what they thought libellous) and a small furore began, which involved most of the press giving a fair amount of space to Smith's 'ban' on *New Worlds*. The *Daily Express* seized on this with glee and rang me up to ask if I'd let my children read *New Worlds* ('I'd be grateful if they'd read anything,' I said). In the House of Commons a Tory asked a question of the Minister for the Arts (Jennie Lee) why public money was being spent on filth, and in Manchester eleven copies were sold by a newsagent to a visiting football team, who were doubtless very disappointed.

I went to see W.H. Smith and Sons and found the head of the magazine division somewhat uncertain of his ground ('someone could sue us for obscenity and make a lot of money'), apparently prejudiced, and unwilling to distribute the magazine. We were not a 'little magazine' – that is, we depended on general distribution to the public. I explained that we were, among other things, objecting to the exploitation of sexuality. He responded to the key words (sex, politics and so on) as I have since seen magistrates respond in court – utterly without reference to their context – and remained disapproving. He told me that they were a family firm and that they had to think of their customers. Their customers would be upset by Smith's stocking *New Worlds*. I pointed to his desk on which lay a modish magazine specialising in soft pornographic photo-stories (it was called *Zeta*). I said that they were prepared to distribute that, which quite specifically exploited sexuality. He murmured that it was a different case. ('That sells 100,000 copies.') He told me that they would rethink their decision if I would agree to modify the magazine's contents and 'kill' the Spinrad serial. I refused. I pointed out that the whole reason for the magazine's existence was to publish fiction which could not otherwise find a publisher. The ideas were so strange to him that he could only answer that W.H. Smith and Sons might be 'sued for libel'. Since all the characters were fictitious, it seemed to me that he was remembering something about *Private Eye* (which his firm had also refused to handle) and was dimly relating the two magazines. The scene was reminiscent of any story involving dumb bureaucracy and I began to go mad. I left.

New Worlds did not benefit from this notoriety. Our circulation depended on Smiths and Menzies. We needed regular newsstand sales to justify our policy. We needed to be available across the country. Moreover, of course, our finances depended completely on maintaining our original distribution. We were not prepared to become another Arts Council-supported little magazine. In the end, rather surprised and upset by the bad publicity, Smith's agreed to take the magazine back. This agreement, however, proved to be ineffective. Our circulation was never to be the same, and Stonehart began to lose enthusiasm for the project. The printers were not paid. There was a nasty quarrel over the Arts Council grant (another reason, I think, why I have never approved of such grants) and Stonehart refused to pay contributors (they had agreed that the Arts Council money should go to contributors since by this time I was broke). The magazine schedules began to be affected as the printer refused to deliver until Stonehart paid his bill. No issues were published for May and June 1968. The July issue, like earlier issues, was largely financed by income from fantasy novels I was writing at a horrible rate, and bore on its cover the slogan WHAT IS THE EXACT NATURE OF THE CATASTROPHE? We were getting into another fresh period of work in which our ambition to blend the artistic avant garde with the worlds of science and popular fiction seemed to be fulfilled at last. There were no August and September issues for 1968. When the October issue was finally published, with its cover by Mal Dean, it bore the question WHAT DO YOU NEED? and was the first issue to be wholly published by me, with full responsibility for all the finance of the magazine. Fearing that we must fold soon, we next ran a special All New Writers Issue, which published the work of Brian Vickers, Robert Holdstock, Graham Charnock, Chris Lockesley and M. John Harrison, among others. We had an office in Portobello Road, we shared typesetters with *Oz*, *International Times* and other 'underground' magazines, but we were still determinedly following our own policies. The next issue ran an Aldiss story in his earlier mode ' . . . And the Stagnation of the Heart', an excellent story by a new writer, Joel Zoss ('The New Agent') and Disch's strange fantasy about heroin addiction, 'The Colours'. We also ran – reluctantly as far as I was concerned – Samuel R. Delany's 'Time Considered as a Helix of Semi-Precious Stones'. I never liked the story. I found it inconsequential, very ordinary conventional stuff. It subsequently won both the Nebula Award (presented by the Science Fiction Writers of America) and the Hugo Award (presented at the World Science Fiction Convention every year). That issue also ran my second Jerry Cornelius short (the first to be published) 'The Delhi Division'. The Cornelius stories caught the imagination of Jim Sallis, then an editor on *New Worlds*, and various other writers, who spontaneously began to write stories around the Cornelius themes or the character of Cornelius. The Cornelius stories were a form in themselves, and this, I think, is what attracted so many writers of such various talents as Sallis, Spinrad, Aldiss, Harrison and a good many others. Langdon Jones wrote a narrative poem with Cornelius as the central character.

We were now beginning to find our feet and the work was, for the first time as far as I was concerned, showing an even quality of inventive writing and original subject matter. We continued to sing the praises of Peake (whom we published regularly: usually his drawings and fragments of prose) and of foreign imaginative writers then beginning to appear in England and America. We were enthusiastic, the majority of us, about Kosinski, Barthelme, Vian and others. We continued to try to formulate a theory of criticism which could deal with such writers, since it was still obvious that modern criticism was unable to cope with this kind of work, whether the critic praised or condemned. We were further inconvenienced, on a basic level, by our distributor, who had quarrelled with Stonehart Publications and as a result pulped all our back numbers! We started fresher than we had planned with a larger and more ambitious series of issues beginning with No. 186. Lord Goodman, then Chairman of the Arts Council, had in the meantime become a little worried about the Council's support of the magazine but apparently had seen the name of Paolozzi on the masthead (still Aeronautics Advisor) and been reassured. By now we had a number of regular contributors who included myself, Ballard, Sladek, Harvey Jacobs, John Clute, D.M. Thomas, Brian Aldiss, Langdon Jones, John Brunner, Thomas M. Disch, M. John Harrison, Charles Platt, Michael Butterworth, Hilary Bailey, George MacBeth, Giles Gordon and Graham Charnock, and we were attracting an increasing number of writers, both new and established. Our graphics became more interesting. We ran drawings and photographs by a variety of artists and photographers. As well as features on artists like Richard Hamilton, Peter Phillips and Colin Self, we ran original graphics by Peake,

Nasemann, Mal Dean, Haberfield, Zoline, Vivienne Young, Glyn Jones, Jay Myrdahl, Douthwaite and others; for a brief while the film-maker Stephen Dwoskin was our designer. It seemed that we were receiving more good work than it was possible to publish. Our schedules were still, however, erratic and our sales poor. We ran on schedule as a monthly between January 1969 (in the March issue we published Harlan Ellison's 'A Boy and his Dog') and July 1969, when we realised that we were getting huge numbers of returns from the wholesalers in the form of boxes which had never actually been distributed. We had built up an enormous debt (because of course we had to pay for the printed copies) and the wholesalers had 'sat' on the copies rather than send them out to their own retail shops. We were forced to reduce the number of pages and work within a budget that was stricter than ever. We dealt with our new printer on a cash basis so that we could not run into the kind of debt we had already incurred and I began work again to pay off the bills, turning over the editorship almost entirely to Charles Platt, who typeset, balanced the books, dealt with the printer, supervised the design (by Nigel Francis) and fulfilled almost every other function virtually single-handedly.

The first of the issues with fewer pages appeared in August 1969. The next issue was for September/October. The issue for November featured Ian Watson's first story, 'Roof Garden Under Saturn'. Platt began to specialise in 'theme' issues. No. 197 (for January 1970) bore the slogan FORGET ABOUT 1970. WHAT ABOUT 1980? Platt's editorial began: 'There has been a monumental dullness about predictions for 1970. Laborious extrapolations of trends in technology, communications, population, food supply – man himself has been included only as a rudimentary button-pusher, a mere unit of society.' Ed Bryant was another new young American writer to appear in that issue. No. 198 contained work by Gwyneth Craven, Paul Green and Ian Watson. The 200th issue featured these and others, as well as Philip Jose Farmer's 'The Jungle Rot Kid on the Nod': Tarzan as written by William rather than Edgar Rice Burroughs. I had a 'guest editorial' in that issue which concluded, '*New Worlds* was the first magazine to see that a serious, coherent and vital modern literature could be developed from the stuff of science fiction. Very few people took it seriously when it was first proposed but the truth has since been demonstrated. I hope *New Worlds* will continue to demonstrate that truth for many more issues.' No. 200 was in fact the last of its particular series to be sold to the general public. Charles Platt's health collapsed and he came close to having a nervous breakdown. Debts had become too large to cope with and my own private problems had to take precedence. I couldn't take on any more epics (I was already committed to several). With No. 201, the Special Good Taste Issue, featuring 'Feathers from the Wings of an Angel' by Thomas M. Disch, an Index and various reprints from nineteenth-century magazines, sent out only to subscribers, we wound things up, wrote to the Arts Council saying we no longer needed a grant, and Charles went to live in America, where he has been ever since. We had already made plans for *New Worlds Quarterly*. We were back to paperback format, published simultaneously in America and Britain, running illustrations and editorial matter as a magazine, but distributed and paid for as a conventional book. We ran for a year on the quarterly basis and then became an occasional. We still were mainly living off our fat, publishing some of the best stories we had ever published and determinedly publishing new writers every issue (R.G. Meadley was one), but we had lost the spark which had made the monthly magazine what it was, for all that we were paying contributors regularly at far higher rates. With No. 7 I decided that I no longer had my editorial touch (I couldn't read sf at all) and handed over to Hilary Bailey, who did a refreshing job of editing the paperback issues and finding new writers until disputes with the publisher made us decide to stop.

To this day I don't know if *New Worlds* achieved anything which would not have happened anyway. But perhaps there is some satisfaction in seeing Anthony Burgess express opinions about sf in the *Observer* in almost exactly the terms used in *New Worlds* some fifteen years before. We fought against cynicism. One of the few things which consoles me is that Tom Disch, after delivering the last episode of *Camp Concentration* said, 'I wouldn't have made it as good if I hadn't known it was going to appear in *New Worlds*.'

In Spring 1978 a large-size issue, consisting mainly of reprints of work done for other magazines by *New Worlds* regulars, was distributed on an exceptionally limited scale. The response to this was good enough for me to do a further issue. No. 213 contained no narrative fiction but concentrated primarily on polemics, attacking what it regarded as moribund in the literary world of 1978. The magazine was deliberately published on an irregular basis, by a consortium consisting of an editorial team (including my then wife Jill Riches, Charles Platt and others) and the printer, Charles Partington. This was successful enough for us to publish No. 214 in the autumn of 1978 and sell out the issue. I decided to do with *New Worlds* what I had once done with Jerry Cornelius, and offer the magazine to anyone who wanted to try their hand at an issue. 215 was published that winter in Manchester by Michael Butterworth and David Britton (whose Savoy Editions firm reprinted many of the old *NW* writers). 216 was published in September 1979 by Charles Platt, who subsequently removed most of our remaining stock of back issues to his own flat, which a few months later burnt down destroying the issues (and almost destroying me, for I'd been staying there when the fire broke out). My ideal was to put *New Worlds* on as free a basis as possible; I've since decided that the policy was probably a little over-idealistic. The title of the magazine is still registered in my name and it is probable that I shall eventually produce another series. I still believe that there should be a magazine which bridges the various cultures of our time, which consistently takes a radical policy, which retains a good deal of anger and contempt for literary complacency, which persists in its belief in experiment. So long as they appear fairly regularly, magazines produce their own kind of energy. They can publish work by a lot of people relatively quickly; they are malleable in a way in which books can never be. Cross-fertilisation is often very rapid; contributors and readers become quickly heated over issues which are probably not very important in themselves but which generate more ideas, more work. This anthology cannot possibly reproduce the atmosphere which existed for us between 1964 and 1971. Neither is it possible to imitate what happened then. *New Worlds* in that period was not merely its graphics, its articles, its controversies or, indeed, its fiction. It was an ambience; its contributors and editors were optimistic, often naive, sometimes unskilled. One can occasionally feel nostalgic for that ambience, but one can never bring it back to life. All an anthology like this one can successfully do is to select some of the most interesting examples from what was, in its own small way, a revolutionary and stimulating period and to remind the reader that it is anger, impatience, optimism and idealism, not nostalgia of any sort, which creates the most worthwhile and lasting changes.

Michael Moorcock,
Ladbroke Grove 1978
North Yorkshire 1981

Gravity
HARVEY JACOBS

I am Bogardus Blik. But I use the name *Morris Nucleus* in my writings.

Nucleus, naturally, for direct association with the Atomic Age of which I am the proudest citizen. *Morris* because that name has always been exotic to me – musky, tumescent, hairy, benevolent, and the wise kind of shy.

My actual name will be new to you. My *non de plume* will mean nothing. Don't sweat.

I have been innocuous as a pebble. I work as a computer programmer in a bank just outside Houston, Texas. I hardly socialize. I live alone in a rented room. And I have published nothing. Not yet. With reason. I am saving.

When my work is done to satisfaction I will release it, ah, it will fall off by itself. Then you will know me. I will be a household word in palaces of power and workers' flats. Such fame will follow that a sun will blaze always in my mottled eyes. Notoriety is pain. I despise it. But it is inevitable since the work I am coping with is epic. And I am more *humous* than *posthumous* by nature.

For now I relish privacy and the dank-dark of obscurity. Later I will suffer plenty from flashbulbs burning the skin off my bones. So let these be tranquil years, years of sweet study and discipline, years of peace.

Dammit, why do they pick at me? Am I a dessert? Yes, in a way.

I am watching television. A cub of a poetess in a literary magazine described the light of television as 'blue cellophane'. Lovely and accurate. I wrote her a letter. The blue cellophane crackles through my room. There on the launch pad at Cape Kennedy (Cape Canaveral to my soul – I have never accepted the change) is the latest of our Moonships poised and smouldering like a young phallus. Look at it and sing.

Morris Nucleus sits eating a mallomar straining for flight. I feel the selfish power of that steaming rocket. I have all to do to keep from yanking myself around the room by my organ. Not in the spirit of a *Portnoy* who masturbates to pull things from within. In the spirit of *Icarus*, in an age beyond wings. It is marvelous to be alive at this hour. We are spreading the legs of the Universe. We will be remembered, if there are memories at work.

Only yesterday I read that 53.2 percent of our population would divert funds from the Space Program. The poor idiots fail to comprehend. I am last to blame them. The New Technology has not communicated its mystique or its message. The sheep see Science as a diplomat of death. Why not? Who has shown them a neutron smiling? They have seen smoking Japs. When my book is published things will be different. They will clamor. There will be demonstrations. Flowers will cover our laboratories. Cut the Space budget? Castrate God?

Give me time. I need time and leisure. Cancer, go home.

They are counting down. Emotion puffs my blue cellophane bag. Ten. Nine. Eight. Seven. Six. Aieee. There is trouble. The countdown is holding. My insides are ignited. Let me off the ground!

The smooth voice of Mission Control. The trouble is minor. Nothing. It is repaired. Now. Five. Four. Three. Two. One. Zero. Blastoff. What a word! Oops. I am lifting, I am pushing, I am a rising vibration. I am gone.

Minutes into my flight I detach my first stage. I wait, count seconds, burn. My second stage is gone. My useless leaden ass falls backward into water. I have attained orbital velocity. Glory to this glorious nation and the glories known and unknown and boons and gifts she has bequeathed. Oh beautiful for spacious skies. Oh beautiful. I would not like to be a Bulgarian sulking at home today. Of course we fly for Bulgarians too but it is better to be part of the heart. And this is an American story.

An animation is on the screen. Jules Bergman tells me that my Spaceship is streaking around the globe. We have made another star. Inside there are men and they are giants. I am proud for every race.

Why am I listed? Soon the telephone will ring.

The telephone rings. Little bitch. Our Ship is barely in range of the Canary Islands tracking station much less Jodrell Bank. Fleshmonger. She must begin her dialing, area code and all, at the moment of liftoff. She must wait for the last digit. She knows how I feel about actual staging and confirmation of apogee and perigee. She knows by now. When it is determined that the mission is safely away she tugs at the dial. And my passive turd of a Princess phone does its *dingle*. This cretin answers.

'Huh? What is it?' (My voice is rage and rejection.)

'Morris?' (Honey flows out of my Princess tunnel.)

'Don't ever call me that.' (A spasm, not a voice.)

'Bogardus, then.' (She is really frightened.)

'Yes.' (Mellowing. Why?)

'You know who this is, don't you?' (Bathwater on soapy thighs.)

'I know.' (A shortness of breath. My plague.)

'Did you watch? He got off all right.' (Would she call through tragedy?)

'Of course I watched. What would I do, not watch?' (I am too soft.)

'Then come to me.' (Leaves from last summer blowing in new spring wind.)

'You can't be serious. We pledged . . . ' (Liquid oxygen turning to mist.)

'Bogardus, I need you. I can't help the way I feel. And it's the only time we can be absolutely sure.' (Petulant appetite. I feel her wet.)

'It is not right. It is wrong.'

'How can anything so . . . holy . . . be wrong? You'll come. I know you won't leave me like this.'

'You trade on my worst instincts. You interrupt my work. You make stalactites grow from my soul. You give me such astonishing guilt that I'll end up like a parsnip. Oh, I'll come. I'll lumber over. But you won't get one hot drop out of me, not this time.'

'Let me try.'

'Then try, bitch. You risk a noisy divorce. I risk damnation. A hell of a lot you care.'

'I care so I'm careful. Hurry, dear fool.'

'If I leave now I will arrive before first pictures are sent live. Is your television working?'

'Yes. The color is fabulous. You won't miss anything. And if you do you can see it all on the Late News.'

'I am not interested in the Late News.'

'Then stop talking and move yourself.'

'What about the press?'

'Been and gone. The kids are with mother. They won't be back until splashdown. It's a five-day mission, Bogardus.'

'I was just getting into Chapter Nine.'

'Hurry.'

'Yes. I'm already out the door.'

Forgive me Chapter Nine. Forgive me neighbors in my century. I know your needs. But I have mine.

On the bus going toward the Space Center I have a lovely fantasy, the kind that eats acid at your own intestines. I am dead and being judged by my peers. The charge is procrastination and fornication. They sit listening as my life is read from a lucite roll – Goddard, Melies, Tsiolkovski, Verne, Avicenne, Von Guericke, Von Humboldt, Gauss, da Vinci, Euler, Kepler, Mercator, Stefanic, Caldas, Boskovic, Roemer, Kuang Chi, Nervander, Le Sage, Poincare, Laplace, Flammarion, Newton, Verrier, Pope Sylvestre II, Galileo, Eddin, Maimonides, Einstein, Huyghens, Kimura, Lomonsov, Koulibine, Arrhenius, Swedenborg, Struve, Gokman, Kucera, Planck, Curie, Mrs

Curie, Röntgen, Perrin, Lavosier, Becquerel, Bohrs, Democritus, Mendeliev, Bjerknes and assorted Chinese. Every one has had a postage stamp for a tombstone. Oh, it is old home week.

I stand naked at an aluminum podium struck silent. My jury mutters back and forth in the poetry of equations. As witnesses for the prosecution empty pages fly like unformed foeti through that chamber of dreams. The faces of husbands I have wronged, wearing the helmets and goggles of their occupation, flash wildly on a cinemascope screen.

Then the jury of genius, men I know and love more than my family, begins a slow tapping at their privates. Tap tap. Thump thump. The din grows. Should I plead? It would be out of order. *Responsibility* is the subject, really, and I have no case. Guilty, I am sentenced to eternal wakefulness. I will hang in other as a footnote suspended from a page as blank as the endless light. The bus reaches my stop. I am trembling as I navigate the aisle.

But I am trembling as much from anticipation of her starved, stunning body as I am from the anger of those educated eyes.

Clams on the half-shell and navel oranges. Her fridge is filled with them. And Bonbell cheese, which I also like. Phosphorus, proteins, vitamins and minerals that go straight to the genitals is the name of her game.

'You should live in trees that give fruit every day. Ripe, gushy fruit like fresh figs. You are an animal.'

'I would rather be a bird than an animal, Bogardus, if it's all the same to you.'

'So. A bird. Eat, tweet, flutter, evacuate and lay eggs. I ask myself a thousand times, "Why did *he* marry *you?*"'

'You know we met at college. He was so specialized. I was drifting in Liberal Arts. We had plenty for each other in those long-ago days.'

'Do you have Jules Bergman's station turned on? He is the only one who knows anything about it up there.'

'The TV is on in the bedroom.'

'Naturally. Hey, how do you live with yourself?'

'I don't want to live with myself. That's why you're here, Bogardus. Lord, where did you get that outfit? Green slacks, a blue jacket, a plaid shirt and brown tie. Your hair is standing like Dr Zorba's. And it's receding. You've lost whole tufts since I saw you right over your forehead. Look at your shoes. And that beard looks like an abandoned nest. You don't take care of yourself.'

'Now tell me my belly is hanging over my belt.'

'I noticed.'

'You look lovely. Not a blemish.'

'Thank you, Bogardus. I know how hard it is for you to spare me any candy.'

'It's the truth.'

It is. She looks lovely as a sunshower. I was in a growl when I came sneaking like a mole to her back door. A mole at the bung of the split-level built and furnished by a great national magazine in exchange for the exclusive rights to *his* memoirs. What would they give for hers? An igloo in Zambia. When she opened her door to me she wore only a turkish towel, a pink affair with flowers. She dropped it and came into my arms.

'Are you advertising your thing to the street? Cover yourself.'

'Cover me.'

'This is ridiculous. Impossible. You're getting worse. You carry on like a yippie. Act your age, dammit. Keep some grace and style. We don't live in the zoo.'

'I'm penitent, Bogardus. How do I feel to your touch?'

'Delicious.'

'Come have a surprise. Look in the refrigerator.'

And there they are, clams, oranges and cheese. She knows my taste for bivalves, citrus and Bonbell. They are aphrodisiac. And I am no teenager. My fountain needs priming. I am ugly and slowing down but I always have women. I am some kind of toy to them.

On hard nights I go over the names of the girls I have penetrated. I list them. I divide them into the beautiful, the near-beautiful and the unbeautiful. The married, the unmarried. The young and old. The mothers, the childless. The Christians, Jews, Quakers, Adventists, Buddists, Mohammadans and B'hais. The fat and thin. The white, black, yellow, red and in-between shades. I break them into luscious categories. One time. Twice. Thrice. Good. Bad. Winners, losers. I arrange them by alphabet. I count them. I lump them. Then I sleep.

'Are you hungry, darling?'

'As a whale.'

'Let's nibble, then. I'll take plates into the bedroom. Go, be comfortable and watch the tube.'

'Why do you call the miracle of television "the tube"? I dislike that expression. Do you do it to detract from the marvel? To drag down? Does that give you pleasure, saying "the tube"?'

'It's an expression the children use.'

'And you let them use it?'

'Please, go inside. There's a robe if you want one. And slippers. I'll get the goodies.'

'Goodies. There's another lovely crappy word.'

'The nutrients. The food. Is that better?'

'To my ear, yes. If you're getting food say it that way.'

'I'll get food.'

'Bravo.'

'You are in a mood. You need a long massage, Bogardus, and you're going to get one, toes to nose.'

'Your hands are cool authority. I am grateful for those hands.'

'That's good of you to say, Bogardus, considering how disturbed your feelings are. God, I'm thankful that I'm not a deep person.'

'You are deep. Deeper than deep. Deep.'

'I'll rush.'

'Yes. Rush. Deep as deep. Making love with you is like drilling for offshore gold. Really.'

'You turn me on.'

'I turn you on! That's three gorgeous phrases in three minutes.'

'I'll shut up, Bogardus. I promise to please you soon and make restitution for my lackings.'

'A lick for a lack.'

'What a mind you have, Bogardus. What a sense of humor.'

Later I draw slow circles on her belly with one finger. My perfume is on her breath. I splash into her and my gravy runs through her terrain like vapour. She feeds me a Cherrystone while I peel an orange with one hand.

'You love to take squishy creatures out of the security of their shells. Creatures like me. You pry us open and suck our juices, pearls, everything.'

'It's you who are eating the clams, Bogardus.'

'I saw you eat at least three. Besides, I am speaking in simple symbols.'

'Symbols or thimbles, clams don't make pearls. On top of that, this month has no R in it.'

'Well, you've destroyed this conversation. You make rubble and garbage out of ideas.'

'You're an idea factory, Bogardus. Don't begrudge me a few measly ideas. Be generous.'

Another report from the Spaceship is due in half-an-hour. But the television is left on in case of emergency. In the space race one never knows and the hazards – the terrible hazards – lurk everywhere. We are just babies in the cosmos and an alien form.

'How is your work coming?'

'The words come like snails.'

'Are you pleased with it?'

'Yes and no. I don't know if it's worth it. Yes, I know it's worth it.'

'I'm sure.'

'You are sure of nothing except that you must get yours. The only thing you're sure of is that you want Bogardus Blik's pole in your throbbing hole.'

'Be crass if you want to. But don't sit up to yell at me. Just rest, Bogardus. I have a gift for you.'

'Oh, wow, ah, Jesus Christ, oh darling, how that feels.'

'Thank you, Bogardus. But you don't have to say a single word.'

A sea is torn from me. I let it go. As it flows I think that I have lost enough little sperms to fill a cathedral with bright faces. Where are my unborns? Also, there is more waste. I am sublimating my writing. I do not share those thoughts with her. She is busy anyhow. I stroke her silk hair and rub her shoulders. She moans.

After rest I ask her if she can say that her children are also his.

'Do you want me to answer?'

'Yes.'

'I'm pretty sure of two. The third might be yours.'

'Werner?'

I roll her over and slap her behind. My hand leaves its map. You can see my life line.

'You are getting a varicose vein on your left thigh.'

'Bogardus, love me a little.'

'I love you a lot. I also hate every cell. With red hate. Pus hate. Hate.'

'I know all that.'

'You have no patriotism. You have no sense of what your husband is doing. You have no comprehension of the religious nature of his vocation much less of the blind courage and dedication. Married to him you should feel like the priestess of a gleaming tomorrow. You shouldn't involve yourself in adultery.'

'It's partly that they train them so hard, Bogardus. Everything is hardwear, hardwear. Have some mercy for me. The only part of the whole ball of wax that I like is when they talk about the umbilical cords. The rest is cold glass and berillium.'

'Do you know how much I envy your husband?'

'Yes, I do.'

'He is perfectly Apollonian, pure, strong, clear as a lamp. He is an action man. In me dregs of seminal wine pollute my blood. I moved across the land to Houston to be near the great computers that direct the Space Program and I meet you.'

'At a supermarket no less. You were arguing about the plumpness of a barbecued chicken. And you turned to me to act as impartial arbitrator. Impartial. You didn't even suspect that I had watched you push your cart in that bent-over way you have for days and weeks before we ever spoke. I dreamed of knowing you.'

'And I of knowing you. Which does not alter the fact that your husband walks in space. I walk on ladies.'

'Don't pluralize. That's insulting. You walk on me.'

'Imagine stepping out into a weightless world.'

'Bogardus, if a person ejaculates in space are they propelled backwards?'

'Ask your husband.'

'He would give me a programmed answer. Don't you see?'

'Imagine making love in a weightless world.'

'Attached to the mother ship by an umbilical.'

'Look, frankly that word *umbilical* bothers me. It downgrades the entire vocabulary of the Program. Do you notice how Jules Bergman winces when he uses that word? He must feel in his heart as I do. *Tether* is enough.'

'You put me down every chance you get, Bogardus. Well, go ahead. Put me down. So long as you jump on top of me. I don't care for your words. I don't care if you roast a billion years with recrimination. I am only selfish when it comes to you. I adore the way you glump around like a teddy bear. I go to butter when you touch me with your chubby hands. When I feel you swelling up despite yourself I die. When I kiss you I let myself go into you and I get me back down below. As for the marriage, I do my part. I give interviews about how I wasn't nervous while he was up there and how glad I am that he came down intact. And I do worry about him. Do you think I don't remember how it was back in college? He's the father of most of my children. I love him, Bogardus, in my fashion. If that's what bothers you, know I love him. But you are simply another story. And that's the way of it.'

'Give me a clam.'

'Give me a section of orange.'

Why do I come here? Discovery would mean instant dismissal from the bank and international mortification. Chapter Nine was moving like water. It's a crucial chapter. It relates my theory to the emotions. Why don't I have my scrotum filled with plaster?

'Take me.'

'But there is a report due in seconds from the capsule.'

'Do me and watch at the same time.'

'Your own husband is reporting live on the first attempt at docking and you want me to do you and watch at the same time?'

'They dock. We dock.'

'Now it's you with the humor. Did He who made the lamb make thee?'

'Yes. I swear it. Now take me, Bogardus, Morris, whoever you are.'

There is Jules Bergman with urgency in his voice.

'Gently. Please. Gently. Nice.'

I suspected complication. There is a slow water leak into a battery that connects with a generator.

'Oh, good. Good. There, yes. Like that.'

The generator is vital. It helps cool a motor involved with recirculation of coolants involved with the heating system. If the heating system should be impaired in the sub-frigid void of hostile space, all is lost.

'Quicker. You're breaking me. Quicker. You're touching my center. I'm coming. I'm coming.'

Jules Bergman is definitely worried.

'Ow. Yow. Oooo. Yes. More. Now. Now.'

If he is worried there is worry. Here comes the announcement. They will scrap the mission. The mission is failed. Down they come.

'Now. Now. Now. Now. Oh, dear, wonderful, splendid, man.'

Down. Millions of dollars, gone. Hours of preparation, gone. So what? We will try again and next time we will prevail.

'I am exhausted. I feel like a beach. Oh, thank you.'

Failure is the price of success. Now, I suppose 55.4 percent will vote to cut funds.

'The mission is over. They are bringing them down.'

'Oh no.'

'Say at least thank heaven the men are spared.'

'Thank heaven the men are spared. Give me a towel or build us an ark. I'm making a lake.'

'Won't reporters ask for your reaction?'

'Any minute. I've got to get to the shower.'

'You see? You see the price of our shame?'

'It was worth any price, Bogardus.'

'Shower. And change your facial expression. You are smiling slightly with that enigmatic it's-still-inside grin. Your face is flushed. Compose yourself, please.'

'Don't worry.'

'The doorbell. I hear the doorbell.'

'Just take your clothes and go into the broom closet. I'll say I'm too upset to talk. I'll use statement A-15 which covers this. I'll say I'm upset but confident.'

'You want me to stand in the broom closet?'

'Take an orange, darling, I'll be back in a jif. Then we'll take one of our famous bubble baths.'

'Oh sure. We'll splish-splash for the Associated Press. Maybe the President will call. They do that.'

'The broom closet, Bogardus.'

I go into the broom closet. I close the door. There is me. And some brooms. A mop. A folded ironing board. And detergent. We make a quaint grouping.

I eat my orange in the dark. I hear her running on bare feet. Even the sound of her arches excites my outrageous balls.

While I wait I will use the time to think. About repression, elimination, definition, construction, conquest and liberation. The repression of war. The elimination of disease and hunger. A clear definition of life and death. The construction of alabaster cities. Conquest of the galaxy. The liberation of love through vigorously applied Technology. I will think about Chapter Ten.

Concentrate 3
MICHAEL BUTTERWORTH

Space is communication. To a human being space is realisation. No imagination could. But the awareness of himself on a planet in the universe is psychedelic.

Matter measures time. Having experienced the highways of space and seen the stars and below him the planet earth . . .?

The Astronaut

Oceans of scrambled knowledge are in his head – they form a conflict between awareness and balance. Space scrambles his mind.

His suit protects him from the real cold and the real vacuum. But his confused mind (accustomed to a keen perception of space/time) flips:

'Space became claustrophobic – suddenly there was no space, no time . . .'

'*He's screaming. Hurry up with him. Get his hat off.*'

The struggling body was brought through the hatch into the station boarding bay. An attendant wearing a white gown removed the casualty's headpiece.

'I experienced the stars crawling over me . . . really I was struggling. My head became hot and buzzed. It really buzzed. There was nothing . . . I felt there was nothing but the stars crawling over my face suddenly drowning in water/space.'

Valve

avenues of space of
spiralling currents
of low pressure ran
within the vacuum

fields of gravity
wakes of magnetic
debris called the hip
astronaut into line

his mind was filledup
with the works of man

he was a technical
part of the capsule

one country's gain of
name over another's

they led his frail
pressurised head into
the regions of low
pressure
              and emptied it

Dr Gelabius
HILARY BAILEY

Dr Gelabius stood at midnight in the laboratory among his foetuses, all heaving and rolling gently and monotonously in the glass jars around him.

Beyond the white frames of the laboratory windows it was quiet and solidly dark. Even the trees of the campus were hidden by the thickness of the night.

Short, fat and shining-bald Dr Gelabius stood, considering, as his foetuses rolled in their jars, three deep on the walls of the small laboratory. Apparatus, gleaming bright under the harsh central light, was laid out neatly on the white work benches. On the central bench lay Dr Gelabius's notebook. Hands behind small foreshortened back, round brown eyes blank and intent, Gelabius moved, began to tour shelves on which embryos were arranged in order of age: from skinny huge-headed three-month foetuses to the large six-or seven-pounders, complete with toe-nails and tiny moving mouths in small, finished faces.

Tour over, Dr Gelabius sat down on his stool opposite the nearly-mature foetuses and, removing a ball point pen, one of three, from his pocket, began to write. Around the walls mute mouths opened and shut, tiny hands slowly clenched and unclenched, monkey bodies rolled in their placid, individual amniotic seas.

Notes done, Dr Gelabius crossed the silent room with his slow, heaving fat-man's walk and began to pace past the forty biggest foetuses, nearly mature in their labelled bottles.

He worked calmly on the contents of the jars, studying the thermometer and pseudo-placenta set in each, touching one embryo gently with a spatula and studying its movements, gazing, huge-faced, through the jar at the tiny features inside. With thirty years' practice behind him, Gelabius could judge the potential of an embryo as well as an experienced mother can sum up her newborn.

Work on each bottle completed, Dr Gelabius marked the labels, some with the date, some with a tiny inked cross.

Dr Gelabius headed one of five research teams – two in Germany, one in Britain and two in the United States – all working on specialized breedings. Fertile cells from selected women were brought together with sperm from selected men, and the results encased in jars, surrounded by pseudo-amniotic fluid and fed by an artificial placenta. Brought forth at maturity, the ex-embryos were placed with approved parents, chosen for their emotional stability and social normality. At a few years old they began to attend special schools part-time, and finally became boarders at institutions designed to reinforce their healthy psyches and extend their already superior mental, moral and physical powers.

For Dr Gelabius had spent his thirty years improving the race; making combinations of beauty, strength and intelligence and sanity, putting to shame the haphazard genetic results of ordinary matings. The end products, by their merits, moved ever upwards and onwards, spreading light in darkness, shaping and forming, continually increasing the sum of human knowledge and pleasure.

By law their natural parents had to be informed of their existence from the beginning – lawyers in all civilized countries had made a last-ditch stand, a desperate and out-dated assertion in favour of those who produced those tiny dots of tissue which fed Dr Gelabius's jars.

Nevertheless, in the laboratory Dr Gelabius was king.

He finished his examination and marking of the jars and stepped back: under the glaring light, a short, insignificant figure in the middle of his shining bottles and instruments.

With the sad but dutiful smile of a parent who must punish he moved forward again towards his slowly-turning foetuses. His pale, steady short-fingered hands reached for the first jar marked with a cross.

He ripped the artificial placenta from its feeder. The foetus gave a sudden jerk. He took the jar, plastic placenta trailing across the floor, contents tossing and moving a little in its water, to the gleaming stainless steel sink. He unstoppered the jar, tipped it up and, one hand splayed across the top of the jar and the embryo's soft head, neatly poured the fluid down the sink. Inside the jar limbs moved feebly, mouth opened and shut soundlessly, fingers closed and loosened in slow spasms. Gravely Dr Gelabius carried the bottle to the door of the laboratory and placed it outside. The foetus heaved a little and, as Dr Gelabius closed the door, stopped moving.

Sadly, borne by necessity, Dr Gelabius removed nine more bottles from the shelves until there were ten shining jars standing in a line in the corridor, each with an unmoving homunculus collapsed on its glass floor.

Dr Gelabius moved back to his bench, opened his record book and began to write.

Suddenly the door crashed back against the wall. In the entrance to the laboratory stood a woman in a torn red coat. Her grey hair hung in wild tangles around her head, her eyes burned in a lined, pinched face. In one thin hand she held a revolver.

'You killed my baby,' she screamed, and as Dr Gelabius stood up she fired four shots into him.

She turned and ran, her feet banging along the corridor and gradually fading away.

Dr Gelabius fell down, hand clutched against his white-coated belly which was pierced by two bullets. He lay, knees drawn up, arms around his body. He rolled a little, made a soundless mouthing, turned on to his back, and died.

All around him in the silent laboratory his embryos continued their determined, senseless rolling; naked monkeys heaving like ships at anchor in their bland, amniotic swell.

But Gelabius, mother and father to them all, did not move.

The Four-Colour Problem
BARRINGTON BAYLEY

The Satellite Mapping Survey undertaken in 1990 revealed that the Earth contains vast areas of undiscovered land surface overlooked by previous explorers and cartographers. Despite disquiet in scientific quarters the US Congress voted a thousand billion dollars towards exploiting the new regions and opening operations were conducted from Strategic Air Command, Omaha.

Every morning at dawn eight-jet *Vulture* bombers took off and by dint of great mathematical expertise were guided by Mission Control over the new countries. Each bomber had an onboard computer drawing random maps on a display screen purporting to relate to the landscape below. The crew meanwhile made pencilled notes of mountains rivers and plains. It was hard to get two maps to agree —

Unease at MIT and Caltech over the Satellite Survey's findings delayed plans for surface missions by land or sea. The papers appearing in professional journals carried such titles as: 'IS TOPOLOGY WRONG?' 'IS GEOMETRY WRONG?' 'IS THE EARTH A SIMPLY-CONNECTED SURFACE?'

The Congressional Inquiry five years later found it hard to decide at what point the character of the project changed. It was evident however that by the third month the mathematical faculties of the major research centres had already established control of SAC, putting out their control lines first through Washington by means of an insidious advisory claim, then drawing up schematics until finally they were right there in SAC Mission Control having captured the chain of command.

(The maths men were already adept at taking over the nation like the SS used to take over – The reasons and methods were the same – *Weltanschauung* – Belief in correctness of technique – Professor M. M. was putting infants in sealed metal chambers and irradiating them with alien equations – They started by running the economy – Look they said economics should be left to us not to untrained psychotics – You have to align the growth vectors – Formulas and differential equations a mile long put them through logic units look we got pulse trains a light year long – Dynamic topology – Structural morphology – Soon there was nothing in the White House but a big computer with direct lines to MIT and Caltech – The President sits hypnotised by a stroboscope – MIT and Caltech start fighting it out they got different ideas see they send the electronic word war streaming through respective landlines – Hostile pulse trains contend in White House computer while Soviet satellite is beaming subversive equations of surplus value to confuse the parameters – The technician spoke out of the corner of his mouth – 'Don't let the computer cotton on to those Marxist surplus value pulse trains from outside the ecliptic' – He picked up a bucket of water and threw it over the consoles to cool them down – Steam drifted through the white rooms – Outside the city continuous explosion of lifting Moon rocket washes over the suburbs fluttering flags – 'Those outer space vectors sure pack a punch'—)

Look they said exploit new lands according to precise formula otherwise returns are not maximised. We know formula have trained forebrain will travel. But once installed in SAC Mission Control they pursue their own interests and convert the whole fucking issue into a world-spanning trillion-dollar exercise in abstract mathematics.

'We have an unprecedented opportunity,' said Professor Gottram, 'to solve the four-colour problem.'

Briefly the four-colour problem concerns the colouring of maps on a plane or spherical surface (the two being the same topologically, known in the jargon as simply-connected surfaces). Map-makers have known for centuries that no more than four colours are ever needed to colour a map so that no two adjoining countries bear the same one. The four colour problem is something of a curiosity in mathematics. Attempts to prove the proposition yielded only a proof of five colours and all efforts to reduce it to one of four colours have not satisfied the rigours of logic. However unlikely it seems to common sense, the possibility therefore remains open that a planar map requiring five colours might be feasible – The bearing it might have on the structure of space is of some interest – Current advances in the field consist mainly of upping the number of countries (140 at last count) below which a map cannot be five-colour – Editors of mathematical journals frequently receive lengthy manuscripts from amateurs purporting to prove the four-colour theorem and involving a tedious task in finding the flaw —

Some regard the four-colour theorem as true but unproven, others regard it as untrue. Professor Gottram, speaking to his students on the eve of his departure to SAC Omaha said: 'The additional extensibility of the Earth has removed the question from the realm of the abstract to the realm of the concrete. Territories – Borders – Hegemonies – Armies march and counter-march – The defender thinks himself surrounded by enemies – Suddenly a new avenue appears and the beleaguered inhabitants vanish into the promised land – The bearing on the structure of space is of immediate interest – No effort can be too great – Gentlemen, in view of the fact that the planet Earth has unanalysed topological properties it is a not unreasonable assumption that the five-colour relation *exists upon it.* We must find it before—' Align vectors – Compass needles waver – Directions uncertain – *Hold your course! Don't look back!*

So they went streaking off in search of El Dorado, Shangri La, the Elixir, the Philosopher's Stone, perpetual motion, the six hundred year orgasm.

At first the crews saw an Eden of lakes, islands and rivers. But all was not well. The scenes gave way to alien landscapes with no oxygen – All burned up by the heat – The chromanauts' perils irradiate the news media with flickering images of despair – For the crews on the end of the line vital links with SAC sometimes fade out, leaving bombers groping desperately for navigation beams precessing to pick up guiding pulse trains – The lid of an underground silo peels back and a monstrous scorpion with wings whirrs up to devour the bombers in mid-air, dashing to and fro like a fox in a chicken run – One squadron suicides with a nuclear blast – In Pentagon crew-cut general with cancer of the larynx adjusts his cardiac pace-maker and barks in a harsh electronic voice 'Want more proof they're Reds?' – The crew of *Happy-Go-Lucky* forgot they were airborne and thought they were in a flight simulator – At Mission Control they are running all kinds of programs on the hardware – Computer display screens flicker with sometimes a hundred experimental maps per second – Burning bombers sinking into bottomless black pit – Last contact is frantic reel of equations meaning nothing to Mission Control —

'Hello Mission Control – We appear to be riding on worldlines of deformed sex energy – Pressure varying – Can you give us fix for phallic heat and return to normal temperature?'

'Mission Control to Cosmo Blair – Sorry, you are on your own – *Don't look back!* – Keep us informed of degree of curvature of sex space – sex tensors vary with stress and longing—'

'We keep trying – Pilot wants to jettison nuclear armament – Says we are riding loaded roller-coaster—' Vectors sear the air. – Burning bomber sinking down black bottomless pit – Controllers stare at equations stupefied – Blazing flags flutter – Surplus value pulse train sets out for Andromeda Galaxy 'to relieve the confusion of the masses exploited there'—

'Wanta buy an army surplus pulse train? It works the settings on an export reject hydrogen bomb I got off a sergeant in the Saigon PX' The man from Chicago held up a reel of tape. 'It works on the human nervous system too to get explosions of orgasms but wear a cardiac pace-maker or your heart can hardly stand it. Try it on your girl friend or you can use it long range maybe on some cutie you're watching on television or on a girls' school the teacher too.'

– Red glow of pleasure – Hot iron runs in biologic furnace – Ovens sigh giving off red heat – 'Shall we try again Mission Control?'

'Withdraw if you can – Appropriations are falling – Pulse train vectors meshing in biologic social computer are radiating moiré patterns of pain—' The bombers seared by heat and pressure streaked over grumbling landscapes turned liquid and exploding in blasts of poison gas—

TECHNICAL SECTION (I)

Note on social computer: Basically any human society is a machine operating on the computer principle of binary (off/on) logic units. The binary notation is provided by the Pleasure/Pain principle expressed in a social Fortran in all its correlatives such as Praise/Blame, Like/Dislike, Admiration/Contempt, Esteem/Disgust, Enthusiasm/Apathy, Why-hello-there!/Get-out-of-my-sight-you-disgusting-little-man. All social gatherings can more or less be translated into social Fortran. The social logic unit (known as a person in the trade) forms input and output leads during an encounter and passes on an emotional charge taking its place in the transmission of a long pulse train. Encounters are not formed by the will of the units concerned as they often think but locations and times are all programmed by the previous state of the computer. Pulse trains are immortal, outliving the units that process and transmit them – So we have the basic structure of social life – Social pulse trains are constantly intersecting the vectors that are flitting through social space-time —

Note on vectors: We owe to William Burroughs the discovery that life is addiction. To be alive is to be addicted, if not to one thing then to another. The reason is that in terms of the world-frame consciousness is addiction, being a vector quantity not a scalar quantity, not a passive screen but a direction and power at any given moment. Just as matter cannot exist without an associated vector, awareness cannot exist without vector. 'The algebra of absolute need' consequent on physical entrapment is endemic and varies only in intensity. Hence consciousness is known as 'the body of desire' in Eastern philosophies. As all instances and correlatives of Pleasure/Pain can be subsumed under Experience we are all Experience Addicts.

The social pulse train works by the simple off/on principle of permitting or stopping the passage of desire vectors. Pleasure is felt when a vector is enabled to go forward. Pain is felt when a vector is stopped or deflected.

Stopping or deflecting vector damages basic being and pain, disappointment and loss of consciousness are experienced. Physical pain is stopped vector of biological body integrity – Other pain is stopped desire vector – In Scientology all losses and no gains sends a man down the tone scale towards Grief – Apathy – Death—

Most vectors are aligned *in planar social space* – i.e. they are aimed into the computer, human society. – Planar space is in general the condition of operation of the social computer, being spread one unit thick on the surface of a sphere – Hence they mesh and oppose one another for available experience-materials – Addiction of all parties to biological energy and mutual emotional need ends in 'extreme untenable positions' (quote). In conditions of stress due to heat and pressure the parties resort to distorted vectors, reflected vectors and other tactics. Binary pulse trains moiré through social space-time – Meshing vectors – Laser light beams diffract untenable circumstances – When the heat is on and communications dry up the units feel their sources failing – Situation of extreme peril – Vital life-support technique in such times is the use of *virtual images*.

Note on virtual images: A virtual image is one that appears to show an object where no object is – As for instance a reflection in a mirror makes the image appear to emanate from a position behind the mirror – Laser holograms also produce virtual images at various angles – It is absolutely vitally necessary that an addicted unit be able to intercept a pulse train – To do this he must have effective output leads which means vector – When the oven is stepped up and the pressure is high pulse trains mesh in pain moiré – At this stage the transmission lines begin to seize up and there is nothing in the whole fucking issue but twisted vectors, deflected vectors and reversed vectors – The atmosphere is something horrible and the units choke for lack of air – So what they do is fight to acquire virtual images to set up a ghost network that allows some sort of power to pass – Virtual images are prized for their reality index that is they mostly arise from genuine entities who died long ago – The units are all scrambling for effective virtual images to validate claims to what remains of the available materials in the by this time festering dungheap or as Burroughs puts it 'rush the lifeboat in drag'.

Note on ovens: An oven is an enclosed space bringing about chemical changes by means of stress heat and pressure – Any human society is an oven situation varying only in the level of the settings – The social computer is designed to be contained within an oven that cooks the logic units so as to specify their responses – Four or five programmed responses to any stimuli whatsoever is regarded by most as a safe level of activity – Hence the inner state of the computer can be controlled by means of a few simple external oven controls – Beings from space sometimes use these controls to cook something tasty as they pass through – A whole range of chemical changes can be induced by combinations of pressure stress heat to synthesise specialised addictions – The atmosphere in many ovens is indescribable – The ovens of Belsen and Buchenwald were simply ritual symbols of the Oven of Germany – Not so different really from the ritual ovens of English drawing rooms – However the chief oven function is the multiplication of virtual images which goes on with viral efficiency even at little more than room temperature.

No one has ever escaped an oven once thrown in by the brutal heavy-helmeted Guards posted at the uterine opening made of brick creaking with white heat. The only possible palliative for the occupants is in the opinion of some authorities random switching, which they are of course unable to achieve even if given this information. Galactic judges sometimes order a criminal to be absorbed into a virtual image thereby effectively banishing him from existence —

'Wanta buy a government ex-issue pulse train? It works the settings on a hydrogen fusion oven. Try it on the orgasm centres while your girl friend is squatting astride you—' Ow-ow-ow-OW-OW Ooooohhh fu-u-u-u-ck . . .

DON'T BLAME ME

'Do we stand a chance, Ed?'

Ed was doodling on four-dimensional graph paper.

'Chance? Chance? Nobody stands a chance in this universe of blame.' He coughed, blew ash from the sheaved papers, wiped hand over rheumy face.

'But you said—'

'I said, I said! Don't believe all you're told, boy. Give me some more of that Red Biddy.' He lurched, nearly scattering his notes to Professor Gottram.

The boy passed him the bottle, kicking aside a rusty tin can and pulling closer his thin jacket. The wind was beginning to cut across the waste ground. This was sure no way to live in winter.

Of late the boy was getting disappointed in Ed. The old feller not as inspiring as he used to be – Getting peevish and selfish – The boy sighed – Maybe he should split and leave the old soak to die in his dirty raincoat – Not many valuable epigrams left in that old corpse.

'Whoever solves the four-colour problem will become world-famous overnight.' Ed smiled dreamily. He had been trying to solve it now for ten years, right after he left off trying to square the circle.

'Give me the Biddy and I'll instruct you in the secret doctrine of the world,' said Ed. 'What you need is *religion*. Things are easier if you *believe*. Believe that there's a God and his Number One Motto is: Never Give a Sucker an Even Break. Know that and you'll never be disappointed.'

'You said that before,' the boy told him irritably. 'Years ago, in fact.'

'Well, don't blame me.' Ed looked into the boy's deep brown eyes, drinking his sulky frown. His heart began to hurt again. Scarcely a year since his last suicide attempt. And what did that damn fool kid do? Rushes off and comes back with an ambulance. The surgeon transplanted a new heart. Ah well, nobody dies in dignity these days ... Ed always had a headache now. If he masturbated the new heart couldn't take the strain and he wasn't able to afford a pace-maker For weeks after that he had refused to speak to his protégé ... disappointed to find that the boy lacked *insouciance*.

'You'll never lick that thing, will you?' the boy said in a flat tone. 'You old fake!'

'Don't be so sure. Did I ever tell you about my old buddy Grafton Street Gus, one-time President of Paraguay? Used to call himself El Supremo-For-Life XIV, Chief Ass-Tearer and Commander of the Grand Inner Space Fleet. That's right, he used to say, my country's got a space fleet anchored in inner space. Come the showdown with the Yanks they'll never find us but our special radar sets can always know where they are, scanning the news media continuously—'

'For Christ's sake can't you spare me your corn.'

'Your trouble is you lack imagination, the nerve to seek outlandish solutions. Let me tell you of a fellow I knew once who had the most brilliant idea I ever heard in my life.' Ed squeezed his heart painfully. 'I won't bother with the preamble ... the upshot is one day he tells his psychiatrist that he's decided the answer to his problems is to buy a helicopter.' Ed laughed. 'Imagine the poor mug seated at the controls for the first time – The powerful downdraft – The skids lift – The machine soars clear of the ground – Everything is laid out below like a map and you can go where you like—

'He was right, of course,' Ed finished. 'A sheer fucking genius. The answer *is* to buy a helicopter.'

'My God what a clapped out old creep you are!' The boy sighed.

– The ovens are always producing phantom images – Dreamily Ed remembered long ago in his youth going to a party – He felt ineffectual there – 'This is Ed, an awfully brainy fellow, he writes for the Mathematical Journal' – Sex vectors zipped about the room like bees in a hive – Ed was passed from hand to hand, referred to always in the third person – Suddenly he had to go beserk or bust – He couldn't stand their attention any longer – '*Stop projecting virtual images on me!* CUNTS*!*' – He dashed about the room, trying to kick everybody, male and female, in the crutch – The party collapsed in hoots of laughter —

Vertigo. He closed his eyes briefly, fascinated by the images that folded and unfolded in his mind. Glimpses of the rooms and apartments lining Grafton Street. A girl painted carefully on a canvas in a white room streaked with raw colour. A few yards away, through walls, an electric fire glowed on a red carpet. On a nearby couch two naked bodies rocked gently, clinging together so as to resemble a big crab.

'Is that a copy of "Battling Laboratory Stories" you have there?' said Ed, squinting. 'That reminds me of my promise to teach you Cabbalistic science. A zig-zag flash, a continuous vibration of energy, puts the Absolute in the same circuit as the densest palpable matter. It's Kether, the Absolute, you have to stay away from. As the magus says, too much straining after Kether, results in suicides, schizophrenia and like tragedies. Not surprising: Kether touches the veils of negative existence. No vectors in negativity. Keep your vectors in good order, lad, if you want to make it.'

'Fuck your vectors!' The boy went back to reading his magazine, where the incredible Man With the X-Ray Eyes fought with slimy green monsters that clawed and oozed, alien robots that dropped from space, and countless other horrors that he had brought down on his own head as a result of his ill-considered experiments.

'Nobody wants to know any more.' Ed spilled Biddy on the pages of the exercise books where he made his notes – Many are the stopped vectors littering the waste grounds – An old man sat in a cellar dreaming of what never happens – In a tiny village up in the hills in Europe was a girl, no longer young, who had never met anybody and who had never left her village – For some reason it was always five o'clock on a winter's afternoon, the pine trees cast long final shadows, the water of the pond was still and cold – She always went home at the same time – A hint of spice was in the air – A blazing bomber plunged headlong down the bottomless pit —

Ed muttered to himself and pored over his sheaves of pencilled notes.

Theorem 3.1.1: – Warm sighing night in July – Bedroom in Omaha – Moon shining through window and on to face of young man sleeping alone – A bird flapped against the pane and flurried in panic before disappearing – The young man woke suddenly —

– You've all had this happen – He lay on his back hearing the sound of the trees – He couldn't fight down the feeling of terror – Weird howling rising and falling outside the window – He was paralysed, couldn't move, couldn't speak – Frantic effort – Big Bird rushed at the window – This time it came on and on, flapped into the inside of his consciousness where it fluttered and winged around his mind—

– 'I found a way in, I found a way in!' —

– At last he forced a tiny croak from his throat, frightening the bird away. Unable to sleep, he rose at dawn and went on a long walk through the countryside, discovering after some miles a place he had never seen before, a dusty complex of concrete runways and low, camouflaged buildings. Eight-jet bombers were lined up for take-off, deafening him with the shriek of their engines – Everything wavered in the heat-haze from their exhausts – As they taxied past he saw mystic mathematical symbols painted on their fuselages —

Theorem 4.88.20: Space-rocket 4-Simplex lifted off from Cape Oswald* today on one of the longest missions yet. *4-Simplex* is not going to any planet or asteroid but deep into space where nothing exists in the hope of locating the rebel astronauts who refused to return home ten years ago.

Cdr. Grüber was interviewed before blast-off. Had the astronauts vanished into a geodesic enclave? Said Cdr. Grüber: 'We have word of a Marxist pulse train taking out instrumentation access.'

Later at Cape Oswald NASA Chief Dr Everard was asked what had gone wrong with the erring astronauts. Why did they evince non-typical psychisms? 'I can only say we relaxed our screening too much to get larger numbers for back-up crews – What can ya do with such crummy hardware like ours? – In the beginning our standards were strict – The astronaut has to have nerves of steel, no imagination so that nothing frightens him – What for instance if a guy stands on the Moon and looks around him and starts *really* looking? – What if he looks up at the Earth? – He has to have strong Momism so as to maintain a subconscious umbilical cord when separated from Mother Earth – "I'm not really anywhere I wasn't before" – We aim to control the solar system – We need that u-cord – Future astronauts will be cyborgs censored for imaginative intelligence—'

London's Astronomer Royal commented later: 'Quite right. I would certainly not go into space if I thought anyone of intelligence was on board.' Also in London, the Chairman of the British Interplanetary Society said that despite setbacks he still believed in the possibility of space-flight and it would become a reality 'probably within the next hundred years'.

People with a stake in the addiction business – governments, newspapers

*Misnamed by many news media – What I want to know is who shot who? – Who perpetrated the deed? – If Kennedy shot Oswald they could call it Cape Kennedy–

and public-minded citizens of every degree – fear rival operations like narcotics and new ideologies because they see in them a threat to their own sources —

The President tapped his fingers on his desk. 'How does this social pulse train work, Joe?'

'Well Mr President, when a personal logical unit receives a pulse it's an emotional charge either Pleasure/Pain and he stores it until he meets an analogous situation and he discharges it in an encounter either stopping or enabling the other party's vector. That way every social act is repeated indefinitely – a man gets hurt so he hurts somebody next time. Of course a considerable period can elapse between charge and discharge so the timebase is pretty complicated.'

'Just like that?'

'Well . . . ' The adviser shifted uneasily. 'Of course that's a simplification. Often the pulse is processed in storage – not always easy to quantify emotion. Occasionally a pulse train fades through processing and dies out. Mostly though the stop trains are on high gain.'

'Sound like quite a build-up of information, Joe.'

'Yes *sir!* That's what we need, Mr President – high stress information. Remember the opposition over the water is building up his own pressure and we got to keep pace.'

The President went through the stock motions that link together dialogue in novels – lit a cigarette, bit an apple, stroked his chin and drummed his fingers on the table. 'Hmmm. Now about those Terminals . . . '

'That's our main problem, sir. A few units appear to have begun acting as terminals to pain charge and refuse to pass on pain load to others. Like that girl took off her clothes *right there in the street!* By constituting pain stop these units are essentially anti-social and can reduce pressure below working level – Loss of control – The ship fills with water—'

'What are we doing about it, Joe?'

'Well, we can pinpoint some terminals. CIA agents posing as National Guardsmen shot down twelve known campus terminals last week. Otherwise chief stratagem is provocation forcing terminals to pass on or reciprocate emotional charge through sheer frustration and so re-enter pulse train pain moiré. Of course we have our sonic vibrations out on the streets – Certain sonic frequencies cause unendurable stress make everybody lash out around him—'

'Chicken-shit! Results! Results!'

'We are getting results, sir – Definitely promising symptoms: the suicide rate is up: yesterday campus pacifists tortured a policeman to death—'

The President grinned at his adviser while his feet danced a jig beneath his desk.

'Results! Results!'

What is real answer? Real answer is step up external oven controls increase pressure stress heat.

– Steam drifted everywhere through the rooms of Mission Control – Outside on the baking plain ovens hummed with electric tension –

'The out-range squadrons are requesting guidance, Professor – What shall we tell them?'

– Professor Gottram looked up wild-eyed and paralytic drunk – 'What are you, some kind of gutless wonder straight out of basic training? Tell them anything, you cunt! Across the universe pushers are setting up ovens on a million planets—'

– He shambled towards the display screens, pushing aside assistants and scattering sheaves of graph-paper. Slack-mouthed, he attempted to read the figures—

'Somewhere somebody'll make it – In laboratories across the universe—'

The President spoke in slow, nasal tones. 'What became of the greatness and might of the Military-Industrial Complex? This Mathematico-Air Force Complex has a funny taste ... Like somebody is trying to take over our pitch.'

Joe nodded gravely, drawing on a fifty dollar cigar and drumming his fingers on the table. 'We were wise to it the minute we saw the Soviets didn't send out any missions of their own. Wanta know why? They got too good a control over their pulse trains. No cracks in their oven.'

When control is slipping a good technique is to send in the examiners. Have you noticed how you have to be examined for everything lately? Steadily they push in on previously unsupervised areas of life – 'Why do you want to live there? Can you support your reasons? Why do you want to work at that profession? Do you think you're qualified – no, I mean have you got the *ability* – That man over there has twenty certificates – Please answer these few questions relating to aptitude tests—' Once established they move to test every instance of every act, sit in watching every move and make obtrusive notes any time the examinee needs undivided attention.

Part of basic training is to radiate a feeling of contempt. The examiner usually begins by suggesting there is something wrong with the basic equipment. 'Don't you think your chances are rather slight in this car? All right it's up to you if you want to go on with it ... You want to talk to that girl? Is it probable she'll take any notice of you, what with your personality and ... well, *appearance?* Well, if you insist on trying—'

'*Why do you walk like that?*'

'Is it necessary to visit the toilet so often?'

'Can't you speak in a more *normal* tone of voice?'

'You are practising a perversion *unique to you alone.*'

The examiner writes devastating remarks on the failure certificates he hands out which the examinee must keep and read every day. After a few years the citizens are all nervous wrecks or in a state of paralytic shock.

– Gentlemen let us remove our hats as a mark of respect to Danny Barlowe, who after failing his driving test twelve times finally got a death-wish about the matter and on the thirteenth engineered a crash killing himself and the examiner outright—

Calling all examiners – Logic units to be tested to destruction – Harsh electronic voice vibrates through packed skyscrapers —

Joe took a long drag on his cigar making the tip glow red. 'Fact is there are parties running the four-colour program at SAC who see success as *possible route of escape from oven.* Question of connectivity in Earth space. If a map needing five colours is possible maybe process of entrapment in normal space-time conditions is not absolute – Uterine guards cannot be everywhere – Pressure would fall if they found it – *Calling all examiners—*'

'God dammit,' the President nodded slowly. 'God dammit.'

'Don't worry. They won't find anything. There is no five-colour map. Entrapment process is absolute in universal space conditions. Conditioning process total and final. No escape from progressive process of compulsion-addiction-blame.' Joe stubbed out his glowing cigar in an ashtray shaped like a gaping cunt. The cunt squirmed and steamed. 'No way out for cock-sucking escapist Red Bastards *God dammit.*'

Theorem 9.56.7: The boards of the church shuddered slightly to the heavy tread of the Reverend Kludd. He mounted the pulpit and pulled back his hood – Heavy face and thick jaw – Startling blue eyes —

'Brothers and sisters in Christ,' – In the front row were little old ladies with lips pressed tightly together – 'The Phantom Phighters Phor Phreedom are today giving their lives to defend this land' – Geodesics curved through the church with electric tension – Burning bombers plunged to stained glass windows of Klansmen and weeping niggers – 'The highest authority in the land' – 'What with Slopehead and Chicom' – '*It is no sin to kill a nigger, for in God's eyes a nigger is no more'n a dawg*' —

The rail of the lectern creaked in the Reverend's incredibly powerful grip. He called to mind the case of Joe Hackenback, an upright God-fearing man and a good Klansman until one year he went on holiday to Chicago and got his balls mashed in an auto accident – Anyway the surgeon decided to carry out the first testicle transplant – He took the left testicle from a nigger shot by the cops and the right testicle from a dockworker from Hong Kong – So there was Joe's wife giving birth to niggers and chinks one after the other and nobody believed Joe was the father – 'A warning to us all'—

Scene: TV cameras roll across concrete expanse to screen husky young men in flying suits beneath the predatory beaks of *Vulture* bombers. 'Can you comment on the theory, that the fifth-colour country is a secret communist enclave or else the legendary Christian kingdom of Prester John sought by Prince Henry and Vasco Da Gama?'

'What-all difference?' drawls the blue-eyed pilot. 'Whether it's the commie enclave or the Pope-kissers' kingdom, when we find it we'll bomb it back to the Stone Age.'

Theorem 652.1.1: Few in the whole world knew of the secret meeting chamber of the World Law Fund. Built with great constructive genius a hundred miles underground, its walls were of stressed carbon with properties very close to diamond, faced with layers of concrete, mica and asbestos. The walls formed sheaves of arches holding.back the pressure of the Earth's mantle with almost visible effort – Like Atlas holding up the Earth —

The lift from the surface arrived at exactly seven. About thirty people filed silently into the chamber and took their seats. The tutor appeared and without introduction launched into his lecture, speaking in quiet, matter-of-fact tones. His eyes were mild but steady. Short, slim, dark hair flecked with grey, he was noticeably older than his years and though his composure was unimpeachable there was an unmistakable feeling of weariness about him, a weariness that no effort could overcome —

'The Communist Party was described in its time as one of the few successful movements of pure will in history – We shall now examine the secret of the Party's success and the cause of its ultimate failure—'

– The tutor paused for a moment and coughed slightly –

– 'To preserve its unwavering will was the Party's first consideration. The Party demanded absolute precision of concept and an attitude of ruthlessness to even the smallest deviations. Left deviations, right deviations, were chopped off mercilessly and their perpetrators degraded, banished or liquidated. "Only the bourgeois persists in thinking that nothing results from these nuances of thoughts," wrote Czeslaw Milosz. "The Party knows that much can come of them ... The difference of a tiny fraction in the premises yields dizzying differences after the calculation is completed." – Hence the ethic of action directed towards control —

'The drawback to such a procedure is that errors in the original philosophical basis of the movement, or in its scientific analysis, remain in force to the bitter end and show themselves in enormous distortions and malformations in the final result —

'The World Law Fund sees itself as the successor to the Party's mission to rescue humanity – No matter that our backs are to the wall – However the Fund sets itself infinitely more difficult criteria in that it must be not conditionally right but absolutely right – The Fund demands of itself the Party's invincible will together with the ability to correct initial error – An almost impossible combination – To reconcile unwavering determination with the ability to re-align vectors and rectify errors of intent nevertheless remains the ultimate test of the developed will.'

He continued in the special terminology of the Fund, outlining its plan for world order based on unique researches. Never did he allow his alertness to be affected by the all-too-evident existential weariness that pervaded his being.

'You may now ask questions.'

A man rose to speak. But at that moment the surrounding basalt shifted due to some trivial geological event and the straining carbon arches were unable to hold back the intolerable pressure any longer. The first crack in the wall was accompanied by a searing wave of mantlar heat. The lift shaft went first, folding up above their heads like a cardboard box. In the next instant the Earth's mantle closed in, fusing the chamber and all its contents into a solid continuum of dense, hot rock.

Theorem 625.1.2: The annihilation of the deep room registered as an insignificant kink on the trace records of Monitor 437 as he strained to catch the faint echoes of his probes and the fragmentary pictures they built up on the television reconstruction screens. He ignored it – only a geological shift, obviously. No-event, politics-wise. He redoubled his vigilance to study the faint rebounds, the distant echoes that pinged, scattered and felt their way through the caverns, buildings, highways and airways and extra-atmospheric space.

Monitor 437 was one of several thousand units embedded a bare half-mile in the skin of the Earth, their beams sweeping underground, over the surface of the world and out into surrounding space in search of sites of subversive activity. Suddenly he was aware of a slight *click* in his earphones, followed by the harsh electronic voice of the political overseer.

'*Anything to report?*'

'I think I might be on to something.' Monitor 437 licked his lips. For the past ten minutes he had been getting faint echoes and was trying to build them into a picture.

'*I am waiting.*'

Sweating slightly, Monitor 437 tuned up his antronoscope. The beams lunged through granite, shale and concrete, searching for all those activities that hide from the sun. 'It's underground – Faint, on the edge of my district – Sounds strange—'

'*Proceed. I am waiting.*'

'Underground – A small chamber – Something unusual going on—' Sharpening of images – 'It's an operating theatre' – A hint of disappointment entered his voice – 'I appear to be observing an organ transplant.'

Click. '*A what? Repeat that phrase.*'

'An organ transplant – It's a man-woman operation – They are exchanging gonads with one another—' Monitor 437 felt a thrilling shiver go through him.

The overseer cut him off, its voice chilling and harsh. '*ORG-AN is Fund jargon for institutionalised hostility, otherwise organic animosity – Your use of a subversive term has been noted —*'

'But I didn't mean!—'

Click click – '*Mental tendencies are never intentional – Unconsciously you have accepted subversive thought – It has been noted and will remain on record – Stay alert, Monitor—*'

Shocked, Monitor 437 opened his mouth to speak – *Click* – he was left alone, sweating and listening with dismay to the pings and cold harmonies of his probes —

TECHNICAL SECTION (II)*

In the jargon of topology as applied to the four-colour problem countries are called *faces*, boundaries *arcs* or *edges* and the points where boundaries converge *vertices*. An equivalent presentation of the problem is to replace countries by a net or *graph* consisting of nodes or vertices connected by *arcs* (i.e. lines). In the latter case it is the vertices that are to be coloured. It will readily be seen that any map can be converted into its corresponding graph by taking a point anywhere within each face and drawing connecting arcs through all common boundaries. Since the following arguments are more

*Readers who are uninterested in mathematics may omit this section without much loss.

easily visualised as graphs than as maps, that terminology will be adopted for the most part.

Coloration is of course only a convenient way of grasping the essence of the question, which is one of the *intensity of connectivity*. The degree of inter-connectivity in a map or graph can be measured by the number of colours that are sufficient to colour it. Taking the simplest cases, two connected vertices have 2-connectivity, three interconnected vertices have 3-connectivity, and four 4-connectivity. It will be evident that in such simple cases 4-connectivity is as far as we can go, the enclosure of one vertex by the other three preventing the addition of a fifth:

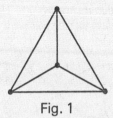

Fig. 1

But the above does not prove the four-colour theorem. Consider the slightly more complicated graph:

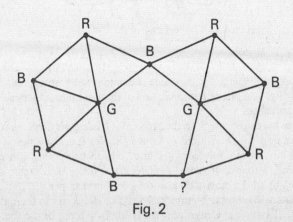

Fig. 2

Three colours would be sufficient to colour any small part of this graph, since no more than three vertices are anywhere inter-connected. But when the whole is put together the graph cannot be coloured with less than four colours. By analogy a map or graph might exist that by its complexity transcended 4-connectivity, even though only 4-connectivity was possible in any small part of it. Arguments similar to this one, using maps for which it is artificially presumed that only three colours are available, go as far back as the 19th century.

A five-colour map would have to be extremely complicated. Much of the work on the problem has consisted of simplifying or contracting graphs by eliminating or merging some of their vertices in order to reduce them to basic structures. Thus if we examine Fig. 2, we see that it contains a ring of vertices around a double axis and that this ring can be reduced without sacrifice of connectivity. The graph would then be coloured:

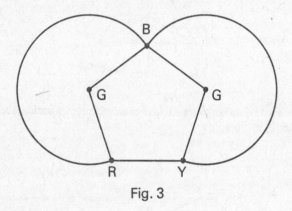

Fig. 3

We could also merge the two same-coloured green vertices, reducing the graph to Fig. 1, a planar representation of the 4-simplex, otherwise known as the tetrahedron.

Perhaps the closest attack on the problem is *Hadwiger's Conjecture* that any graph can be similarly reduced to form a simplex (i.e. the simplest regular figure in any set of dimensions – a line between two points, a triangle, a tetrahedron, a four-dimensional pentatope etc. Since each vertex must be connected to all the others, there is only one simplex per continuum. The nomenclature 2-simplex, 3-simplex, 4-simplex etc. refers to the number of vertices). If true, the Conjecture would imply a proof of the four-colour theorem since it means that a five-colour map could be contracted to a 5-simplex. By the Kuratowski criterion this is not possible, because a 5-simplex cannot be drawn as a planar graph (the arcs would cross one another).

A method other than Hadwiger's for reducing graphs to a simplex can be suggested, one that does not involve any elimination or alteration but leaves the graph intact. Imagine a generalised graph that is to represent all possible graphs, containing an indefinite number of vertices in optimum connectivity, so that if a five-colour graph is possible then this is such a graph. It has already been coloured in the most economical way and therefore possesses either four or five colours.

The next step is to abolish the planar space on which it is drawn, substituting n-space of an indefinite number of dimensions. The graph is then folded or deformed in 3-dimensional or 4-dimensional space (assuming the arcs to be perfectly elastic) so as to collect and separate the vertices into colour-classes, bringing all like-coloured vertices to the same loci or nodes. The result will be a skein in the form of either a 4-simplex (a tetrahedron with four nodes and four triangles) or a 5-simplex (a pentatope with five nodes and ten triangles).

If we now attempt to return the 'simplexified' graph to its original planar continuum (if we like we can first carry the 'simplexification' further by coalescing like-coloured vertices into single nodal vertices and the connecting arcs likewise) we once again come up against the Kuratowski criterion: the tetrahedron can of course be transferred back to the plane, but the five-pointed pentatope cannot. This suggests that the hypothetical five-colour map must possess contradictory properties: it is planar before folding, but it is not planar after folding, even though it has not been altered in any other way.

The situation might emerge more vividly in a slightly different context. Kempe pointed out that any planar graph is a generalised polyhedron. If represented on a sphere (planar and spherical surfaces are indistinguishable topologically) it can be regarded as 'sculptured sphere', the areas bounded by arcs being carved into flat surfaces. A 5-simplex (pentatope) is not a polyhedron, however, but a polytope, an example of a four-dimensional figure, and it cannot be sculptured from a sphere – or rather, it could only be sculptured from a 4-dimensional sphere (a hypersphere). Neither can its three-dimensional projection, the pentagram, be sculptured from a sphere because some of the arcs would have to pass inside the sphere. So once again we have the contradictory conclusion that a five-colour map, while being *polyhedral* before folding, is *polytopal* after folding.

The question crucial to these considerations is whether the folding could actually take place; or whether the same complexity that led to the necessity for five colours would also lead to the arcs fouling. This snag need not worry us when we have any number of dimensions to play with – the arcs will not foul where there are no interior lines – but the rigours of argument might require that the folding of the five-colour map be carried out not in imaginary four-dimensional space but in real three-dimensional space. Since the three-dimensional projection of the pentatope involves interior lines, the danger of fouling presents itself.

The treatment of the question might be clarified by converting the graph to a network of triangles. This can be done without any alteration of connectivity, simply by filling in additional connections between vertices wherever there are openings. If it can be shown that *all* such networks can be folded without fouling, then this is equivalent to the four-colour problem.*

Is the four-colour problem a tautology? Very likely. The surfaces to which it refers, those of the plane and the sphere, are known technically as *simply-connected*. The meaning of this is that a single cut will divide them into two separate pieces (whereas it may leave a torus, for instance, in one piece). One example of a 'cut' is a closed curve, which may be defined by taking three points not all on the same straight line and connecting them.

So already we have arrived back at Fig. 1. Any three points define a closed curve separating the surface into two pieces. By the same token the surface we are dealing with is defined by saying that it is such as to be divided by this operation.

But true surfaces do not exist in nature: real space is three-dimensional. Even though the surfaces of solids and liquids *suggest* two-dimensionality to our minds, we must acknowledge them to be projections of our intellects since in actuality they possess depth. It is hard to avoid the proposition that planar space is a mental construction and that in posing the four-colour theorem we are merely restating the conditions whereby we specify such space, namely that it is to be simply-connected. Therefore the four-colour theorem is tautologous.

Maps as message networks: A blue vertex is assigned the colour 'blue' because it is unconnected to any other 'blue' vertex. Conversely we can take the view that it is transmitting to all other vertices to which it is connected the message

Kempe proved that the average number of arcs belonging to a vertex is less than six. The exact average for the above network is $6(n-2)$.

'not blue'. They in turn are transmitting to their neighbours (including the blue one) their own negative messages 'not red', 'not yellow', 'not green'.

This concept of information is a useful one. We can see a graph as a dynamic reticulation of information, influences, vectors, messages, spreading and reacting throughout the graph.

The possibility of a five-colour map relies largely upon such a view. At first sight five-colour maps appear to be excluded from possibility on the grounds that a closed curve (a circuit of three or more vertices) divides a simply-connected surface in two and therefore no messages can pass between the two parts. The supposition is wrong, however. Messages of a sort *can* be passed through the barrier offered by a closed circuit. If, for instance, a vertex-member of a circuit receives the message 'not blue' from outside, then it will be prevented from relaying the same message to the space inside the circuit and will be limited to other colours. Bearing in mind that a map's information universe usually has only four degrees of freedom (red, blue, yellow and green), then by aiming a number of carefully chosen messages at a circuit it would be possible to control the coloration of some vertex lying inside it.

With this in mind, let us examine the conditions that would appertain, in a five-colour map, to the vertex bearing the fifth colour (it is neither here nor there that such a map might offer several alternative sites for the fifth colour). The vertex would be surrounded by a 4-connectivity complex whose immediate adjoinment to the vertex took the form of a closed circuit with the vertex as its central hub. The circuit must contain four colours, and it must be impossible by any shift or arrangement to eliminate one of them from the circuit. Now, a circuit normally need contain only three colours. So the problem becomes one of how messages passing between the members of the circuit could maintain its unique 4-connectivity.

The degree of complexity would be great. The circuit would need to contain hundreds or even thousands of members among whom, with alternative colourings, the colours would run as in a super-kaleidoscope. The back-up graph conveying the messages would probably be even larger. Symbolically, however, we will represent the circuit with only four vertices, one for each colour. The elaborate reticulations and messages that maintain the four colours will be symbolised by dotted arcs (Fig. 4a). This is in keeping with our defining of complex combinations in terms of their *connectivity*.

Fig. 4a represents the abstract notion of *informational connectivity*. In other words it portrays 5-connectivity in terms of messages. As a real graph, it is not planar: two of the arcs obstruct one another. Let us deal with the figure as a normal graph for a moment, in order to see how the requisite information might be conveyed between members of the circuit.

Let us approach the problem as being one of how to convey the message 'not blue' from vertex 3 to vertex 1 through the dotted arc that isolates the latter vertex:

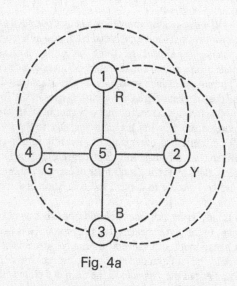

Fig. 4a

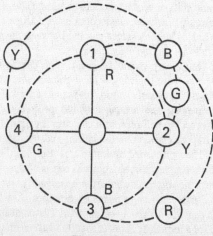

Fig. 4b

This can be done (Fig. 4b) by inserting a vertex in the intersection of the two arcs. So as to keep other things equal, we elaborate the process by making it part of a red-blue chain stretching between vertices 1 and 3, and also of a yellow-blue-green chain stretching between vertices 2 and 4.

The vertices of the inner circuit are now receiving all the right messages, their coloration is stable, and as far as the fifth vertex at the hub is concerned they are 4-connective. Actually, of course, they are not. Their dependency on the messages received is a false, artificial one for the purpose of demonstration. It might have meaning if we were restricted to two or three colours (as in the 19th-century demonstration) but with four colours available the red-blue and yellow-blue-green chains are arbitrary. What *has* been achieved is to transmit 2-connectivity through a barrier (i.e. through the one separating vertices 1 and 3).

2-connectivity is of a rather low order in an environment where the degree of freedom amounts to four, of course, but it is a very simple graph. More serious is what transpired in the course of the operation. To maintain 2-connectivity between the two pairs of vertices (1 & 3, 2 & 4), a *3-connectivity* chain (yellow-blue-green) was required. The lesson of this is that to transmit 3-connectivity we would need a 4-connected mechanism, and if we wished to transmit 4-connectivity – the precondition for a five-colour map – we would require the aid of a *5-connected* mechanism. In other words the specification for a five-colour map involves an infinite regression. The conclusion is that a five-colour map would have to have an infinite number of faces, and any map with a finite number of faces is inescapably four-colour or less.

(*Note by Congressional Inquiry:* Therefore there is no escape for biologic creatures in conditions of planar-social space-time.)

SEND US YOUR HUDDLED MASSES – IF YOU CAN

'So we rounded up a hundred or so citizens and put them together to study what happens when you put people together.' The man from Chicago took careful drags on a butt-end, frowning thoughtfully. 'First we give them the Teacher Test to make sure they are average citizens* – Then we go on to

---

*In the Teacher Test a citizen is persuaded that he is helping in an experiment to study the effect of punishment on learning. His task is to inflict electric shocks of increasing severity 'to another helper like himself' whenever the latter gives wrong answers to a series of questions. The Teacher Test confirms unequivocally that 'Mr Average' will torture his neighbour to order, bringing him to the point of death and ignoring all his screams and pleadings.

subject them to a spectrum of situations and conditions, stressful, peaceful, happy, unhappy, ranging from the euphoric to the morbid and watch to see how they behave to one another. Our investigations reveal that social space is planar space, governed by the limitations of the Four-Colour Theorem. You probably know already that nobody can hold more than four objects in his mind at the same time. Likewise, we find that social interconnectivity does not go beyond the fourth integer at any moment in time. Hence social relations follow the dynamic patterns of maps on a plane.'

He threw away the used butt-end, pushed back his slouch hat and began to unbutton his dirty raincoat. Before entering the field of social research he had been engaged on a project to inject mentally deficient children with animal diseases and canine parasites. 'The normal social encounter entails 2-connectivity. Mere numbers mean little, by the way. Groups, gangs, circles of acquaintances and whole nations are frequently only 2-connective. A man lecturing an audience is engaged on 2-connectivity because the audience reciprocates to him alone. 3- and even 4-connectivity do also occur, with less frequency. People capable of 4-connectivity become organisers and leaders. Kinky mystic groups have 4-connectivity sometimes, 4-part sex is wild. However if anybody tries to push connectivity beyond the fourth integer the result is disintegration and shake-up into new social pattern. Have you ever noticed how friendships and associations rearrange themselves now and then? Nevertheless we here at Mission Control are experimenting with the human brain, replacing some lobes with cyborg extensions, so as to try to create people capable of the connectivity of the twenty-two paths between the Cabbalistic Sephiroth—' (Were it not that the Great Bird crashed screaming through the barrier and squeezed till the DNA popped)—

'Psst.' The agent spoke out of the corner of his mouth. 'Have procured formula for lowering pressure by means of pain stop: "refusal to relay received hurt" is all and everything of appropriate technique – pass it on to—' A blast of sunlight pulverised the Fund agent to dust swirling down the highway amid diesel fumes – 'If anyone's interested,' cooed a coy voice above the creaking of ovens —

The Great Bird crashed through the membrane and stood screaming – Glittering wings akimbo – Legs thrust out in goose-step rape posture – Eyes blazing and beak agape in terrible grin – *I found a way in* – 'Did I say I would repay you for your addictions and allow you to find release in a better land? Unfortunately you do not have the comeback to make me keep my promise and therefore you are *fair game*—'

How had the dynamism of the world placed him here? Ed slouched slumbering against the wall while the man from Chicago went through his pockets looking for pennies – His eyes opened – Sunlight, the Daddy of all geodesic vectors, pounded the rubble of the waste ground – The Bird was explaining, in a voice alternately coy and shrieking, the formulas for stopping and retarding vectors – 'Positive reinforcement enables vectors to go forward, negative reinforcement blunts personal force – So tactic is for every move to meet with a sneering NO – What happens to man the world consistently says NO to? – He sinks into miasma of virtual images without even the energy to rush the lifeboat in drag—' Flicker-picture of Central Telegraph Office: the manager, a gaunt figure in frock coat and straggle bow tie, smiles grimly: 'Only negative messages of sneering refusal are sent out from here—'

'Life is a series of pressure chambers beginning WOMB, FAMILY, and so on progressively – Trick is to build up pressure unbearable tension of Compulsion-Addiction – Blame so like bacteria the marks ferment poignant liqueurs for our delicate pleasure – Hence our ideology is progressive emplacement of conscious entities into fucking awful situations largely through their own efforts—' The Bird's laughter shrieked skirling up the electromagnetic spectrum to a background of humming ovens —

'One delightful effect of progressive pressurisation is explosion of biologic body vector into cancer – Cancer is the ultimate disease, total vector dispersal (hence the intense suffering attached to cancer) – In other words we squeeze till the DNA pops – Apply enough pressure and it will crack every time, the nervous system co-operates beautifully, too, synthesising destructive chemicals in response to stress and spreading them through the body—' The Bird preened, voice fading coyly.

'On Earth we maintain a number of institutions for pressure-cooking the cells and spreading stressful ambiguity, dejection and apathy – As for instance *News of the World*,* one of our most successful cancer-inducing agents—' Creaking steam blasted up at the probing bombers – Burning plane sank down pit with never-ending howl –

'Some among us even advocate abolition of biological directiveness altogether – As you know, my approach is different – Be that as it may, the Anti-Biologic Party recently sent an Expeditionary Force to Galaxy K5, arming its troops with cancer-ray guns – Zap-Zap-Zap – Bodies disintegrate in biologic vector explosions —

'Actually an isolated platoon scouted as far as Earth (Zap-Zap) – However they were machine-gunned to death by the Galactic Gangsters protecting our pitch – Later they were found to be mercenaries in the pay of the Negativity Kings – These lurking non-beings squat sulking like aggrieved totems out at

*A mental pollutant in the form of a British Sunday newspaper specialising in anything that by any twist of posture could be given a sordid or morbid aspect. Its circulation embraces the larger part of the population, with appalling consequences to the mental and physical health of the community.

the back of space beyond the reach of perception—' Sullenly over the aeons searchlights of black minus-light played over the dark foothills –

'Lemme do you a Cabbalistic favour—' White light flashed in Ed's eyes to give subliminal glimpses of the Atziluthal World – Reverberating at the rate of a trillion a second between Binah and Chochmah were transient space-time continua, each one with a unique geometry – Ed knew the Bird was faking it just to keep him hooked —

'Shit!' he croaked harshly, forcing the Bird to flee to Galactic Wastes —

KINGS OF NEGATIVITY

Weeping and snarling, Professor Gottram flung tangled masses of tape in the faces of his assistants. 'Incompetent mother-fuckers! Where were you when the spunk hit the ovum? Copping out, I bet, as don't you always? You've got shit for brains!'

Wearily he rubbed a hand across his fevered brow. 'Program this quick and transmit it subliminally.'

Previously Gottram had declared all programs null and void. The only possible basis for future work lay, he believed, in the form of a final message from a far-out ranging bomber: 'Radio contact fading – Future instructions can only be received subconsciously—'

'We still have a field of operations,' he announced to his dishevelled crew, '*in the inner landscape of psychic space.* That's where we'll make our maps now . . .'

'Hell,' said a buck-toothed young technician, 'we got a head start already. I've been reading *Cabbalistic Science Fiction Stories* for years.'

'Yes, I've noticed for some time how you techs go skiving into the can to read those trash magazines,' Gottram commented. 'That's how I know we're going to make it.' After space fiction came rockets. So after Cabbalistic fiction . . . *

'Ask me about it,' chimed in another youngster. 'I know how to equilibrate Yetzirah. Shucks, there ain't nothin' to it. Yesod, Hod, Netzach, then over the Gulf to Tiphareth, base of the Briatic Tree and centre of mystic consciousness. Exploration of the upper paths—'

'You're not reading the adventures of *The Magus with the X-Rays* now,' Gottram growled. 'This is serious work – a *Cabbalistic Crash Program.* Get busy with that hardware. Let's see those strobes flickering.'

*The Cabbala is a mystic doctrine purporting to map the dynamic morphology of the universe, including the inner landscape peopled by symbols and images.

Professor Gottram retired to a secret library of Jungian volumes and ancient, iron-bound books with curses to whoever should open them engraved on their massive seals. In the Mission Control Centre, for long a shambles, chaos compounded on chaos as his staff applied themselves assiduously to tracking the paths between Sephiroth:

'We need more computer capacity. We're overloading everything trying to simulate the Seventeenth Path of the Disposing Intelligence—'

'You'll have to arrange the confluences differently—'

'What answer does it give now?'

'Seven of Swords, Lord of Unstable Effort—'

'Could the Invisible Sephira be the answer? Put another process in the Abyss—'

'What does it say now?'

'Five of Cups, Lord of Loss in Pleasure.'

An enigmatic, imposing construction rose in the main room of the Control Centre, consisting chiefly of an assemblage of giant discharge tubes and radiant globes, crackling, humming and glowing in all colours. Eerily beautiful hues flickered about the place. The air was heavy with ozone and the buzz of escaping electricity.

A sphere of expanding golden light represented Tiphareth, whose symbol was the sun. 'Might try for a bit of hydrogen fusion in there.' Rivers of weird light rose and fell in alternation. While at the base of it all solid panels of meter boards and print-outs told them how it was going. The crew-cut young men sat before these boards, watching calmly and glancing up at their electronic Tree of Life.

They beamed the output of the Tree to Chuck, standing on an insulated plate. Spheres of light appeared on him in a sequence, white at the crown of his head, lavender at his throat, red at the solar plexus, blue at the genitals and russet at the feet. Streams of light passed down his left side and returned up his right.

'Man, you look as pretty as a Christmas tree!'

A vast lightning flash connected Heaven and Earth.

In the close confines of the battered radio cabin thick cigarette smoke obscured everything. The two operators, their faces smudged with smoke and cinders, wore 21st-century-style military helmets and listened to their crackling equipment with cynical weariness.

Their post, which was in the rear of the battle zone, overlooked the sea. Recently they had received an almost direct hit from a hydrogen bomb. Only an efficient use of the appropriate magical images, chiefly the displaying of the Stars and Stripes and a harmonised rendering of 'Turn them Wagons in a Circle' had warded off the main force of the explosion.

– Radio transmission from Galaxy K5, percolating weakly through the atmosphere, pinged and moiréed off the cold, swelling surface of the ocean – The Operator picked it up, one hand to his earphone while he chatted inconsequentially to his buddy –

The message read as follows: //The most penetrating research has shown that there is no hope of escape from environmental conditions // A conscious entity, on encountering Environment, will either conquer it or succumb to it // The Environment is an active Enemy seeking to enter the consciousness of living beings and inhabit them // Calling Biologic Creatures everywhere, we are under attack from the Environmental Enemy //—

'Some new kind of code,' the operator said, hearing in his earphone the intermittent crackle and hiss that constituted the message.

'Naw, just interference. These Nuke explosions play hell with the ionosphere.'

Despite all efforts on the part of officers and crew, the submarine was steadily filling with water. The influx of the sea was relentless. For a long time the struggle had been waged beneath the swelling waves, and now it was very nearly over.

Messages and commands crackled in clipped, controlled voices along the submerged lines to and from the bridge, the engine room, the torpedo room, the damage control section. The Captain, with the backing of his crew, had throughout stolidly refused to abandon ship. Almost open to the ocean, now, and filled with sea water in all but isolated pockets, the sub lost momentum and began to sink. The escape hatch was inaccessible – There was no decompression equipment, only an inexorable knowledge of the vessel's condition—

The dream of the drowning sub was a recurring one with Ed. Always it brought with it a peculiar sensation of something glimpsed and vanishing. It came to him for the last time during a hypnagogic doze when he lay dying of exposure on a bench facing the sea front.

Said the Chicagoan: 'We all go down with the water-filled submarine to crushing depths. As they sink, the crew thinks longingly of flight in space: no resisting medium seeking to enter, only emptiness, free-fall, freedom of motion: nothing to stop needle-sharp spacecraft all alone in the void lancing towards Galaxy K5 —

'Who could describe the euphoria of a spaceship coasting without effort on geodesic in free-fall? In blissful abandonment the crew opens the hatch and empties all oxygen into the void – Sextants, ball-point pens, space helmets,

World War II Lugers, stale crusts and torn copies of *The News of the World* tumble into space – Support systems coast timelessly—'

They know different.

All the agents and servants of the Negativity Kings who lurch sneering about the galaxies, all the fawning narks, sidekicks and sycophants, all can tell you different –

'DNA traps you – Womb traps you – Environment traps you – Geometry traps you – Topology traps you – *You* traps you – Submarine disaster stressfully symbolises the situation but contrary to all your wishful poetics anywhere in the space frame is no different however you twist and turn —

'All your Environmental defiance is useless – Space brings need for vector – Vector brings contingency and hazard and all modifying conditions – Contingency brings heat and pressure, brings radiant moiré patterns of pain – Needless to say whereas underwater vessels may sometimes carry decompression equipment, decompression apparatus that might allow escape from topological space is, in the words of Klaus the Klever Kraut, strictly *verboten,* hence the unforgiving character of space-time dynamic conditions—'

An additional voice broke into the lecture like radio interference, croaking, shrieking, fading – 'So you think you can fight His Environmental Majesty? Fools! You are merely impulses we ourselves set in motion, irresistible marks we used to lure the Milky Way Mob into a long overdue showdown—'

In the Mission Control Centre the air was growing murky and lurid. The discharge globes sizzled, giving out vibrations that zoomed up and down the scale from ultrasonics to infrasound, from radio waves to gamma rays. The connecting wave guides and discharge tubes were hot, colourful and smoking, giving off a haze of mercury vapour. Gottram and his underlings, wearing padded suits because of the increasingly harsh conditions in the hall, doggedly continued their work of charting the collective unconscious.

The base boards were tremendously extended. The system had a life of its own now, beyond the control of its creators, who concerned themselves mainly with metering and interpreting its unpredictable complexities. Constantly they engaged in various projects to achieve a stable configuration in it: the relations between the electronic Sephiroth oscillated in wild states of imbalance. The glowing globes ebbed and strengthened at each others' expense and their compelling hues brought about unexpected changes in the mood of the hall's atmosphere and the feelings of the people working there. Several times powerful infrasound vibrations had picked up operators and flung them bodily across the work space, and had inflicted serious internal injuries on others. At other times workers had been rendered colour-blind by the supernal colour-changes.

'We are getting an exaggerated emphasis of charge down the Pillar of Severity. Can't we put more power into the counter-balancing Pillar of Mercy?'

'Everything we put in gets shunted back to the Pillar of Severity via the Fourteenth Plan of the Illuminatory Intelligence. The Tree is decidedly biased and not in equilibrium.'

'There is a dangerously heavy load on the Twenty-Third Path of the Stable Intelligence that we are unable to interrupt.'

'Definitely we are being dominated by Binah—'

Gottram frowned and looked worried – You could expect trouble from Binah, the origin of the Pillar of Severity, defined as undifferentiated form or topological space, and whose magical images were the mature woman, the cunt, the cup – The desirable female, the dark sterile mother —

'What readings are we getting now?'

'Eight of Swords, Lord of Shortened Force.'

'Ten of Wands, Lord of Oppression.'

'Eight of Cups, Lord of Abandoned Success.'

'Five of Pentacles, Lord of Material Trouble.'

Struggling to handle the outputs of his board, Chuck spoke with difficulty over the threatful vibrations – 'Professor, Binah is taking over – Putting us in contact with the Neutron Star of the Crab Nebula—' (The material of the Neutron Star is of such density that one teaspoonful weighs a hundred million tons – There is no conceivable structure that could withstand its clamping gravitation pull, for which it is aptly nicknamed the Cunt of Binah – Its emission of light, heat and radio waves is interrupted several thousand times per second to produce a rapidly pulsing off/on vibration – The space surrounding the Neutron Star undergoes an incredible degree of negative curvature and is swamped, blanketed, by the clattering hum of light and power—)

Hovering amid the discharging branches of the tree, a shadow form emerged in coloured smoke – A harsh bird-shape, shimmering feathers, outspread wings, vibrating with a golden hum, glittering eyes capable of switching up and down the electromagnetic spectrum – 'So you are the marks, creatures, addicts of DNA still soliciting for your due back pay? – Forget it there is no escape from your pitiable condition in absolute space-time – Better for you if you surrender yourselves to sucking the beautiful protruding nipples of Binah and Her clamping cunt, as you must—'

DON'T SAY STOP

So I was coasting on geodesic with the examiner on my back watching everything – Vector explodes in glitter of light like cheap firework to send useless ripples across green stagnant pools of the Galaxy – The cry of irremediable loss pines through the emptiness – Fragments of images flicker in your eyes who I knew long ago –

– To harsh electronic voice the falcon hurtles out – The Galactic Carnie explodes in cheap tawdry glitter – With piteous howl the burning bomber hurtles down – The water of the pond is cold and still, the pine trees cast long final shadows – (Flicker of images in your eyes) – Squeeze till the DNA cracks – The message of absolute blame wailed through the desolate spaces of the Galaxy –

A hot wind blew across the plain and went through the deserted skyscrapers with a sound like a foghorn – Lucy drew up her legs and opened them as far as they would go; closing her eyes she felt the pulse of his fucking – Temporarily he pulled out the hot prick, revealing her red-hot valley – Deliciously her cunt throbbed and creaked, smoking faintly —

'Oh boy!' she breathed, groaning faintly —

– Out beyond Galaxy K5 the Grand Inner Space Fleet riding on a geodesic of deformed sex energy* picked up her message on the special transceiver tuned to ten thousand million vibrations per second —

'Don't stop,' whimpered Lucy in little-girl voice —

– So to escape exploding Galactic Carnie they bravely manned their lance-shaped spacecraft to go skimming over stagnant green pools – Eventually they were riding majestically on grand sex tensor – Incredible degree of negative curvature – Suddenly broke through all limitations to explore the sex universe— The pulse of his fucking— Next instant mantle fusing continuum hot dense rock —

Professor Gottram smiled quietly to himself, sipping beer in a New York bar. All day long he had been playing the Cabbalistic pin-ball machine.† Putting down his glass on a nearby shelf, he began again.

The steel ball entered the play at Kether and ricocheted rapidly about a trillion times between the powerful springs of Binah and Chocmah.

*Because the space-time continuum undergoes deformations in the presence of matter vectors do not travel in straight lines but follow curving worldlines called geodesics – Sex energy is also a continuum and therefore has its own deformations of all degrees of curvature —
†Funnily enough the lay-out of the average pin-ball table resembles the Cabbalistic Tree of Life.

Then it dropped down to bounce lazily off Geburah and crossed the Veil of the Temple. Using the side-flicks he managed to keep it rebounding for a fair while off Tiphareth, the central stud. The paths were only ten points each. Moving more slowly, the ball crossed the Gulf, swung between Netzach and Hod a number of times, hit Yesod once and disappeared down the slot at Malkuth.

Gottram glanced up to read his score – At that moment the basalt shifted—Searing wave of mantlar heat—The pulse of his fucking – Next instant mantle closing in, fusing into solid continuum of hot dense rock.

(The Congressional Inquiry was discontinued at this point.)

Running Down

M. JOHN HARRISON

I knew Lyall, certainly, and I was in the Great Langdale Valley at the time: but I had no place in the events of that Autumn in the late 70s – no active place, that is; and I could no more have prevented them than the eroded heather of the rhacomitrium-heath can 'prevent' the wind. More important, perhaps, I could not have foreseen, much less averted, Lyall's end. He may have been insane (myself, too) long before the insensate nightmare of Jack's Rake, but that does not explain why the earth shook; he may have murdered the hapless woman who lived with him to further some fantastic metaphysical image he had of himself, but that relates in no way you or I could understand to what I saw on the summit of Pavey Ark in the early hours of a haunted morning, the *ascent* that has remained with me, waking or sleeping ever since.

Lyall was never more than an acquaintance of mine even at Cambridge, where we shared a room and might have been described as 'close'; in fact, there were times when we found it difficult to disguise our dislike for one another. Nevertheless, we clung together, embittered and hurt – neither of us could make any warm contact with our contemporaries. To be honest: no one else would put up with us, so we put up with each other. It's common enough. Even now, Cambridge is all comfortable November mists, nostalgic ancient quadrangles, the conspiracy of the choir practising at King's – pure, ecstatic, and a constant wound to the outsider. It was inevitable that Lyall and I press those wounds together to achieve some sort of sour blood-fraternity. I suppose that's hard to understand; but it must be a common enough human compulsion.

Lyall was tall and ectomorphic, with a manner already measured, academic, middle-aged. His face was long and equine, its watery eyes, pursed mouth and raw cheeks accusatory, as if he blamed the world outside for his own desperate awkwardness. He did: and affected a callow but remorseless cynicism to cover it. He was a brilliant student, but already comically accident-prone – constantly scratched and bruised, his clothes stained with oil and ink and food. His background (he had been brought up by two impoverished, determined maiden ladies in Bath) chafed the tender flesh of my own early experience under the bleak shadow of the southern end of the

Pennines – the open-coffin funerals of a failing industrial town, a savage unemployment, black methodism.

We must have made a strange pair in those endless winter fogs: Lyall as thin as a stick, hopeless in the tweed jacket and college scarf his aunts insisted he wear, his inflamed nose always running, his wrists and ankles protruding dismally from the awful clothes; and myself, short of leg, barrel-chested and heavily muscled about the shoulders and ridiculous long arms for the solitary climbing and fell-walking that had in adolescence become my passionate escape from the back-terraces of the North. In those days, before the Dru accident, I could do a hundred press-ups with a fifty-pound pack on my back. I was sullen, dark, aggressive, and so terrified of being nicknamed 'Ape' by the fragile, intellectual young women of the modern languages faculty that no one buy Lyall ever had the miserable chance. God knows why we do these things to ourselves.

So: it was a temporary alliance. I have memories of Lyall's high, complaining voice, his ruthless wit and feral disappointment as we separated on the last day of the last term. He took a poor Honours, due to an unfortunate bicycle accident a week before Finals: but mine was poorer (although somewhat ameliorated by the offer of a junior instructorship I'd received from an Outward Bound school in Kenya). His handclasp was curt, mine cursory. We were both faintly relieved, I think.

We never sought each other out. I believe he tried several jobs in the provinces before becoming the junior personnel officer of a small manufacturing firm in London, which was where I met him again, quite by chance, some two or three years later.

A week off the boat from North Africa – and finding it almost as difficult to adjust to the dirty chill of late autumn in the city as to accept bacon at a hundred pence a pound after Kenya's steak at twenty-five the kilo – I was wandering rather morosely about in the West End, wondering grimly if I could afford to go into a cinema and waste another evening, when I spotted him teetering at a kerb trying to hail a taxi. Two ignored him while I watched. He hadn't changed much: his ghastly college scarf was now tucked into the neck of a thin raincoat, and he was carrying one of those wretched little plastic 'executive' cases. The contemptuous grooves round his mouth had deepened.

'Oh, hallo Egerton,' he said off-handedly, staring away from me down the road. He looked drunk. One of his hands was inexpertly bandaged with a great wad of dirty white gauze. He fiddled with his case. 'Why on earth did *you* come back to this rat-hole? I'd have thought you were better off out of it.'

I felt like a deserter returning to some doomed ship only to find its captain still alive and brooding alone over the white water and foul ground: but I was surprised to be remembered at all, and, when he finally captured his taxi, I agreed to go home with him.

It turned out that he'd been in another taxi when it became involved in some minor fracas with a pedestrian, and he had to get out. 'I should have been home bloody hours ago,' he said sourly. That was all: and by the time we reached his flat I was beginning to regret an impulse which had basically been one of sympathy. There was an argument with the driver, too, over a malfunctioning meter. It was always like that with Lyall. But Holloway isn't Cambridge.

He had two poky, unwelcoming rooms at the top of a large furnished house. the place had a sink, a filthy gas-stove and some carpets glazed with ancient grease: it was littered with dirty crocks, empty milk bottles, every kind of rubbish conceivable; everything in it seemed to be damaged and old; it was indescribably cheerless.

When I declined the offer of a can of soup (partly because he was at pains to let me see he had nothing else in the cupboard where he kept his food, and partly out of horror at that mephitic stove) he shrugged ungraciously, sat cross-legged on the floor among the old newspapers and political pamphlets – he seemed to have become interested in some popular nationalist organisation, to the extent anyway of scrawling 'Rubbish!' or 'A reasonable assumption' in the margins of some of the stuff – and ate it ravenously straight out of the pan. He was preoccupied by some slight he'd received at work. 'Bloody jumped up filing clerks,' he explained, 'every one of them. You'd better sit on the bed, Egerton. There's nothing else, so you needn't bother to look for it.'

Later, he insisted on going out to an off-licence and fetching back some half-pint bottles of stout. This produced a parody of fellowship, strung with gaunt silences. We really had nothing in common any more, especially since Lyall would mention Cambridge only in the cryptical, barbed asides of which he was so fond.

But he seemed determined; and I took it as a desperate attempt on his part to achieve some sort of contact, some sort of human feeling among all that cold squalor. His loneliness was apparent – in deference to it, I talked; and I was quite happy to fall in with his mood until I realised that he had adopted a most curious conversational procedure.

This consisted in first eliciting from me some reminiscence of my time in Africa, then blatantly ignoring me as I talked – flicking through the pages of a girlie magazine, picking up books only to toss them aside again, staring out of the uncurtained windows at the ominous pall of sodium light outside;

even whistling or humming. He took to breaking in on my anecdotes to say, apropos of nothing, 'I really ought to have that scarf cleaned,' or 'What's that racket in the street? Damned lunatics;' and then when (perfectly relieved to escape from what had become an agonising monologue) I made some answering remark about the London air or traffic, demanding: 'What? Oh, go on, go on, you mustn't pay me any attention.'

I talked desperately. I found myself becoming more and more determined to overcome his scarcely-veiled sneers and capture his attention, inventing at one point an adventure on Mount Nyiru that I simply hadn't had – although it did happen to a fellow instructor of mine shortly after his arrival at the school.

It was an eerie experience. What satisfaction he could have had from it, I can't imagine.

'Fairly pleased with yourself then, are you?' he said suddenly. He went on to repeat it to himself, rocking to and fro. 'Fairly pleased—' And he laughed.

In the end, I got up and made some excuse, a train, a matter of an hotel key: what else could I have done?

He leapt immediately to his feet, the most ludicrous expression of regret on his face. 'Wait, Egerton!' he said. He glanced desperately round the room. 'Look here,' he said, 'you can't go without finishing the last bottle, can you?' I shrugged. 'I'll only chuck it out. I'll just—' He lurched about, kicking up drifts of rubbish. He hadn't taken that flimsy raincoat off all night. 'I can't seem—'

'Let me.' And I took the bottle away from him.

I bought my knife at Frank Davies's in Ambleside, more than twenty years ago. Among its extensible, obsessive gadgets is a thing like a claw, for leavering off the caps of bottles. I'd used it a thousand times before that night; more. I latched it on to the cap with my right hand, holding the neck of the bottle with my left. An odd thing happened. The cap resisted; I pulled hard; the bottle broke in my hand, producing a murderous fork of brown glass.

Beer welled up over a deep and painful gash between my thumb and forefinger, pink and frothy. I stared at it. 'Christ.'

But if the accident was odd, Lyall's reaction was odder.

He groaned. Then he began to laugh. I sucked at the wound, staring helplessly at him over my hand. He turned away, fell on his knees in front of his bed and beat his hands on it. 'Bugger off, Egerton!' he croaked. His laughter turned suddenly into great heaving sobs. 'Get out of my sight!' I stood looking stupidly down at him for a moment, at the thin shoulders crawling beneath that dirty raincoat, the miserable drift of *Guardian* and girlie magazines and Patriotic Front literature: then turned and stumbled down the stairs like a blind man.

It wasn't until I'd slammed the outside door that the full realisation of what had happened hit me. I sat down for a minute among the dented bins and rotting planks of the concrete area, shivering in what I suppose must have been shock. I remember trying to read what was daubed on the door. Then an upstairs window was flung open, and I could hear him again, half laughing, half sobbing. I got up and went down the street; he leant out of the window and shouted after me.

I was terrified that he might follow me, to some lighted, crowded tube station, still laughing and shouting. He'd been expecting that accident all evening; he'd been waiting all evening for it.

For a couple of weeks after that, a thin, surly ghost, he haunted me through the city. I kept imagining him on escalators, staring bitterly through the dirty glass at the breasts of the girls trapped in the advertisement cases; a question mark made of cynical and lonely ectoplasm.

Why he chose to live in squalor; why he had shouted 'You aren't the first, Egerton, and you won't be the bloody last!' as I fled past the broken milk machines and dreary frontages of his street; how he – or anyone – could have predicted the incident of the last bottle: all questions I never expected to have answered, since I intended to avoid him like the plague if I ever caught sight of him again. I had four stitches put in my hand.

Then the Chamonix climbing school post I had been waiting for came free, and I forgot him in the subsequent rush of preparation.

He stayed forgotten during a decade which ended for me – along with a lot of other things – on a stiffish overhang some way up the Dru, in a wind I can still feel on sleepless nights, like a razor at the bone.

When I left Chamonix I could still walk (many can't after the amputation of a great toe), but I left counting only losses. The English were just then becoming unpopular on the Continent – but I returned to Britain more out of the lairing instinct of a hurt animal than as a response to some fairly good-humoured jostling outside Snell's sports shop. I simply couldn't stand to be in the same country as the Alps.

At home, I took a job in the English department of a crowded comprehensive school in Wandsworth; hobbled round classrooms for a year or so, no more bored than the children who had to sit day after day in front of me; while on Saturday mornings I received, at the Hampstead hospital, treatment for the lingering effect of the frost-bite on my fingers and remaining toes.

I found quickly that walking returned to me something of what I'd lost to a bit of frayed webbing and a twelve-hour Alpine night. During the long vacations that are the sole reward of the indifferent teacher, I rediscovered the Pennines, the Grampians, Snowdonia – and found that while Capel Curig and Sergeant Man are no substitute for the Aiguille Verte group, I could at least recapture something of what I'd felt there in Cambridge days and before. I walked alone, despite the lesson of the Dru (which I am still paying for in a more literal way: French mountain rescue is efficient, but it can cost you twenty years of whatever sort of life you have left to you; up there, many people pray *not* to be taken off the mountain); and I discouraged that obsessive desire to converse which seems to afflict hikers.

It was on one of these holidays that I heard next from Lyall.

I was staying in the 'Three Peaks' district north and west of Settle, and was beginning to find its long, impressionistic sweeps of moorland arduous and unrewarding. Lyall's letter caught up with me after a day spent stumping half-heartedly over Scales Moor in the kind of morose warm drizzle only Yorkshire can produce. I was sufficiently browned-off on returning, I recall, to assassinate a perfectly good pair of boots by leaving them too long on top of Mrs Bailey's ravenous kitchen stove.

So the surge of sentiment which took hold of me when I recognised Lyall's miserly handwriting may be put down to this: I was soaked to the skin, and receptive.

The letter had been forwarded from Chamonix (which led me to wonder if he'd been as drunk as he seemed on the night of the accident – or as indifferent), and again from my digs in Wandsworth: a round trip of absurd length for something which bore a Westmorland postmark. That in itself was curious; but it was the contents that kept me some time from my shepherd's pie.

It seemed that Lyall's maiden ladies had finally succumbed, within two months of one another and despite all that Bath could do, to the inroads of heart-disease; leaving him – 'Almost as an afterthought,' as he described it, 'among two reams of sound advice –' a property in the Langdale Valley. He had nothing good to say of the place, but was 'hard up' and couldn't afford to sell it. He had 'funked' his personnel officership in London because the place had begun to 'stink of appeasement' – an apparently political comment I couldn't unravel, although by now, like all of us, I knew a little more about the aims of the Patriotic Front. He had married: this I found almost incredible.

He suggested with a sort of contemptuous bonhomie that if I was 'tired of grubbing about on the Continental muckheap', I might do an old friend the favour of dropping by to see him.

There was something else there; he was his usual mixture of cold formality and old colloquialisms; 'It's not much to ask' and 'Please yourself of course' were there; but underneath it all I sensed again the desperation I had witnessed in that squalid flat twelve or thirteen years before – a horrified sense of his own condition, like a sick man with a mirror. And his last sentence was in the form of an admission he had, I'm quite sure, never in his life made before:

'Since you seem to like that sort of mucking about,' he finished, 'I thought we might walk up some of those precious hills of yours together. It's what I need to cheer me up.'

That, tempered no doubt by a twin curiosity as to the nature of his inheritance and the temperament of his unnamed wife, decided me. I packed my rucksack that night, and in the morning left Mrs Bailey's inestimable boarding house to its long contemplation of Ingleborough Common. Why I was so quick to respond to him, I don't know; and if I'd suspected one half of the events that were to follow my decision, I would have been content with any amount of rain, moss and moorland.

Ingleborough Hill itself is a snare and a delusion, since a full third of its imposing height is attained by way of an endless gentle slope bare of interest and a punishment to the ankles: but that morning it thrust up into the weather like a warning – three hundred million years of geological time lost without trace in the unconformity between its base and its flat summit, from which the spectre of the brigand Celt chuckles down at that of his bemused, drenched Roman foe.

The Ambleside bus was empty but for a few peaky, pinch-faced children in darned pullovers and cracked shoes. Their eyes were large and austere and dignified, but for all that they taunted the driver unmercifully until they spilled out to ravage the self-involved streets of Kendal, leaving him to remark, 'It don't bother the kids, though, does it?' It didn't seem to bother him much, either. He was a city man, he went on to explain, and you had to admit that things were easier out here.

In the score or so of miles that separate Ingleton from Ambleside, geomorphology takes hold of the landscape and gives it a cruel wrench; and the moorland – where a five-hour walk may mean, if you are lucky, a vertical gain of a few hundred feet – gives way to a mass of threatening peaks among which for his effort a man may rise two thousand feet in half a mile of forward travel. If I saw the crowding, the steepness, of those hills as Alpine, it may be that the memory dulls in proportion to the wound's ripening, no more.

The weather, too, is prone to startling mutation in that journey between Yorkshire and Westmorland, and I found the Langdales stuporous under a heat wave of a week's standing (it works, as often as not, the other way round). Ambleside was lifeless. Being too early for the valley bus, and tiring finally of Frank Davies's display window, I decided to walk to Lyall's 'property'.

Heat vibrated from the greenstone walls of the new cottages at Skelwith Bridge, and the Force was muted. A peculiar diffused light hung over the fellsides, browning the haunted fern; Elterwater and Chapel were quiet, deserted; the sky was like brass. I had some conversation with a hard-eyed pony in the paddock by the Co-op forecourt when I stopped to drink a can of mineral water; but none with the proprietor, who was languid even among the cool of his breakfast cereals and string.

Outside Chapel I took to the shade of the trees and discovered a dead hare, the flies quite silent and enervated as they crawled over its face; a little further on, in the dark well of shadow at the base of the drystone, a motionless adder, eyeless and dried up. The valley had undergone some deterioration in the fifteen years since I had last seen it: shortly after I got my first sight of the Bowfell crags and Mickleden (the Rosset Gill path a trembling vertical scar in the haze), I came upon the rusting corpse of a motor car that had run off the difficult narrow road and into the beck.

Here and there, drystone scattered in similar incidents simply lay in the pasture, white clumps infested by nettles, like heaps of skulls; and when I came finally to the address Lyall had given me, I found the fellside below Raw Pike blackened up to the five hundred foot line by fire. I didn't know then what I began to suspect later; I saw it all in terms of the children on the Ambleside bus, the price of bacon in Wandsworth – symptomatic of another kind of disorder.

And none of it prepared me for Lyall's 'property', a low shambling affair of local stone, facing directly on to the road; the main cottage having two rooms on each floor, and a couple of ancillary buildings leaning up against it as if they would prefer not to but had no choice.

It was amazingly dilapidated. Much of the glass at the front had been replaced by inaccurately-cut oblongs of hardboard; something seemed to have been spilt out of one of the upper windows to dry as an unpleasant brown smear on the stone. The barn roofs sagged, and wanted slates; uncovered rafters are an agony and here crude patches of corrugated iron did little to mitigate it. One corner of the cottage had been battered repeatedly by confused motorists returning at night from the pubs of Ambleside to the National Trust camp site at the head of the valley; the same fire that had wasted the fern on the slope above had charred it; small stones and mortar made a litter of the road.

I untied the binder twine that fastened the gate and wandered round, knocking shyly on doors and calling out. The valley, bludgeoned into stillness by the sun, gave back lethargic echoes.

Road-walking tires my mutilated foot quite quickly. I keep a stick clipped to my pack where an ice axe would normally go, and try to have as little recourse to it as possible: the first two miles had forced it on me that day. I knocked down a few nettles with it, watched the sap evaporate. Two or three minute figures were working their way slowly down the Band, heat and light resonating ecstatically from the 2900-foot contour behind them. I sat on an upturned water trough, blinking, and cursing Lyall for his absence.

I'd been there for perhaps a quarter of an hour, wondering if I could hear the valley bus, when he came out of the house, swirling dirty water round an enamel bowl.

'Good God!' he exclaimed sarcastically, and the stuff in the bowl slopped down the front of his trousers. 'The famous Alpinist deigns to visit.' He shot the water carelessly into the nettles. 'Why the hell didn't you knock, Egerton? Shy?' I had the impression that he'd been watching me ever since I arrived. It wouldn't have been beyond him.

'You'd better come in,' he said, staring off into the distance, 'now you're here.'

The intervening years had made him a parody of himself – lined and raw, all bone and raging, unconscious self-concern; he'd developed a stoop, a 'dowager's hump', during his London days; a small burn on his neck seemed to be giving him trouble, and he kept his head at a constant slight angle to ease the inflammation caused by his collar. He remembered I was there, nodded at my stick. An old cruelty heliographed out like the light from the peaks.

'Your fine mountaineering cronies won't be so interested in you now, then? Not that I'd have thought that thing stopped you buying their beer.'

It may have been true. I honestly hadn't thought of it until then. 'I've learnt to live with it,' I said, as lightly as I could.

He paused in the doorway – Lyall always walked ahead – and looked me up and down. 'You don't know the half of it, Egerton,' he said. 'You never will.' Then, sharply: 'Are you coming in, or not?' The crags of Bowfell broadcast their heat across Mickleden, and the Pikes gave it back like a thin, high song of triumph.

What the outer dilapidation of the cottage led me to expect, I don't know: but it was nothing to what I found inside; and despite all that has happened since it still unnerves me to think of that place.

Plaster had fallen from the ceiling of the grim cubby-hole of a kitchen, and still lay on the cracked tile floor; an atrocious wallpaper meant to represent blond Swedish panelling, put up by the maiden ladies or one of their tenants in an attempt to modernise, bellied slackly off the walls. In the living room there was only plaster, and one wall had actually fissured enough to admit a thin, wandering line of sunlight – just as well, since the windows let in very little. Across this tenuous wafer of illumination, motes danced madly; and the place stank.

All the furniture was scarred and loose-jointed. Everywhere, objects: table-lamps, ashtrays and paltry little ornaments of greenstone: and nothing whole. Everything he owned had become grubby and tired and used in a way that only time uses things, so that it looked as if it had been broken thirty years before: a litter of last month's paper-backed thrillers, spilling with broken spines and dull covers and an atmosphere of the second-hand shop from the bookcases; gramophone records underfoot, scratched and warped and covered in bits of dried food from the dinnerplates, with their remains of week-old meals, scattered over the carpet.

It was as if some new shift of his personality, some radical escalation of his *morgue* and his bitterness, had coated everything about him with a grease of hopelessness and age. I was appalled; and he must have sensed it, because he grinned savagely and said:

'Don't twitch your nose like that, Egerton. Sit down, if you can find something that won't offend your lilywhite bum.' But he must have regretted it almost immediately – making tea with an air of apology that was the nearest he ever came to the real thing, he admitted, 'I don't know what I'm doing in this hole. I don't seem to be any better off than I was.' He had got a job correcting publishers' proofs, but it gave him nothing, 'Not even much of a living.' While I drank my tea, he stared at the floor.

I got nothing but the weather from him for about half an hour. Then he said suddenly: 'I haven't seen – what was his name? – *Oxlade* – lately. You remember him. The guitarist.'

I was astonished. Probably the last time either of us had seen Oxlade was at Cambridge, just before he went down in the middle of his second year to sing with some sort of band; and then Lyall had loathed the man even more than the music, if that were possible.

I chuckled embarrassedly. All I could think of to say was, 'No. I suppose not.' This threw him into a temper.

'Christ, Egerton,' he complained, 'I'm doing my bit. You might join in. We've got little enough in common—'

'I'm sorry,' I began, 'I—'

'You've brought some bloody funny habits home with you, I must say.' He was silent again for a moment, hunched forward in his seat looking at something between his feet. He raised his eyes and said quietly: 'We're stuck with each other, Egerton. You need me again now. That's why you came crawling back here.' This with a dreadful flatness of tone.

I looked for my rucksack. 'There's a place where I can camp farther up the valley,' I told him stiffly; perhaps because I suspected he was correct.

We were both on our feet when a large vehicle drew up in the road outside, darkening the room further and filling it with a smell of dust and diesel oil; airbrakes hissed. It was the valley bus, and down from it stepped Lyall's wife. Lyall, tensed in the gloom, seemed to shrug a little – we both welcomed the interruption. 'Look, Egerton—' he said.

He went to let her in.

She was a tall, haggard woman, ten or even fifteen years older than him and wearing a headscarf tied in a strangely dated fashion. Her legs were swollen, and one of them was bandaged below the knee. From under the headscarf escaped thin wisps of brownish hair, framing a quiet, passive face. She was carrying two huge shopping bags. They greeted one another disinterestedly; she nodded briefly at me, her lips a thin line, and went immediately into the kitchen, swaying a little as if suffering from the heat.

'You didn't tell me we'd run out of coffee,' she called. When she returned, it was to throw a couple of paperbacks on the floor in front of him. 'There weren't any papers,' she said. 'Only the local one.' She went upstairs, and I didn't see her again that day. Lyall hadn't introduced her, and I don't think he ever told me her name.

I didn't want to stay, but he insisted. 'Forget all that,' he said. Later, he opened some cans into a saucepan. While we ate, I stuck to Cambridge, the safe topic, and was glad to see his customary sense of the ridiculous steadily replacing the earnestness with which he'd introduced the subject of Oxlade. Afterwards, 'Let me do the washing up,' I offered: and so cleared enough floor space to unroll my sleeping bag. Nobody had unpacked the shopping; I couldn't coax more than a trickle from the kitchen taps. Lyall looked cynically on.

After he'd gone to bed, I heard them arguing in tight suppressed voices. The sound carried all over the house – hypnotic but meaningless. The darkness was stuffy and electrical, and I hadn't got rid of the smell.

They were up and sparring covertly over some domestic lapse before I got out of my sleeping bag the following morning – the woman throwing things round the sink, Lyall prowling restlessly out into the garden and back again. If my presence had acted as a brake the night before, it was clearly losing its effect; by the time breakfast was ready, they were nagging openly at one another over the eggs. I would have been more embarrassed if the argument had not been over who was to unpack yesterday's shopping.

'I emptied the bloody Elsan yesterday,' said Lyall defensively. 'You do the shopping, not me.'

'For God's sake who eats it?'

I drank some reconstituted orange juice and bent my head over my plate. The woman laughed a bit wildly and retreated into the kitchen. '"For God's sake who *eats* it?"' mimicked Lyall, ignoring me. I heard her scraping something into the sink tidy. There was a sudden sharp intake of breath. A moment later she reappeared, holding up her left hand. Blood was trickling slowly down the wrist.

'I'm sorry,' she said desperately. 'I cut it on a tin-lid. I couldn't help it.'

'Oh, *Christ!*' shouted Lyall. He smashed his fist down on the table, jumped to his feet and stalked out.

She looked bemusedly after him. 'Where are you going?' she called.

The cut was a ragged lip running across the base of her thumb, shallow but unpleasant. Worried by the grey tinge to her sallow, ageing face, I made her sit down while I rummaged through the place looking for some sort of dressing. In the end I had to raid my pack for a bit of plaster. When I got back to her she was slumped head-down on the table, her thin bony shoulders trembling. I saw to her hand, wishing Lyall would come back. While I was doing it, she said:

'You wonder why I stay here, don't you?'

The palm of her hand was cross-hatched with other, older scars. I might have been tempted to chuckle at the thought of these two sour accident-prones, trapped together in their crumbling backwater and taking miserable revenges on one another, if I hadn't had recollections of my own – chilly images of London in late autumn, the pall of sodium light outside Lyall's poky rooms, the last bottle of beer.

'Lyall's hard to live with,' I temporised. I didn't want her confidences, any more than I wanted his. 'At Cambridge—'

She took hold of my wrist and squeezed it with a queer fervour. 'It's because he needs someone.' I shrugged. She hung on. 'I love him, you know,' she said challengingly. I tried to free my wrist. 'So do you,' she pressed. 'You could be anywhere but here, but you're his best friend—'

'Look,' I said angrily, 'you're making this very difficult. Do you want you hand bandaged or not?' And when she simply stared: 'Lyall just invited me to stay here. We knew each other at Cambridge, that's all. Hasn't he told you that?'

She shook her head. 'No.' Colour had come back into her face. 'He needs help. I made him write to you. He thinks—' Her mouth thinned; she seemed to withdraw. 'Let him tell you himself.' She looked down at her hand. 'Thank you,' she said formally.

I spent the rest of the day sitting on the water trough, staring out across the valley at quite another range of hills and wondering who I'd meet if I went to one of the hotels for a drink. At about midday she came out of the house, squinting into the sunlight.

'I'm sorry about this morning,' she said. I muttered something, and drew her attention to a hawk of some kind hanging in the updraught over Raw Pike. She glanced at it impatiently. 'I don't know anything about birds. I was in social work.' She made a vague motion that took in the whole valley, the hot inverted bowl of the sky. 'Sometimes I blame this place, but it isn't that.' She had come out to say something else, but I gave her no encouragement. Perhaps I should have done. 'Do you want any lunch?' she said.

Lyall returned with the valley bus.

'I suppose she's been talking to you,' he said. He avoided my eyes. A little bit disgusted by the whole thing, I walked up to the New Dungeon Ghyll and spent the evening drinking beer. The place was full of tourists who'd been running up and down Mill Gill all day in tennis shoes, making the rest of us look like old men. When I got back. Lyall and his wife were in bed, the eternal dull complaint rising and falling soporifically through the cottage. I was half-asleep when the woman suddenly shouted:

'I'm twenty-five years old! *Twenty-five years!* What's happening? What's happened to me?'

After that, I got up and paced around until dawn, thinking.

Heat pumped down the valley from the secret fastnesses of Flat Crags, from the dry fall at Hell Ghyll; up in the high gullies, the rock sang with it. Further down, the hanging Langdale oakwoods were sapless, submissive – heat had them by the throat. A sense of imminence filled the unlovely living room of the Lyall cottage, reeked on the stairs, fingered out from the bedroom like ectoplasm from a medium. Lyall took to staring for hours at the crack in the wall, hands clasped between his knees. His wife was quiet and tense. Her despairing cry in the dark still hung between them.

Into this strange stasis or prostration, like a low, insistent voice, a thousand small accidents introduced themselves: the insect bite, the hand slipping on the can-opener, a loss of balance on the stair – cuts, rashes, saucepans dropped, items lost or broken; a constant, ludicrous, nerve-wracking communication from the realm of random incidence. For half a day the kitchen taps refused to give water of any sort, then leaked a slow, rusty liquor even when turned off; four slates fell from the roof in an afternoon of motionless air; Lyall's wife suddenly became allergic to the sun, and walked about disfigured.

Lyall's response to these events was divided equally between irritation and apathy. He brooded. Several times he took me aside as if to broach some mutually embarrassing subject, and on each occasion failed. I couldn't help him: the raging contempt of his Cambridge days, applied with as much rigour to his own motives as to those of others, was by now a memory. Out in one of the barns, cutting a piece of zinc to mend the roof, he said, 'Don't you ever regret your childhood, Egerton?'

I didn't think I did; I didn't think childhood meant much after a certain age. I had to shout this over the screech of the hacksaw. He watched my lips for a while, like a botanist with an interesting but fairly common specimen, then stopped working.

'In Bath, you know,' he said, brushing his lank hair off his face, 'it was all so clear-cut. A sort of model of the future, with neat sharp edges: English, Classics, Cambridge; and after that, God knows what – the Foreign Service, if the old dears had a thought in their heads.' He laughed bitterly. 'I had to play the piano.' He held up the hand with the dirty ball of bandage on the thumb. 'With this.' He looked disgusted for a moment, but when he turned away, his eyes were watering.

'I was really rather good at it.'

This picture of the young Lyall, shut in some faded Regency drawing-room with a piano (his limbs protruding amazed and raw from the tubular worsted shorts and red blazer his maiden ladies would doubtless have insisted upon), was ludicrous enough. He compounded it by yearning. 'We never deserve the future, Egerton. They never tell us what it's going to be like.'

When I tried to laugh him out of it, he went angrily off with 'You might show a bit of interest in someone else's problems. It'd take your mind off your precious bloody foot.'

He came back to the house late, with a half-empty bottle of brandy. God knows what fells he had been staggering across, red-faced and watery-eyed, his shirt pulled open to the waist. His wife and I had been listening to Bach: when he entered the room, she glanced at me and went straight upstairs. Lyall cocked his head, laughed, kicked out at the radiogram. 'All that bloody Lovelace we had, eh?' he said, making some equation I couldn't follow.

'I don't know what I am, Egerton,' he went on, pulling a chair up close to mine. 'You don't, either. We'll never know the half of it,' he said companionably. 'Eh?' He was bent on baring his soul (or so I imagined): yearning for the emotional storm I was equally determined to avoid – Cambridge, recrimination, the maudlin reaffirmation of our interdependence. 'Have a bloody drink, Egerton,' he demanded.

'I think you ought to have some coffee,' I said. 'I'll make you some.' I went into the kitchen.

'You bloody prig,' he said quietly.

When I went back, he had gone upstairs. I listened for a moment, but could hear nothing. In the end I drank the coffee myself and went to bed. That night was one of vast heat and discomfort: the rancid smell I had noticed on my first day in the cottage oozed from the furniture as if the heat were rendering from the stuffing of the cushions some foul grease no scrubbing brush could touch; my sleeping bag was sticky and intolerable, and no amount of force would move the windows; I lay for hours in an exhausted doze poisoned by nightmares and incoherent, half-conscious fantasies.

Groaning from upstairs disturbed that dreary reverie. A sleepy moan, the dull thump of feet on the bedroom floor; something fell over. There was a moment of perfect silence, then Lyall saying loudly, 'Oh Christ, I'm *sorry* then.' Somebody came stumbling down through the thick, stale darkness of the staircase. My watch had stopped.

'Egerton?' called Lyall, bumping about in the dark. 'Egerton? Egerton?'

He sounded like a dead child discovering that eternity is some buzzing, languorous dream of Bath. I heard him cough once or twice into the sink; then the brandy bottle gurgled, fell onto the kitchen tiles and was smashed. 'Oh God,' whispered Lyall. 'Do you ever have nightmares, Egerton? Real ones, where you might just as well be awake?' I felt him coming closer through that ancient velvet darkness. 'All this is my fault, you know.' He swallowed loudly. He tried to touch my shoulder.

'You could get another job,' I suggested cautiously, moving away. 'The proof reading doesn't seem to make you much.'

'When we came here, this place was perfect. Now look at it.' There was a pause, as he scratched irritably about for the light switch. He failed to find it. 'It's a slum, *and I'm doing it*. What difference can a job make?'

'Look,' I said, 'I don't quite understand.' I couldn't bear the confines of the sleeping bag any more, but out there in the dark I was as lost as Lyall. I perched on what I hoped was the arm of a chair. 'You'd better tell me about it,' I invited, since there seemed to be no alternative; and added, feeling disgusted with myself even as I did it, 'old chap.' I needn't have worried. He hardly noticed.

'Everything I touch falls to pieces,' he said. 'It's been happening since I was a kid.' Then, with a dull attempt at dignity – 'It's held me back, of course: I'd have had a First if it hadn't been for that bloody bicycle; the last job went down the shute with the office duplicator; I can't even get on a bus without it smashing into something.'

'Everybody feels like that at some time or another,' I said. 'In the Alps—'

'Bugger the Alps, Egerton!' he hissed. 'Listen to me for once!'

His mind was a back drain, it was an attic with a trap full of dry, eviscerated mice. In it he'd stored up every incident of his childhood – a nursery *faux pas*, a blocked lavatory bowl, a favourite animal run down in the street – making no distinction between the act and the accident, between the cup and the lip. With a kind of quiet hysteria in his voice, he detailed every anti-climax of his maturity – each imagined slight carefully catalogued, each spillage, each coin lost among the rubbish beneath a basement grid; every single inkblot gathered and sorted into a relentless, unselective system of culpability.

It was nonsensical and terrifying. Typists, tutors and maiden ladies, his victims and pursuers, haunted him through that attic; *I* haunted him, it seemed, for he ended with: 'It was me that cut your hand in London, Egerton, not that bottle. I couldn't help it. Something flows out of me, and I can't control it any more—

'Look at this place. Look at it!' And he began to sob.

A dim, cobwebby light was filtering through the remaining panes of glass, greying his face, his scrawny, hopeless body. I have a horror of confession; I was angry with him for burdening me, and at the same time full of an awful empty pity; what could I have said to him – That I thought he was mad? Self concern makes us all mad. All I could do then was pat his shoulder reassuringly.

'Look,' I said, 'it's getting light, Lyall. Let's both have a bit of sleep. We can work it out later. You've obviously got a bit depressed, that's all. You'll feel better now.'

He stiffened. One moment he was blubbering helplessly, the next he had said quite clearly, 'I might have known. You've had it easy all your life, you bloody pompous bastard—'

I got to my feet. I thought of Chamonix, and the razor of wind that shaves the Aiguilles. I should have kept my temper; instead, I simply felt relieved to have a reason for losing it. I waited for a moment before saying, 'Nobody paid my way through Cambridge, Lyall.' Then, deliberately, 'For God's sake pull yourself together. You're not a child any more. And you never were a Jonah – just a bloody great bag of self-pity.'

He was hitting me the moment I turned away. I fell over the chair, upset more by the things he was screaming than by his clumsy attempts to re-enact some schoolyard fight of twenty years before. 'Christ, Lyall, don't be silly!' I shouted. I got the chair between us, but he roared and knocked it away. I made a grab for his windmilling arms; found myself backed into a corner. I got a knock on my cheek which stung my pride. 'You little fucker,' I said, and hit him in the stomach. He fell down, belching and coughing.

I pulled him back into the room and stood over him. His wife discovered us there in our underpants – too old to be scrabbling about on a greasy carpet, too white and ugly to be anything but foolish. 'What's the matter?' she pleaded, befuddled with sleep and staring at my mutilated foot. Lyall said something filthy. 'You'd better look after the baby,' I told her viciously. And then that old terrible boyhood cry of triumph. 'He shouldn't start things he can't finish.'

I got dressed and packed my rucksack, Lyall sniffing and moaning throughout. As I left, the woman was kneeling over him, wiping his runny nose – but she was gazing up at me. 'No!' I said. 'No more. Not from me. He needs a bloody doctor—' Turning in the doorway: 'Why did you have to lie to him about your age? Couldn't *you* get anybody, either?' I felt a little sick.

It might have ended there, I might have taken away the simplest and most comforting solution to the enigma of Lyall, if I hadn't decided that while (for the second, or, now I could admit it, the third time in my life) I never wanted to see him again, I didn't intend to let him ruin the week or so of holiday I had left to me. It was unthinkable to return to Wandsworth with only that sordid squabble to remember through the winter.

So instead of catching the bus back to Ambleside I moved up the valley to the National Trust site, put up my little Ultimate tent, and for a week at least had some recompense for my stay beneath Raw Pike; pottering about in the silent, stone-choked ghylls of Oxendale, where nobody ever seems to go; drowsing among the glacial moraines of Stake Pass, where dragonflies clatter mournfully through the brittle reed-stems and the path tumbles down its spur into the Langstrath like an invitation; watching the evening climbers on Gimmer, coloured motes against the archaic face of the rock, infinitely slow-moving and precarious.

It was a peculiar time. The heat-wave, rather than abating, merely consolidated its grip and moved into its third week, during which temperatures of a hundred degrees were recorded in Keswick. Dead sheep dotted the fells like *roches moutonées*, and in dry gullies gaped silently over bleached pebbles. A middle-aged couple on a coach outing for the blind wandered somehow on to the screes at Wastwater, to be discovered on the 1700-foot line by an astonished rescue team and brought down suffering from heat prostration and amnesia. Mickleden Beck diminished to a trickle – at the dam beneath Stickle Breast, exhausted birds littered the old waterline, staring passively up at the quivering peaks.

The camp site was empty, and curiously lethargic. A handful of climbers from Durham University had set up in one field, some boys on an Outward Bound exercise in the other: but there were none of the great blue-and-orange canvas palaces which normally spread their wings beneath Side Pike all summer long, none of the children who in a moment of boredom trip over your guylines on their way to pee secretly in the brook. After dark each night, a few of us clustered round the warden's caravan to hear the ten o'clock national news, while heat-lightning played round Pike o'Stickle then danced gleefully away across Martcrag Moor. Under a fat moon, the valley was greenish and ingenuous, like an ill-lit diorama.

Despite my anger – or perhaps because of it – I couldn't exorcise the Lyalls, and their dreamlike embrace of inadvertency and pain continued to fascinate me. I even broke an excursion to Blea Rigg and Codale to sit on the fellside for half an hour and muse over the cottage, small and precise in the valley; but from up there it was uncommunicative. One of the barn roofs had sagged; there was fresh rubble in the road; the whole place had an air of abandonment and stupefaction in the heat. Where was Lyall? —Prowling hungrily through the Ambleside bookshops, haggling sourly over the price of a papercover thriller now that he couldn't get *The Times?*

And the woman – what elusive thoughts, what trancelike afternoons, staring out into the sunlight and the nettles? Her calm was mysterious. Lyall was destroying her, but she stayed; she was a liar – but there was something dreadfully apt in her vision, her metaphor of entropy. If this seems a detached, academic attitude to her essential misery, it was not one I was able to hold for long. The heat wave mounted past bearing; the valley lay smashed and submissive beneath it; and eight days after my brawl with Lyall, on a night when events human and geological seemed to reach almost consciously toward a state of metaphysical marriage, I was forced from the speculative view and into the full and veritable nightmare.

Sleep was impossible. Later than usual, we gathered round the warden's radio. But for the vibrant greenish haze in the sky, it might have been day. Sweat poured off us. Confused by the evil half-light and the heat rolling out of Mickleden, a pair of wrens were piping miserably and intermittently from the undergrowth by the brook, where a thousand insects hung in the air over an inch of slow water.

With oil-tariff revelations compromising the minority government, public anger mounting over the French agricultural betrayal, and the constant spectre of the Patriotic Front demanding proportional representation from the wings of an already shaky Parliament, the political organism had begun to look like some fossil survivor of another age. That night, it seemed to wake up suddenly to its situation; it thrashed and bled in the malarial air of the twentieth century, and over the transistor we followed its final throes; the government fell, and something became extinct in Britain while we slapped our necks to kill midges.

After the announcement a group of the Durham students hung uneasily about in the wedge of yellow light issuing from the warden's door, speechless and shrugging. Later, they probed the bleeding gum cautiously, in undertones, while the warden's wife made tea and the radio mumbled unconvincingly into the night. They seemed reluctant to separate and cross the empty site to empty tents, alone.

It was one of them who, turning eventually to go, drew our attention to a curious noise in the night – a low, spasmodic bubbling, like some thick liquid simmering up out of a hole in the ground. We cocked our heads, laughed at him, and he deferred shyly to our judgement that it was only the brook on the stones beneath the little bridge. But shortly afterwards it came again, closer; and then a third time, not twenty yards away across the car-park.

'There's someone out there,' he said wonderingly. He was a tall, wispy lad with a thin yellow beard and large feet, his face young and concerned and decent even in that peculiar beryline gloom. When we laughed at him again, he said gently, 'I think I'll go and have a look, though.' The gate creaked open, we heard his boots on the gravel. With an edgy grin, one of his friends explained to us, 'Too much ale tonight.' Silence.

Then, 'Oh my God,' he said in a surprised voice. 'You'd better come and do something,' he called, and gave himself up suddenly to a fit of choking and coughing. We found him sitting on the gravel with his head between his knees. He had vomited extensively. On the ground in front of him lay Lyall's wife.

'How did she walk?' he whispered. 'Oh, how did she walk?' He wrapped his arms round his knees and rocked himself to and fro.

She was hideously burnt. Her clothes were inseparable from the charred flesh in which they had become embedded; one ruined eye glared sightlessly out of a massive swelling of the facial tissue; plasma leaked from the less damaged areas, and she stank of the oven. Whatever fear or determination had driven her from under the shadow of Raw Pike now kept her conscious, staring passively upwards from her good eye, her body quivering gently with shock.

'Egerton,' she said, 'Egerton, Egerton, Egerton—'

I knelt over her.

'—Egerton, Egerton—'

'Someone get that bloody Land-Rover across here,' said the warden thickly.

'What happened?' I said. She lay like a blackened log, staring up at the sky. She shuddered convulsively. 'Where's Lyall?'

'—Egerton, Egerton, Egerton, Egerton—'

'I'm here.'

But she was dead.

I staggered away to squirt up a thin, painful stream of bile. The warden followed me. 'Did she know you?' he said. 'Where did she come from? What's happened?' I wiped my mouth. How could I tell? She had come to get help from me, but not for herself. I hang on to that thought, even now. With some idea of protecting Lyall, at least until I could get to him, I said, 'I've never seen her before in my life. Look, I've got to go. Excuse me.'

I felt him staring after me. The Land-Rover was manoeuvring nervously round the car-park, but now they had nowhere to take her. The boy from Durham was asking himself, over and over again, 'How did she *get* here?' He appealed to his friends, but they were shaken and grey-faced and they didn't know what to say.

It was past midnight when I left the camp site. An almost constant flicker of heat-lightening lent a macabre formality to the lane, the hills and the dry-stone walls – like subjects in some steel engraving or high-contrast photograph, they were perfectly defined but quite unreal. At Middlefell Farm the lights were all out. Some sheep stared at me from a paddock, their sides heaving and their eyes unearthly.

I lurched along under that hot green sky for forty minutes, but it seemed longer. Like a fool, I kept looking for signs of the woman's blind agonised flight: had she fallen here, and dragged herself a little way? —And there, had it seemed impossible to drive the quivering insensate hulk a yard further? I was brought up short, stupid and horrified, by every smear of melted tar on the road; yet I ignored the only real event of the journey.

I had stopped for a moment to put my back against a drystone and massage the cramped calf of my left leg. A curlew was fluting tentatively from the deep Gothic cleft of Dungeon Ghyll. I had been gazing vacantly down the valley for perhaps half a minute, trying to control my erratic breathing, when the sky over Ambleside seemed to *pulse* suddenly, as if some curious shift of energy states had taken place. Simultaneously, the road lurched beneath me.

I felt it distinctly: a brief, queasy swaying motion. And when I touched the wall behind me, a faint tremor was in it, a fading vibration. I was dazed through lack of proper sleep; I was obsessed – and knew it – by the grim odyssey of Lyall's wife: I put the tremor down to dizziness, and attributed that strange transitional flicker of the air to a flare of lightning somewhere over Troutbeck, a flash partially occluded by the mass of the fells between. But when I moved on, the peculiar hue of the sky was brighter; and although the event seemed to have no meaning at the time, it was to prove of central significance in the culminating nightmare.

The smoke was visible from quite a long way off, drifting filmy and exhausted up the fellside, clinging to the spongy ash and shrivelled bracken stems of that previous fire, to be trapped by an inversion about a hundred feet below Raw Pike and spread out in a thin cloudbank the colour of watered milk.

Lyall's cottage was ruined. Both barns were down in a heap of lamp-blacked stone, here and there an unconsumed rafter or beam sticking up out of the mess; the roof of the main building had caved in, taking the upper floor with it, so that there remained only a shell full of smoking slates and white soft ash. It radiated an intense heat, and the odd glowing cinder raced erratically up from it on the updraughts, but the fire *per se* had burnt itself out long before.

The wreckage was curiously uncompact. An explosion, probably of the kitchen gas-cylinders, had flung rubble into the nettle patch; and for some reason most of the face of the building lay in the road.

There among a tangle of smashed window frames and furniture, motionless in contemplation of the wreck and looking infinitely lonely, stood the long, ungainly figure of Lyall. His tweed jacket had gone through at the elbows, his trousers were charred and filthy, and his shoes were falling to pieces, as if he'd been trampling about in the embers looking for something. I began to shout his name long before I reached him. He studied my limping, hasty progress down the road for a moment; then, as I got close, seemed to lose interest.

'Lyall!' I called. 'Are you all right?'

I kicked my way through the rubbish and shook his shoulder. He watched a swirl of ash dance over the deep embers. Something popped and cracked comfortably down in that hot pit. When he faced me, his eyes, red and sore, glowed out of his stubbled, smoke-blackened face with another kind of heat. But his voice was quite inoffensive when he said, 'Hello, Egerton. I didn't get much stuff out, you see.' Stacked neatly in the road a few yards off were twenty or thirty charred paperbacks. 'She came to fetch you, then?'

He stared absently at the ruin. I had expected to find something more than a drowsy child, parching its skin in some reverie over the remains of a garden bonfire. I was sickened. 'Lyall, you bloody moron!' I shouted: 'She's *dead!*' He moved his shoulders slightly, stared on. I caught hold of his arm and shook him. He was relaxed, unresistant. 'Did you send her away in that condition? Are you mad? She was burnt to pieces!' I might have been talking to myself. 'What's been *happening* here?'

When he finally pulled up out of the dry trap of ashes, it was to shake his head slowly and say, 'What? I don't know.' He gaped, he blinked, he whispered, 'She was getting so old. It was my fault—' He seemed about to explain something, but never did. That open-mouthed pain, that terrible passive acceptance of guilt, was probably the last glimpse I had of Lyall the human being. Had he, at some point during the dreadful events of that night, actually faced and recognised the corroding power of his self-concern? At the time I thought I understood it all – and standing uselessly amid all that rubble I needed to believe he had.

'I'm sorry,' I said.

At this the most inhuman paroxysm of misery and loathing took hold of his swollen, grimy features. 'Fuck you, Egerton!' he cried. He threw off my hand. For a second, I was physically afraid, and backed quickly away from him. He followed me, with, 'What's it got to do with you? What's any of it got to do with you?' Then, quieter, 'I can't seem to—'

The spasm passed. He looked down at his blistered hands as if seeing them for the first time. He laughed. His eyes flickered over me, cruel as heat lightning. 'Bugger off back home then, Egerton, if you feel like that,' he said. He put his hands in his trouser pockets and stirred the rubble with his toe. '*I* didn't break the bloody piano, and I'll tell the old bitch I didn't—' He whirled away and strode off rapidly across the scorched fellside, stopping only to pick up an armful of books and call: 'I'm sick of all this filthy rubbish anyway.'

Smoke wreathed round him. I saw him turn north and begin to climb.

With this absurd transition into the dimension of height began what must surely be the most extraordinary episode of the entire business. Lyall stalked away from me up the fell. Amazed, I shouted after him. When he ignored me, I could only follow: he may or may not have had suicidal intentions, but he was certainly mad; in either case, if only out of common humanity, I couldn't just stand there and watch him go.

It might have been better if I had.

He made straight for Raw Pike, and then, his torso seeming to drift legless above the pall of white smoke that hung beneath the outcrop, bore west to begin a traverse which took us into the deep and difficult gullies between Whitegill Crag and Mill Gill. Here, he seemed to become lost for a while, and I gained on him.

He blundered about those stony vegetation-choked clefts like a sick animal, trying to scale waterslides or scrape his way up the low but steep rock walls. His shoes had fallen off his feet, and he was leaving a damp, urgent trail. He ignored me if I called his name, but he was quite aware of my presence, and took a patent delight in picking at his emotional scabs, real or imagined, whenever I got close enough to hear him. His voice drifted eerily down the defiles. The piano seemed to preoccupy him.

'*I* never broke it,' I heard, in a self-congratulatory tone, then: 'Nowhere near it, miss,' mumbled as part of a dialogue in which he took both parts. She didn't believe him, of course, and he became progressively more sullen. Later, groping for a handhold three feet above his head, he burst out angrily, 'You can tell him I *won't* be responsible for the bloody things. Staff loss isn't *my* problem.' His hold turned out to be a clump of shallow-rooted heather, which came out when he put his weight on it. He laughed. 'Go and lick her arse then—'

In this way, he visited almost every period of his life. He met his wife down by the Thames, in a filthy March wind; later they whispered to one another at night in his Holloway flat. He conjured up mutual acquaintances from Cambridge, and set them posturing like the dowdy flamingos they had undoubtedly been. And once my own voice startled me, echoing pompously over the fells as part of some student dispute which must have seemed excruciatingly important at the time, and which I still can't remember.

When he finally broke out on to the east bank of Mill Gill, he stared back at me for a moment as if reassuring himself that I was still there. He even nodded to me, with a sort of grim approval. Then he lurched unsteadily through the bracken to the ghyll itself and dropped his paperbacks into it one by one, looking over his shoulder each time to see if I was watching. He crouched there like a child, studying each bright jacket as it slipped beneath the surface of the water and was whirled away. His shoulders were moving, but I couldn't tell whether he was laughing or crying.

It was during the latter part of this unburdening that the earth began to shake again – and this time in earnest. I sensed rather than saw that energetic transition of the air. The whole sky pulsed, flickered with lightning, seemed to stabilise. Then, with an enormous rustling noise, the fell beneath my feet shifted and heaved, lifting itself into a long curved wave which raced away from me up the slopes to explode against the dark rock of Tarn Crag in a shower of small stones and uprooted bracken.

I tottered about, shouting, 'Lyall! Lyall!' until a second, more powerful shock threw me off my feet and sent me rolling twenty or thirty feet down toward the road.

Mill Gill gaped. The last paperback vanished. A groan came up out of the earth. Abruptly, the air was full of loose soil and rock-chippings, mud and spray from the banks of the ghyll. Lyall stared up through it at the throbbing sky; spun round and set off up the path to Stickle Tarn at a terrific rate, his long legs pumping up and down. Rocks blundered and rumbled round him – he brandished his fist at the hills. 'Lyall, for God's sake come back!' I begged, but my voice was sucked away into the filthy air, and all I could see of him was a dim untiring figure, splashing across the ghyll where Tarn Crag blocks the direct route.

I put my head down into the murk and scrambled upward. Black water vomited suddenly down the ghyll, full of dead sheep and matted vegetation. Through the spray of a new waterfall I had a glimpse of Lyall waving his arms about and croaking demented challenges at a landscape that changed even as he opened his mouth. Twice, I got quite close behind him; once, I grabbed his arm, but he only thrashed about and shouted 'Bugger off home, Egerton!' over the booming of the water.

Five hundred feet of ascent opened up the gully and spread Stickle Tarn before us, the colour of lead: fifty acres of sullen water simmering in its dammed-up glacial bowl. Up there on the 1500-foot line, out of the confines of the ghyll, it was quieter and the earth seemed less agitated. But the dam was cracked; a hot wind rumbled through the high passes and gusted across the cirque; and up out of the black screes on the far bank of the tarn there loomed like a threat the massive, seamed face of the Borrowdale Volcanics –

Pavey Ark lowered down at us, crawling with boulder slides and crowned with heat-lightning: the highest sheer drop in the Central Fells, four hundred and eighty million years old – impassive, unbending, orogenetic. A constant stream of material was pouring like fine dust from the bilberry terraces at its summit two thousand feet above sea level, crushed volcanic agglomerate whirling and smoking across the face; while, down by the water, larger rocks dislodged from the uneasy heights bounced a hundred feet into the air in explosions of scree.

Lyall stood stock-still, staring up at it.

Beside him, the dam creaked and flexed. A ton of water spilled over the parapet and roared away down Mill Gill. He paid it not the slightest attention, simply stood there, drenched and muddy, moving his head fractionally from side to side as he traced one by one the scars of that horrific cliff, like a man following a page of print with his index finger: Great Gully, unclimbable without equipment, Gwynne's Chimney, Little Gully, and, tumbling from the western pinnacle to the base of East Buttress, the long precipitous grooves and terraces of Jack's Rake.

He was looking for a way up.

'Lyall,' I said, 'haven't you come far enough?'

He shrugged. Without a word, he set off round the margin of the tarn.

I'm convinced that following him farther would have done no good: he had been determined on this course perhaps as far back as Cambridge, certainly since his crisis of self-confidence in the cottage. Anyway, my foot had become unbearably painful: it was as much as I could do to catch up with him half-way round the tarn, and, by actually grabbing the tail of his jacket, force him to stop.

We struggled stupidly for a moment, tottering in and out of the warm shallows – the Ark towering above us like a repository of all uncommitted Ordovician time. Lyall disengaged himself and ran off a little way. He put his head on one side and regarded me warily, chest heaving.

Then he nodded to himself, returned, and, keeping well out of my reach, said quite amiably, 'I'm going up, Egerton. It's too late to stop me, you know.' Something detached itself from the cliff and fell into the tarn like a small bomb going off. He spun round, screaming and waving his fist. 'Leave me alone! Fuck off!' He watched the water subside. He showed his teeth. 'Listen, you bastard,' he said quietly: 'Why don't you just chuck yourself in *that?*' And he pointed to the torrent rumbling over the dam and down Mill Gill. 'For all the help you've ever been to me, you might as well –'

He began to walk away. He stopped, tore at his hair, made an apologetic gesture in my direction. His face crumpled, and the Lyall I had beaten up in the living room of his own house looked out of it. 'I can't seem to stop going up, Egerton,' he whispered, 'I can't seem to stop doing it––'

But when I stepped forward, he shook with laughter. 'That got you going, you bloody oaf!' he gasped. And he stumbled off toward the screes.

It really would have done no good to go with him. Once or twice on the long walk back to the dam, I actually turned and began to follow him again. But it was useless: by then, distance and the Ark had made of him a small mechanical toy. I called for him to wait, but he couldn't have heard me; in the end, I made my way up the northern slopes of Tarn Crag (I had to cross the dam to do it – I waited for a lull, but even so my feet were in six inches of fast water as I went over, and my skin crawled with every step) and from there watched his inevitable ascent.

He crabbed about at the base of the Great Gully for a while, presumably looking for a way up; when this proved impracticable, he made a high easterly traverse of the screes and vanished into the shadow of East Buttress: to reappear ten minutes later, inching his way up Jack's Rake – an infinitely tiny, vulnerable mote against the face.

I didn't really imagine he would do it. God knows why I chose that moment to be 'sensible' about him. I sat down and unlaced my boots, petulantly determined to see him through what was after all a rather childish adventure, and then say nothing about it when the cliff itself had sent him chastened away. There was so little excuse for this that it seems mad now, of course: the Ark was shaking and shifting, the very air about it groaned and rang with heat; St Elmo's fire writhed along its great humped outline. How on earth I expected him to survive, I don't know.

He was invisible for minutes at a time even on the easy stretch up to the ashtree at the entrance of Rake End Chimney, inundated by that curtain of debris blowing across the sheer walls above him. He tried confusedly to scale the chimney; failed; trudged doggedly on up, the temperature rising as he went. A smell of dust and lightning filled the air. Negotiating the fifty-degree slope of the second pitch, he was forced to cling to the rock for nearly half an hour while tons of rubble thundered past him and into the tarn below. He should have been crushed; he must have been injured in some way, for it took him almost as long to complete fifteen yards of fairly simple scrambling along the Easy Terrace.

Perhaps I remembered too late that Lyall was a human being; but from that point on, I could no longer minimise the obsession that had driven him up there. When some internal rupture of the cliff flooded the channels above him and turned the Rake into a high-level drainage culvert, I could hear only that despairing mumble in the cottage at night, the voice of his wife; when he windmilled his arms against the rush of the water, regained his balance and crawled on up, insensate and determined, I bit my lip until it bled. Perhaps it's never too late.

In some peculiar way the Ark too seemed to respond to his efforts: two thousand feet up, spidering across the Great Gully and heading for the summit wall, he moved into quietude; the boulder slides diminished, the cliff stood heavy and passive, like a cow in heat. Down below, on Tarn Crag, the earth ceased to tremble. Stickle Tarn calmed, and lay like a vat of molten beryl, reflecting the vibrant, acid sky: there were no more shadows, and, when I took off my shirt to dip it in the Tarn Crag pool, I felt no movement of the air. Hundreds of small birds were rustling uncomfortably about in the heather; while up above the blind, blunt head of Harrison Stickle, one hawk wheeled in slow, magnificent circles.

Twenty minutes after his successful negotiation of the Great Gully intersection, Lyall crossed the summit wall. There I lost him for a short period. What he did there, I have no clue. Perhaps he simply wandered among the strange nodulate boulders and shallow rock pools of the region. But if any transition took place, if his sour and ludicrous metaphysic received its final unimaginable blessing, it must have come there, between summit wall and summit cairn, between the cup and the lip, while I fretted and stalked below.

All this aside: suddenly, the peaks about me flared and wavered ecstatically; and he was standing by the cairn—

He was almost invisible: but I can imagine him there, with his arms upraised, his raw wrists poking out of the sleeves of his tweed jacket: no more unengaging or desperate, no stranger than he had ever been among the evening mists of Cambridge or the broken milk machines of Holloway: except that, now, static electricity is playing over him like fire, and his mouth is open in a great disgusted shout that reaches me quite clearly through the still, haunted air—

For a moment, everything seemed to pause. The sky broadcast a heat triumphant – a long, high, crystalline song, taken up and echoed by summit after summit, from Wetherlam and the Coniston Old Man, from Scafell Pike and the unbearable resonant fastnesses of Glaramara, never fading. For a moment, Lyall stood transfigured, perched between his own madness and the madness of an old geography. Then, as his cry died away to leave the cry of the sky supreme, a series of huge cracks and ruptures spread out across the cliff face from beneath his feet; and, with a sound like the tearing of vast lace, the whole immense façade of Pavey Ark began to slide slowly into the tarn beneath.

Dust plumed half a mile into the air; on a mounting roar the cliff, like an old sick woman, fell to its knees in the cirque; the high bilberry terraces poised themselves for a long instant, then, lowering themselves gently down, evaporated into dust. Millions of tons of displaced water smashed the dam and went howling down Mill Gill, crashing from wall to wall; to spill – black and invincible, capped with a dirty grey spume – across the valley and break like a giant sea against the lower slopes of Oak Howe and Side Pike. Before the Ark had finished its weary slide, the valley road was no more, the New Hotel and Side House were rubbish on a long wave – and that pit of ashes, Lyall's house, was extinguished forever.

I watched the ruin without believing it. I remember saying something like, 'For God's sake, Lyall—' Then I turned and ran for my life over the quaking crag, east toward the safety of Blea Rigg and the fell route to an Ambleside I was almost frightened to reach. As I went, an ordinary darkness was filtering across the sky; a cool wind sprang up; and there were rain clouds already racing in from the Irish Sea along a stormy front.

Even allowing for the new unreliability of the press, exoteric explanations of the Great Langdale earth movement – activity renewed among the Borrowdale Volcanics after nearly five hundred million years; the unplanned landing of some enormous Russian space probe – seem ridiculous to me. Beyond the discovery of that poor woman, there were no witnesses other than myself in the immediate area. Was *Lyall*, then, responsible for the destruction of Pavey Ark?

It seems incredible: and yet, in the face of his death, insignificant. He carried his own entropy around with him, which makes him seem monstrous, perhaps; I don't know. He believed in an executive misery, and that should be enough for any of us. It hardly matters to me now. Other events swept it away almost immediately.

As I stumbled through the dim, panicky streets of Ambleside in the aftermath of the earthquake, the Patriotic Front was issuing from dusty suburban drill halls and Boy Scout-huts all over the country; and by noon England, seventy years too late, was taking her first hesitant but heady steps into this century of violence. Grouped about the warden's radio in the still, stupefied night, we would have guessed at something of the sort. I understand now why the Durham students were so affected: students have suffered more than most as the Front tightens its political grip.

In dreams, I blame Lyall for that, too; equate the death of reason with the collapse of Pavey Ark; and watch England crawl past me over and again in the guise of a burnt woman on her desperate journey to the head of a valley that turns out every time to be impassive and arid. But awake I am more reasonable, and I have a job at the new sports shop in Chamonix. It's no hardship to sell other climbers their perlon and pitons – although the younger ones will keep going up alone, against all advice. Like many of the more fortunate refugees I have been allowed to take a limited French nationality; I even have a second-class passport, but I doubt if I shall ever go back.

Walking about the town, I still hate to look up, in case the cruel and naked peaks surprise me from between the housetops: but the pain of that wound is at least explicable, whereas Lyall—

Everyone who ever met Lyall contributed in some small way to his death. It might have been averted perhaps, if, in some Cambridge mist of long ago, I had only come upon the right thing to say; and I behaved very badly toward him later: but it seems as futile to judge myself on that account as to be continually interpreting and reinterpreting the moment at which I was forced to realise that one man's raw and gaping self-concern had brought down a mountain.

And I prefer to picture Stickle Tarn not as it looked from the 1600-foot contour during Lyall's final access of rage and despair, but as I remember it from my Cambridge days and before – a wide, cold pool in the shadow of an ancient and beautiful cliff, where on grey windy days a seabird you can never identify seems always to be trawling twenty feet above the water in search of something it probably can't even define to itself.

The Eye of the Lens
LANGDON JONES

THE HALL OF MACHINES

Many great thinkers have attempted to analyse the nature of the hall. However, all their different approaches have been characterized by a lack of agreement and often blatant contradiction of fact. The appearance of the hall is generally well known, but as soon as we try to unearth specific detail we realize that all is conjecture.

The hall is vast. We would expect the descriptions of its contents to vary – one person could not be expected to cover the whole area of its interior. However, there has been a great deal of superstitious rumour concerning its contents, and it is often difficult to separate the true from the wholly fallacious.

There has been much conjecture concerning the size of the hall, but no results have actually been confirmed by any kind of measurement. It has been postulated by at least one writer that the hall is in fact infinite in extent. Others, no doubt influenced by exaggerated reports, have maintained that the hall covers a variable area, its size altering by a factor of at least fifty. Other evidence, however, suggests that both of these ideas bear, in all probability, little relationship to the facts.

During the last few years I have found it a rewarding task to research all the material I could find that related in any way to the hall. The task has been difficult, but illuminating. I have now in my files a vast amount of information in the form of books, articles, newspaper cuttings, recorded tapes, and ciné film as well as a large number of transcribed interviews, on a subject which I have found to become daily more fascinating. My research has become, to a degree, obsessional. I now find that my normal routine has been disturbed to quite a large extent over the last three years. I have devoted a complete room to this work, my ultimate intention being to shape the material into a comprehensive book. All over the wall are pinned the relevant newspaper cuttings, their arrangement depending on whichever aspect of the hall I am currently researching; set in the middle of the room is my ciné projector (frequently I watch the five hours of film I have accumulated at one sitting), and beside it is the tape recorder. On tape I have, apart from interviews and commentaries, at least an hour of the recorded sounds of some of the machines actually in operation. I have taken these sounds down, as accurately as possible, into musical notation. I have permutated the resultant patterns of notes and have found interesting relationships between the basic shapes, but, as yet, nothing more concrete.

I now spend a large proportion of my day in carrying out this research. I sit for hours, cutting out newspaper articles or developing film in the darkroom I have constructed. And so, with scissors, photographic chemicals, music paper, paste, tape recorder, and projector, I have built up a picture that is far from complete, but which is remarkable in its specific detail.

I now present some of the more striking of the descriptions I have unearthed. They are not delivered in a planned order, but have been assembled to give, rather than a dry academic account, a series of interesting impressions. I believe that one of the most fascinating aspects of the hall is in the diversity of impression it creates within the minds of the observers.

When my book is complete (which will not be for some years – it will run to at least five large volumes) I shall have sufficient confidence in the correctness of my results, and also the scope, to present them in detail. Until then, these extracts are intended only to communicate the atmosphere of the hall as it appeared to some people.

THE WATER MACHINE

The troughs and gulleys of the Water Machine extend over a very large area of this section of the hall, and although it is enclosed by false 'walls' of board, it still gives a sprawling impression. All about are convex metal surfaces; the floor is intersected by runnels and gulleys. The Water Machine is constructed primarily of cast iron, but certain of its parts are made of a lighter metal; probably an alloy, such as aluminium. The machine consists of a complexity of large components which stretch probably twenty feet in height, and the whole mass is supported by a surprisingly small number of slim metal struts.

Water is being pumped in from a large pipe at the very top of the machine. It is conducted by a series of ingenious mechanical movements through a series of gulleys and out of this part of the hall. I thought it likely that the water was moving in a large enclosed cycle, and dropped into a nearby channel a small piece of white paper. As I suspected, within about three minutes, the paper came floating past my feet again.

The noise of the water is almost deafening at times. Constantly there is the hissing of the jet at the top of the machine and a rushing of the liquid as it bubbles its way through its course; also there is the loud creaking of the metal parts as they operate. Every few seconds there is an enormous crash as a metal part is activated, and the water momentarily redoubles its volume.

Water drips constantly from the supporting members, gathers on the floor, and runs down the slope towards the many drains: concrete channels sweep in graceful lines about my feet: cast-iron conduits curve in black roundness, globules of condensation running along their undersides.

Situated at the top of the machine is the vast silver belly of the top water-container, spatulate and curved, like a vast silver spoon. The lead-in pipe, about six inches in diameter, is pointing into this tank, and a great jet of water, like a column of glass, is sluicing into its interior.

After a while, the container begins to groan, loudly. Suddenly the critical balance is attained. The groaning reaches a climax under the enormous weight of water, and the tank begins to shudder under a volume of liquid that it is incapable of supporting. Overspill slops to the floor and runs down to the square drains. Slowly, inch by inch, the tank begins to tip its vast bulk. Water spills over its thick pouring lip and falls in a glistening ribbon into a reservoir a couple of yards below. The tank begins to accelerate its rate of movement, and more water gushes down. Faster moves the container, and then, with a crash, it inverts itself. A solid mass of water falls into the reservoir, and the ground shudders with the impact. The container, meanwhile, is pulled back to a creaking vertical by a counterweight.

Water leaks from the reservoir, jetting out with great force from a circle of six holes at its convex base. These six separate streams are all conducted by diverse methods to the ground. One of the streams gushes into a smaller version of the water-barrel. Another enters one of the hinged containers set between the double rim of a large wheel, its weight causing the wheel to rotate slowly; after a quarter-revolution the container will snag on a projection and tip up, letting the water escape into one of the channels. Another stream strikes a sprung flange which bounces constantly in and out of the flow, the other end of the flange operating a mechanism like the escapement of a clock.

All the streams eventually reach the dark channels of wet concrete set in the floor, and are then conducted away from sight through holes set in the surrounding 'walls'.

Behind the wall can be heard the sound of great pumps.
Up above, I know, a fountain is playing.

MACHINES OF MOVEMENT

I was passing through a rather enclosed part of the hall, its spaciousness not apparent owing to the large bulk of the partitions enclosing various machines, when I passed a small wooden doorway set into one of the partitions. On the door was a plaque, printed black on white. It said:

INTERLOCKING MACHINE ROOM

On entering the room I found it to be full of giant metal crabs.

Great struts of thin metal rod criss-cross from ceiling to floor, making it impossible to see very far into the room. The very air shudders with the vibration of these machines. Although the constructions vary considerably, one from the other, a large number of them have the same basic shape. Their nucleus is a mass of rods and other interlocking members, and they stand about ten feet high. The arrangement of these rods is infinitely complex. At their apex they are thickly composed, and are surrounded by other parts which join them and permit their motion. They branch out, and at floor level each machine covers a considerable area.

All of the legs of these machines are connected by free-moving joints to the legs of the other units, and a movement of one causes an adjustment to the position of the other. The whole room is in motion, and the machines twitch each other with an action that appears almost lascivious in nature.

A rod near me is moved by the action of a neighbour's leg. This movement is communicated at the top of the unit to another of the legs, and it, in turn, imparts motion to a machine further away. As these machines work, a constant metallic clattering fills the air, as if the room is filled with typewriters.

The machines are slick and oiled; their movement is smooth, but gives an impression of great nervousness. All over this chamber are various other parts, all of which seem affected in some way by the movement of the rods. On the wall, near me, is fixed a plaque with a jointed arm extending from it. Taut wires radiate from either extremity into the skeletal grey. One end is angled up, the other down. As the wire of the higher end is pulled by some motion in the mass of interlocking parts, the arm reverses its position jerkily.

Perhaps, a million years ago, these machines were constructed in a delicate static balance, a frozen wave; and with the locking of the final link in the circuit, the fixing of the last jointed leg against leg, the balance was tripped. A motion would have run its path, twisting and turning about the machines, splitting itself, dividing again, until today this movement still ran about the constructions, diffused and unpredictable. A million strands of current, still splitting. And perhaps the machines had been so carefully designed that in another million years all the currents would begin to amalgamate, becoming less and less complex, until they finally became two, meeting in opposition and deadlock, all movement ceasing.

The mind drowns among the interlocking machines. Perhaps the reason is in the similarity of this abstract maze to that pattern formed by the neural current. Perhaps these patterns of motion parallel too closely the patterns of electricity that we call personality, and the one is disturbed by the other. Conversely, perhaps the very existence of a human mind in the room causes little eddies and whirls in the motion of the machines.

I was unable to stay in the interlocking machine room for more than a minute or two before the psychological effects became more than I could bear.

THE CLOCK

A large number of the machines in the hall are partitioned off by boards, so that one sometimes feels that one is walking in a constricted space, and loses completely the feeling of immensity that one often experiences in the hall. It was in such a place that I found, set against one 'wall', the mechanism of an enormous clock. It was all of shining brass, and it stood no less than ten feet high. It was facing the wall, the dial and hands (if, in fact, any such existed) being completely invisible. The clock was triangular in shape, and was supported by a framework of sturdy brass, front and back, that curved down to provide four feet. There was no plate at the back of the clock, its arbors being seated in strips of brass that curved in beautiful shapes from the main framework.

Despite the largeness of the clock, it was built to delicate proportions. The wheels were all narrow-rimmed, and the pallets that engaged the escape wheel were long and curved, like the fingernails of a woman. It was as if the mechanism of an ordinary domestic clock had been magnified to a great degree; there was none of the solidity and cumbersomeness of the turret clock here. I discovered to my surprise that this clock was powered, as most domestic clocks, by a spring. However, this spring was immense, and must have exerted a tremendous pressure to operate the mechanism.

Although the whole movement was surmounted by the escape wheel and anchor, which perched on the apex of the triangle, the pendulum was disproportionately short, stretching down little more than six feet. The slow tick of this enormous clock was lacking in the lower partials, and as a consequence was not disturbing.

As the clock was so large, motion could be seen among the wheels, which moved, each to a varying degree, with each tick of the clock. This was a fascinating sight, and I stayed watching the clock for a considerable period of time.

I wish that I could have seen the clock illuminated by strong morning sunlight from a window.

MACHINES OF DEATH – 1

There is darkness in this part of the hall. Stray light illuminates black, pitted metal. I can see little of the machine of death; it is to my right, and is a bleak high wall of metal. The end of a thick chain extrudes here, turns, and plunges back into the metal wall. The chain is a foot wide and four inches thick. The only other feature of this machine is a waste pipe which is sticking out from the wall. Underneath this pipe is a channel set into the floor, which conducts the waste to a nearby drain. The all-pervasive stink of this drain makes breathing difficult.

The pipe is pouring blood into the channel.

MACHINES OF DEATH – 2

This machine is very large, sprawling, and complicated. It appears to be completely functionless. It is possible that it was constructed to be entirely symbolic in nature, or alternatively that the things – creatures – upon which it operated are here no longer.

It consists of a vast network of girders, all of which are vibrating with a strange jogging motion. The only parts of the machine not affected by this movement are the two great supports at either end. The supports are each a framework of girders, and they contain various driving chains and gearing devices. At the top of each of these frames is a long jointed arm, of tremendous proportion. These arms also carry chains and gears. At the end of each arm is an enormous blade, made of a silver metal that catches the small amount of light. The blades have complete mobility, and appear to be fixed on the arms by some kind of ball joint.

The motion of the arms and the blades is difficult to observe in detail and even more difficult to describe. Analysing the action in words tends to give an impression of slowness, when in fact, considering the bulk of the parts, it is very swift indeed.

The arms rest close to their supports, their joints extending downward like elbows, the blades upright. Keeping the blades in the same position, they move together across the thirty-yard space. When they are only about a yard apart, the arms are almost fully extended, and the motion stops for an instant. Then abruptly the blades begin to move independently. They execute, in the space of only a few seconds, a complicated system of movements – thrusts, parries, arabesques – the motion of each blade being the mirror of the other. Then again comes the pause, and the arms bend again, carrying the blades back to the supports.

The action of these blades certainly suggests physical mutilation, and I found, as I watched, that I was wondering whether in fact the machine was still complete. Was there once a feeding mechanism that carried the bodies over to the knives to be sculptured within a few seconds to a raw, twitching mass?

Despite the unpleasant feelings that the machine arouses, I found it a fascinating experience to watch the blades, and also the complex system of vibrating girders beneath them. It is strange to see such large objects in such rapid motion; the throbbing of the floor testified to the weight of the mechanism, which must have been in the hundreds of tons.

On the occasion that I observed the machine, there were two other people there as well; a man and a woman. At first I thought that they were part of the machine, but my attention was caught by the fact that their own vibrating motion was slightly lagging behind that of the machine as their soft bodies absorbed their impetus.

They were both naked, and they were on one of the girders directly below the high knives. The man was lying on his back, stretched along the girder, and the woman was squatting astride his hips. The jogging of the girder was throwing their bodies up and down in a mechanical travesty of copulation. The man was grasping the woman's thighs tightly, and her face, turned towards me, with her bottom lip between her teeth, was florid and beaded with sweat. I could see her nostrils contracting with each gasped breath she took.

A drop of oil fell from the knives as they clashed above, and dropped unnoticed onto her shoulder. As it ran down the pale flesh of her arm, it looked like a single drop of ancient blood.

MACHINES OF DEATH – 3*

The machine sits in distance unheard. I walk on dry sin, on the shit of us all, a man by my side who points out all his bones. The well has now dried and all that remains is a glowing, radioactive silt. The universe is shaped like a whirlpool, and the vortex is here. Here is the end of all time, the end of all space. The ultimate nil. I have eaten my fill; here is my place; there is no single way left to climb, and the rest is just fear. This cul-de-sac is arid and death-cool. It is bleakness, a focus-point built by man and his pains. The door must be tried; I pull and it groans, and opens up wide. The chamber is small, but light is let in to show me a word ——
Auschwitz!

THE MOTHER

This machine is standing in isolation; it is surrounded by space on all sides. It is extremely large, standing almost a hundred feet high, and it is shaped like an elongated onion, tapering at the top to a high spire. From one side of the machine, from about ten feet up, a flaccid rubbery tube hangs down and outward to ground level.

The onion-belly of the Mother is completely featureless, and light catches its curves; the tube is of a dull red shade.

There are sounds coming from inside the metal body, soft but constant. But then, abruptly, they stop, and all is silent.

At the top of the tube, a bulge becomes apparent, swelling outward all the time. Slowly, this bulge begins to travel inside the tube, away from the machine and down to the ground. While all this is going on, one obtains an impression of supreme effort, and, strangely, pain. Perhaps it is because the whole process is so slow. The object creeping down the tube will eventually reach the end and emerge into the light; one realizes this, and feels an almost claustrophobic impatience with the slowness of the event. There is a feeling too of compression and relaxation, and one finds one's own muscles clenching in time to the imagined contractions.

Eventually the bulge reaches the end of the tube at ground level. This is where the real struggle begins. One becomes aware that the end of the tube is beginning to dilate, slowly and rhythmically. The belly of the machine is

---

*This machine consists of a flat surface of metal with a circular metal door which leads to a small chamber, called the 'compressor', or 'pot'. Apart from this the wall is featureless except for a switch by the side of the door. This area seems to be the most dismal place in the entire hall.

as smooth and unevocative of any emotion as ever, but it is impossible for the observer not to feel that agonies are now being endured. One realizes that the process is completely irreversible; that there is no way of forcing the bulge back up the tube and inside the metal shell again.

Wider and wider grows the aperture at the end of the tube, affording one an occasional glimpse of shiny moisture within. A glint of metal is now and then apparent.

The tube dilates to its fullest extent, and a metal form is suddenly revealed, covered in dripping brown fluid. The rubber slides over its surface, releasing it more and more by the second. Abruptly, it bursts free in a wash of amniotic oil.

All is still.

The oil begins to drain away, and the new machine stands there motionlessly as the liquid drains from its surfaces. It is a small mechanism on caterpillar tracks, with various appendages at its front end which seem to be designed for working metal, or stone.

With a whirr, it jerks into action, and it moves softly away from the great Mother. There is a click from the parent machine, and the noises inside begin again.

I have watched this mechanism for long periods, and it appears to create only two kinds of machine. They are both on the same basic design, but one appears to be made for erection, the other for demolition.

The Mother has probably been working thus for hundreds of years.

ELECTRONICS

Electric machines stare at me with warm green eyes. I see nothing but bright plastic surfaces, inset with pieces of glass. These are still machines, active but unmoving, and in my ears is the faint hum of their life. The only movement here which indicates that the machines are in operation is the kicking of metres and the occasional jog of an empty tape spool.

Their function is not apparent; they work here at nameless tasks, performing them all with electronic precision and smoothness.

There are wires all over the room, and their bright, primary colours contrast strikingly with the overall pastel tones of the plastic bodies.

Sonata in the style of machines

In a small chamber to the rear of the room of electric machines, there are some more of a different kind. The door to this small room is of wood, with a square glass set into it. The room appears to have remained undisturbed for many years.

They line three walls of the chamber, and are covered with switches and meters. They hum in strange configurations of sound, and appear to be making electric music together.

DEATH OF MACHINES – 1

In this part of the hall, all is still. Spiked mounds of time rise round me, their hulks encrusted with brown decay. The floor is totally covered by a soft carpet of rust, and its acrid odour stings the nostrils. A piece detaches itself from one of the tall machines and drifts to the floor, a flake of time. Many such flakes have fallen here in this part of the hall.

Time burns fire in my eyes, and I turn my head, looking for escape. But everywhere I see seconds and hours frozen into these red shapes. Here is a wheel, its rim completely eaten through; there is a piston, its movable parts now fixed in a mechanical *rigor mortis*. A reel of wire has been thrown into a corner, ages in the past, and all that remain are its circular traces in the dust.

My feet have left prints in the rust-carpet.

DEATH OF MACHINES – 2

I had come into the hall with my girl, and we had spent a long time wandering about, hand in hand, when we suddenly came on the remains of a machine.

It stood about six feet in height, and I could see that at one time it had been of great complexity. For some reason my girl was not very interested, and went off to see something else, but I found that this particular machine made me feel very sad. It appeared to be entirely composed of needles of metal, arranged in a thick pattern. The largest of these needles was about three inches long, and there appeared to be no way for the machine to hold together. My guess is that when it was made, the needles were fitted in such a way that the whole thing struck an internal balance. The machine was now little more than a gossamer web of rust; it must have had tremendous stability to have remained standing for such a long time.

It was fascinating to look closely at its construction, to see the red lines fitting together so densely. It was like looking into a labyrinth; a system of blood-red caves. With every movement of my head a whole new landscape was presented to me. I called my girl over, and we stood hand in hand, looking at the dead machine.

I think that it must have been our body heat, for neither of us made an excessive movement, but at that moment the entire construction creaked, and sank a few inches. Then there was a sigh, and the whole thing dissolved into dust about our feet.

Both of us felt very subdued when we left the hall.

I hope that the above information has enabled my readers to gain an impression of this strange and exciting hall. There is little that I can add, except the following point.

You will remember from one of the accounts I have printed here, the one giving details of the creation of new machines, the following passages: 'It is a small mechanism on caterpillar tracks, with various appendages at its front end which seem to be designed for working metal, or stone.' ' . . . .it appears to create only two kinds of machine . . . one appears to be made for erection, the other for demolition.' These two passages, together with some other material that I have not published here, suggest an interesting point.

I believe that the machines mentioned are the same as those described in another account, in which the writer stood by one of the outer walls of the hall. He watched one set of machines building a wall about six inches further out than the old one, which was being torn down by the other mechanisms. This seems to be a process which is going on all the time, all over the hall; a new wall is built, slightly further out, and this in its turn will be demolished as another is put up.

I believe that the hall has been, from the time of its creation and always will be, increasing in size!

However, only more research will be able to establish this radical idea as an incontrovertible fact.

THE COMING OF THE SUN

Cellar Fire

Rudolf opened the cellar door, spilling light into the dim chamber. He walked carefully down the wooden steps, the yellow light shining on his bald scalp. He coughed as fumes from the dormant paraffin-fired boiler caught at his throat, and as he reached the bottom of the steps he muttered slow obscenities.

Normally Michael would come down here with him to supervise this preparing of the boiler, but Michael couldn't make it this time. He was in the hospital after being attacked by someone. Rudolf smiled to himself and a silver line coursed down his chin.

Rudolf was tall, but stooped. All his movements were slow and deliberate and accompanied by gruntings and pantings as if each one caused him supreme effort or pleasure. A pink scar traced a smooth curve over the surface of his shaven head, as if following the sutures of the skull beneath. He was dressed in a formless garment of rough grey cloth. In his mind there was very little, save for a general hatred of a world that had done him some unspecified wrong. His hatred was generalized, directed toward tables, chairs, walls, as well as people.

His life was here. His past was now far buried, and his half-formed thoughts swirled about his skull like mist rising on a marsh.

He shuffled across the room to the cans of paraffin. 'Bastards ... ' he muttered to the cans, as he bent to pick one up. If he was capable of liking any place, then he liked it here in the cellar. He liked the wet brick walls, the dark corners; he liked the cobwebs and the wooden boxes stacked in the far corner; he liked the silence and the electric light bulb which swung on its flex, swaying the room back and forth beneath his feet. He liked the smells of the cellar, the smells of mustiness and decay.

He moved to the boiler with his can of paraffin swaying in his hand, and lowered the can to the floor. He unscrewed the fuel cap on the pump and inserted the funnel. Bending down slowly, he lifted and tilted the can, watching the blue liquid bubbling down the vortex of the funnel. When the can was empty he threw it, smiling, into the corner, enjoying the clanging sound it made. Michael wouldn't have allowed him to throw the can. He primed the boiler, and when the pressure was up, pressed the green button. A glow came to life behind a small square of glass and a chugging sound began. There was a flash, a bang, and the boiler fired, a jet of flame appearing behind the glass. He enjoyed looking at the fire; that was why he had come down here without supervision, to press his nose, as he was doing now, against the glass and to watch the potent flare jetting and roaring.

After a while he became tired of looking at the flame, and turned once again to the collection of cans in the corner. He shuffled across, his ragged clothes trailing on the dirty floor. He unscrewed the cap of one of the cans, and drew in, his nose pressed into the can, the oily softness of the paraffin's odour. Then he raised the can slowly above his head, in both hands, and inverted it so that the liquid fell in a broken stream, splashing onto the floor, soaking the bottoms of his trouser legs. He felt an unusual excitement, and breathed in deeply.

When the can was empty, the floor was swimming with liquid. He looked at the other cans; they reminded him of policemen. He didn't like policemen; a vague freak of memory told him that policemen didn't believe in Jesus. He went to the other cans and, one by one, he twisted off the caps, and threw them about the room. There were about thirty cans, and they stood at his feet, their round mouths open in surprise. He was like a king, and they stood at his feet like subjects. He felt happy.

He kicked at them, and one fell over, bubbling away its life.

'Bastards ... '

He picked up one of the cans and swung it round, creating a transient parabola of blueness that sparkled in the light and then sprayed both him and the room. His skull was throbbing, and something began to grow in his throat; he had to gasp for breath. His big hands clenched and unclenched at his sides, and the breath whistled through his teeth. He picked up another of the cans, held it upside-down and deliberately sprayed his feet. He threw its corpse away, and as it bounced into the corner shouted, 'Clatter!'

He had no memory of feeling like this before. Actually he had, many times in childhood, and he had last felt it in a woodyard between the thighs of an anonymous woman.

He picked up another can, emptied and killed it, and threw it away. Another. Another. He strode among the cans, kicking, pushing aside, growing in stature all the time. The smell of paraffin was strong in the air now, and he gloried in the odour, filling his chest with its stickiness.

When all the cans had been emptied, he stood with his feet in the paraffin, beating his chest with a large hand, his scar bright red and appearing to glow in the dim cellar light.

An idea began to grow in his mind. He found that he was shaking with excitement. A stirring began in his groin, and he put out long and clumsy arms, wanting to embrace anything. He walked over to the boiler and picked up a metal rod that had been standing nearby. His throat was nearly blocked now, and his body was constantly shaken by small shudders.

He plunged down the rod and smashed the thick glass. The flame was free, to breathe!

For a while he watched the flame, smiling at it, then he abruptly bent down and ripped a strip of cloth from his trouser leg. He dipped it into the paraffin until it was soaked. He suddenly found tears filling his eyes. He lowered the cloth on to the roaring flame, and through the tears saw it burst with dancing fire that was reflected a million times to become a universe of light.

He wiped his eyes and, while he could still see, threw the flaming cloth into the centre of the floor. For a while, nothing happened, but suddenly the fire widened and widened, from a drop, to a pool, to a lake, to a sea of fire. He felt a rising and a swelling, and as the fire grew, so did he. Fumes were in the air, and the cellar was lit with a brightness that it had never known before. It was hot, and as the fire came closer to him, hotter.

At the end he stood there, arms and legs outstretched, erect and potent, shouting with happiness at the flame, his friend and creation.

Finally he knew the glorious pain of self-immolation.

In the Lounge

Light comes through the french windows and splashes warmly across the parquet floor, reflecting into the far corners of the room. Near the window is a grand piano, and a man sits at it, dressed in rough grey clothing. On his face is a look of complete involvement in what he is playing; his eyes are half-closed and he sways his head from side to side. His hands rise and fall, jerkily and mechanically, and he plays a constant series of random and dissonant chords.

Also in the room, sitting in armchairs facing each other, are two people: a man and a woman.

JOHN: Are you sure you feel all right this morning, Mary?

MARY: Yes thanks, John, fine; it's just that poor Robert sitting there makes me feel a bit depressed. (They both glance at the pianist.)

JOHN (to the pianist): Good morning, Eusebius!

PIANIST (turning quickly and speaking swiftly and angrily): *Florestan!*

MARY (shivering): Oh! I hate this place!

JOHN: Well, I don't think you're alone in that. I think we all hate it – even the ones who don't know anything.

MARY: Yes. So many of them don't understand, but you can sense that they feel fear, just the same as us. (She glances at the piano again.)

One, two, three, four ... I wonder how many chords he plays each day. I wonder whether he enjoys it, or whether each note is a torment.

JOHN: And there's Colin, every day, curled up in the bathroom, his hairy legs in front of him like a trembling shield. It's like living constantly in some kind of disaster area.

MARY: Yes, a moment after the disaster has occurred; there is the same feeling here of mute horror, just like the first few seconds after an accident.

JOHN: The *Hindenburg* falls in smoking ruins by breakfast time; at lunch the *Titanic* meets its end, and Christ is crucified by dinner time.

MARY: Oh, I wish I could *leave!*

JOHN. How can we? There's no way out for us past the eyes of authority. Two mistakes have been made; we are forgotten, and here we shall remain until we're too old to care any more . . . .

MARY: Oh, please don't! The whole thing depresses me so much. Let's go out somewhere; would you like a walk in the garden?

JOHN (preoccupied): Yes . . . yes . . . in a while.

(MARY suddenly inclines her head and sniffs at the air.)

MARY: John – can you smell something?

JOHN (vaguely): What?

MARY: It's almost . . . as if something's . . . burning.

JOHN: I saw . . . two dogs once . . .

MARY: John – I'm sure there's something burning! I think we should get out!

JOHN : . . . two dogs in the street . . .

MARY: Perhaps it's just a bonfire.

JOHN: . . . not doing anybody any harm . . . .

A Scene in the Street

The scene is a medium-sized suburban shopping centre. Fairly heavy traffic is moving past, but there are not many people on the pavements. Outside one of the shops, a grocer's, the shopkeeper is talking to two women shoppers.

There are two dogs padding about the pavement, sniffing each other. The shopkeeper looks disapprovingly at the dogs, and then turns his bright attention back to the women. One of the dogs makes an attempt to mount the other, but then drops back to all fours again, and they continue to move about from one side of the pavement to the other.

The grocer is a tall man, and he prides himself on his friendliness towards his customers. He had a hard time when he was younger, trying to establish himself, but now he is the owner of a thriving shop, and is able to spare the time to chat to his young housewives. Also he is not sure about one of the women to whom he is talking. She has only been here for a short time, and she seems to be exceptionally friendly. He wonders if, one day, she might be good for a turn. He is beginning to develop a paunch, but is rather proud of it, and likes to rest his hands on it.

The smaller of the dogs again mounts the other, and they begin to copulate there on the pavement. The grocer and the housewives see this copulation out of the corners of their eyes, but the housewives carry on talking brightly. The grocer however, is annoyed. He sees the behaviour of the dogs as an annoyance, almost as an insult. The ladies are, for a moment, talking to each other.

The grocer seizes his opportunity, walks over and gives the dogs a kick.

However, his boot strikes only the male dog. The animal is spun round so that he is facing away from the female, but is still in her. As the grocer walks back, the dog screams in agony. Its twisted penis is still congested with blood, which now cannot escape. A permanent erection now binds him fast to the female in an agonizing union. The female dog is frightened and begins to run, dragging the male backwards.

The grocer and the ladies, embarrassed, try not to notice, and carry on their conversation.

The screams of the trapped dog become even more pitiful as the creature is dragged away swiftly by the female. The level of sound in the street drops as people become aware of the suffering dogs. People turn to watch as the creatures disappear down the street.

The grocer is very embarrassed, and more than a little angry.

In the Courtyard

He found himself alone in a dark courtyard. He had been there for a long, long time. He remembered sunlight and contentment, but now his world was filled with his desire for escape.

To his right, curving down to the dark tarmac of the yard was a wind vent, its black throat yawning in air noisily. It was a silver structure, square in outline, and he kept away from its mouth. The yard was in shadow, made even blacker by the sunlight above. The sun never reached down here. On three sides black buildings rose in the air, and loomed beside and behind him, but on the fourth, a long way above, sunlight broke across the wall like glass and splintered a rude balcony with light. At the balcony was a door, and he knew that behind the door was a small chamber, big enough to accommodate the small staircase that led through the manhole to the grassy field above.

All round the courtyard were the corpses of small animals, and in the far corner lay a crazed donkey, a silver spoon buried in its neck, ready for someone to come along to scoop out a mouthful of melting flesh. All about the donkey were flies, feeding off its craziness, and it gave to the world its foetid odour without shame or pride.

Fire escapes jutted blackly above him. He clawed back the life bulging in his throat. A shaft of black brick, a basic buttress, sloped from one side of the courtyard to the other. In this enclosed place it was like a beam from some black and dusty sun. He leaned against a wall, and brick crumbled under his twitching fingers. In front of him was a steel ladder that reached up to the balcony, but he was scared to climb. There was everything to lose.

But now the odour of burning oil reached his nostrils, and fear for his life came to him. He must leave!

He grasped the rungs of the ladder and began to climb. But he could not; his feet would not respond to him. He fell back, almost screaming.

There was a movement above him on the balcony. It was a slim Jewish girl. She was shouting something down to him, but he couldn't hear what she was saying.

'I can't hear you!' he called, but she indicated her ears and shook her head sadly. He realized that she was deaf. She reached down to him with an imploring expression on her face. He realized what he must do. He began to climb the ladder again, but found it now a little easier. As he climbed towards her, so she strained her hands down to him. As their flesh closed in contact he felt a wild crackling strength coursing into him. He climbed over the railing and on to the balcony, she helping him. Once over, he stood and looked into her large, dark eyes, still holding her hands.

'You saved me,' he said.

'No, you helped me as well. And I haven't saved you; you can't beat geometry.'

'I couldn't hear you down there.'

'I know. I've been in a very similar place.'

He looked back over his shoulder. The yard, from up here, was much smaller than he remembered it. The donkey, far below, twitched his tail with mad contempt.

'I shall never go back there,' he said. 'And I shall never leave you.'

She smiled. 'You will. The answer is written in the very curves of space, the geometry of time. Kiss me.'

The power from her was welling through him, and his body floated with the breeze that blew about. He took her in his arms, and pressed his lips gently against hers. She was warm in his arms and his mouth; he closed his eyes, and let his body sing the song they had begun.

And then she was gone.

There was nothing. He turned wildly, his arms flailing the air. As he turned he slipped, and fell back into the yard. But he fell slowly, descending like a feather into darkness. He sprawled on the cold tarmac, sobbing into the dust.

He got up on his knees and stared at the balcony which swam in his gaze. There was another woman there, and as he watched her hair changed colour, her features flowed like treacle into new combinations of line and form.

Sometimes she seemed old, sometimes she was young and fresh. Each time she reached down to him, but he could not hear what she was saying; he couldn't reach up to touch her hands. Sometimes she was too weak to lift him; sometimes she just looked at the sky; sometimes she reached for someone else whom he could not see. Once she was sad and beautiful, and he rushed for the ladder, but she didn't see him, and was lost in contemplation of her own feet.

'I remember a neater arrangement than this!' he called to her.

Time danced like fireflies across his brow. He sensed the years falling, brown skeletal leaves of age, and he put out his hand to brush them as they fell.

And all the time he could feel the ground shaking and the angry fire nearing him for its revenge . . . .

Finally her features changed again. Above him stood a girl with blue eyes and with pale musicians moving in a procession through her mind.

'Help me!' he called to her. 'I NEED *YOU!*' just realizing that he did.

Her mouth began to move anxiously, but a second after her lips moved, a cracked voice spoke a foreign tongue into his ears. The sounds she made brought agony to him. 'Go!' he shouted. 'Go away!' He ran to the other side of the courtyard to escape the pain she was causing him. She began to grow transparent, fading into nothing. Just before she disappeared he realized that he could understand what she was saying.

But now all was bright; the fire was coming to claim him.

In the Lounge

All is unchanged. JOHN and MARY still sit in their facing chairs. ROBERT still plays the piano like an automaton. There is a strong smell of smoke in the air.

JOHN: The strange thing about this place is that no one really knows anything about anybody else. None of us has a past life. We are all here, living in the immediate present with nothing at all behind us. Perhaps we were all created here; perhaps there is nothing outside at all. Perhaps this whole place is the only thing in the universe, and that what we see from our windows is nothing but a backdrop painted to deceive us. I often worry about this, you know. In fact the other day I put my arm through the bars over my window, right up to the shoulder, but I didn't touch anything.

MARY: I had a terrible dream last night.

JOHN: Mary – I'm sure I can smell smoke.

MARY: I dreamed I had a husband . . . . I dreamed a past life for myself.

JOHN: I'll swear there's something on fire.

MARY: I dreamed a complete past . . . . I dreamed love and pain and death and friends and enemies.

JOHN: I think we should see what is burning.

MARY: I dreamed that I fed from my husband. When he loved me I would draw sweetness and strength from his body. He would enter my body with his, and my soul with his. He would move inside me, shaking me, and my body would respond, and twist and turn to receive the power and love of him. This was my dream: He is loving me. *This is me!* I feel, *this responsive, mindless creature is me! Everything else is false.* I cling to him, my fingers pressing into his back. My head is moving from side to side, but all I can feel is him in me and my body responding to his power. He penetrates my bowels, my chest, my eyes; he is everywhere in me, there is nothing but him. I call his name out into the world, but the world is him, and he is moving in me. Our bodies stiffen in one. I strain up to him, and his body gasps rigidly down to me. And then there is nothing but the soundless explosion to which I abandon myself.

And then we are both quiet. His face is on the pillow by my shoulder, and his weight presses me down.

I didn't tell you about my husband, did I? He is a very big man. When he was younger, he was powerful and muscled. He is still strong, but now the flesh of middle age swells his belly. He is heavy on me as we lie there, but I do not care. Nothing matters but the strength I have drawn from him. He is quieter than usual, and so am I. I lie, staring up peacefully at the ceiling, illuminated by the bedside light. I stroke his shoulder, and decide eventually that he has gone to sleep. I will give him a few minutes before I wake him. His weight is now uncomfortable, but I vow to endure it for a while until I am forced to disturb him. (MARY's voice is gradually getting higher, and a light of hysteria is coming into her eyes.)

His shoulders feel cold, and I pull up the blankets to cover them. And then . . . and then I try to wake him. I push his shoulder gently, but he does not wake. I smile indulgently, and push again a little harder. The flesh gives under my hand, but he does not respond. I call his name . . . again . . . and then I smell it. The smell of death.

(The last part of MARY's story is screamed out.)

I smelt the death of him in that bed. Have you ever read in the papers, 'He died in his sleep'? I was pinned under him. I tried desperately to get him away from me. I hit his shoulder again and again, but I could not get a response from him. I tried to escape from under him ... he was still in me ... but I could not. I cried and screamed and tried to force life back in. I held his face up, and saw his dead eyes. His eyes stared at me like a dead fish's eyes. His face was distorted in a terrible twisted smile.

I tried to push his head away, but it fell back on to my shoulder, giving me a dead man's kiss – cold saliva on my flesh. I remember that I felt now nothing but a terrible revulsion for him. I must try to escape ... I must unjoin myself from him. I remember that I twisted and turned, moving my hips as if I were loving this crushing body. I strained myself, careless of myself, saying something, I forget what. And at last his dead prick no longer touched my body. I couldn't get from underneath him .... I put my hands under his corpse and tried to lift it off ... but even with the strength of panic I couldn't do it. Time went past. His flesh cooled. I cursed him, I jerked and twitched under him .... I remember spittle drooling all over my face, and I remember calling and crying and punching and groaning ... but his weight pinned me flat on the bed. And I remember that at last someone heard my screams and came ... and they brought me here! HERE! THEY BROUGHT ME HERE!

(MARY begins to scream and writhe in her chair. JOHN is not looking at her, but is talking quietly to himself. The pianist continues to play his chords.)

The Burning Clock —

It is an American wall clock. Its case is made of wood, square, with two supporting columns that rise from the bottom to the top. A large arch of glass is in front, and two side panels form gothic curves. The face and mechanism is supported behind the front arch, at the top, and the pendulum, with a large, flat brass bob, hangs almost to the bottom of the case.

Flames have just caught at the bottom of the case, and the watching man leans closer to see better. The wood at the bottom of the right-hand column is beginning to char. The flames have caught quickly, and begin to reach up the sides of the clock. The fire also burns at the base of the clock, and a discoloured patch can be seen on the 'floor' through the front glass. He looks at the burning column on the right. Varnish has peeled off all the way up, and the whole column is now burning fiercely. There is a crack, and the side glass splinters. The back of the clock has now caught fire.

Suddenly a flame appears inside the clock, as the baseboard burns completely through. The flames engulf the pendulum bob as it swings gently to and fro. Now flames are rising inside the clock and, for a while, the clock resembles a glass case of fire. Then the fire outside the clock gains a better hold, and abruptly the front glass cracks. Half of the glass falls to the floor and shatters; the other half clings to the blackening wood. Now the bob can only be seen as it emerges from the fire at the extreme ends of its swing; it can be seen now that parts of the pendulum are glowing red. Although the hands, which he can just distinguish in the flare, are not pointing to the hour or the half, the clock begins to strike. The clock strikes twelve, and then goes on.

The baseboard falls to the floor, trailing smoke behind it, and smoulders there. The striking of the clock is becoming erratic; the strokes are irregular, and slowing. The front part of the clock swings open on its hinges, the warping of the frame freeing it, and the remainder of the glass crashes down. The flames are concentrated at the top of the clock now; the pendulum is a glowing shaft of red. The clock's striking mechanism seizes, and the sound stops. The pendulum is now moving under its own momentum, and its arc is diminishing; the clock is now like a burning skeleton.

Metal drips down from the interior of the clock mechanism in bright, hurried drops. The clock is now completely still, only the flames dancing over its surface. He moves round to the side of the clock, and sees its cogs, warped and glowing. The sight disturbs him. It is as if the flames are the only moving things in a petrified universe. Great calcified images loom in his mind, and he presses the back of his hand to his teeth to subdue his fear.

But then he sees that the clock has not burned at all; it is just that the intense heat has caused it to stop.

Three Catatonic Stories

A man runs across the room, fear glinting in his eyes. In the corner, curled up like a slug, is the naked body of a man called Colin. Beside him is a sheet of paper. The man picks up the paper and reads:

1. A man is sitting at a table. The surface in front of him is supporting a large block of gold, on a red silk cushion. Lying on the table beside the nugget is a sharp silver knife. The man licks his lips and rolls up his sleeves with delicacy. Then he puts out his hands, grasping the knife with one and holding

the block with thumb and forefinger of the other. The gold is pure, and much softer than gold usually is. Its outside surface has a dull gleam. The man picks up the knife, and brings it deliberately to a point above the block. He lowers it to the dull golden surface and carefully draws it across, scoring a straight bright line across the top. For a few seconds he holds the knife poised, regarding his work critically. Then he brings down the knife again and draws it across once more, but this time with more pressure, slicing through the gold as if it were butter and exposing the bright gleam of its inner surface.

He neatly bisects the block, and with the knife, moves the two pieces apart. This is the moment of consummation. A few heavy seconds pass. Then he puts down the knife, with gold adhering to its blade, and picks up one of the sections of the golden block. His lips are full and wet; he parts them and pushes in the gold. He licks the moist gold from his fingers.

FIRE

2. There is a plain. It is dark in colour and absolutely flat, like the polished top of a table. There is an impression of depth about the plain, and it gleams faintly.

In the centre of the plain, standing like a passion translated into stone, is a cathedral. At this distance the cathedral cannot be seen in detail, but its general shape, the light on its windows, can just be made out.

A man is riding a motorcycle across the plain, at high speed. The plain is intensely cold, and the temperature is dropping by the minute. The man is trying to reach the cathedral before the cold is enough to cause his consciousness to fail and make him plunge to the ground. The roar of his engine echoes from unseen obstacles. He rockets across the ground, nearing the cathedral swiftly. Soon the shape of the building is towering over him, and he throttles down, gradually slowing. He overshoots the cathedral and circles it, its features flashing past him in a jumble of grey stonework.

On his second circuit he turns in and travels through the door, right into the nave. Inside, the cathedral is very spacious and warm. Light comes in and makes the stone warm and sensual with its stained-glass colours. About three-quarters down the cathedral nave is the altar. The rest of the floor space is empty, save for a few benches cluttered in the centre.

The man turns his motorcycle to the right, and travels slowly down one side of the nave. The sound of the engine comes booming back at him from the high roof. He circles the nave, the light turning his flesh into a shifting sequence of colour and texture. As he twists the throttle control his engine noise becomes higher and rises to a recognizable note. The engine backfires, and the tremendous report echoes into a continuous sound. The stonework throws back throbbing reflections of the engine noise; it is as if all the sound he has made since entering the door is still winging about from one side of the building to the other. The air brushes his face, and he speeds up, dipping his machine at the corners. The note of his engine rises still more.

And abruptly there is something else in the air. A disturbance shudders in the nave. A response – a conflict. Still faster he travels, flinging his motorcycle round the nave. The note of the engine rises in a roar.

And suddenly he has it.

His engine note hits one of the harmonics of the basic resonance frequency of the cathedral, and all the air in the building begins to vibrate in a sympathetic resonance.

As he speeds round, he coaxes the sound from the depths. The air shudders deeply, louder and louder, until the cathedral-note has been completely evoked, and the deep shuddering is almost unbearable. Now he knows he will never leave the cathedral. As he cycles round, holding the throttle steady, he begins to laugh, an act that is noiseless in the great mass of vibrating air, his motorcycle sound lost in the giant organ note of the building.

On the plain, the cathedral sounds.

FIRE BRIGHT

3. A man is born, whose body is constructed in such a way that positive space exerts a tremendous pressure on his cellular structure. He may only obtain a lessening of these sensations by standing in front of large mirrors, when positive space is balanced to a degree by the residual pressure from negative space. By placing two mirrors, one each side of him, both facing inward, the balancing of tensions affords him exquisite relief.

One day the pressures become intolerable, and he tries to escape them by leaping into a full-length mirror. He becomes trapped, merged with his 'negative' image. He is forced to hang motionless, caught in the interstices of positive and negative space, at the point where the two intersect. He doesn't have the strength to move himself; the power-weight ratio permits him only to move one finger. This he does often, projecting it into normal or negative space, but each time the finger is two-dimensional, and the stresses are immense.

He hangs, trapped in a glacier of force.

FIRE BURN BRIGHT

The man puts down the paper and turns to the foetus beside him, but now in his eyes there is an expression of lost despair. He speaks without conviction. 'You must come with me – we must escape.' The door at the end of the room blossoms into orange light. ' . . . must come with me . . . ' says the foetus. ' . . . must escape . . . ' A faint hint of urgency and panic comes into the man's voice. 'Come . . . quickly!' 'Come . . . quickly!' Tongues roar into the room. The man turns, ignoring the hunched form on the floor, and begins to scream, in a high childish voice. He drops to his hands and knees and begins to wail like a baby, beating his fists on the parquet flooring. It is very warm in the room.

Black Wave, Take Me Away With You

Flat and polished tables of black glass – head of flutes shrilling like Cocteau's opium pipes – wide grey façade 'Charing Cross Hotel' through rain going in distance and past – sun drips blood into a sea of tears making the green one red ... weave your bandages of gold – flat façade, wide and grey filled out with deperspectived spaces – bully shouldered perverts take each other sexually, and us – men sob in the lavatory – paraschizophrenic moves walls and time by psychokinesis – Eusebius plucks dead chords from the piano, crying – the walls weep with memories of you – time-men lurk round corners waiting for more time to destroy – locked in the washroom, naked people cry out as ice-water jets their flesh, fiercely – dirty old men communicate telepathically with God – my own legs tremble before me with beautiful fear – rimed with blue glory they await the coming of the sun ....

Smoke comes from the sky like a scent of lemons – I am coming – I am coming ...

Soleil de Sang, d'Oiseaux

It is quiet in this house behind my windows
My Jesus, my universe of silence and bells
There are only more windows; layers of glass
Throw to me the lance of love, my Love
And I can look out through the layers of glass
Make of yourself a cauldron for my heart
See the slow flower-garden and the ghosts of love

Give me the red and the green of your love
Inside this house it is very quiet
Rainbow of love, desert of love
Like a cave and I am here
Your golden pillars are singing to me
I am here in a cave in a house behind glass

They slowly swing, the bells of the depths
And I am falling apart and dying
Do not wake me: it is the time of the bird!

Events in Hell

Time sinks wells into my brain – sutures hum with electrical circuits –
Russian death machines swing wide barrels and project electrical rays into my
eyes – faces, fatty, broken, and degenerate, strain at the sun's glory – fantasies
of life crackle among dendrides – an old man masturbates his death-tool and
spits white glory at the sun – morons concentrate on the intellectual promise
of a piece of wood – my head is a gramophone horn sounding music-hall songs
out to the stars.

Dead Book Images Spin in My Mind Like Snow

Book jackets fall spinning to my floor – God rises in me like a vapour from
snow – the sound of my voice echoes in levels of light – a rainbow of love to
the vision of your face – Give me the thirst of your love; the tumescence of
your love.

Motorcycles ride across the plain of snow – black mosquito squadrons of
desire – The snow lies on my soul like the seal of your name – Send your
motorcycles to me – Give me the red and the green of your love – my man,
my woman, my child, my God.

Levels of consciousness hide your bells in light – Sound waves of glory put
my soul to flight – The sun of blood is trembling on the bleeding snow – The
colours of your love flux in a brilliant flow – Your core of acquiescence swells
in me – Dead images are floating on the sea.

Book jackets are trampled by jack boots – a dead web stretches across the
swelling surfaces of dead water – the smiling, deep surfaces – they welcome
the laxness of my new body – they hide their bowels in night – they clasp soft
hands under me and receive my weakness – I see your light far above me,
your sun, your blood – but I feel the warmth of their embrace, the kiss of
their foul water-skin touches my lips – Your snow is burying me, and your
sun is burning my flesh – My ears are blinded by the melody of your light
– Their web is enfolding me, and I can't escape its mesh – My body is sighing
in a velvet field of white – I am dying for you – your bells, your colours, your
heart – your heart is red and it pulses like the sun – the clangour of your

sunlight strikes my eyes like metal – book images stir dust in my brain – I
die for your colours, your name.

Catatonic Sun, Fill My Valleys

Sun-mist, you are in me
Sun-fire, my foetus fills me with heat
Sun-death, your touch rests on my body
Sun, you are drying my leaves – my foliage moves under your hand
Sun, you are piercing my womb
Sun, my mouth is full of you
Sun, you are burning away my heart

Red Piano

Across the room the red piano is playing – piano of pain – Florestan plays
desert chords, and the flame-piano answers with cracks like a cannon. Strings
curl over him like a benediction.

This Is Sun

This is sun
Sun is blood
And the bone, gouged and crackling
Sun is the laughing of a pretty woman
And the voice of a great multitude
Sun is semen
Ejaculated in a spurt of blood
Sun is dust and the memory of old wounds
Sun is water in the softness of flood
Sun of the waters, here am I
I await you
This is Sun

Sun!

We are here sun sun glorious we wait for your rays to lick us
with tongues sun we call on you bring your anger to bear on
our flesh clean us with your venom sun magic sun-spear of
deadly passion sun take us in to your burning embrace sun
potent sun glorious to join sun sun sun for the end of burning
the concerted rush to your condensed sun-energy bloom for us
sun unfold sun like a glowing rose and wrap us in your burning
petals ...

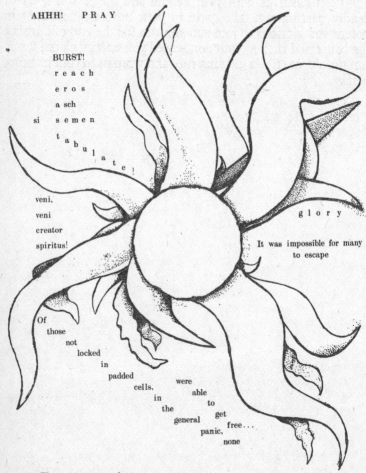

AHHH! PRAY

BURST!
r e a c h
e r o s
a sch
si   s e m e n
t
a
b
u
l
a
t e !

veni,
veni
creator
spiritus!

g l o r y

It was impossible for many
to escape

Of
those
not
locked
in
padded
cells,   were
in   able
the   to
general   get
free...
panic,
none

There were no survivors

THE EYE OF THE LENS

The Film

The film is shot on Agfacolour 16 mm stock on a Bell & Howell camera. It is shot at 24 frames per second, and lasts for fifteen minutes, thirty-two seconds. The film has an optical sound track, and is ideally projected with a screen width of eight feet.

At certain points in the film colour filters have been used. The filters are very light, and serve only to give a predominance to a particular colour, rather than the effect of a dense wash. At other points the same effect is achieved by the selection of particular objects in the field of vision. Thus objects of the chosen colour appear on the screen either isolated or as predominant elements.

The Cast

A girl.
A florist.
A holy man.
Throughout the film, the girl wears a white, pleated dress, caught at the waist by a length of gold chain, the end of which hangs down her thigh.

She is slender, and moves with a light grace. Her hair is long and dark; it is parted at the centre, drawn back, and hangs down between her shoulder blades. Her neck is long, and her face has, despite its appearance of fragility, a strong bone structure. In bare feet she stands at five feet seven, and she has brown eyes.

Her teeth have been extensively filled, and when she laughs one may see the glint of silver in her mouth. Her body hair is rather slight, and on her legs there is an almost invisible covering of sparse, dark hair. She sometimes tries to be cool and off-hand, but she never succeeds with any conviction.

Her skin is more brown than one would expect of a girl with such a delicate appearance, but at her neck one is able to see traceries of veins beneath the skin. Although she has a nervous temperament, she is capable of deep serenity and objectivity, and this is the mood she most often projects through the film.

She is deeply ashamed of her breasts, slight, with long light nipples. Without realizing that this would spoil the proportions of her body, she feels that her breasts should be much larger than they are. This shame diffuses over her whole being, and she is genuinely convinced that she is rather unpleasantly ugly.

The florist and holy man are played by the same actor. In the case of the holy man, he wears a short russet beard.

There is a large cast of extras, and the voice on the sound track is that of a man.

The Images

The sound track is silent, save for the hissing that comes through the loudspeakers. The screen is dark. Fade in. The girl enters from the left. She walks ankle-deep through a forest of broken icons. Gods with upturned faces, blind eyes staring heavenward. Arms are broken off and stretch up from the sea of figures, hands stretching out in supplicant tension. The sun shines brightly, and casts deep shadows among the bodies of the figurines. The screen is in parts intolerably bright and absolutely black.

SOUND TRACK: 'Love me red – love me green – my serenity of soul fills all the places of earth – it calms the tempest and quietens the wild beast.

'Love me red with bloody arrows and anoint my feet with oil – let me plunge my arms into your wounds and cleanse myself in the bubbling red stream. Give me the red of your tortured eyes, the red of your bloody limbs – I will take the red and build it into strength for my arms – into wrath to fight the hatred of my life.

'Love me green – green of palm-leaf, of glory, that I might some day rise to your feet and sing praises to your name.

'Love me gold – gold of riches, that I might spread your word throughout the land – that I might raise temples in your name and spread your teachings to the ends of the earth.

'Love me brown – the brown of leather, that I might fashion whips for my flesh – to suffer the mortification of your love – to live in the glory of fearful pain to the end of my days.

'Give me all the colours of your being, that I might form them into the pure white of resurrection and eternal life.'

The girl clearly has been hearing the voice on the sound track, and she stands for a moment, looking reflective, and then moves on. She passes out of the frame, kicking the statuettes idly as she walks. The picture remains for a few seconds, the idols looking, in the strong sunlight, like a field of motionless grey corn.

Fade out, with a silent sound track.

The Sandstone Bust

The girl is walking through the desert. The sand is lit brightly by the sun, almost white, and her footprints are softened by the shifting of the sand. The rounded contours of the desert stretch to the horizon.

She passes an upturned bicycle, half buried in sand, like the bones of a graceful creature. Its front wheel is twisted towards her, and as she passes the machine appears to be watching her with little interest and with patience born of decay. She goes past the bicycle at a considerable distance. The camera lifts as she passes, and a helicopter comes into view, its belly sunk deep into the sand. The fractured vanes move slightly in the breeze. Although, apart from this corpse-like movement, the helicopter is quite still, the canted mechanism appears as if it is trying to struggle up from the sand to fly away. It is like a photograph of a wounded creature. It is almost as though the film has seized in the projector, and if it started again the helicopter would hump and flap dreadfully on the desert sand.

The girl looks at the helicopter as she passes, and then turns her head back to the front, stopping abruptly as she comes face to face with something else.

It is a bust, made of sandstone, and it stands on a waist-high pedestal. Although it is the likeness of a man, the features are so rough as to be almost unrecognizable. The sandstone bust has about it a tremendous sense of time, and it is clear that the roughness is caused by erosion.

All the parts of the bust have been carefully labelled, and stencilled letters of dark green paint, spelling FOREHEAD, CHEEK, RIGHT EAR, LEFT EAR, add to the general grotesqueness of the figure. The face, with its disfiguring words, has an expression of such comic sadness that it could never be considered frightening. She tries to rock the statue on its pedestal, but it seems to be firmly bolted into place. She rubs the surface of the bust, and sandstone can be seen crumbling into her hand. Now we see the statue closely it looks very old indeed, as if it has been in this desert for an immense period of time.

She takes out a handkerchief from her handbag, dampens part of it, and tries to rub off part of the 'N' in the word 'NOSE', and after considerable effort, the green begins to fade. She runs her fingers over the forehead, and smiles at the 'MOUTH' and 'CHIN' notices.

She appears to be delighted with the statue.

Slow cello music is now on the sound track.

It is now obvious that the bust is severely eroded. Although quite clearly signposted, the right and left nipples are no longer distinguishable, and the right armpit is badly chipped. The girl walks behind the statue, and the next shot is from this position, with the girl walking across the frame, round to the front again. From here the bust is even less like a person, and it seems also to lose all its identity as an object, and to fuse into the contours of the desert.

The cello music becomes grotesque and poignant.

From the front again. The girl is peering closely at the statue's face. A dark mark is running across the letters of the 'LEFT EYE' notice, making it difficult to read. It can be seen that the mark is in fact moisture, black against the dry stone. She puts out her finger to the dampness, and then touches her tongue to fingertip. The wet area seems to be increasing in size, and the girl begins to look a little apprehensive.

Then she drops her handbag and stares with a profound horror, as a drop of water comes from the left eye and merges with the general wetness. Now an identical darkness is spreading across the other cheek. Another drop comes from the left eye and courses its way down to the chin, leaving a trail that glistens in the sunlight. There is no movement, no sound other than the wide sweeps of the cello melody. The only motion is of the little drops that roll down the figure's rough cheeks.

She steps back appalled. She seems to be incapable of action.

A drop comes from the right eye, and rolls down the craggy face.

She stands with her mouth open, her hands clenching at her sides, staring helplessly at the old, old statue that is now weeping before her. The tears of the statue somehow make real the weight of centuries that have passed in this place. She buries her face in her hands, and looks at the bust no longer.

After about half a minute she takes her hands away. A certain calmness has spread over her. She slowly picks up her handbag and feels into it, bringing out a large note-book. She tears out a page and fashions the paper into a rectangular shape, then tears one end to a point. She takes out a fountain pen and writes a single word on the paper. She fixes the notice to the cheek with a pin, in such a way that the arrowhead is indicating the water which is now streaming down the face.

The notice says, simply, 'TEARS'.

She turns, and swiftly walks away across the desert.

The Florists

Now the cello has stopped. All that can be heard is the ironic funeral march from the first symphony of Mahler. The girl is walking across the desert towards a hill, the only feature in the otherwise gently sloping terrain, apart from a black plume of smoke which is rising distantly in the air. As she gets nearer to this oily cloud of smoke, scurrying human activity can be seen on the ground beneath. Occasionally a gout of bright flame bursts along the ground, and more smoke is added to the cloud, rising swiftly in the air. Now the camera, in a tracking shot, reveals a close-up of the girl's face as she walks along. At first lines of concentration furrow her forehead as she tries to make out what is going on, then the concentration is replaced by bewilderment, and then, a little later, by anger. Now the camera is static, and we see the whole scene as the girl walks up.

Men in shirt sleeves are rushing about, their faces grimy and shining with sweat. They look bewildered and panic-stricken, but this is obviously their normal state of mind. On their backs they carry the large chemical tanks of flamethrowers, and the straps have rubbed into their shoulders for so long that they are obviously in great pain. All around, the ground is seared and black. It appears that nothing could possibly grow in such a devastated place, but straggly vegetation is visibly thrusting itself up through the soil. Every moment one of the strange plants is beginning to bloom. A bud appears, almost instantaneously, and begins to open. Lush, coloured petals are visible, promising future beauty. But as soon as one of the men sees this he moves up and immerses the plant in a bath of flame from the nozzle of the weapon he is carrying. All that is left when the fire dies away is charred black soil. But after only a few seconds, pushing up through this inhospitable earth, can be seen a new plant.

The girl clearly doesn't like this place, but when one of the men comes close to her, a fevered expression on his face, she lightly touches his arm.

GIRL: What is this? What are you doing?

MAN: Killing them.

GIRL: But – why?

MAN: To stop them from growing.

(The man turns away to spread a carpet of flame, and then turns back to the girl.)

The only way is to kill them. If we weren't doing this good work they'd be spreading all over the desert.

GIRL: But why do you want to stop them?

MAN: We don't want these – these filthy blossoms all over the desert. For one thing they'd encourage laxness – all our men would be too lazy to do any useful work, like they're doing now.

GIRL: But the only reason they're working is to kill the flowers.

MAN: And besides which, we're used to the desert. When I see those disgusting petals coming out I feel a strange – tension – inside me. What would happen if I gave way to that, and watched them evolving all the way?

And anyway, why are you so interested? I don't like the kind of talk you're giving me.

GIRL: It's just that I can't understand you. You're killing something that's beautiful and alive, something that can grow and give you pleasure . . . .

The man looks at the girl with a disgusted expression on his face, and quite deliberately spits at the ground by her feet. Then he turns back to his work. But just before his face goes out of frame his expression can be seen to change from one of disgust to an infinite sadness. The music fades.

The Flagellants

The girl is now standing on one of the foothills of the large natural mound in the desert. She stands with her back to the camera, watching an extraordinary scene taking place about fifty feet below on the sand. There is a vast circle of naked people on the plain. Their heads are downcast, and they tramp slowly round, their eyes to the ground, like prisoners exercising in a large yard. As they slowly move, each person brings down the lash of a large whip on the back of the person before him. This whipping is so arranged that as one man feels the bite of the lash on his flesh, his own whip is whistling down, striking the person in front a fraction of a second later, the lash of this man about to contact the back of the man before him. Thus, from a distance, this movement can be seen to form a wave of energy, which ripples quickly round the circle, much faster than the people are walking, a wave of pain which circles eternally.

The Eye

The girl is walking through a complex of corridors, green walls rapidly moving across the screen. The floors are of black polished marble, and the sounds of her steps are echoed by the walls. She turns right, down another identical corridor, and quickly left again. All the corridors are the same, and the wooden doors have to distinguish them only small silver numbers set above them, but the individual figures cannot be seen. The sounds of her shoes are now very loud on the sound track, and the echoes build up in feedback, echoes of echoes, until there is nothing but a continuous hollow sound, the resonance of the corridors forming a throbbing note, punctuated by the clicking of the shoes, which, all the time, are adding still more sound to the whole.

She suddenly turns and opens one of the doors. We see her from inside the room as she slams the door shut and leans against it. The slam of the door terminates the sound on the optical track, and there is now no noise at all, nothing but an unnatural silence.

On a table in the middle of the room is a ciné projector. The girl switches off the room light, and goes across to this table. Light filters into the room through the drawn venetian blinds, and a large white screen can be seen dimly at the end of the room. The girl switches on the projector, and the screen is filled with light. We see, projected onto the screen, a picture of a girl, walking hurriedly down a series of green corridors, the floors of which are of black polished marble. She turns right and then quickly left again, moving rapidly past many wooden doors with small silver figures above them. She opens one of the doors, and can then be seen from inside the room as she slams the door and leans against it. On a table in the middle of the room is a ciné projector. The girl switches off the light, and goes across to the projector. A large white screen can be seen dimly at the end of the room. She bends down and presses a switch on the side of the projector.

On the screen is projected the gigantic image of a human eye. The iris is a light watery blue, and the eye itself, separated as it is from the rest of the face, expresses nothing at all. It is just a blue eye, watching all the time.

On the film in the room, the camera begins to approach the eye, and the silhouetted shape of the girl disappears on one side of the screen. Now on that film there is nothing but the blue eye. The girl turns off the projector, and the picture dies. She turns to face the camera, which tracks in, closer and closer, until now only her face can be seen, now only the brow, eye, and cheek, and now just her staring eye.

The Switched-on Psychedelic Auto-destructive Cathedral

The inside of the cathedral batters the eyes and the ears. Everywhere there is colour; the pastel mosaics of the altar, tapestries, stonework; and bright garish colours, the lights, the revolving stained-glass windows, the projected beams staining the clouds of steam. A notice in pseudo-gothic script, painted in dayglo colours says PSYCHEDELIC FREAK-OUT – TONITE! In the nave of the cathedral, in front of the altar, are enormous steam engines. Great pistons, their brass-work reflecting back the iridescent greens and reds of the projector, operate powerfully, flashing and gleaming. Wheels are turning, and great clouds of steam are rising to the cathedral ceiling, almost invisible due to the sea of colour below. These steam engines drive the windows and the other moving parts of the cathedral. The windows are circular, and are of stained glass. They are built in two layers, each with a bright mosaic pattern. The inner of each pair of windows is set in a ball-race and revolves slowly, the colours of both windows combining and separating, forming new colours, and the patterns of the mosaics working together, forming moving lines and swirling shapes. A projector is throwing incandescent colours on to a large screen set behind the altar, which there form swiftly alternating patterns of red, green, blue, blinding white, purple, bright yellow, mauve, orange, in hundreds of shades. Set all round the cathedral, stroboscopic lights are flashing, all out of synchronization, and here and there, among the large numbers of people in the nave, one or two figures are on the floor, writhing in the throes of *grand mal*.

The cathedral is full of sound. Multichannelled electronic noises are booming through loudspeakers set in a ring round the nave, and the sounds chase each other in circles; three cardinals play electric guitars, and a trio of women, their long hair streaming, scream loudly and trace with their hands the shapes of space. The steam engines cannot be heard. A man is standing at the altar with a microphone, brandishing a crucifix. 'Turn on!' he shrieks. 'Tune in! Drop out!' The robes of the cardinals swirl as their synchronized arms smash down, electronic chords bursting from the loudspeakers.

The girl, her dress now a rainbow-dress, gleaming in the lights of the cathedral, turns and goes through the door. Outside we see her emerge. Here it is as it was before; there is the desert and the sun, and only faintly can be heard the sounds of the cathedral. She walks hurriedly away. For a long time can be seen nothing but her feet, treading swiftly over the desert sand. When she is a long way from the building, there is a loud crack, and she turns to look. The cathedral appears for a moment to shake, and, abruptly, there is no longer a cathedral, but a vast moving mass, pouring to the ground like a waterfall, surrounded by clouds of dust which obscure the end. On the sound track there is an enormous rumbling crash, and when it has died, and when the dust has settled, there is nothing but a pile of rubble in the desert and a silence that seems infinite. She turns and walks out of frame, leaving, for a moment, the camera trained on the pile of debris, which looks as if it has been there for a million years.

The Crucifixion

The girl is again walking across the white sand of the desert. The camera pans to follow her as she walks past. On the sound track is the noise of a strong wind. As she stops and looks up, into the picture comes the base of a black marble construction. It is very large and is oval in shape; only part of it is in the field of view. It consists of oval slabs, each a little smaller than the one below it, forming an oval staircase. The marble gleams in sunlight.

Looking down from the top of the edifice. The girl can be seen climbing the staircase. A black shadow falls across her, but its outlines cannot be seen clearly. As she climbs the camera zooms back, so that we see that the black construction is much larger than it had appeared. As more and more comes into our field of view, we are able to see more clearly the shape of the shadow. Abruptly we see that the shadow is in the form of a cross.

She reaches the top of the construction, walks forward, and stops. There is blood running down the base of the cross and forming a small pool beneath it.

From the side. Her face is in frame, at the bottom left. On the right is the cross, with two bent legs, nailed by the feet, at the top of the frame.

GIRL: Oh! What have they done to you?

The man on the cross can now been seen entirely. The upper half of his body is sagging away from the cross, only the great nails driven through his wrists holding his weight. Congealed blood lines his arms. His head is hanging forward, and he regards the girl from under his brows, with great burning eyes. His flesh is very white, and his whole body hangs like that of a corpse.

GIRL: Oh! You're in such pain!

MAN (irritably): Of course I'm in pain.

GIRL (almost crying): I must get you down.

MAN: No, you must not. For my name is Jesus Christ of Nazareth and it is ordained that I die in this way.

GIRL: But I can't let you suffer like this!

JESUS CHRIST (irritably): My dear girl, this is bad enough, without you adding to my misery with your witless comments. If you knew how much this hurt you'd have more consideration than to make me worry about anything else. Now leave me alone, and don't attempt to get me down.

GIRL: Well – do you mind if I talk? Perhaps I will be able to ease your last hours. And I – I want to talk to you.

JESUS CHRIST: It's immaterial to me; I'll be joining my Father soon, and I don't give a damn about anything else.

GIRL: Well, what I need really – I know it's not fair to ask you at a time like this, but – well – I need help, you see.

JESUS CHRIST: That's my job.

GIRL: You see, I've seen so much today, and well – I just wonder about the things I've seen, I suppose I feel a little confused about it all.

JESUS CHRIST: Don't be confused, my child, for you are like a lamb, and I am your shepherd. Just follow me, take the path I show you, and I will lead you to my heavenly fold.

GIRL: Yes, I appreciate that, but I want to find my own way around. It can't be wrong, I guess, because you made me like this. I don't really want to be led anywhere. I've made mistakes, but I've seen a lot of people today who've made far worse ones than me. I don't want to contradict, but with all respect, I'm not a sheep.

JESUS CHRIST: But my child, you are a sheep. For my Father is in control of the whole universe. He knows all the secrets of the proton, the quasar, and all the millions of things which humans are not even aware. My Father is all.

GIRL: Well, why am I unhappy?

JESUS CHRIST: Because you have sinned. You are black and steeped in the foul brew of fleshly wickedness. You choose the easy path of earthly pleasure, and your soul drips with evil poison, one drop of which will be enough to send it screaming to eternal damnation. And you probably play with yourself.

GIRL: I think you're very rude, and you're not at all as I imagined you to be. Not only that, you seem very stupid, for you know nothing about me, what I am, and yet you criticise me. You seem to me a very shallow person.

JESUS CHRIST (angrily): What do you mean? If I weren't nailed up here I'd come down and ... What do you mean?

GIRL: I know more about you than you do of me. I know that you are a man full of compulsive rituals, neurotic, almost insane. You wouldn't even let me get you down from the cross, because it would upset your precious ceremonies. They say you are kind, but I don't find you to be.

JESUS CHRIST (somewhat nervously): Come now, my child ...

GIRL (dramatically): You claim omnipotence for your Father. Well then, in making that claim you are also claiming for him credit for all the crimes of the universe! I charge your Father with creating starvation. I charge him with cruelty, with disease, with disaster. I charge the God of Love with being the God of Syphilis. I charge the God of Life with being the God of Death!

JESUS CHRIST: You are on earth, my child, as a test. Only when you have been weeded, the good from the bad, can my Father know who to take with him into eternal life.

GIRL: So your Father chooses to test us by suffering? He cannot find another way?

JESUS CHRIST You cannot understand my Father's motives, my stupid child. His ways are mysterious to such as you.

GIRL: But there's no mystery. I am unhappy, and I've seen people today so unhappy that they didn't even know it, frightened and lonely people; what have they done that they should be so punished?

(Dark clouds are banking up very rapidly behind the cross. The girl puts one
hand on her hip, and points at Jesus in a very melodramatic manner.)
So I judge your Father, and I find him guilty. I pronounce your Father evil!
He knows the universe, you claim, the secrets of eternity, yet he cannot
understand the sadness in a young girl's heart!

It has become very dark. Jesus Christ suddenly convulses and vomits, fluid
pouring down the front of his body. He begins to twitch on the cross, the
muscles knotting and relaxing. His convulsions make him hiccough violently
for a long time. Dark clouds are now filling the sky, but the girl can still be
seen, pointing at the tortured hanging figure. A flash of lightning suddenly
strikes the cross with an enormous explosion. The cross rips like a curtain,
and in the flash pieces of wood can be seen flying everywhere. Smoke rises
faintly in the air. It darkens rapidly. Now nothing can be seen but the faint
whiteness of the girl's dress, and the rain which is now falling from
heaven.

The Enchanted Flower-field

It is sunny, and on the sound track the calls of hundreds of birds can be heard.
In front of the camera is a moving mass of colours. This is the flower-field.
Gigantic blossoms are spread in profusion to the horizon. The girl enters the
frame from the side, and stands for a moment looking at the flowers. Their
blossoms are composed of large fleshy petals, red, white, mauve, purple,
orange, sky-blue, bright yellow, every conceivable colour lifted to the sun in
folds of scented flesh. The flower-field is like a thick musky carpet, and the
girl takes a deep breath, as if the air is heady with the perfumes of the flowers.
Round about the bases of these enormous blossoms, green leaves are
intertwined, and large bees are bumbling about from flower to flower.

The girl steps forward, into the field, an expression of happy wonderment
on her face. She looks at the moment like a child, but the colours of the flowers
have changed her face into a thing of radiance. The reds and yellows are
reflected in the surface of her skin, and her face is now the face of a Madonna.
At once she is waist-deep in the flowers. It is as if they strain to meet her.
She puts out her hand and touches the blooms, and they respond to her touch,
the large flat petals stiffening, opening the cups of their flowers to her hand.
She smiles happily, and begins to sink down among the flowers. The sensual
blooms sway toward her and away, unimaginably beautiful. There is a
humming in the air, like the humming of approaching unconsciousness. The
girl disappears into the midst of the field, and now only the colours of the
swaying flowers can be seen, forming bright shapes all over the screen.

But a sudden sense of unreality comes over the whole scene, and then, abruptly, the whole of the flower-field fades away. There is just left the girl, sitting on the sand of the desert. She looks about herself, terrified and unhappy. The picture becomes dimmer; this is the end of the film. But as the picture fades, we notice little green shoots appearing all over the ground, and we know that it will not be long before the flower-field is back, with all its radiant glory.

Fade out.

Polite applause.

The Assassination Weapon
J.G. BALLARD

THORACIC DROP. The spinal landscape, revealed at the level of T-12, is that of the porous rock-towers of Teneriffe, and of the native of the Canaries, Oscar Dominguez, who created the technique of decalcomania and so exposed the first spinal landscape. The clinker-like rock-towers, suspended above the silent swamp, create an impression of profound anguish. The inhospitality of this mineral world, with its inorganic growths, is relieved only by the balloons flying in the clear sky. They are painted with names: Jackie, Lee Harvey, Malcolm. In the mirror of this swamp there are no reflections. Here, time makes no concessions.

AUTOGEDDON. Waking: the concrete embankment of a motorway extension. Roadworks, cars drumming two hundred yards below. In the sunlight the seams between the sections are illuminated like the sutures of an exposed skull. A young woman stands ten feet away from him, watching with unsure eyes. The hyoid bone in her throat flutters as if discharging some subvocal rosary. She points to her car, parked off the verge beside a grader, and then beckons to him. *Kline, Coma, Xero.* He remembered the aloof, cerebral Kline and their long discussions on this terminal concrete beach. Under a different sun. This girl is not Coma. 'My car.' She speaks, the sounds as dissociated as the recording in a doll. 'I can give you a lift. I saw you reach the island. It's like trying to cross the Styx.' He sits up, searching for his Air Force cap. All he can say is: 'Jackie Kennedy.'

GOOGOLPLEX. Dr Lancaster studied the walls of the empty room. The mandalas, scored in the white plaster with a nail file, radiated like suns towards the window. He peered at the objects on the tray offered to him by the nurse. 'So, these are the treasures he has left us – an entry from Oswald's Historic Diary, a much-thumbed reproduction of Margritte's *Annunciation*, and the mass numbers of the first twelve radioactive nuclides. What are we supposed to do with them?' Nurse Nagamatzu gazed at him with cool eyes. 'Permutate them, doctor?' Lancaster lit a cigarette, ignoring the explicit insolence. This elegant bitch, like all women she intruded her sexuality at the most inopportune moments. One day.... He said: 'Perhaps. We might find

Mrs Kennedy there. Or her husband. The Warren Commission has reopened its hearing, you know. Apparently it's not satisfied. Quite unprecedented.' Permutate them? The theoretical number of nucleotide patterns in DNA was a mere 10 to the power of 120,000. What number was vast enough to contain all the possibilities of those three objects?

JACKIE KENNEDY, YOUR EYELIDS DEFLAGRATE. The serene face of the President's widow, painted on clapboard 400 feet high, moves across the rooftops, disappearing into the haze on the outskirts of the city. There are hundreds of the signs, revealing Jackie in countless familiar postures. Next week there may be an SS officer, Beethoven, Christopher Columbus or Fidel Castro. The fragments of these signs litter the suburban streets for weeks afterwards. Bonfires of Jackie's face burn among the reservoirs of Staines and Shepperton. With luck he got a job on one of the municipal disposal teams, warms his hands at a brazier of enigmatic eyes. At night he sleeps beneath an unlit bonfire of breasts.

XERO. Of the three figures who were to accompany him, the strangest was Xero. For most of the time Kline and Coma would remain near him, sitting a few feet away on the embankment of the deserted motorway, following in another car when he drove out to the radio-observatory, pausing behind him as he visited the atrocity exhibition. Coma was too shy, but now and then he would manage to talk to Kline, although he never remembered what they said to each other. By contrast, Xero was an archangel, a figure of galvanic energy and uncertainty. Moving across the abandoned landscape near the flyover, the very perspectives of the air seemed to invert behind him. At times, when Xero approached the forlorn group sitting on the embankment, his shadows formed bizarre patterns on the concrete, transcripts of cryptic formulae and insoluble dreams. These ideograms, like the hieroglyphs of a race of blind seers, remained on the grey concrete after Xero had gone, the detritus of this terrifying psychic totem.

QUESTIONS, ALWAYS QUESTIONS. Karen Novotny watched him move around the apartment, dismantling the mirrors in the hall and bathroom. He stacked them on the table between the settees in the lounge. This strange man, and his obsessions with time, Jackie Kennedy, Oswald and Eniwetok. Who was he? Where had he come from? In the three days since she had found him on the motorway she had discovered only that he was a former H-bomber pilot, for some reason carrying World War III in his head. 'What are you trying to build?' she asked. He assembled the mirrors into a box-like structure. He glanced up at her, face hidden by the peak of his Air Force cap. 'A trap.' She stood beside him as he knelt on the floor. 'For what? Time?' He placed a hand between her knees and gripped her right thigh, handhold of reality. 'For your womb, Karen. You've caught a star there.' But he was thinking of Coma, waiting with Kline in the espresso bar, while Xero roamed the street in his white Pontiac. In Coma's eyes runes glowed.

THE IMPOSSIBLE ROOM. In the dim light he lay on the floor of the room. A perfect cube, its walls and ceiling were formed by what seemed to be a series of cinema screens. Projected on to them in close-up was the face of Nurse Nagamatzu, her mouth, three feet across, moving silently as she spoke in slow motion. Like a cloud, the giant head moved up the wall behind him, then passed across the ceiling and down the opposite corner. Later the inclined, pensive face of Dr Lancaster appeared, rising up from the floor until it filled three walls and the ceiling, a slow, mouthing monster.

BEACH FATIGUE. After climbing the concrete incline, he reached the top of the embankment. The flat, endless terrain stretched away on all sides, a few oil derricks in the distance marking the horizon. Among the spilled sand and burst cement bags lay old tyres and beer bottles, Guam in 1947. He wandered away from here, straddling roadworks and irrigation ditches, towards a rusting quonset near the incline of the disused flyover. Here, in this terminal hut, he began to piece together some sort of existence. Inside the hut he found a set of psychological tests; out of curiosity ran them on himself. Although he had no means of checking them, his answers seemed to establish an identity. He went off to forage, and came back to the hut with some documents and a coke bottle.

PONTIAC STARCHIEF. Two hundred yards from the hut a wheel-less Pontiac sits in the sand. The presence of this car baffles him. Often he spends hours sitting in it, trying out the front and back seats. All sorts of rubbish is lying in the sand: a typewriter with half the keys missing (he picks out fragmentary sentences; sometimes these seem to mean something), a smashed neuro-surgical unit (he pockets a handful of leucotomes, useful for self-defence). Then he cuts his foot on the coke bottle, and spends several feverish days in the hut. Luckily he finds an incomplete isolation drill for trainee astronauts, half of an 80-hour sequence.

COMA: THE MILLION-YEAR GIRL. Coma's arrival coincides with his recovery from the bout of fever. She never enters the hut, but they team up in a left-handed way. To begin with she wants to spend all her time writing poems on the damaged typewriter. Later, when not writing the poems, she wanders away to an old solar energy device and loses herself in the maze of mirrors. Shortly afterwards Kline appears, and sits at a chair and table in the sand twenty yards from the hut. Xero, meanwhile, is moving among the oil derricks half a mile away, assembling immense cinemascope signs that carry the reclining images of Oswald, Jackie Kennedy and Malcolm X.

PRE-UTERINE CLAIMS. 'The author,' Dr Lancaster wrote, 'has found that the patient forms a distinctive type of object relation based on a perpetual and irresistible desire to merge with the object in an undifferentiated mass. Although psychoanalysis cannot reach the primary archaic mechanism of "rapprochement" it can deal with the neurotic superstructure guiding the patient towards the choice of stable and worthwhile objects. In the case under consideration the previous career of the patient as a military pilot should be noted, and the unconscious role of thermonuclear weapons in bringing about the total fusion and non-differentiation of all matter. What the patient is reacting against is, simply, the phenomenology of the universe, the specific and independent existence of separate objects and events, however trivial and inoffensive these may seem. A spoon, for example, offends him by the mere fact of its existence in time and space. More than this, one could say that the precise, if largely random, configuration of atoms in the universe at any given moment, one never again to be repeated, seems to him to be preposterous by the virtue of its unique identity . . .' Dr Lancaster lowered his pen and looked down into the recreation garden. Traven was standing in the sunlight, raising and lowering his arms and legs in a private callisthenic display, which he repeated several times (presumably an attempt to render time and events meaningless by replication?).

'BUT ISN'T KENNEDY ALREADY DEAD?' Captain Webster studies the documents laid out on Dr Lancaster's demonstration table. These were: (1) a spectroheliogram of the sun; (2) tarmac and take-off checks for the B29 Superfortress *Enola Gay*; (3) electroencephalogram of Albert Einstein; (4) transverse section through a Pre-Cambrian Trilobite; (5) photograph taken at noon, August 6, 1945, of the sand-sea, Quattara Depression, Libya; (6) Max Ernst's *Garden Airplane Traps*. He turned to Dr Lancaster. 'You say these constitute an assassination weapon?'

'NOT IN THE SENSE YOU MEAN.' Dr Lancaster covered the exhibits with a sheet. By chance the cabinets took up the contours of a corpse. 'Not in the sense you mean. This is an attempt to bring about the "false" death of the President – false in the sense of coexistent or alternate. The fact that an event has taken place is no proof of its valid occurence.' Dr Lancaster went over to the window. Obviously he would have to begin the search singlehanded. Where to begin? No doubt Nurse Nagamatzu could be used as bait. That vamp had once worked as a taxi-dancer in the world's largest nightclub in Osaka, appropriately named 'The Universe'.

UNIDENTIFIED RADIO-SOURCE, CASSIOPEIA. Karen Novotny waited as he reversed the car onto the farm track. Half a mile across the meadows she could see the steel bowls of the three radio-telescopes in the sun light. So the attempt was to be made here? There seemed to be nothing to kill except the sky. All week they had been chasing about, sitting for hours through the conference on neuro-psychiatry, visiting art galleries, even flying in a rented Rapide across the reservoirs of Staines and Shepperton. Her eyes had ached from keeping a look-out. 'They're four hundred feet high' he told her, 'the last thing you need is a pair of binoculars.' What had he been looking for – the radio-telescopes or the giant madonnas he muttered about as he lay asleep beside her at night. 'Xero!' she heard him shout. With the agility of an acrobat he vaulted over the bonnet of the car, then set off at a run across the meadow. 'Come on!' he shouted over his shoulder. Carrying the black Jackie Kennedy wig as carefully as she could in both hands, she hurried after him. One of the telescopes was moving, its dish turning towards them.

MADAME BUTTERFLY. Holding the wound under her left breast, Nurse Nagamatzu stepped across Webster's body and leaned against the bogie of the telescope pylon. Eighty feet above her the steel bowl had stopped revolving and the echoes of the gun-shots reverberated among the lattice work. Clearing her throat with an effort, she spat out the blood. The flecks of lung tissue speckled the bright ribbon of the rail. The bullet had broken two ribs, then collapsed her left lung and lodged itself below her scapula. As her eyes faded she caught a last glimpse of a white American car setting off across the tarmac apron beyond the control house, where the shells of the old bombers lay heaped together. The runways of the former airfield radiated from her in all directions. Dr Lancaster was kneeling in the path of the car, intently building a sculpture of mirrors. She tried to pull the wig off her head, and then fell sideways across the rail.

THE BRIDE STRIPPED BARE BY HER BACHELORS, EVEN. Pausing outside the entrance to the tea-terrace, Margaret Traven noticed the tall figure of Captain Webster watching her from the sculpture room. Duchamp's glass construction, on loan from the Museum of Modern Art, reminded her of the ambiguous role she might have to play. This was chess in which every move was a counter-gambit. How could she help her husband, that tormented man, pursued by furies more implacable than the four riders, the very facts of time and space. She gave a start as Webster took her elbow. He turned to face her, looking into her eyes. 'You need a drink. Let's sit down – I'll explain again why this is so important.'

VENUS SMILES. The dead face of the President's widow looked up at him from the track. Confused by the Japanese cast of her features, with all their reminders of Nagasaki and Hiroshima, he stared at the bowl of the telescope, searching through the steel lattice for the time-music of the quasars. Twenty yards away Dr Lancaster was watching him in the sunlight, the sculpture beside him reflecting a dozen fragments of his head and arms. Kline and Coma were moving away along the railway track.

EINSTEIN. 'The notion that this great Swiss mathematician is a pornographer may strike you as something of a bad joke,' Dr. Lancaster remarked to Webster. 'However, you must understand that for Traven science is the ultimate pornography, analytic activity whose main aim is to isolate objects or events from their contexts in time and space. This obsession with the specific activity of quantified functions is what science shares with pornography. How different from Lautreamont, who brought together the sewing machine and the umbrella on the operating table, identifying the pudenda of the carpet with the woof of the cadaver.' Dr. Lancaster turned to Webster with a laugh. 'One looks forward to the day when the General Theory of Relativity and the Principia will outsell the Kama Sutra in back-street bookshops.'

RUNE-FILLED EYES. Now, in this concluding phase, the presence of his watching trinity, Coma, Kline and Xero, became even closer. All three were more preoccupied than he remembered them. Kline seemed to avoid his eyes, turning one shoulder as he passed the café where Kline sat with Coma, evidently waiting for something. Only Coma, with her rune-filled eyes, watched him with any sympathy. It was as if they all sensed that something was missing. He remembered the documents he had found near the terminal hut.

IN A TECHNICAL SENSE. Webster's hand hesitated on Karen Novotny's zip. He listened to the last bars of the Mahler symphony playing from the radiogram extension in the warm bedroom. 'The bomber crashed on landing,' he explained 'Four members of the crew were killed. He was alive when they got him out, but at one point in the operating theatre his heart and vital functions failed. In a technical sense he was dead for about two minutes. Now, all this time later, it looks as if something is missing, something that vanished during the short period of his death. Perhaps his soul, the capacity to achieve a state of grace. Lancaster would call it the ability to accept the phenomenology of the universe, or the fact of your own consciousness. This is Traven's hell. You can see he's trying to build bridges between things – this Kennedy business, for example. He wants to kill Kennedy again, but in a way that makes sense.'

THE WATER WORLD. Margaret Traven moved through the darkness along the causeways between the reservoirs. Half a mile away the edge of the embankment formed a raised horizon, enclosing this world of tanks, water and pumping gear with an almost claustrophobic silence. The varying levels of water in the tanks seemed to let an extra dimension into the damp air. A hundred yards away, across two parallel settling beds, she saw her husband moving rapidly along one of the white painted catwalks. He disappeared down a stairway. What was he looking for? Was this watery world the site where he hoped to be reborn, in this quantified womb with its dozens of amniotic levels?

AN EXISTENTIAL YES. They were moving away from him. After his return to the terminal hut he noticed that Kline, Coma and Xero no longer approached him. Their fading figures, a quarter of a mile from the hut, wandered to and fro, half-hidden from him by the hollows and earthworks. The cinemascope hoardings of Jackie, Oswald and Malcolm X were beginning to break up in the wind. One morning he woke to find that they had gone.

THE TERMINAL ZONE. He lay on sand with the rusty bicycle wheel. Now and then he would cover some of the spokes with sand, neutralizing the radial geometry. The rim interested him. Hidden behind a dune, the hut no longer seemed a part of his world. The sky remained constant, the warm air touching the shreds of test papers sticking up from the sand. He continued to examine the wheel. Nothing happened.

The Heat Death of
The Universe
PAMELA ZOLINE

(1) ONTOLOGY.
That branch of metaphysics which concerns itself with the problems of the
nature of existence or being.

(2) Imagine a pale blue morning sky, almost green, with clouds only at the
rims. The earth rolls and the sun appears to mount, mountains erode, fruits
decay, the Foraminifera adds another chamber to its shell, babies' fingernails
grow as does the hair of the dead in their graves, and in egg timers the sands
fall and the eggs cook on.

(3) Sarah Boyle thinks of her nose as too large, though several men have
cherished it. The nose is generous and performs a well-calculated geometric
curve, at the arch of which the skin is drawn very tight and a faint whiteness
of bone can be seen showing through, it has much the same architectural
tension and sense of mathematical calculation as the day after Thanksgiving
breastbone on the carcass of a turkey; her maiden name was Sloss, mixed
German, English and Irish descent; in grade school she was very bad at
playing softball and, besides being chosen last for the team, was always made
to play centre field, no one could ever hit to center field; she loves music best
of all the arts, and of music, Bach, J.S; she lives in California, though she
grew up in Boston and Toledo.

(4) BREAKFAST TIME AT THE BOYLES' HOUSE ON LA FLORIDA STREET,
ALAMEDA, CALIFORNIA, THE CHILDREN DEMAND SUGAR FROSTED
FLAKES.
    With some reluctance Sarah Boyle dishes out Sugar Frosted Flakes to her
children, already hearing the decay set in upon the little white milk teeth, the
bony whine of the dentist's drill. The dentist is a short, gentle man with a
moustache who sometimes reminds Sarah of an Uncle who lives in Ohio. One
bowl per child.

(5) If one can imagine it considered as an abstract object, by members of
a totally separate culture, one can see that the cereal box might seem a
beautiful thing. The solid rectangle is neatly joined and classical in
proportions, on it are squandered wealths of richest colours, virgin blues,

crimsons, dense ochres, precious pigments once reserved for sacred paintings and as cosmetics for the blind faces of marble gods. Giant size. Net Weight 16 ounces, 250 grams. 'They're tigeriffic!' says Tony the Tiger. The box blatts promises. Energy, Nature's Own Goodness, an endless pubescence. On its back is a mask of William Shakespeare to be cut out, folded, worn by thousands of tiny Shakespeares in Kansas City, Detroit, Tucson, San Diego, Tampa. He appears at once more kindly and somewhat more vacant than we are used to seeing him. Two or more of the children lay claim to the mask, but Sarah puts off that Solomon's decision until such time as the box is empty.

(6)   A notice in orange flourishes states that a Surprise Gift is to be found somewhere in the packet, nestled amongst the golden flakes. So far it has not been unearthed, and the children request more cereal than they wish to eat, great yellow heaps of it, to hurry the discovery. Even so, at the end of the meal, some layers of flakes remain in the box and the Gift must still be among them.

(7)   There is even a Special Offer of a secret membership, code and magic ring; these to be obtained by sending in the box top with 50 cents.

(8)   Three offers on one cereal box. To Sarah Boyle this seems to be oversell. Perhaps something is terribly wrong with the cereal and it must be sold quickly, got off the shelves before the news breaks. Perhaps it causes a special, cruel cancer in little children. As Sarah Boyle collects the bowls printed with bunnies and baseball statistics, still slopping half full of milk and wilted flakes, she imagines *in her mind's eye* the headlines, 'Nation's Small Fry Stricken, Fate's Finger Sugar Coated, Lethal Sweetness Socks Tots.'

(9)   Sarah Boyle is a vivacious and intelligent young wife and mother, educated at a fine Eastern college, proud of her growing family which keeps her busy and happy around the house.

(10) BIRTHDAY.
Today is the birthday of one of the children. There will be a party in the late afternoon.

(11) CLEANING UP THE HOUSE. (ONE.)
Cleaning up the kitchen. Sarah Boyle puts the bowls, plates, glasses and silverware into the sink. She scrubs at the stickiness on the yellow-marbled formica table with a blue synthetic sponge, a special blue which we shall see again. There are marks of children's hands in various sizes printed with sugar and grime on all the table's surfaces. The marks catch the light, they appear and disappear according to the position of the observing eye. The floor

sweepings include a triangular half of toast spread with grape jelly, bobby pins, a green Band-Aid, flakes, a doll's eye, dust, dog's hair and a button.

(12) Until we reach the statistically likely planet and begin to converse with whatever green-faced teleporting denizens thereof – considering only this shrunk and communication-ravaged world – can we any more postulate a separate culture? Viewing the metastasis of Western Culture it seems progressively less likely. Sarah Boyle imagines a whole world which has become like California, all topographical inperfections sanded away with the sweet-smelling burr of the plastic surgeon's cosmetic polisher, a world populace dieting, leisured, similar in pink and mauve hair and rhinestone shades. A land Cunt Pink and Avocado Green, brassiered and girdled by monstrous complexities of Super Highways, a California endless and unceasing, embracing and transforming the entire globe, California, California!

(13) INSERT ONE. ON ENTROPY.

ENTROPY: A quantity introduced in the first place to facilitate the calculation, and to give clear expressions to the results of thermodynamics. Changes of entropy can be calculated only for a reversible process, and may then be defined as the ratio of the amount of heat taken up to the absolute temperature at which the heat is absorbed. Entropy changes for actual irreversible processes are calculated by postulating equivalent theoretical reversible changes. The entropy of a system is a measure of its degree of disorder. The total entropy of any isolated system can never decrease in any change; it must either increase (irreversible process) or remain constant (reversible process). The total entropy of the Universe therefore is increasing, tending towards a maximum, corresponding to complete disorder of the particles in it (assuming that it may be regarded as an isolated system). See *Heat Death of the Universe*.

(14) CLEANING UP THE HOUSE. (TWO.)

Washing the baby's diapers. Sarah Boyle writes notes to herself all over the house; a mazed wild script larded with arrows, diagrams, pictures, graffiti on every available surface in a desperate/heroic attempt to index, record, bluff, invoke, order and placate. On the fluted and flowered white plastic lid of the diaper bin she has written in Blushing Pink Nitetime lipstick a phrase to ward off fumey ammoniac despair. 'The nitrogen cycle is the vital round of organic and inorganic exchange on earth. The sweet breath of the Universe.' On the wall by the washing machine are Yin and Yang signs, mandalas, and the words, 'Many young wives feel trapped. It is a contemporary sociological phenomenon which may be explained in part by a gap between changing living patterns and the accommodation of social services to these patterns.' Over the stove she had written 'Help, Help, Help, Help, Help.'

(15) Sometimes she numbers or letters the things in a room, writing the assigned character on each object. There are 819 separate moveable objects in the living-room, counting books. Sometimes she labels objects with their names, or with false names, thus on her bureau the hair brush is labelled HAIR BRUSH, the cologne, COLOGNE, the hand cream, CAT. She is passionately fond of children's dictionaries, encyclopedias, ABCs and all reference books, transfixed and comforted at their simulacra of a complete listing and ordering.

(16) On the door of a bedroom are written two definitions from reference books. 'GOD: An object of worship'; 'HOMEOSTASIS: Maintenance of constancy of internal environment.'

(17) Sarah Boyle washes the diapers, washes the linen, Oh Saint Veronica, changes the sheets on the baby's crib. She begins to put away some of the toys, stepping over and around the organizations of playthings which still seem inhabited. There are various vehicles, and articles of medicine, domesticity and war: whole zoos of stuffed animals, bruised and odorous with years of love; hundreds of small figures, plastic animals, cowboys, cars, spacemen, with which the children make sub and supra worlds in their play. One of Sarah's favourite toys is the Baba, the wooden Russian doll which, opened, reveals a smaller but otherwise identical doll which opens to reveal, etc., a lesson in infinity at least to the number of seven dolls.

(18) Sarah Boyle's mother has been dead for two years. Sarah Boyle thinks of music as the formal articulation of the passage of time, and of Bach as the most poignant rendering of this. Her eyes are sometimes the colour of the aforementioned kitchen sponge. Her hair is natural spaniel-brown; months ago on an hysterical day she dyed it red, so now it is two-toned with a stripe in the middle, like the painted walls of slum buildings or old schools.

(19) INSERT TWO. THE HEAT DEATH OF THE UNIVERSE.
The second law of thermodynamics can be interpreted to mean that the ENTROPY of a closed system tends towards a maximum and that its available ENERGY tends towards a minimum. It has been held that the Universe constitutes a thermodynamically closed system, and if this were true it would mean that a time must finally come when the Universe 'unwinds' itself, no energy being available for use. This state is referred to as the 'heat death of the Universe'. It is by no means certain, however, that the Universe can be considered as a closed system in this sense.

(20) Sarah Boyle pours out a Coke from the refrigerator and lights a

cigarette. The coldness and sweetness of the thick brown liquid make her throat ache and her teeth sting briefly, sweet juice of my youth, her eyes glass with the carbonation, she thinks of the Heat Death of the Universe. A logarithmic of those late summer days, endless as the Irish serpent twisting through jewelled manuscripts forever, tail in mouth, the heat pressing, bloating, doing violence. The Los Angeles sky becomes so filled and bleached with detritus that it loses all colours and silvers like a mirror, reflecting back the fricasseeing earth. Everything becomes warmer and warmer, each particle of matter becoming more agitated, more excited until the bonds shatter, the glues fail, the deodorants lose their seals. She imagines the whole of New York City melting like a Dali into a great chocolate mass, a great soup, the Great Soup of New York.

(21) CLEANING UP THE HOUSE. (THREE.)
Beds made. Vacuuming the hall, a carpet of faded flowers, vines and leaves which endlessly wind and twist into each other in a fevered and permanent ecstasy. Suddenly the vacuum blows instead of sucks, spewing marbles, dolls' eyes, dust, crackers. An old trick. 'Oh my god,' says Sarah. The baby yells on cue for attention/changing/food. Sarah kicks the vacuum cleaner and it retches and begins working again.

(22) AT LUNCH ONLY ONE GLASS OF MILK IS SPILLED.
At lunch only one glass of milk is spilled.
(23) The plants need watering, Geranium, Hyacinth, Lavender, Avocado, Cyclamen. Feed the fish, happy fish with china castles and mermaids in the bowl. The turtle looks more and more unwell and is probably dying.
(24) Sarah Boyle's blue eyes, how blue? Bluer far and of a different quality than the Nature metaphors which were both engine and fuel to so much of precedant literature. A fine, modern, acid, synthetic blue; the shiny cerulean of the skies on postcards sent from lush subtropics, the natives grinning ivory ambivalent grins in their dark faces; the promising fat, unnatural blue of the heavy tranquilizer capsule; the cool mean blue of that fake kitchen sponge; the deepest, most unbelievable azure of the tiled and mossless interiors of California swimming pools. The chemists in their kitchens cooked, cooled and distilled this blue from thousands of colorless and wonderfully constructed crystals, each one unique and nonpareil; and now that color, hisses, bubbles, burns in Sarah's eyes.

(25) INSERT THREE. ON LIGHT.
LIGHT: Name given to the agency by means of which a viewed object influences the observer's eyes. Consists of electromagnetic radiation within

the wave-length range 4 x 10^{-5} cm to 7 x 10^{-5} cm approximately; variations in the wave-length produce different sensations in the eye, corresponding to different colors. See color vision.

(26) LIGHT AND CLEANING THE LIVING ROOM.

All the objects (819) and surfaces in the living room are dusty, gray common dust as though this were the den of a giant molting mouse. Suddenly quantities of waves or particles of very strong sunlight speed in through the window, and everything incandesces, multiple rainbows. Poised in what has become a solid cube of light, like an ancient insect trapped in amber, Sarah Boyle realizes that the dust is indeed the most beautiful stuff in the room, a manna for the eyes. Duchamp, that father of thought, has set with fixative some dust which fell on one of his sculptures, counting it as part of the work. 'That way madness lies, says Sarah,' says Sarah. The thought of ordering a household on Dada principles balloons again. All the rooms would fill up with objects, newspapers and magazines would compost, the potatoes in the rack, the canned green beans in the garbage pale would take new heart and come to life again, reaching out green shoots towards the sun. The plants would grow wild and wind into a jungle around the house, splitting plaster, tearing shingles, the garden would enter in at the door. The goldfish would die, the birds would die, we'd have them stuffed; the dog would die from lack of care, and probably the children – all stuffed and sitting around the house, covered with dust.

(27) INSERT FOUR. DADA.

DADA (Fr., hobby-horse) was a nihilistic precursor of Surrealism, invented in Zurich during World War I, a product of hysteria and shock lasting from about 1915 to 1922. It was deliberately anti-art and anti-sense, intended to outrage and scandalize and its most characteristic production was the reproduction of the *Mona Lisa* decorated with a moustache and the obscene caption LHOOQ (read: *elle a chaud au cul*) 'by' Duchamp. Other manifestations included Arp's collages of coloured paper cut out at random and shuffled, ready-made objects such as the bottle drier and the bicycle wheel 'signed' by Duchamp, Picabia's drawings of bits of machinery with incongruous titles, incoherent poetry, a lecture given by 38 lecturers in unison, and an exhibition in Cologne in 1920, held in an annexe to a café lavatory, at which a chopper was provided for spectators to smash the exhibits with – which they did.

(28) TIME-PIECES AND OTHER MEASURING DEVICES.

In the Boyle house there are four clocks; three watches (one a Mickey Mouse watch which does not work); two calendars and two engagement books; three rulers, a yardstick; a measuring cup; a set of red plastic measuring spoons which includes a tablespoon, a teaspoon, a one-half teaspoon, one-fourth teaspoon and one-eighth teaspoon; an egg timer; an oral thermometer and a rectal thermometer, a Boy Scout compass; a barometer in the shape of a house, in and out of which an old woman and an old man chase each other forever without fulfillment; a bathroom scale; an infant scale; a tape measure which can be pulled out of a stuffed felt strawberry; a wall on which the children's heights are marked; a metronome.

(29) Sarah Boyle finds a new line in her face after lunch while cleaning the bathroom. It is as yet barely visible, running from the midpoint of her forehead to the bridge of her nose. By inward curling of her eyebrows she can etch it clearly as it will come to appear in the future. She marks another mark on the wall where she has drawn out a scoring area. FACE LINES AND OTHER INTIMATIONS OF MORTALITY, the heading says. There are thirty-two marks, counting this latest one.

(30) Sarah Boyle is a vivacious and witty young wife and mother, educated at a fine Eastern college, proud of her growing family which keeps her happy and busy around the house, involved in many hobbies and community activities, and only occasionally given to obsessions concerning Time/Entropy/Chaos and Death.

(31) Sarah Boyle is never quite sure how many children she has.

(32) Sarah thinks from time to time; Sarah is occasionally visited with this thought; at times this thought comes upon Sarah, that there are things to be hoped for, accomplishments to be desired beyond the mere reproductions, mirror reproduction of one's kind. The babies. Lying in bed at night sometimes the memory of the act of birth, always the hue and texture of red plush theatre seats, washes up; the rending which always, at a certain intensity of pain, slipped into landscapes, the sweet breath of the sweating nurse. The wooden Russian doll has bright, perfectly round red spots on her cheeks, she splits in the centre to reveal a doll smaller but in all other respects identical with round bright red spots on her cheeks, etc.

(33) How fortunate for the species, Sarah muses or is mused, that children are as ingratiating as we know them. Otherwise they would soon be salted off for the leeches they are, and the race would extinguish itself in a fair sweet flowering, the last generations' massive achievement in the arts and pursuits of high civilization. The finest women would have their tubes tied off at the age of twelve, or perhaps refrain altogether from the Act of Love? All interests would be bent to a refining and perfecting of each febrile sense, each fluid hour, with no more cowardly investment in immortality via the patchy and too often disappointing vegetables of one's own womb.

(34) INSERT FIVE. LOVE.

LOVE: a typical sentiment involving fondness for, or attachment to, an object, the idea of which is emotionally colored whenever it arises in the mind, and capable, as Shand has pointed out, of evoking any one of a whole gamut of primary emotions, according to the situation in which the object is placed, or represented; often, and by psychoanalysts always, used in the sense of *sex-love* or even *lust* (q.v.)

(35) Sarah Boyle has at times felt a unity with her body, at other times a complete separation. The mind/body duality considered. The time/space duality considered. The male/female duality considered. The matter/energy duality considered. Sometimes, at extremes, her Body seems to her an animal on a leash, taken for walks in the park by her Mind. The lamp posts of experience. Her arms are lightly freckled and when she gets very tired the places under her eyes become violet.

(36) Housework is never completed, the chaos always lurks ready to encroach on any area left unweeded, a jungle filled with dirty pans and the roaring giant stuffed toy animals suddenly turned savage. Terrible glass eyes.

(37) SHOPPING FOR THE BIRTHDAY CAKE.

Shopping in the supermarket with the baby in front of the cart and a larger child holding on. The light from the ice-cube-tray-shaped fluorescent lights is mixed blue and pink and brighter, colder, and cheaper than daylight. The doors swing open just as you reach out your hand for them, Tantalus, moving with a ghastly quiet swing. Hot dogs for the party. Potato chips, gum drops, a paper tablecloth with birthday designs, hot dog buns, catsup, mustard, picalilli, balloons, instant coffee Continental style, dog food, frozen peas, ice cream, frozen lima beans, frozen broccoli in butter sauce, paper birthday hats, paper napkins in three colors, a box of Sugar Frosted Flakes with a Wolfgang Amadeus Mozart mask on the back, bread, pizza mix. The notes of a just-graspable music filter through the giant store, for the most part by-passing the brain and acting directly on the liver, blood and lymph. The air is delicately scented with aluminum. Half and half cream, tea bags, bacon, sandwich meat, strawberry jam. Sarah is in front of the shelves of cleaning products now, and the baby is beginning to whine. Around her are whole libraries of objects, offering themselves. Some of that same old hysteria that had incarnadined her hair rises up again, and she does not refuse it. There is one moment when she can choose direction, like standing on a chalk-drawn X, a hot cross bun, and she does not choose calm and measure. Sarah Boyle begins to pick out, methodically, deliberately and with a careful ecstasy, one of every cleaning product which the store sells. Window Cleaner, Glass

Cleaner, Brass Polish, Silver Polish, Steel Wool, eighteen different brands of Detergent, Disinfectant, Toilet Cleanser, Water Softener, Fabric Softener, Drain Cleanser, Spot Remover, Floor Wax, Furniture Wax, Car Wax, Carpet Shampoo, Dog Shampoo, Shampoo for people with dry, oily and normal hair, for people with dandruff, for people with grey hair. Tooth Paste, Tooth Powder, Denture Cleaner, Deodorants, Antiperspirants, Antiseptics, Soaps, Cleansers, Abrasives, Oven Cleansers, Makeup Removers. When the same products appear in different sizes Sarah takes one of each size. For some products she accumulates whole little families of containers: a giant Father bottle of shampoo, a Mother bottle, an Older Sister bottle just smaller than the Mother bottle, and a very tiny Baby Brother bottle. Sarah fills three shopping carts and has to have help wheeling them all down the aisles. At the checkout counter her laughter and hysteria keep threatening to overflow as the pale blonde clerk with no eyebrows like the *Mona Lisa* pretends normality and disinterest. The bill comes to $57.53 and Sarah has to write a check. Driving home, the baby strapped in the drive-a-cot and the paper bags bulging in the back seat, she cries.

(38) BEFORE THE PARTY.
Mrs David Boyle, mother-in-law of Sarah Boyle, is coming to the party of her grandchild. She brings a toy, a yellow wooden duck on a string, made in Austria: the duck quacks as it is pulled along the floor. Sarah is filling paper cups with gum drops and chocolates, and Mrs David Boyle sits at the kitchen table and talks to her. She is talking about several things, she is talking about her garden which is flourishing except for a plague of rare black beetles, thought to have come from Hong Kong, which are undermining some of the most delicate growths at the roots, and feasting on the leaves of other plants. She is talking about a sale of household linens which she plans to attend on the following Tuesday. She is talking about her neighbor who has cancer and is wasting away. The neighbor is a Catholic woman who had never had a day's illness in her life until the cancer struck, and now she is, apparently, failing with dizzying speed. The doctor says her body's chaos, chaos, cells running wild all over, says Mrs David Boyle. When I visited her she hardly *knew* me, can hardly *speak*, can't keep herself *clean*, says Mrs David Boyle.

(39) Sometimes Sarah can hardly remember how many cute chubby little children she has.

(40) When she used to stand out in centre field far away from the other players, she used to make up songs and sing them to herself.

(41) She thinks of the end of the world by ice.

(42) She thinks of the end of the world by water.

(43) She thinks of the end of the world by nuclear war.

(44) There must be more than this, Sarah Boyle thinks, from time to time. What could one do to justify one's passage? Or less ambitiously, to change, even in the motion of the smallest mote, the course and circulation of the world? Sometimes Sarah's dreams are of heroic girth, a new symphony using laboratories of machinery and all invented instruments, at once giant in scope and intelligible to all, to heal the bloody breach; a series of paintings which would transfigure and astonish and calm the frenzied art world in its panting race; a new novel that would refurbish language. Sometimes she considers the mystical, the streaky and random, and it seems that one change, no matter how small, would be enough. Turtles are supposed to live for many years. To carve a name, date and perhaps a word of hope upon a turtle's shell, then set him free to wend the world, surely this one act might cancel out absurdity?

(45) Mrs David Boyle has a faint moustache, like Duchamp's *Mona Lisa*.

(46) THE BIRTHDAY PARTY.

Many children dressed in pastels, sit around the long table They are exhausted and overexcited from games fiercely played, some are flushed and wet, others unnaturally pale. This general agitation, and the paper party hats they wear, combine to make them appear a dinner party of debauched midgets. It is time for the cake. A huge chocolate cake in the shape of a rocket and launching pad and covered with blue and pink icing is carried in. In the hush the birthday child begins to cry. He stops crying, makes a wish and blows out the candles.

(47) One child will not eat hot dogs, ice cream or cake, and asks for cereal. Sarah pours him out a bowl of Sugar Frosted Flakes, and a moment later he chokes. Sarah pounds him on the back, and out spits a tiny green plastic snake with red glassy eyes, the Surprise Gift. All the children want it.

(48) AFTER THE PARTY THE CHILDREN ARE PUT TO BED.

Bath time. Observing the nakedness of children, pink and slippery as seals, squealing as seals, now the splashing, grunting and smacking of cherry flesh on raspberry flesh reverberate in the pearl tiled steamy cubicle. The nakedness of children is so much more absolute than that of the mature. No musky curling hair to indicate the target points, no knobbly clutch of plane and fat and curvature to ennoble this prince of beasts. All well-fed naked children appear edible, Sarah's teeth hum in her head with memory of bloody feastings, prehistory. Young humans appear too like the young of other species for smugness, and the comparison is not even in their favor, they are much the most peeled and unsupple of those young. Such pinkness, such utter nuded pinkness; the orifices neatly incised, rimmed with a slightly deeper rose, the incessant demands for breast, time, milks of many sorts.

(49) INSERT SIX. WEINER ON ENTROPY.

In Gibbs' Universe order is least probable, chaos most probable. But while the Universe as a whole, if indeed there is a whole Universe, tends to run down, there are local enclaves whose direction seems opposed to that of the Universe at large and in which there is a limited and temporary tendency for organization to increase. Life finds its home in some of these enclaves.

(50) Sarah Boyle imagines, in her mind's eye, cleaning, and ordering the great world, even the Universe. Filling the great spaces of Space with a marvellous sweet smelling, deep cleansing foam. Deodorizing rank caves and volcanoes. Scrubbing rocks.

(51) INSERT SEVEN. TURTLES.

Many different species of carnivorous Turtles live in the fresh waters of the tropical and temperate zones of various continents. Most northerly of the European Turtles (extending as far as Holland and Lithuania) is the European Pond Turtle (*Emys orbicularis*). It is from eight to ten inches long and may live a hundred years.

(52) CLEANING UP AFTER THE PARTY.

Sarah is cleaning up after the party. Gum drops and melted ice cream surge off paper plates, making holes in the paper tablecloth through the printed roses. A fly has died a splendid death in a pool of strawberry ice cream. Wet jelly beans stain all they touch, finally becoming themselves colorless, opaque white flocks of tamed or sleeping maggots. Plastic favors mount half-eaten pieces of blue cake. Strewn about are thin strips of fortune papers from the Japanese poppers. Upon them are printed strangely assorted phrases selected by apparently unilingual Japanese. Crowds of delicate yellow people spending great chunks of their lives in producing these most ephemeral of objects, and inscribing thousands of fine papers with absurd and incomprehensible messages. 'The very hairs of your head are all numbered,' reads one. Most of the balloons have popped. Someone has planted a hot dog in the daffodil pot. A few of the helium balloons have escaped their owners and now ride the ceiling. Another fortune paper reads, 'Emperor's horses meet death worse, numbers, numbers.'

(53) She is very tired, violet under the eyes, mauve beneath the eyes. Her uncle in Ohio used to get the same marks under his eyes. She goes to the kitchen to lay the table for tomorrow's breakfast, then she sees that in the turtle's bowl the turtle is floating, still, on the surface of the water. Sarah

Boyle pokes at it with a pencil but it does not move. She stands for several minutes looking at the dead turtle on the surface of the water. She is crying again.

(54) She begins to cry. She goes to the refrigerator and takes out a carton of eggs, white eggs, extra large. She throws them one by one onto the kitchen floor which is patterned with strawberries in squares. They break beautifully. There is a Secret Society of Dentists, all moustached, with Special Code and Magic Rings. She begins to cry. She takes up three bunny dishes and throws them against the refrigerator; they shatter, and then the floor is covered with shards, chunks of partial bunnies, an ear, an eye here, a paw; Stockton, California, Acton, California, Chico, California, Redding, California Glen Ellen, California, Cadix, California, Angels Camp, California, Half Moon Bay. The total ENTROPY of the Universe therefore is increasing, tending towards a maximum, corresponding to complete disorder of the particles in it. She is crying, her mouth is open. She throws a jar of grape jelly and it smashes the window over the sink. It has been held that the Universe constitutes a thermodynamically closed system, and if this were true it would mean that a time must finally come when the Universe 'unwinds' itself, no energy being available for use. This state is referred to as the 'heat death of the Universe'. Sarah Boyle begins to cry. She throws a jar of strawberry jam against the stove, enamel chips off and the stove begins to bleed. Bach had twenty children, how many children has Sarah Boyle? Her mouth is open. Her mouth is opening. She turns on the water and fills the sink with detergent. She writes on the kitchen wall, 'William Shakespeare has Cancer and lives in California.' She writes, 'Sugar Frosted Flakes are the Food of the Gods.' The water foams up in the sink, overflowing, bubbling onto the strawberry floor. She is about to begin to cry. Her mouth is opening. She is crying. She cries. How can one ever tell whether there are one or many fish? She begins to break glasses and dishes, she throws cups and cooking pots and jars of food, which shatter and break, and spread over the kitchen. The sand keeps falling, very quietly, in the egg timer. The old man and woman in the barometer never catch each other. She picks up eggs and throws them into the air. She begins to cry. She opens her mouth. The eggs arch slowly through the kitchen, like a baseball, hit high against the spring sky, seen from far away. They go higher and higher in the stillness, hesitate at the zenith, then begin to fall away slowly, slowly, through the fine clear air.

The Valve Transcript

JOEL ZOSS

'I was on the day shift. There were about twenty-five of us, and I was the smallest. They always used me when the pipes were small. I could go places the bigger man couldn't go. One guy, I think he was from Plainfield, he was too big for much work below the surface. They didn't know what to do with him because he was a trained pipe man. But to be a valuable linesman you've got to be small. You can be any size you want on the surface, but for the pipes you've got to be small. A lot of your professions can use a good small man.'

'I believe some of that machinery is quite complicated.'

'It's like everything else. I was always interested in cars when I was a kid. One year I made a little car out of a lawnmower engine. We could only drive it up and down our street because it didn't have a licence. All your motor vehicles have to have a licence.'

'How long have you held this job?'

'I've worked for Cammera's eight years. At first I used to rotate shifts sometimes, getting up and going to work at midnight, four o'clock. At the time I was on the day shift. I liked working in the pipes. At the end of the day you come out things are different.'

'Is it true you sometimes spent more time underground than you had to?'

'That depends how you look at it. One guy used to tell me about vitamin D deficiency, or maybe vitamin A, from not being in the sun. From a strict health standpoint you might be correct. It's not bad for your eyes. They've got much better lighting than you think down there. I have my headlamp. They used to use flares. It's much cooler in the summer. It wasn't that that got my goat. I was thinking of something else. He's the foreman and wants to make sure his responsibility comes through. I knew he was the foreman. The bad valve was six hundred yards from the closest hatch. Go down one and come out the other.'

'You didn't intend anything tricky?'

'I didn't intend anything tricky. Ask anybody if I'm known for jokes. More difficult jobs come along all the time. They kept telling me how much money it meant. It takes a lot of money for a vacation too. I used to go canoeing.

They had beaver, moose, loons, everything. The Indians up there all use outboards.'

'Then you insist you acted alone?'

'I went through the one hatch to get to the machinery. Then I was supposed to climb out the other further down instead of coming back the same one. That would have meant climbing back uphill, and they were slippery. The whole thing wouldn't take more than ten minutes. So they would shut everything down for fifteen minutes and start right up again. It amounts to replacing one part, as easy as putting your batteries in a flashlight. Anybody could do it if he wasn't too big. If they didn't start right up again they would lose too much money, it would be better to start up even if the valve wasn't fixed. How would they know I was out? They would have a man where I was supposed to come out, and he would tell them.'

'Were you familiar with this part of the line?'

'If they started up and I was inside that would kill me. They couldn't kill somebody. I worked there eight years. Think of the publicity. I don't blame people looking out for their money. I've spent more time down there than most of the men.'

'Who was supposed to wait for you? Do you recognize him?'

'I have a very bad memory for faces. I would look at my wife and she would be a different person, sometimes even my mother and father would look different. My dog looks the same only. All animals, I guess. Sometimes I thought things didn't stay the same at all. They change all the time. Why not? We use radio cars at construction so Allen would have called right in – "OK, let her go." Once they tried microphones in our helmets, but we never kept them. Everybody's wired up. Did you read about how atoms always change in the newspapers? With those, when you came to a place you did not know, for instance, you weren't sure which turn to take you just speak up and on the surface they had a map. Sure enough, the man would tell you, "Take your right." I always knew the line so well but some guys called all the time. If you have a feel for the pipes, which some of the men have, then you just don't have any trouble. I think the foreman recognized my ability. Who was up top?'

'You knew precisely how much money was involved?'

'Some men just naturally care for the job. For most it's check in and then just drive off in their cars as fast as they can. For a while night shift when I got off at 12.00 o'clock I would hang out at the bar and grill but I got to getting up too late I liked to feel awake. So the foreman says: "We are shutting down for fifteen minutes. It costs Cammera fifty thousand every minute the flow is off, so do not stay down any longer than is absolutely necessary." I have known this foreman for six years. He knows I do a good job. It was a bright day too. When you come out it takes a while to get used to the light. I put on dark glasses for the first few minutes and then take them off when my eyes are used to that, otherwise your eyes are hurt, sensitive. Then it's much hotter too. Up north it would get up to ninety in the day and below forty at night.'

'You didn't have any trouble with the valve?'

'Did you think they would start it back even if I wasn't out? When it comes to repairs I never take very long. On the way down I figured that's seven hundred fifty thousand dollars. It wasn't very slippery at all, when you have to be careful. Some people want you to be what you aren't. I got to the valve right away because of my size, the seals on those models are worn. They have to be soft because your harder metals don't seal as well, which means they wear out. All the coffee cups have "Delays are Costly" on them. For a while they had them with safety messages. I didn't like the way the little men were drawn. Then we got the new service where the truck comes around to you and the back opens up. There are a lot of opportunities in the services. I fixed the valve just like that, and by then I was thinking it was time for coffee. I like to sit down for fifteen minutes, not stand around a truck. Paper cups always taste bad.'

'Then you proceeded to the other hatch.'

'In a few minutes sitting down I can relax. I earn my living. The days come and go, the day shift you spend underground in the damp. Some guys make more money than me, but I do good work. What's the fuss? I couldn't understand everybody so serious – you'd think we were invading Japan. Would they start it up anyway even if I didn't come out? Time is money. I never saw a minute but you can see money. What's money? Made at the bank. I was doing my job.'

'Why didn't you leave from the hatch you were supposed to?'

'When the gas is off a man can get through the pipes without any trouble at all, otherwise it would kill you. We have very few casualties. In fact, the foreman says we came close to getting a safety award. But I never pay much attention to that. I didn't like it in the army either. You know what they do when some kids get caught in a cave? What's so special about getting caught in a cave. They get on the Ed Sullivan show. You don't see TV cameras when I come out of the ground. For instance, what if some kids were trapped in a cave and the foreman yelled, "OK, you better come out. In fifteen minutes we're going to turn on the gas." Would you believe him? I know there are a lot of crazy things in this world. When you start getting all excited and worrying about money that's crazy. My wife worries if the milkman got the bill right. I don't even drink milk.'

'Didn't you realize how much money was involved?'

'Actually milk is good for you even when you're grown. When you work below the surface you need all the vitamins you can get. When the valve was fixed I started for the hatch, but then it occurs to me another wasn't much farther down, where the access road comes in. I used to go to the diner when we worked more down that end. The one waitress doesn't tease you like the others. She has such a friendly smile. It is a pleasure to have her bring you a cup of coffee on sunny days. Now the others always try to act sexy. They make too many promises, but I bet she gets more tips. Who wants to get all sexy when you're drinking a cup of coffee? They knew I was doing my job. I was never slow before. I got a little chill and went out the other hatch to the diner instead.'

The Tank Trapeze

MICHAEL MOORCOCK

01.11 hours. Prague Radio announced the move and said the Praesidium of the Czechoslovak Communist Party regarded it as a violation of international law, and that Czechoslovak forces had been ordered not to resist.

Perfection had always been his goal, but a sense of justice had usually hampered him. Jerry Cornelius wouldn't be seeing the burning city again. His only luggage an expensive cricket bag, he rode a scheduled corpse boat to the Dubrovnik depot and boarded the SS *Kao An* bound for Burma, arriving just in time.

After the ship had jostled through the junks to find a berth, Jerry disembarked, making his way to the Rangoon public baths where, in a three-kyat cubicle, he took off his brown serge suit and turban, changing into an elaborately embroidered Russian blouse loose enough to hide his shoulder holster. From his bag he took a pair of white flannels, soft Arabian boots and an old-fashioned astrakhan shako. Disguised to his satisfaction he left the baths and went by pedicab to the checkpoint where the Buddhist monk waited for him.

The monk's moody face was fringed by a black 'Bergman' beard making him look like an unfrocked BBC producer. Signing the safe-conduct order with a Pentel pen that had been recharged in some local ink, he blinked at Jerry. 'He's here today.'

'Too bad.' Jerry adjusted his shako with the tips of his fingers then gave the monk his heater. The monk shrugged, looked at it curiously and handed it back. 'OK. Come on. There's a car.'

'*Every gun makes its own tune,*' murmured Jerry.

As they headed for the old Bentley tourer parked beyond the guard hut, the monk's woolly saffron cardigan billowed in the breeze.

02.15: All telephone lines between Vienna and Czechoslovakia were cut.

They drove between the green paddy fields and in the distance saw the walls of Mandalay. Jerry rubbed his face. 'I hadn't expected it to be so hot.'

'Hell, isn't it? It'll be cooler in the temple.' The monk's eyes were on the twisting white road.

Jerry wound down the window. Dust spotted his blouse but he didn't bother to brush it off. 'Lai's waiting in the temple, is he?'

The monk nodded. 'Is that what you call him? Could you kill a child, Mr Cornelius?'

'I could try.'

03.30: *Prague Radio and some of its transmitters were off the air.*

All the roofs of Mandalay were of gold or burnished brass. Jerry put on his dark glasses as they drove through the glazed gates. The architecture was almost primitive and somewhat fierce. Hindu rather than Buddhist in inspiration, it featured as decoration a variety of boldly painted devils, fabulous beasts and minor deities.

'You keep it up nicely.'

'We do our best. Most of the buildings, of course, are in the later Pala-Sena style.'

'The spires in particular.'

'Wait till you see the temple.'

The temple was rather like an Anuradhapuran ziggurat, rising in twelve ornate tiers of enamelled metal inlaid with silver, bronze, gold, onyx, ebony and semi-precious stones. Its entrance was overhung by three arches, each like an inverted V, one upon the other. The building seemed overburdened, like a tree weighted with too much ripe fruit. They went inside, making their way between pillars of carved ivory and teak. Of the gods in the carvings, Ganesh was the one most frequently featured.

'The expense, of course, is enormous,' whispered the monk. 'Here's where we turn off.'

A little light entered the area occupied chiefly by a reclining Buddha of pure gold, resting on a green marble plinth. The Buddha was twenty feet long and about ten feet high, a decadent copy in the manner of the Siamese school of U Thong. The statue's thick lips were supposed to be curved in a smile but instead seemed fatuously pursed.

From the shadow of the Buddha a man moved into the light. He was fat, the colour of oil, with a crimson fez perched on his bald head. His hands were buried in the pockets of his beige jacket. 'You're Jeremiah Cornelius? You're pale. Haven't been out East long. . . .'

'This is Captain Maxwell,' said the monk eagerly.

'I was to meet a Mr Lai.'

'This is Mr Lai.'

'How do you do.' Jerry put down his cricket bag.

'How do you do, Mr Cornelius.'

'It depends what you mean.'

Captain Maxwell pressed his lips in a red smile. 'I find your manner instructive.' He waved the monk away and returned to the shadows. 'Will it matter, I wonder, if we are not simpatico?'

03.30: *Russian troops took up positions outside the Prague Radio building.*

In the bamboo bar of the Mandalay Statler-Hilton Jerry looked through the net curtains at the rickshaws passing rapidly on both sides of the wide street. The bar was faded and poorly stocked and its only other occupants, two German railway technicians on their way through to Laos, crossed the room to the far corner and began a game of bar billiards.

Jerry took the stool next to Captain Maxwell, who had registered at the same time, giving his religion as Protestant and his occupation as engineer. Jerry asked the Malayan barman for a Jack Daniels that cost him fourteen kyats and tasted like clock oil.

'This place doesn't change,' Maxwell said. His Slavic face was morose as he sipped his sherbet. 'I don't know why I come back. Nowhere else, I suppose. Came here first. . . .' He rubbed his toothbrush moustache with his finger and used the same finger to push a ridge of sweat from his forehead. Fidgeting for a moment on his stool he dismounted to tug at the material that had stuck to the sweat of his backside. 'Don't touch the curries here. They're murder. The other grub's OK though. A bit dull.' He picked up his glass and was surprised to find it empty. 'You flew in, did you?'

'Boat in. Flying out.'

Maxwell rolled his sleeves up over his heavy arms and slapped at a mosquito that had settled among the black hairs and the pink, torn bites. 'God almighty. Looking for women?'

Jerry shrugged.

'They're down the street. You can't miss the place.'

'See you.' Jerry left the bar. He got into a taxi and gave an address in the suburbs beyond the wall.

As they moved slowly through the teeming streets the taxi driver leaned back and studied Jerry's thin face and long blond hair. 'Boring now, sir. Worse than the Japs now, sir.'

03.45: *Soviet tanks and armoured cars surrounded the party Central Committee's building in Prague.*

From the other side of the apartment's oak door Jerry heard the radio, badly tuned to some foreign station, playing the younger Dvorak's lugubrious piano piece, *The Railway Station at Cierna nad Tisov*. He rang the bell. Somebody changed the channel and the radio began to play *Alexander's Ragtime Band*, obviously performed by one of the many Russian traditional jazz bands that had become so popular in recent years. A small woman in a blue cheongsam, her black hair piled on her head, opened the door and stepped demurely back to let him in. He winked at her.

'You're Anna Ne Win?'

She bowed her head and smiled.

'You're something.'

'And so are you.'

On the heavy chest in the hallway stood a large Ming vase of crimson roses.

The rest of the apartment was full of the heavy scent of carnations. It was a little overpowering.

03.47: *Prague Radio went off the air completely.*

The child's body was covered from throat to ankles by a gown onto which intricately cut jewels had been stitched so that none of the material showed through. On his shaven head was a similarly worked cap. His skin was a light, soft brown and he seemed a sturdy little boy, grave and good looking. When Jerry entered the gloomy, scented room, the child let out a huge sigh, as if he had been holding his breath for several minutes. His hands emerged from his long sleeves and he placed one on each arm of the ornate wooden chair over which his legs dangled. 'Please sit down.'

Jerry took off his shako and looked carefully into the boy's large almond eyes before lowering himself to the cushion near the base of the chair.

'You've seen Lai?'

Jerry grinned. 'You could be twins.'

The boy smiled and relaxed in the chair. 'Do you like children, Mr Cornelius?'

'I try to like whatever's going.'

'Children like me, I am different, you see.' The boy unbuttoned his coat, exposing his downy brown chest. 'Reach up, Mr Cornelius, and put your hand on my heart.'

Jerry leaned forward and stretched out his hand. He placed his palm against the child's smooth chest. The beat was rapid and irregular. Again he looked into the child's eyes and was interested by the ambiguities he saw in them. For a moment he was afraid.

'Can I see your gun, Mr Cornelius?'

Jerry took his hand away and reached under his blouse tugging his heater from its holster. He gave it to the child, who drew it up close to his face to inspect it. 'I have never seen a gun like this before.'

'It's a side-product,' Jerry said, retrieving the weapon, 'of the communications industry.'

'Ah, of course. What do you think will happen?'

'Who knows? We live in hope.'

Anna Ne Win, dressed in beautiful brocade, with her hair hanging free, returned with a tray, picking her way among the cushions that were scattered everywhere on the floor of the gloomy room. 'Here is some tea. I hope you'll dally with us.'

'I'd love to.'

04.20: *The Soviet Tass Agency said that Soviet troops had been called into Czechoslovakia by Czechoslovak leaders.*

In the hotel room Maxwell picked his nails with a splintered chopstick while Jerry checked his kit.

'You'll be playing for the visitors, of course. Hope the weather won't get you down.'

'It's got to get hotter before it gets cooler.'

'What do you mean by that?' Maxwell lit a Corona from the butt of a native cheroot he had just dropped in the ashtray, watching Jerry undo the straps of his bag.

Jerry up-ended the cricket bag. All the equipment tumbled noisily onto the bamboo table and hit the floor. A red cricket ball rolled under the bed. Maxwell was momentarily disconcerted, then leaned down and recovered it. His chair creaked as he tossed the ball to Jerry.

Jerry put the ball in his bag and picked up a protector and a pair of bails. 'The smell of brand new cricket gear. Lovely, isn't it?'

'I've never played cricket.'

Jerry laughed. 'Neither have I. Not since I had my teeth knocked out when I was five.'

'You're considering violence, then?'

'I don't get you.'

'What is it you dislike about me?'

'I hadn't noticed. Maybe I'm jealous.'

'That's quite likely.'

'I've been aboard your yacht, you see. The *Teddy Bear*. In the Pool of London. Registered in Hamburg , isn't she?'

'The *Teddy Bear* isn't my yacht, Mr Cornelius. If only she were. Is that all? . . . .'

'Then it must be Tsarapkin's, eh?'

'You came to Mandalay to do a job for me, Mr Cornelius, not to discuss the price of flying fish.'

Jerry shrugged. 'You raised the matter.'

'That's rich.'

04.45: *Prague Radio came back on the air and urged the people of Prague to heed only the legal voice of Czechoslovakia. It repeated the request not to resist. 'We are incapable of defending these frontiers,' it said.*

Caught at the wicket for sixteen off U Shi Jheon, Jerry now sat in his deckchair watching the game. Things looked sticky for the visitors.

It was the first few months of 1948 that had been crucial. A detailed almanac for that period would reveal a lot. That was when the psychosis had really started to manifest itself. It had been intensifying ever since. There was only a certain amount one could do, after all.

06.25: *Russian troops began shooting at Czechoslovak demonstrators outside the Prague Radio building.*

While Jerry was changing, Captain Maxwell entered the dressing room and stood leaning against a metal locker, rubbing his right foot against his fat left leg while Jerry combed his hair.

'How did the match go?'

'A draw. What did you expect?'

'No less.'

'You didn't do too badly out there, old boy. Tough luck, being caught like that.'

Jerry blew him a kiss and left the pavilion, carrying his cricket bag across the empty field towards the waiting car that could just be seen through the trees.

06.30: *Machine-gun fire broke out near the Hotel Esplanade.*

Jerry strolled among the pagodas as the sun rose and struck their bright roofs. Shaven-headed monks in saffron moved slowly here and there. Jerry's boots made no sound on the mosaic paths. Looking back, he saw that Anna Ne Win was watching him from the corner of a pagoda. At that moment the child appeared and took her hand, leading her out of sight. Jerry walked on.

06.30: *Prague television was occupied.*

Maxwell stared down through the window, trying to smooth the wrinkles in his suit. 'Rangoon contacted me last night.'

'Ah.'

'They said: "It is better to go out in the street."' Maxwell removed his fez. 'It's all a matter of profits in the long run I suppose.' He chuckled.

'You seem better this morning. The news must have been good.'

'Positive. You could call it positive. I must admit I was beginning to get a little nervy. I'm a man of action, you see, like yourself.'

06.37: *Czech National Anthem played.*

Anna Ne Win moved her soft body against his in the narrow bed, pushing his legs apart with her knee. Raising himself on one elbow he reached out and brushed her black hair from her face. It was almost afternoon. Her delicate eyes opened and she smiled.

He turned away.

'Are you crying, Jerry?'

Peering through the slit in the blind he saw a squadron of L-29 Delfins fly shrieking over the golden rooftops. Were they part of an occupation force? He couldn't make out the markings. For a moment he felt depressed, then he cheered up, anticipating a pleasant event.

06.36: *Prague Radio announced: 'When you hear the Czech National Anthem you will know it's all over.'*

Jerry hung around the post office the whole day. No reply came to his telegram but that was probably a good sign. He went to a bar in the older part of the city where a Swedish folk-singer drove him out. He took a rickshaw ride around the wall. He brought a necklace and a comb. In Ba Swe Street he was almost hit by a racing tram and while he leaned against a telephone pole two *Kalan cacsa* security policemen made him show them his safe conduct. It impressed them. He watched them saunter through the crowd on the pavement and arrest a shoeshine boy, pushing him aboard the truck which had been crawling behind them. A cathartic act, if not a kindly one.

Jerry found himself in a deserted street. He picked up the brushes and rags and the polish. He fitted them into the box and placed it neatly in a doorway. A few people began to reappear. A tram came down the street. On the opposite pavement, Jerry saw Captain Maxwell. The engineer stared at him suspiciously until he realised Jerry had seen him, then he waved cheerfully.

Jerry pretended he hadn't noticed and withdrew into the shade of a tattered awning. The shop itself, like so many in the street, had been closed for some time and its door and shutters were fastened by heavy iron padlocks. A proclamation had been pasted on one door panel. Jerry made out the words *Pyee-Duang-Su Myanma-Nainggan-Daw*. It was an official notice, then. Jerry watched the rickshaws and cars, the trams and the occasional truck pass in the street.

After a while the shoeshine boy returned. Jerry pointed out his equipment. The boy picked it up and walked with it under his arm towards the square where the Statler-Hilton could be seen. Jerry decided he might as well follow him, but the boy began to run and turned hastily into a side street.

Jerry spat into the gutter.

07.00: *President Svoboda made a personal appeal over the radio for calm. He said he could offer no explanation for the invasion.*

As Jerry checked the heater's transistors, Maxwell lay on the unmade bed watching him. 'Have you any other occupation, Mr Cornelius?'

'I do this and that.'

'And what about political persuasions?'

'There you have me, Captain Maxwell.'

'Our monk told me you said it was as primitive to hold political convictions as it was to maintain belief in God.' Maxwell loosened his cummerbund.

'Is that a fact?'

'Or was he putting words into your mouth?'

Jerry clipped the heater back together. 'It's a possibility.'

08.20: *Pilsen Radio described itself as 'the last free radio station in Czechoslovakia'.*

A Kamov Ka-15 helicopter was waiting for them on the cricket field near the pavilion. Maxwell offered the pilot seat to Jerry. The clambered in and adjusted their flying helmets.

'You've flown these before,' said Maxwell.

'That's right.' Jerry lit a cheroot.

'*The gestures of conflict keep the peace,*' murmured Maxwell nostalgically.

10.00: *The Czechoslovak agency Ceteka said that at least ten ambulances had arrived outside Prague Radio station, where a Soviet tank was on fire.*

When they had crossed the Irrawaddy, Jerry entered the forest and headed for the shrine. He had a map in one hand and a compass in the other.

The atmosphere of the forest was moist and cool. It would begin to rain soon; already the sky was becoming overcast. The air was full of little clusters of flies and mosquitoes, like star systems encircling an invisible sun, and in avoiding them Jerry knocked off his shako several times. His boots were now muddy and his blouse and trousers stained by the bark and foliage. He stumbled on.

About an hour later the birches began to thin out and he knew he was close to the clearing. He breathed heavily, moving more cautiously.

He saw the chipped green tiles of the roof first, then the dirty ivory columns that supported it, then the shrine itself. Under the roof, on a base of rusting steel sheeting, stood a fat Buddha carved from local stone and painted in dark reds, yellows and blues. The statue smiled. Jerry crawled through the damp undergrowth until he could get a good view of the boy.

A few drops of rain fell loudly on the roof. Already the ground surrounding the shrine was churned to mud by a previous rainfall. The boy lay in the mud, face down, arms flung out towards the shrine, legs stiffly together, his jewelled gown covering his body. One ankle was just visible; the brown flesh showing in the gap between the slipper and the hem. Jerry touched his lips with the tip of his finger.

Above his head monkeys flung themselves through the green branches as they looked for cover from the rain. The noise they made helped Jerry creep into the clearing unobserved. He frowned.

The boy lifted his head and smiled up at Jerry. 'Do you feel like a woman?'

'You stick to your prayers, I'll stick to mine.'

The boy obeyed. Jerry stood looking down at the little figure as it murmured the prayers. He took out his heater and cleared his throat, then he adjusted the beam width and burned a thin hole through the child's anus. He screamed.

Later Maxwell emerged from the undergrowth and began removing the various quarters from the jewelled material. There was hardly any blood, just the stench. He shook out the bits of flesh and folded the parts of the gown across his arm. He put one slipper in his right pocket and the other in his left. Lastly he plucked the cap from the severed head and offered it to Jerry.

'You'd better hurry. The rain's getting worse. We'll be drowned at this rate. That should cover your expenses. You'll be able to convert it fairly easily in Singapore.'

'I don't often get expenses,' said Jerry.

10.25: *Ceteka said shooting in the centre of Prague had intensified and that the* Rude Pravo *offices had been seized by 'occupation units'.*

Waiting near the Irrawaddy for the Ka-15 to come back, Jerry watched the rain splash into the river. He was already soaked.

The flying field had only recently been cleared from the jungle and it went right down to the banks of the river. Jerry picked his teeth with his thumbnail and looked at the broad brown water and the forest on the other side. A wooden landing stage had been built out into the river and a family of fishermen were tying up their sampan. Why should crossing this particular river seem so important?

Jerry shook his umbrella and looked up at the sound of the helicopter's engines. He was completely drenched; he felt cold and he felt sorry for himself. The sooner he could get to the Galapagos the better.

11.50: *Pilsen Radio said: 'The occupation has already cost twenty-five lives.'*

He just got to the post office before it closed. Anna Ne Win was standing inside reading a copy of *Dandy*. She looked up. 'You're British, aren't you? Want to hear the Test results?'

Jerry shook his head. It was pointless asking for his telegram now. He no longer had any use for assurances. What he needed most at this stage was a good, solid, undeniable fact; something to get his teeth into.

'A Captain Maxwell was in earlier for some money that was being cabled to him,' she said. 'Apparently he was disappointed. Have you found it yet – the belt?'

'I'm sorry, no.'

'You should have watched where you threw it.'

'Yes.'

'That Captain Maxwell. He's staying at your hotel, isn't he?'

'Yes. I've got to leave now. Going to Singapore. I'll buy you two new ones there. Send them along.' He ran from the post office.

'Cheerio,' she called. 'Keep smiling.'

12.28: *Ceteka said Mr Dubcek was under restriction in the Central Committee building.*

Naked, Jerry sat down on his bed and smoked a cheroot. He was fed up with the East. It wasn't doing his identity any good.

The door opened and Maxwell came in with a revolver in his hand and a look of disgust on his fat face. 'You're not wearing any damned clothes!'

'I wasn't expecting you.'

Maxwell cocked the revolver. 'Who do you think you are, anyway?'

'Who do you think?'

Maxwell sneered. 'You'd welcome suggestions, eh? I want to puke when I look at you.'

'Couldn't I help you get a transfer?'

'I don't need one.'

Jerry looked at the disordered bed, at the laddered stockings Anna Ne Win had left behind, at the trousers hanging on the string over the washbasin, at the woollen mat on the floor by the bed, at the cricket bag on top of the wardrobe. 'It would make me feel better, though.' He drew on his cheroot. 'Do you want the hat back?'

'Don't be revolting, Cornelius.'

'What do you want, then, Captain Maxwell?'

'Justice.'

'I'm with you.' Jerry stood up and reached for his flannels. Maxwell raised the Webley and Scott .45 and fired the first bullet. Jerry was thrust against the washbasin and he blinked rapidly as his vision dimmed. There was a bruise five inches in diameter on his right breast and in its centre was a hole with red, puckered sides; around the edges of the bruise a little blood was beginning to force its way out. 'There certainly are some shits in the worlds,' he said.

A couple of shots later, when Jerry was lying on the floor, he had the impression that Maxwell's trousers had fallen down. He grinned. Maxwell's voice was faint but insulting. 'Bloody gangster! Murderer! Fucking killer!'

Jerry turned on his side and noticed that Anna Ne Win's cerise suspender belt was hanging on a spring under the bed. He reached out and touched it and a tremor of pleasure ran through his body. The last shot he felt hit the base of his spine.

He shuddered and was vaguely aware of the weight of Maxwell's lumpen body on his, of the insect-bitten wrists, of the warm Webley and Scott still in one hand and the cordite smell on the captain's breath. Then Maxwell whispered something in his ear and reaching around his face carefully folded down his eyelids.

(All quotes from *The Guardian* 22.8.68)

Angouleme

THOMAS M. DISCH

There were seven Alexandrians involved in the Battery plot – Jack, who was the youngest and from the Bronx, Celeste DiCecca, Sniffles and MaryJane, Tancred Miller, Amparo (of course), and *of course*, the leader and mastermind, Bill Harper, better known as Little Mister Kissy Lips. Who was passionately, hopelessly in love with Amparo. Who was nearly thirteen (she would be, fully, by September this year), and breasts just beginning. Very very beautiful skin, like lucite. Amparo Martinez.

Their first, nothing operation was in the East 60s, a broker or something like that. All they netted was cufflinks, a watch, a leather satchel that wasn't leather after all, some buttons, and the usual lot of useless credit-cards. He stayed calm through the whole thing, even with Sniffles slicing off buttons, and *soothing*. None of them had the nerve to ask, though they all wondered, how often he'd been through this scene before. What they were about wasn't an innovation. It was partly that, the need to innovate, that led them to think up the plot. The only really memorable part of the holdup was the name laminated on the cards, which was, weirdly enough, Lowen, Richard W. An omen (the connection being that they were all at the Alexander Lowen School), but of what?

Little Mister Kissy Lips kept the cufflinks for himself, gave the buttons to Amparo (who gave them to her uncle), and donated the rest (the watch was a piece of crap) to the Conservation booth outside the Plaza right where he lived.

His father was a teevee executive. In, as he would quip, both senses. They had got married, his Mama and Papa, young and divorced soon after, but not before he'd come to fill out their quota. Papa, the executive, remarried, a man this time and somewhat more happily. Anyhow it lasted long enough that the offspring, the leader and mastermind, had to learn to adjust to the situation, it being permanent. Mama simply went down to the Everglades and disappeared, sploosh.

In short, he was well-to-do. Which is how, more than by overwhelming talent, he got into the Lowen School in the first place. He had the right kind of body though, so with half a desire there was no reason in the city of New

York he couldn't grow up to be a professional dancer, even a choreographer. He'd have the connections for it, as Papa was fond of pointing out.

For the time being, however, his bent was literary and religious rather than balletic. He loved, and what seventh grader doesn't, the abstracter foxtrots and more metaphysical twists of a Dostoevsky, a Gide, a Mailer. He longed for the experience of some vivider pain than the mere daily hollowness knotted into his tight young belly, and no weekly stomp-and-holler of group therapy with other jejune eleven-year-olds was going to get him his stripes in the major leagues of suffering, crime and resurrection. Only a bonafide crime would do that, and of all the crimes available murder certainly carried the most prestige, as no less an authority than Loretta Couplard was ready to attest. Loretta Couplard being not only the director and co-owner of the Lowen School but the author, as well, of two nationally televised scripts, both about famous murders of the twentieth century. They'd even done a unit in social studies on the topic: A History of Crime in Urban America.

The first of Loretta's murders was a comedy involving Pauline Campbell, RN of Ann Arbor, Michigan, circa 1951, whose skull had been smashed by three drunken teenagers. They had meant to knock her unconscious so they could screw her, which was 1951 in a nutshell. The eighteen-year-olds, Bill Morey and Max Pell, got life; Dave Royal (Loretta's hero) was a year younger and got off with twenty-two years.

Her second murder was tragic in tone and consequently inspired more respect, though not among the critics unfortunately. Possibly because her heroine, also a Pauline (Pauline Wichura), though more interesting and complicated, had also been more famous in her own day and ever since. Which made the competition, one best-selling novel and a serious film biography, considerably stiffer. Miss Wichura had been a welfare worker in Atlanta, Georgia, very much into environment and the population problem, this being the immediate pre-REGENTS period when anyone and everyone was legitimately starting to fret. Pauline decided to do something, viz, reduce the population herself and in the fairest way possible. So whenever any of the families she visited produced one child above the three she'd fixed, rather generously, as the upward limit, she found some unobtrusive way of thinning that family back to the preferred maximal size. Between 1989 and 1993 Pauline's journals (Random House, 1994) record twenty-six murders, plus an additional fourteen failed attempts. In addition she had the highest welfare department record in the US for abortions and sterilizations among the families whom she advised.

'Which proves, I think,' Little Mister Kissy Lips had explained one day after school to his friend Jack, 'that a murder doesn't have to be of someone *famous* to be a form of idealism.'

But of course idealism was only half the story; the other half was curiosity. And beyond idealism *and* curiosity there was probably even another half, the basic childhood need to grow up and kill someone.

They settled on the Battery because: 1) none of them ever was there ordinarily; 2) it was posh and at the same time relatively, 3), uncrowded, at least once the night shift were snug in their towers tending their machines. The night shift seldom ate their lunches down in the park.

And 4) because it was beautiful, especially now at the beginning of summer. The dark water, chromed with oil, flopping against the buttressed shore; the silences blowing in off the Upper Bay, silences large enough sometimes that you could sort out the different noises of the city behind them, the purr and quaver of the skyscrapers, the ground-shivering *mysterioso* of the expressways, and every now and then the strange sourceless screams that are the melody of New York's themesong; the blue-pink of sunsets in a visible sky; the people's faces, calmed by the sea and their own nearness to death, lined up in rhythmic rows on the green benches. Why even the statues looked beautiful here, as though someone had believed in them once, the way people must have believed in the statues in the Cloisters, so long ago.

His favorite was the gigantic killer-eagle landing in the middle of the monoliths in the memorial for the soldiers, sailors, and airmen killed in World War II. The largest eagle, probably, in all Manhattan. His talons ripped apart what was *surely* the largest artichoke.

Amparo, who went along with some of Miss Couplard's ideas, preferred the more humanistic qualities of the memorial (him on top, and an angel gently probing an enormous book with her sword) for Verrazzano, who was not, as it turned out, the contractor who put up the bridge that had, so famously, collapsed. Instead, as the bronze plate in back proclaimed:

IN APRIL 1524
THE FLORENTINE BORN NAVIGATOR
VERRAZZANO
LED THE FRENCH CARAVEL LA DAUPHINE
TO THE DISCOVERY OF THE HARBOR OF
NEW YORK
AND NAMED THESE SHORES ANGOULEME
IN HONOR OF FRANCIS I KING OF FRANCE

'Angouleme' they all agreed, except Tancred, who favored the more prevalent and briefer name, was much classier. Tancred was ruled out of order, and the decision became unanimous.

It was there, by the statue, looking across the bay of Angouleme to Jersey, that they took the oath that bound them to perpetual secrecy. Whoever spoke of what they were about to do, unless he were being tortured by the Police, solemnly called upon his co-conspirators to insure his silence by other means. Death. All revolutionary organizations take similar precautions, as the history unit on Modern Revolutions had made clear.

How he got the name: it had been Papa's theory that what modern life cried out for was a sweetening of old-fashioned sentimentality. Ergo, among all the other indignities this theory gave rise to, scenes like the following: 'Who's my Little Mister Kissy Lips!' Papa would bawl out, sweetly, right in the middle of Rockefeller Center (or a restaurant, or in front of the school), and he'd shout right back, 'I am!' At least until he knew better.

Mama had been, variously, 'Rosebud,' 'Peg O' My Heart,' and (this only at the end) 'The Snow Queen.' Mama, being adult, had been able to vanish with no other trace than the postcard that still came every Xmas postmarked from Key Largo, but Little Mister Kissy Lips was stuck with the New Sentimentality willy-nilly. True, by age seven he'd been able to insist on being called 'Bill' around the house (or, as Papa would have it, 'Just Plain Bill'). But that left the staff at the Plaza to contend with, and Papa's assistants, schoolmates, anyone who'd ever heard the name. Then a year ago, aged ten and able to reason, he laid down the new law – that his name *was* Little Mister Kissy Lips, the whole awful mouthful, each and every time. His reasoning being that if anyone would be getting his face rubbed in shit by this it would be Papa, who deserved it. Papa didn't seem to get the point, or else he got it and another point besides, you could never be sure how stupid or how subtle he really was, which is the worst kind of enemy.

Meanwhile at the nationwide level, the New Sentimentality had been a rather overwhelming smash. *The Orphans*, which Papa produced and sometimes was credited with writing, pulled down the top Thursday evening ratings for two years. Now it was being overhauled for a daytime slot. For one hour every day our lives were going to be a lot sweeter, and chances were Papa would be a millionaire or more as a result. On the sunny side this meant that *he'd* be the son of a millionaire. Though he generally had contempt for the way money corrupted everything it touched, he had to admit that in certain cases it didn't have to be a bad thing. It boiled down to this (which he'd always known): that Papa was a necessary evil.

This was why every evening when Papa buzzed himself into the suite he'd shout out, 'Where's my Little Mister Kissy Lips,' and he'd reply, 'Here Papa!' The cherry on this sundae of love was a big wet kiss, and then one more for their new 'Rosebud', Jimmy Ness. (Who drank, and was not in all likelihood going to last much longer.) They'd all three sit down to the nice *family* dinner Jimmyness had cooked, and Papa would tell them about the cheerful, positive things that had happened that day at CBS, and Little Mister Kissy Lips would tell all about the bright fine things that had happened to *him*. Jimmy would sulk. Then Papa and Jimmy would go somewhere or just disappear into the private Everglades of sex, and Little Mister Kissy Lips would buzz himself out into the corridor (Papa knew better than to be repressive about hours), and within half an hour he'd be at the Verrazzano statue with the six other Alexandrians, five if Celeste had a lesson, to plot the murder of the victim they'd all finally agreed on.

No one had been able to find out his name. They called him Alyona Ivanovna, after the old pawnbroker woman that Raskolnikov kills with an axe.

The spectrum of possible victims had never been wide. The common financial types of the area would be carrying credit cards like Lowen, Richard W., while the generality of pensioners filling the benches were even less tempting. As Miss Couplard had explained, our economy was being refeudalized and cash was going the way of the ostrich, the octopus, and the moccasin flower.

It was such extinctions as these, but especially seagulls, that were the worry of the first lady they'd considered, a Miss Kraus, unless the name at the bottom of her handlettered poster (STOP THE SLAUGHTER of The *Innocents!!*, etc.) belonged to someone else. Why, if she were Miss Kraus, was she wearing what seemed to be the old-fashioned diamond ring and gold band of a Mrs? But the more crucial problem, which they couldn't see how to solve, was: was the diamond real?

Possibility Number Two was in the tradition of the original Orphans of the Storm, the Gish sisters. A lovely semi-professional who whiled away the daylight pretending to be blind and serenading the benches. Her pathos was rich, if a bit worked-up; her repertoire was archeological; and her gross was fair, especially when the rain added its own bit of too-much. However: Sniffles (who'd done this research) was certain she had a gun tucked away under the rags.

Three was the least poetic possibility, just the concessionaire in back of the giant eagle selling Fun and Synthamon. His appeal was commercial. But he had a licensed Weimaraner, and though Weimaraners can be dealt with, Amparo liked them.

'You're just a Romantic,' Little Mister Kissy Lips said. 'Give me one good reason.'

'His eyes,' she said. 'They're amber. He'd haunt us.'

They were snuggling together in one of the deep embrasures cut into the stone of Castle Clinton, her head wedged into his armpit, his fingers gliding across the lotion on her breasts (summer was just beginning). Silence, warm breezes, sunlight on water, it was all ineffable, as though only the sheerest of veils intruded between them and an understanding of something (all this) really meaningful. Because they thought it was their own innocence that was to blame, like a smog in their souls' atmosphere, they wanted more than ever to be rid of it at times, like this, when they approached so close.

'Why not the dirty old man, then?' she asked, meaning Alyona.

'Because he *is* a dirty old man.'

'That's no reason. He must take in at least as much money as that singer.'

'That's not what I mean.' What he meant wasn't easy to define. It was as though he'd be too easy to kill. If you'd seen him in the first minutes of a program, you'd know he was marked for destruction by the second commercial. He was the defiant homesteader, the crusty senior member of a research team who understood Algol and Fortran but couldn't read the secrets of his own heart. He was the Senator from South Carolina with his own peculiar brand of integrity but a racist nevertheless. Killing that sort was too much like one of Papa's scripts to be a satisfying gesture of rebellion.

But what he said, mistaking his own deeper meaning, was: 'It's because he deserves it, because we'd be doing society a favor. Don't ask me to give *reasons.*'

'Well, I won't pretend I understand that, but do you know what I think, Little Mister Kissy Lips?' She pushed his hand away.

'You think I'm scared.'

'Maybe you *should* be scared.'

'Maybe you should shut up and leave this to me. I said we're going to do it. We'll do it.'

'To him then?'

'Okay. But for gosh sakes, Amparo, we've got to think of something to call the bastard besides "the dirty old man"!'

She rolled over out of his armpit and kissed him. They glittered all over with little beads of sweat. The summer began to shimmer with the excitement of first night. They had been waiting so long, and now the curtain was rising.

M-Day was scheduled for the first weekend in July, a patriotic holiday. The computers would have time to tend to their own needs (which have been variously described as 'confession,' 'dreaming,' and 'throwing up'), and the Battery would be as empty as it ever gets.

Meanwhile their problem was the same as any kids face anywhere during summer vacation, how to fill the time.

There were books, there were the Shakespeare puppets if you were willing to queue up for that long, there was always teevee, and when you couldn't stand sitting any longer there were the obstacle courses in Central Park, but the density there was at lemming level. The Battery, because it didn't try to meet anyone's needs, seldom got so overpopulated. If there had been more Alexandrians and all willing to fight for the space, they might have played ball. Well, another summer. . . .

What else? There were marches for the political, and religions at various energy levels for the apolitical. There would have been dancing, but the Lowen School had spoiled them for most amateur events around the city.

As for the supreme pastime of sex, for all of them except Little Mister Kissy Lips and Amparo (and even for them, when it came right down to orgasm) this was still something that happened on a screen, a wonderful hypothesis that lacked empirical proof.

One way or another it was all consumership, everything they might have done, and they were tired, who isn't, of being passive. They were twelve years old, or eleven, or ten, and they couldn't wait any longer. For what? they wanted to know.

So, except when they were just loafing around solo, all these putative resources, the books, the puppets, the sports, arts, politics, and religions, were in the same category of usefulness as merit badges or weekends in Calcutta, which is a name you can still find on a few old maps of India. Their lives were not enhanced, and their summer passed as summers have passed immemorially. They slumped and moped and lounged about and teased each other and complained. They acted out desultory, shy fantasies and had long pointless arguments about the more peripheral facts of existence – the habits of jungle animals or how bricks had been made or the history of World War II.

One day they added up all the names on the monoliths set up for the soldiers, sailors, and airmen. The final figure they got was 4,800.

'Wow,' said Tancred.

'But that can't be *all* of them,' MaryJane insisted, speaking for the rest. Even that 'wow' had sounded half ironic.

'Why not?' asked Tancred, who could never resist disagreeing. 'They came from every different state and every branch of the service. It has to be complete or the people who had relatives left off would have protested.'

'But so *few*? It wouldn't be possible to have fought more than one battle at that rate.'

'Maybe. . . .' Sniffles began quietly. But he was seldom listened to.

'Wars were different then,' Tancred explained with the authority of a prime time news analyst. 'In those days more people were killed by their own automobiles than in wars. It's a fact.'

'Four thousand, eight *hundred*?'

'. . . a lottery?'

Celeste waved away everything Sniffles had said or would ever say. 'MaryJane is right, Tancred. It's simply a *ludicrous* number. Why, in that same war the Germans gassed seven *million* Jews.'

'Six million Jews,' Little Mister Kissy Lips corrected. 'But it's the same idea. Maybe the ones here got killed in a particular campaign.'

'Then it would say so.' Tancred was adamant, and he even got them to admit at last that 4,800 was an impressive figure, especially with every name spelled out in stone letters.

One other amazing statistic was commemorated in the park: over a 35-year period Castle Clinton had processed 7.7 million immigrants into the United States.

Little Mister Kissy Lips sat down and figured out that it would take 12,800 stone slabs the size of the ones listing the soldiers, sailors, and airmen in order to write out all the immigrants' names, with country of origin, and an area of five square miles to set that many slabs up in, or all of Manhattan from here to 26th Street. But would it be worth the trouble, after all? Would it be that much different from the way things were already?

Alyona Ivanovna:

An archipelago of irregular brown islands were mapped on the tan sea of his bald head. The mainlands of his hair were marble outcroppings, especially his beard, white and crisp and coiling. The teeth were standard MODICUM issue; clothes, as clean as any fabric that old can be. Nor did he smell, particularly. And yet . . . .

Had he bathed every morning you'd still have looked at him and thought he was filthy, the way floorboards in old brownstones seem to need cleaning moments after they've been scrubbed. The dirt had been bonded to the wrinkled flesh and the wrinkled clothes, and nothing less than surgery, or burning, would get it out.

His habits were as orderly as a polka-dot napkin. He lived at a Chelsea dorm for the elderly, a discovery they owed to a rainstorm that had forced him to take the subway home one day instead of, as usual, walking. On the hottest nights he might sleep over in the park, nesting in one of the Castle windows. He bought his lunches from a Water Street speciality shop, *Dumas Fils:* cheeses, imported fruit, smoked fish, bottles of cream, food for the gods. Otherwise he did without, though his dorm must have supplied prosaic necessities like Breakfast. It was a strange way for a panhandler to spend his quarters, drugs being the norm.

His professional approach was out-and-out aggression. For instance, his hand in your face and, 'How about it, Jack?' Or, confidingly, 'I need sixty cents to get home.' It was amazing how often he scored, but actually it wasn't amazing. He had charisma.

And someone who relies on charisma *wouldn't* have a gun.

Agewise he might have been sixty, seventy, seventy-five, a bit more even, or much less. It all depended on the kind of life he'd led, and where. He had an accent none of them could identify. It was not English, not French, not Spanish, and probably not Russian.

Aside from his burrow in the Castle wall there were two distinct places he preferred. One, the wide-open stretch of pavement along the water. This was where he worked, walking up past the Castle and down as far as the concession stand. The passage of one of the great Navy cruisers, the USS *Dana* or the USS *Melville*, would bring him, and the better part of the Battery, to a standstill, as though a whole parade were going by, white, soundless, slow as a dream. It was part of history, and even the Alexandrians were impressed, though three of them had taken the cruise down to Andros Island and back. Sometimes, though, he'd stand by the guardrail for long stretches of time without any real reason, just looking at the Jersey sky and the Jersey shore. After a while he might start talking to himself, the barest whisper but very much in earnest to judge by the way his forehead wrinkled. They never once saw him sit on one of the benches.

The other place he liked was the aviary. On days when they'd been ignored he'd contribute peanuts and breadcrumbs to the cause of the birds' existence. There were pigeons, parrots, a family of robins, and a proletarian swarm of what the sign declared to be chickadees, though Celeste, who'd gone to the library to make sure, said they were nothing more than a rather swank breed of sparrow. Here too, naturally, the militant Miss Kraus stationed herself when she bore testimony. One of her peculiarities (and the reason, probably, she was never asked to move on) was that under no circumstances did she ever deign to argue. Even sympathizers pried no more out of her than a grim smile and curt nod.

One Tuesday a week before M-Day (it was the early a.m. and only three Alexandrians were on hand to witness this confrontation) Alyona so far put aside his own reticence as to try to start a conversation going with Miss Kraus.

He stood squarely in front of her and began by reading aloud, slowly, in that distressingly indefinite accent, from the text of STOP THE SLAUGHTER: 'The Department of the Interior of the United States Government, under the secret direction of the Zionist Ford Foundation is *systematically* poisoning the oceans of the World with so-called "food farms". Is this "peaceful application of Nuclear Power"? Unquote, *The New York Times*, August 2, 2024. Or a new Moondoggle!! *Nature World*, Jan. Can we afford to remain indifferent any longer? Every day 15,000 Seagulls die as a direct result of Systematic Genocides while elected Officials falsify and distort the evidence. Learn the facts. Write to the Congressmen. *Make your voice heard!!*'

As Alyona had droned on, Miss Kraus turned a deeper and deeper red. Tightening her fingers about the turquoise broomhandle to which the placard was stapled, she began to jerk the poster up and down rapidly, as though this man with his foreign accent were some bird of prey who'd perched on it.

'Is that what you think?' he asked, having read all the way down to the signature despite her jiggling tactic. He touched his bushy white beard and wrinkled his face into a philosophical expression. 'I'd *like* to know more about it, yes I would. I'd be interested in hearing what *you* think.'

Horror had frozen up every motion of her limbs. Her eyes blinked shut, but she forced them open again.

'Maybe,' he went on remorselessly, 'we can discuss this whole thing. Some time when you feel more like talking. All right?'

She mustered her smile, and a minimal nod. He went away then. She was safe, temporarily, but even so she waited till he'd gone halfway to the other end of the seafront promenade before she let the air collapse into her lungs. After a single deep breath the muscles of her hands thawed into trembling.

M-Day was an oil of summer, a catalog of everything painters are happiest painting – clouds, flags, leaves, sexy people, and in back of it all the flat empty baby-blue of the sky. Little Mister Kissy Lips was the first one there, and Tancred, in a kind of kimono (it hid the pilfered Luger), was the last. Celeste never came. (She'd just learned she'd been awarded the exchange scholarship to Sofia.) They decided they could do without Celeste, but the other non-appearance was more crucial. Their victim had neglected to be on hand for M-Day. Sniffles, whose voice was most like an adult's over the phone, was delegated to go to the Citibank lobby and call the West 16th Street dorm.

The nurse who answered was a temporary. Sniffles, always an inspired liar, insisted that his mother—'Mrs *Anderson*, of course she lives there, Mrs Alma F. Anderson'—had to be called to the phone. This was 248 West 16th, wasn't it? Where *was* she if she wasn't there? The nurse, flustered, explained that the residents, all who were fit, had been driven off to a July 4th picnic at Lake Hopatcong as guests of a giant Jersey retirement condominium. If he called bright and early tomorrow they'd be back, and he could talk to his mother then.

So the initiation rites were postponed, it couldn't be helped. Amparo passed around some pills she'd taken from her mother's jar, a consolation prize. Jack left, apologizing that he was a borderline psychotic, which was the last that anyone saw of Jack till September. The gang was disintegrating, like a sugarcube soaking up saliva, then crumbling into the tongue. But what the hell – the sea still mirrored the same blue sky, the pigeons behind their wicket were no less iridescent, and trees grew for all of that.

They decided to be silly and made jokes about what the M *really* stood for in M-Day, Sniffles started off with 'Miss Nomer, Miss Carriage, and Miss Steak.' Tancred, whose sense of humor did not exist or was very private, couldn't do better than 'Mnemone, mother of the Muses'. Little Mister Kissy Lips said, 'Merciful Heavens!' MaryJane maintained reasonably that M was for MaryJane. But Amparo said it stood for 'Aplomb' and carried the day.

Then, proving that when you're sailing the wind always blows from behind you, they found Terry Riley's day-long *Orfeo* at 99.5 on the FM dial. They'd studied *Orfeo* in mime class, and by now it was part of their muscle and nerve. As Orpheus descended into a hell that mushroomed from the size of a pea to the size of a planet, the Alexandrians metamorphosed into as credible a tribe of souls in torment as any since the days of Jacopo Peri. Throughout the afternoon little audiences collected and dispersed to flood the sidewalk with libations of adult attention. Expressively they surpassed themselves, both one by one and all together, and though they couldn't have held out till the apotheosis (at 9.30) without a stiff psychochemical wind in their sails, what they had danced was authentic and very much their own. When they left the Battery that night they felt better than they'd felt all summer long. In a sense they had been exorcised.

But back at the Plaza Little Mister Kissy Lips couldn't sleep. No sooner was he through the locks than his guts knotted up into a Chinese puzzle. Only after he'd unsealed his window and crawled out onto the ledge did he get rid of the bad feelings. The city was real. His room was not. The stone ledge was real, and his bare buttocks absorbed reality from it. He watched slow movements in enormous distances and pulled his thoughts together.

He knew without having to talk to the rest that the murder would never take place. The idea had never meant for them what it had meant for him. One pill and they were actors again, content to be images in a mirror.

Slowly, as he watched, the city turned itself off. Slowly the dawn divided the sky into an east and a west. Had a pedestrian been going past on 58th

Street and had that pedestrian looked up, he would have seen the bare soles
of a boy's feet swinging back and forth, angelically.

He would have to kill Alyona Ivanovna himself. Nothing else was
possible.

Back in his bedroom, long ago, the phone was ringing its fuzzy nighttime
ring. That would be Tancred (or Amparo?) trying to talk him out of it. He
foresaw their arguments. Celeste and Jack couldn't be trusted now. Or, more
subtly: they'd all made themselves too visible with their *Orfeo*. If there were
even a small investigation, the benches would remember them, remember
how well they had danced, and the police would know where to look.

But the real reason, which at least Amparo would have been ashamed to
mention now that the pill was wearing off, was that they'd begun to feel sorry
for their victim. They'd got to know him too well over the last month, and
their resolve had been eroded by compassion.

A light came on in Papa's window. Time to begin. He stood up, golden
in the sunbeams of another perfect day, and walked back along the foot-wide
ledge to his own window. His legs tingled from having sat so long.

He waited till Papa was in the shower, then tippytoed to the old secretaire
in his bedroom (W. & J. Sloan, 1952). Papa's keychain was coiled atop the
walnut veneer. Inside the secretaire's drawer was an antique Mexican cigar
box, and in the cigar box a velvet bag, and in the velvet bag Papa's replica
of a French dueling pistol, circa 1790. These precautions were less for his
son's sake than on account of Jimmyness, who every so often felt obliged to
show he was serious with his suicide threats.

He'd studied the booklet carefully when Papa had bought the pistol and
was able to execute the loading procedure quickly and without error, tamping
the premeasured twist of powder into the barrel, and then the lead ball on
top of it.

He cocked the hammer back a single click.

He locked the drawer. He replaced the keys, just so. He buried, for now,
the pistol in the stuffs and cushions of the Turkish corner, tilted upright to
keep the ball from rolling out. Then with what remained of yesterday's
ebullience he bounced into the bathroom and kissed Papa's cheek, damp with
the morning's allotted two gallons and redolent of 47-11.

They had a cheery breakfast together in the coffee room, which was
identical to the breakfast they would have made for themselves except for the
ritual of being waited on by a waitress. Little Mister Kissy Lips gave an
enthusiastic account of the Alexandrians' performance of *Orfeo*, and Papa
made his best effort of seeming not to condescend. When he'd been driven
to the limit of this pretense, Little Mister Kissy Lips touched him for a second

pill, and since it was better for a boy to get these things from his father than from a stranger on the street, he got it.

He reached the South Ferry stop at noon, bursting with a sense of his own imminent liberation. The weather was M-Day all over again, as though at midnight out on the ledge he'd forced time to go backwards to the point when things had started going wrong. He'd dressed in his most anonymous shorts, and the pistol hung from his belt in a dun dittybag.

Alyona Ivanovna was sitting on one of the benches near the aviary, listening to Miss Kraus. Her ring hand gripped the poster firmly, while the right chopped at the air, eloquently awkward, like a mute's first words following a miraculous cure.

Little Mister Kissy Lips went down the path and squatted in the shadow of his memorial. It had lost its magic yesterday, when the statues had begun to look so silly to everyone. They still looked silly. Verrazzano was dressed like a Victorian industrialist taking a holiday in the Alps. The angel was wearing an angel's usual bronze nightgown.

His good feelings were leaving his head by little and little, like aeolian sandstone attrided by the centuries of wind. He thought of calling up Amparo, but any comfort she might bring to him would be a mirage so long as his purpose in coming here remained unfulfilled.

He looked at his wrist, then remembered he'd left his watch home. The gigantic advertising block on the facade of the First National Citibank said it was fifteen after two. That wasn't possible.

Miss Kraus was *still* yammering away.

There was time to watch a cloud move across the sky from Jersey, over the Hudson, and past the sun. Unseen winds nibbled at its wispy edges. The cloud became his life, which would disappear without ever having turned into rain.

Later, and the old man was walking up the sea promenade toward the Castle. He stalked him, for miles. And then they were alone, together, at the far end of the park.

'Hello,' he said, with the smile reserved for grown-ups of doubtful importance.

He looked directly at the dittybag, but Little Mister Kissy Lips didn't lose his composure. He would be wondering whether to ask for money, which would be kept, if he'd had any, in the bag. The pistol made a noticeable bulge but not the kind of bulge one would ordinarily associate with a pistol.

'Sorry,' he said coolly. 'I'm broke.'

'Did I ask?'

'You were going to.'

The old man made as if to return in the other direction, so he had to speak quickly, something that would hold him here.

'I saw you speaking with Miss Kraus.'

He was held.

'Congratulations – you broke through the ice!'

The old man half-smiled, half-frowned. 'You know her?'

'Mm. You could say that we're *aware* of her.' The 'we' had been a deliberate risk, an hors d'oeuvre. Touching a finger to each side of the strings by which the heavy bag hung from his belt, he urged on it a lazy pendular motion. 'Do you mind if I ask you a question?'

There was nothing indulgent now in the man's face. 'I probably do.'

His smile had lost the hard edge of calculation. It was the same smile he'd have smiled for Papa, for Amparo, for Miss Couplard, for anyone he liked. 'Where do you come from? I mean, what country?'

'That's none of your business, is it?'

'Well, I just wanted . . . to know.'

The old man (he had ceased, somehow, to be Alyona Ivanovna) turned away and walked directly toward the squat stone cylinder of the fortress.

He remembered how the plaque at the entrance – the same that had cited the 7.7 million – had said that Jenny Lind had sung there and it had been a great success.

The old man unzipped his fly and, lifting out his cock, began pissing on the wall.

Little Mister Kissy Lips fumbled with the strings of the bag. It was remarkable how long the old man stood there pissing because despite every effort of the stupid knot to stay tied he had the pistol out before the final sprinkle had been shaken out.

He laid the fulminate cap on the exposed nipple, drew the hammer back two clicks, past the safety, and aimed.

The man made no haste zipping up. Only then did he glance in Little Mister Kissy Lips' direction. He saw the pistol aimed at him. They stood not twenty feet apart, so he must have seen it.

He said, 'Ha!' And even this, rather than being addressed to the boy with the gun, was only a paranthesis from the faintly aggrieved monologue he resumed each day at the edge of the water. He turned away and a moment later he was back on the job, hand out, asking some fellow for a quarter.

Scream
GILES GORDON

Traffic – thousands of cars. Feet, transistors, engines, shouting, calling, breathing. A ball bouncing in an asphalt playground and being chased by nine, ten, eleven kids. The number blurs, goes out of focus, is on top of the ball, panting, laughing, shouting. Bodies in the foreground, playing. Noisily. A plane roaring across the sky, ripping the blue sheet. Ten planes in the afternoon, no, in an hour and a half. Raised voices outside the Blind Beggar. Then fists, and men running in different directions. The rattle of the Tube train and the gust of wind as it crashes through Mornington Crescent. People, individuals pushing, yawning, shopping. Tired, but continuing. Keeping at it, keeping at it. The heat, the humidity, the closeness of the afternoon. But closeness isn't togetherness. Which afternoon? Choose your afternoon. The sweat on men's brows, and drips running down the shaven skin in front of the ears, to be mopped, blotted by absorbent shirts. The bell of an ambulance, and its gazelle-like zig-zag progress through the traffic. A hooter at lunch time. At lunch time, many hooters, then men and women spreading out into the streets away from the direction of the hooters. More planes, more heavy lorries. Motorbikes farting in the faces of pedestrians. The noise, the noise. The air even hums, shimmers with haze, movement, disturbance.

> *Aaaaaaaaaaaaaaaahhh!*
> The scream. The screeeeaaaaam.
> *Aaaaaaaaaaaahhh!*

Another? No, only one. Only the one. The echo? No, not the echo. There was none, no echo. Just the memory of it, immediately afterwards. It came first, isolated the afternoon, shattered it. Pinpointed it. The scream, that is.

And yet, and yet . . .

Some were aware of the echo – no, not the echo. There was no echo. Or if there was it was not heard. The memory, the foreboding – before the scream. Some had been aware of it for years. Either continually or intermittently. Or both. The premonition had been welling up for years, for lifetimes. And they had prayed against the scream, in the several ways they knew how to pray, and in ways they didn't know. Some who didn't believe in praying, or didn't believe, believed. It wasn't a matter of faith but of certainty. They believed that the scream, when it came, when it would come, would be for the worst. Would be the worst. The very worst.

The scream.

Tap, tap, tap. Plod, plod. The noise wasn't subtle enough to account for the creaking of leather in new shoes. Stares, many stares. Stares everywhere, everyone staring. With eyes; eyes, eyes, eyes. And the hopeless machines behind the eyes. A machine to each pair, that is except for those with disfigured sight. Some of them wore black glasses. Some with good eyes wore black glasses. They appeared to be less emotional, less involved. This was an illusion. They were involved, everyone was involved. Wanted to be, though embarrassed. Eyes everywhere, and for an instant everyone riveted in their minds, movements. Only for an instant. Then ... Feet/Feet running/Feet running away/Feet running away faster/Feet running away faster, faster/Feet running away faster, faster to escape/Feet running away faster, faster to escape the scream/Feet running away faster, faster to escape the scream, the scream, the scream, the scream, the scream.... The feet were panting, beating at the pavements; the breath of their possessors rasped and they were doubled-up with stitches.

O that they could be sewn up so easily!

Others stopped, stayed that way. Stock still. Averted their eyes. Looked anywhere, anywhere but at the scream. Shuffled a little in their leather or suede, even looked at their feet without seeing them, without realising they had them. Tickled, twitched their toes. Hot, sweaty, sticky toes. Other eyes sought the scream. Pursued it, sought it out, discovered it. By elimination. Would have hypnotised it. How they would have hypnotised a devil had they not known how to do it. Out Satan, out Satan.

The scream was a warning. Whether the two events – scream, warning – were connected is probably irrelevant, certainly coincidental. The first was a symptom of the malaise, a harbinger. Of what? Who will say? Let's leave it as a symptom.

Aaaaaaaaaaaaaaaahhh!

The scream again? No, for the first time

No one remembers, knows how long it lasted. A few seconds – five, seven, twelve, grappled with from the face of a clock – a minute, a few minutes, days, years, a generation, longer? Those not there say it was for twenty-four hours. Come, sir; come, *sir*. It wasn't twenty-four hours. How could it have been?

No one could scream for twenty-four hours non-stop. Now, could they? I ask you. It's not possible, not possible. It was almost definitely for well under half a minute. Not that it matters, the *time* doesn't matter, one way or another. ... No, I wasn't there, I wasn't present. I freely admit that, freely. What, what? How then can I know its significance? I know its significance. I don't know how long it lasted, nor am I interested. I know it happened. Of course it did, no question of it. No question of *that*. That's what interests me, that it happened. Sir, you have told me yourself that you've no proof.

I know it happened, I tell you. I choose to.

I had a premonition that it would happen.

We all did, in our different ways. If only we'd admit it. But it makes no difference, none at all. What happened, happened. That is what happened.

The scream. The scream.

Some of them are still there, there now, trying to discover the exact, precise spot. Even though the scream took place more than five feet from the ground. So that they may tell generations unborn that will, because of the scream or in spite of it, remain unborn. They are trying to record history, write it. Create it. Recreate it. Recreate what happened, with their consciences (so-called), their umbilical cords. They are trying to destroy history, right it. Put it to right. With actors, representing the real, live actors. Now the dead actors. Actors playing at acting, playing at living.

What else is there? Indeed, indeed. They are trying, trying. . . .

Crying? No, trying. . . .

Oh no, I don't, won't comment. I won't say it's invalid. It's better to do something, to make an effort, *the* effort.

To try.

To cry again and laugh and cross yourself; if that's your inclination.

To scream if you will. Or won't.

To scream again.

And again. Ten years after the scream, *the* scream, if necessary. Or has the scream, the one and only scream perhaps been going on for that length of time? Maybe it began in the Pentagon, was taken up on Mount Olympus, in Kentish Town, Algeria, Vietnam, and is continuing on its way to some unclassified planet millions of light years away. Maybe.

The scream. You are in danger of loving it. It will be the cause and the effect. You must be dispassionate.

The scream. A little, short one that hardly anyone noticed. Maybe you were trying too hard. To draw attention to yourself. In retrospect – if it now is retrospective – it is easy to be detached, clinical, cynical. The rising, roaring bellow; the sustained note; the trembling, dying fall; the hysterical collapse and all those faces on top of you, on top of you, on top of you. Blocking out your view of the sky. The voices buzzing like robots. The scream pushed out into the afternoon, contracted it, shrivelled it into a globule of evaporating air.

It lay on the ground. On the street. On the road. On the pedestrian crossing. You lay on your back on the road, like a turned-over tortoise free-wheeling.

Like old flesh, old human flesh. Like the genesis and disintegration of a flower, disposed of in a handful of seconds. The time and the petals were snatched at, crushed, spat out. And the remains lay gasping, gasping. Or a meringue lodged in the palm of a hand, its brittle whipped surface being crumpled by encroaching finger tips. Like old flesh, old human flesh. Ancient and modern, but old. Capture the scream, isolate it, pinpoint it. Prick it with a pin, a lance, the unwieldiest sharp surface or edge and it cannot be erased. Let the breath that makes it, the scream, freeze in the air at the moment of sound. Like an icicle; and it can prick itself past melting point. Then you can walk away nonchalantly, leaving the scream suspended roughly five feet, seven inches from the road's surface.

Lower if it's a woman. Unless it's a tall woman.

The authorities could build a glass case round it. Custodians in a specially devised uniform could guard it. They could work in three shifts round the clock, not excluding Sundays and public holidays. Annual leave would depend upon the state of the State's economy. No one wants to prejudge the issue.

The scream would be a national memorial. An institution, in time. The Unknown Scream – Our Destiny; and the scream begat a scream; and the latter scream begat a scream; and the third scream begat a fourth; etcetera. The original scream in a glass cage where it occurred. If there was anyone to visit it. Alas, alas! Pessimism to this extent must not intrude. It could scream away to its heart's content within the glass cage. No one would mind that. Once people were used to it, they would even walk past – shopping or doing the things that people do when out walking – without noticing. Yes, it could come to that. For the first fifty years or so, the men would doff their hats as they passed the scream. Thereafter not even that courtesy would be accorded it. How many people notice the statue of Cromwell in Piccadilly Circus?

But if the scream were to break out, if the glass were to be shattered? From within, or without! From without? Would anybody pierce it, could they? Would they? Certainly they *could*, even with guards, armed guards permanently in attendance. It would need only one man, one fanatic and the scream would be out. Then what chances for the world?

Human nature being.... Reflect for a moment; a digression. In 196—, whenever it was, Lee Harvey Oswald killed John Fitzgerald Kennedy. Right? Or wrong? Are you certain it wasn't John Fitzgerald Kennedy who killed Lee Harvey Oswald? One the American dream, the other the American nightmare. But which was which, and which will be which?

Safer not to enshrine the scream....

Like old flesh, old human flesh. A decaying woman, a widow. Five children, all grown up (that's a laugh), and with the reeking stumps of her teeth squelching and oozing over her flabby, bloodless gums.

She can scream hoarsely, like a horse.

When her mouth is thrown open, flung open in laughter or coughing or to grasp air from the atmosphere, or prised open by her non-existent enemy, you see the rottenness of her teeth erupting like wind or quicksands turning over and over themselves.

Not a pleasant sight, or smell. Not a pleasant image.

There are more gaps than teeth; and more fillings than gaps. The tongue, too, lolls forward from the throat. It wobbles erratically, obsequiously like a snake that has lost its venom but doesn't realise it, or accept it. No one has told the poor dear. No one could expect a fellow snake to tell its fellow of its plight; and no one is going to do a similar service for her. She hobbles up the hill with one leg two inches shorter than the other, and enormous, voluminous dark brown skirts covering her shapeless massiveness.

She can scream.

Womankind can scream; mankind can scream.

In the desert a tortoise is pushed over on its back by another tortoise. This, after they have fought one another for more than three hours. The accidental victor stumbles off, the vanquished kicks and pushes, kicks and pushes, kicks, kicks its dry leathery feet upwards and outwards. It gasps for breath, noiselessly but for the odd tiny whimper. If nobody turns it over, half a revolution on to its feet, it will die. In time. Was the fight for fun, for exercise, over a female? Tortoises will not tell the likes of us.

The screeeeeeeeeeeeeeaaaaaaaaaaaam seemed to lengthen and louden after it was silent; even immediately afterwards, seconds afterwards. Not that it could be exactly ignored at the moment of its inception, realisation. Execution. No journalist was there to witness it, to report it. That is something. Nor a BBC man with a microphone, nor a television man with a camera. One must be grateful for certain things.

At the same moment other screams may have been made elsewhere. May have occurred elsewhere. May have been screamed elsewhere. The scream. A scream.

Screams.

They may have heard each other, been aware of each other simultaneously. But no one screaming was aware of anyone else screaming. Each scream was in a vacuum. Was a vacuum.

Like new, young smooth flesh. A young woman screaming.

A virgin. With child. Without child. A virgin screaming.

In Vietnam on, say, 10 July, 1966, too many people screaming for any of them, for even one, to be heard above the din of the gunfire. Bang, bang, bang, bang. Not that any individual noise of the composite roar resembled that word. But it was loud all right. The noise.

Do the deaf hear no sound, no noise? Or do they have their own noises, their own sounds, their own screams? Screams we are unable, mercifully, to hear?

On the hill, outside the newspaper kiosk parallel to the angle of the slope of the hill, hundreds of people. People entering, leaving the Tube station. Gusts of wind, swirling paper up into paper chases. People, people, people.

The scream. No beginning, no end – though it stopped.

A middle, a middle, a middle.

AAAAAAAAAAAAAAAAAAAhhhhhhhhh
AAAAAAAAAAAAAhhh
AAAAAAAAAhh

or

```
                                        A
    SSSSSSCCC                           A
      SS        CRRE                    A
       S          E            AMMMMMM
                EEEEEEEEEAAAAMMM
                  E                     A
                  E                     A
                                        A
```

Clip, clip, clip, clip. The legs hurrying away, walking away quickly. Feet, shoes, running, running. Out of breath, below the crest of a hill, round the corner, out of sight. A man peered back from round the corner. To view the scream, to track it, lodge it for ever, for ever in his memory. Did he think he'd forget it? Even with his hands locked against his ears, crushing them into his head? He withdrew his hands. The scream had stopped, yet like an awl was twisting into his skull.

Other eyes hurried away from the scene. Or were fixated upon it, transfixed. Impaled.

They waited for it to happen again, not realising yet that its second coming was theirs to create. Not realising that they couldn't avoid not creating it.

At least one eye hung in the air, suspended until skewered by the scream.

It was only minutes afterwards that the men with the tubular scaffolding arrived, clanging it on to the ground, off their lorry. Erected it piece by hollow piece. When it was sixty feet high the men with cameras appeared, clambered up the scaffolding, photographed the spot where the scream was. Where it had been. Where it took place. Where it was said to have taken place.

It was a warning. An augury. It was the beginning, the scream. The scream was the beginning.

That scream? The same one? The beginning? The end, more likely – though that is easily said. Even more likely, the beginning of the end. Even more likely, the end of the beginning. Depending upon where you like the interval – *if* you like an interval.

But it was none of these things. If it had been one of them, or the lot, the total, the sum, the aftermath might have been clearer. As it was she just screamed. Just screamed.

Just screamed.

Her age, status is irrelevant, immaterial. Even to her grandchildren, which she did not have. She was thirty. But to say that, which – so far as we can record truth as being the truth – gives the game away, reduces truth to untruth – specific is not the universal but the universal is the specific, certainly contains the specific – falsified the false position. Though to indulge in too many paradoxes endangers the validity of the argument, if it must still be so designated.

Thirty is – what? Young? Yes, young, that's what they'd say, all of them. All of you. All of us. And if she'd had ten children, which she could easily have done, what then? Is she still young, or does that depend on her shape and looks? What . . . ? You didn't know that? Didn't know she'd had any children, let alone ten? How could you have done, how could you have done indeed? I didn't tell you, nobody told you; ten minutes ago – one minute for one child? – you didn't know she existed. But – I say again – it is irrelevant, all of it is.

Except that she screamed. Accept that she screamed. You have? You have to. And that too is irrelevant. That she screamed is not the point, not even to the point. But human beings thrive on human irrelevancies, so . . .

Having ten children seemed in retrospect so much more important than the scream. The fact of the scream. If it was a fact, if, if. Pin down that 'if' again and again and again so that its repetition ceases to mean anything. The fact may be questioned, or may be left as a fact. The scream in retrospect is from the point. Other, other very different screams and noises will occur in the future as they occur in the present. It is the heartbeats, the pulses that you may in the future be incapable of hearing.

Take a day, a date. Pick it at random. Don't even pick it, take it. Please. Thank you. Saturday, 23 July, 1966, at 4.15 p.m. That will do. You selected it by some process, not I. Listen: noises; aircraft taking off, and landing. The first Brandenburg on the record player switched to the crowd slow handclapping at Wembley as Rattin of Argentina protests at being sent off by a referee who doesn't understand his protest. The Bach, to some ears is more offensive as noise than the cheers, screams. Oh yes oh *yes*! And the birds, the cats, the traffic generally.

A drop of silence. You will? You can? You have the right, the authority? You don't mind? Julie Christie for Jesus Christ? No, there would be more noise, more ructure throughout history. Twentieth Century Noise would promote it with its roaring lion vomit.

You know what they did to Gordon of Cartoon? Or was it Lawrence of Olivier? Or J. Robert Oppenheimer, he who personifies more of the century's tragedy than you or me? They pinned him down on a seat, or on the ground, or against a wall or a post. That part of it doesn't matter. Then they blinded the poor bugger, whichever he was, fired rifles close to his ears. Being blindfolded he didn't know when the triggers would be squeezed, when the bullets were coming, or going. He was deafened. His ear drums were exploded, and his ears hung down all bloodily afterwards. Can you imagine how they looked?

The date you picked, out of the blue – or is it the red now? – was the date she screamed. Telepathetic, that's what you are. What a blue scream it proved, or didn't prove. The scream, then ... no, not then, as it happened, concurrently, she sunk in a pile, a heap onto the zebra crossing with the exploded belisha head and the winking naked bulk or naked winking bulb or bulb winking naked, and was still.

Still still.
Is still still.
Still is still.
Is still still.

Who is she? Was she? *That* was what they wanted to know. They wondered that, even in the silence between the end of the scream and the beginning again of breathing afterwards. Let her be analysed, disciplined, torn apart, ignored, congratulated, disregarded, left to recompose herself; gather her wits, control, self-control. Let her be ignored, let her be, let her.

Don't let her. Don't allow her. Hush her up, cover her up. Pretend she doesn't exist. She doesn't exist. She must be some sort of horrible pervert, some sort of awful pervert.

To the sperm, silence is a marginal subject, to the juice it's at least worth a poem. What then is the scream, a scream worth? Silence is worth a little one, a silent one.

Sssssssssssssssssshh!
Aaaaaaaaaaaaaaaaaahh,
etc., as the scream goes, erupts.

Evaporates, expires. But is remembered even if it hasn't a memory.

And they, sirs, will remember it, mourn it all the way to the graveyard if not beyond. Slowly there, with dignity and decorum, but back rapidly. Perhaps they forgot it half-way back. Certainly they won't wake up in the night screaming. If the telephone bell clatters through, across, down or just into their deep breathing they'll turn over and dissolve within the crisp linen. But they will have followed the scream in the coffin, the coffin carrying the scream. For it was likely, had it been put on, to have proved most noisy. Dracula had nothing on it as six of them in black and billowing crepe marched, no, stumbled across the field after field with the coffin on their half shoulders. The bullets whistled, whispered past with thuds and made little dust clouds when they hit the earth. Whether or not they were seen.

Arriving at the grave hole, which had not been dug specially but would be useful, the six of them quarrelled. One thought burial was too good for the scream. One wanted all six of them to pray for it but the others refused. They claimed to be true Christians and that consequently their prayers would be unnecessary acts of self indulgence.

She crumpled on to the zebra stripes by the newspaper kiosk outside Belsize Park Tube station. Which is on Haverstock Hill. Having ten children – bastards, bastards all and not one of them illegitimate – all born one at a time, not twins or triplets or quads or quins, being young is she old or young? Or ageless, or is that too easy? Having ten children and permanently shaven-off pubic hair is she a girl, a woman, a female? A whore? A countess? A whore countess? A screamer? A scream? What would you have her? – you can insist, if you insist. Would you feel happier, less embarrassed if she was a nutty Hungarian refugee who chats to herself? Or a black, a wog? You hadn't thought of her as black, had you? Are you embarrassed that you hadn't, you liberal ass? You haven't been told she wasn't black. Or yellow. Or luv-from-sunny-Blackhead-wish-you-was-queer-pink-holiday-rock. Or any other colour. Specifically. Or nationality. Specifically. You see what happens if you insist?

Go on, what would you have her? You wouldn't have her. Not afterwards maybe, you being you, but what about before? She collapsed sexily enough. Thighs, legs, breasts spilling out, long streaming hair on top. Or didn't you notice her with her pram and her infants piling and pulling at her ankles as she tried to battle through up down across on on up across the crowded, so crowded hot sticky, dusty dazzling bright pavements and streets? And then panting up Haverstock Hill, if that doesn't cause the mind to wander. If conception is a blessing, do not bless her. Has she conceived, has she? You tell me.

She has no children, bastards or otherwise, and is thirty. No, you were not misled. If you feel misled you have misled yourself. So much for prejudices, misconceptions, preconceptions. Read it again, paying heed to the sense. To the senselessness. If you like, *if* you like. Having no children, who is to say she cannot scream? Not cannot, she can. Can and has. May not, rather, should not and all the other little, petty nots. Who is to say she may not scream? Who heard her, or her sister, when she was pushed under the wheels of the Tube train near Euston station? Did she scream, did she? Or was the train screeching, heaving to a halt too noisily? Did the iron wheels suffocate her mouth? They couldn't really ask her an hour later when they jacked the train up and removed her body because it was only a body. How long, O Lord, how long?

Could be she likes noise. Enjoys it. Listening to it, contributing to it, making it. Could be she takes it for granted and when if when if when if when if she screamed she was not aware. Of adding to it. Could be she was screaming for an utterly different reason, nothing to do with sound, noise. Unlikely, but possible. Could have been a private frustration, some sort of personal dilemma or response.

At night, so it was stated in evidence against her, she moved furniture around in her own flat, thumping it about from one room to the other. The time varied but was usually between two and four a.m. Nobody objected to her moving furniture about in her own flat at any hour she chose but when, as in her case, it meant that other tenants in the house, living on the floors immediately below and above her, were awakened night after night by her nocturnal activity, a case could be made out that she was, however unintentionally, a disturber of the peace. However, the case against her was dismissed when the prosecution could offer no evidence that this was the woman who screamed.

Now she is lying on the black and white stripes, bags and petticoats and hems of clothes around her, like a flurry of foam tilting at a rock moving out to meet the incoming tide. Cars were honking at her from below the hill and above, and what the children of Hiroshima were doing was no one's business, least of all theirs. Conveniently she had collapsed around the centre of the road, blocking traffic in both directions. Cars were in two long thin lines, like lengthening saliva. Whoever wherever was screaming now would have difficulty being heard above the car hooters. Were people taking advantage of this opportunity, screaming their heads off?

A policeman observed the scene, clinically – whatever that means. Practising alienation. Had he heard the scream? Had he wanted to hear it? Had he added it to the scream he had previously recorded in his shiny kinky black notebook? Or had he joined the Force to escape from noise, to escape from being a witness, hopeful that when people saw a bobby, or a man in bobby's uniform, they would behave, be quiet, not scream?

'You sir, you. No not you, you. Yes, you. Excuse me a minute. What do you feel about that woman screaming?'

'I feel much more alarmed at her lying there on the road. No right to cause an obstruction. I don't care whether it's wilful of not, that's hardly the point. It's the inconvenience.'

He walks away. You ask the same question of another man. He looks at you without stopping, as if you're deranged. Walks on down the hill, faster than before you accosted him. Then he stops, comes almost to a standstill when he is twenty paces past you. You watch. He will come back, turn round, come back. You wish him, will him. What is all this social conscience bit? you imagine him saying. He approaches you but doesn't eye you, deliberately doesn't. Walks back up the hill past you, having forgotten to buy his evening paper. These are his standards, are they? The lunchtime edition. Maybe he follows the dogs. Maybe. Most people like that, most people follow ... no, that is gratuitous, irrelevant. Delete it, please. He walks away, half looking round but there is no camera for him to smile at.

You stop a man coming out of the station. He may have heard the scream.

'Sir, did you—?'

'Yes. I did. Disgraceful. As if there isn't enough noise already.'

'But did you know that that woman—'

'I know nothing. About her. I choose to ignore her. What's the alternative? Now, if you'll excuse me ... '

And he walks away, stands by the belisha beacon. Scuttles across the zebra, avoiding the body when the traffic stops breathing even. Inside the station, the doors of the lifts clang shut. Their noise is indescribable but my job is to describe it. They fired rifles at T. E. Lawrence's ears to deafen him, as has already been noticed once. To explode his ear drums. When his ears were raw and obliterated, he heard the sound, the noise of what had just happened, in his deaf ears for the rest of his days. She had flinched from the clang of the lift gates the previous afternoon, so recently. Was that why she screamed, why they had to run her down? To count her down and out? No longer reasonable, beyond reason?

She is crying now, crying. She has no children, no memories. That is not why she is crying. She might have had ten. And would still be crying. She is crying because of the noise. The noise everywhere. In the silence. Throughout the world. Yes, yes, oh yes.

'... a woman aged about thirty screamed at fifteen minutes past four this afternoon on Haverstock Hill, London. A few passers-by and bystanders looked away in embarrassment. Otherwise, no one took any notice. That is the end of the news.'

She didn't hear it herself. A friend told her. There is a point where things snap, they have to. With most people the things that have to snap snap invisibly, silently. No one notices. No one who had been a witness, so-called, remembered her scream an hour later. If they had been reminded, they would have recalled, smiled: 'It was a scream, was it? There was so much noise.'

She clung to him that night, the two of them naked between the clean sheets. She screamed louder than she had ever screamed; louder than she had ever screamed when his love juice entered her.

Masterson and the Clerks
JOHN T. SLADEK

'Whoever is in charge of operations should be designated with real authority
to be used in case of an emergency.'

A.P. SLOAN
My Life with General Motors

PART ONE: CLERKS ALL

SECTION I: THE LUTTE AGENCY
Division A: Mr Gelford

Henry found that, when he had filled out the orange card listing his
education, work experience and hobbies, he was permitted to pass beyond
the railing next to the receptionist's desk. The receptionist was a fat, pretty
girl whose bare feet would be soft and pink. Being bored in the evenings,
especially Sunday evenings, she would draw on black silk stockings and fuck
someone in front of a movie camera. Once a famous American executive,
watching her in a movie, had had an unusual experience.

Henry moved down the light green hall to a barn-like room where each stall
was equipped with a desk and a living soul. The black wooden floor was wavy.
Little incandescent bulbs, strung on wires, pumped light into the room, but
dark corners drained it away too fast. Henry sat down in the second rank of
folding chairs, along with a blind man and a Negro who would someday be
a well-known boxer. The blind man's dog looked at Henry, seeing him.

Henry remembered visiting the dentist with just such an orange card in his
hand. He was thinking of some way of explaining this to the blind man or
the Negro, when far down the barn a tall man stood up and beckoned.

'Henry,' he called. Henry and the blind man stood up together.

'Did he say Amory?' asked the blind man.

'No, Henry.'

'Eh? Henry?'

'Henry.'

'Henry!' called the tall man again, beckoning over the waves. Henry walked towards him, past the desks of Mr Blair and Mr Clemens and Mrs Dudevant and Mr Beyle and Miss Knye.

Division B: Mr Nind

Mr Gelford asked Henry to call him Al. With a special pen, Al initialled the orange card in several places, maintaining the attitude of a dentist marking caries. His eyes, small and dark – like human nipples, they were surrounded with tiny white bumps – looked searchingly at Henry's hair or teeth.

'Henry C. Henry, eh? What does the C. stand for?'

Henry looked at him in silence until Al turned his nipples to a mimeographed list. 'Nothing here, I'm afraid, for someone with almost no experience. I'll turn you over to Mr Nind.'

Don kept a telephone receiver well in front of his mouth as he spoke, because the inside of his lip had developed a terrible cold sore he wished to hide. It was, as he already suspected, syphilis.

'I have a really challenging job in a small, friendly engineering company,' he said. 'No experience necessary, and there is no limit to how far you can work your way up. What do you say, fella?'

Henry leaned forward and laid a hand on Nind's desk calendar. 'Fine, Don,' he said softly.

SECTION II: AN INTERVIEW

In an almost bare room evenly coated with dust, Mr Masterson toyed with a slide rule, a clipboard, a retractable ballpoint pen and a thin book, *Steam Tables*, by Keynes and Keyes. Henry sat motionless before him. Out of the window he could see a soup line, and in the distance a building was being demolished. A man in uniform walked up to the soup line, pulled a man out of it and began hitting him in the face. Perhaps later the victim would go to a movie theatre, buy a ticket, enter the Gents and comb his hair.

'Are you a good, steady worker?' asked Masterson.

'Yes.'

Fingers like white slugs curled around the slide rule. Undoubtedly Masterson was puffy and white all over, like a drowned corpse. His unpleasant glasses were hinged in the centre like motorcycle goggles, and folded hard against the colourless bubbles of his eyes. Mr Masterson contained a great quantity of liquid.

'Do you work good?' he asked.

'Yes.'

'If you work good, we'll do good by you.' Henry was never to forget this sentence, for he wrote it on a sheet of paper and taped it in the drawer of his desk, where it became a kind of motto.

'You start at fifty.' The corner of Mr Masterson's mouth lifted in a kind of smile, revealing a rotten tooth.

SECTION III: THE ARRANGEMENT

The Masterson Engineering Company occupied the third and fourth floors of the building. Henry was to work on the third floor. An old man, whose tie was fastened with a paper clip, whose sleeves were rolled high above his parched elbows, led Henry downstairs into a room full of clerks at oak desks. There were in the room perhaps a dozen, perhaps a hundred men of various sizes and ages.

Gesticulating wildly with his skinny arms, the old man began in a high, clear voice to explain Henry's duties:

> See this here form
> This here is the system sheet.
> You've got to mark it down every time
> An assignment bill comes in
> You've got to mark it down every time
> An assignment bill goes out
> And put the tally number here off the spec
> Or else the item identification.
>
> See this here list
> This here is the transfer list,
> Where you put the part number here
> From the compiled list of numerical transfers
> Where you put the description number here
> From the B column of the changeover schedule
> And mark it down.
>
> We have always intialled our work
> We always will.
> Be sure you initial the backlist
> When you add a serial number
> Be sure you initial the adjustment form
> When you check this here.
> Fill out the job number;
> Fill out the item identification index
> (Blue and yellow copies),
> Make a note on the margin of the drawing
> Or on the margin of the transfer book
> If the alphabetical register is stamped
> And initialled by the proper authority.

'You'll catch on ... ' Winking, the old man gave his sketches of arms a final flourish and went away. Henry fingered various piles of clean forms tentatively murmuring fragments of the old clerk's song; he picked up a coloured pencil and laid it down again. It seems that being a clerk is not all fun!

Henry consulted with himself and decided to learn by observing and imitating the other clerks around him. There were eight clerks around him in the following arrangement:

Clark Markey	Robert Kegel	Harold Kelmscott
Willard Bask	Henry C. Henry	Edward Warner
Karl Henkersmahl	Rodney Klumpf	Edwin Futch

Henry was never to learn the names of any of the sixteen or forty clerks outside this circle of desks, but soon he caught on, or moved into the general work rhythm. He accepted from Rod or Ed Warner a batch of forms, removed paper clips from some, marked a few of them with numbers and initials, erased the numbers or initials from others, sorted them by his own arrangement, clipped them together, and gave them to either Bob or Willard.

Willard was born and raised in the Southern part of the United States, while Bob's younger sister was sure to become salutatorian of her high school class. Meanwhile Bob or Willard was undoing part or all of Henry's work, then passing the stuff on to Clark or Harold or Karl, who in turn undid part or all of his (Bob's or Willard's) work, then passed the stuff on to Rod or Ed W. or callow Eddie Futch; each man along the chain approaching the work as if no one had gone before and no one would come after. Numbers would be erased, altered, changed back to their original   values.   Forms might be sorted by names, then dates, then colour, then in numerical order, alphabetical order and alphanumerical order. Often enough, work came back to Henry from two to three times. This was indeed a vicious circle!

SECTION IV: THE HAPPY ENDING

Happily, sooner or later, every form ended up with Karl, the stapler, who might put a staple in it and send it out of the department for good. Work flow was thus:

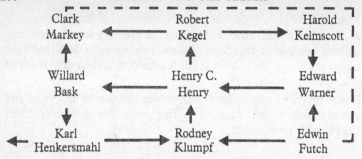

Thus a kind of progress was achieved, without, however, sacrificing routine. The happy days blended into one another like molten glass.

Section V: The Departures

No one ever saw Mr Masterson on the third floor. He seemed to send all his orders through the old clerk, who descended every morning with a memorandum to be tacked to the bulletin board.

The speaker of the intercom, fixed in the ceiling, made crackling noises that might have been the voice of Masterson. The shape of a name emerged from the static. A clerk at once rose, squared his shoulders and climbed the stairs. He did not come back.

The room was filled with the anxious murmur of the clerks, discussing his departure. The same thing had happened a dozen times or more, it was said. They never came back.

The discussion stamped everyone. Some clerks stood leaning against their desks, arms akimbo. Some tapped pencils on their blotters, made spitting motions, or leaned back. Others pretended to move their jaws sideways, while still more others sharpened pencils and drank water from paper 'cups'. Bob Kegel continued to read numbers from a list to Rod Klumpf who punched the buttons of a small adding machine. Karl picked at his stapler with a preoccupied air. Big Ed Warner, an older man known for his leaky heart and halitosis, was swivelled around to talk to Eddie Futch. Had the bomb (or a Hiroshima-size atomic bomb) gone off at this moment, at 5,000 feet above Fifth Avenue and 42nd Street, the shadow of Ed would no doubt have protected the acne-riddled face of Eddie from the direct effects of the blast, or is this just wishful thinking?

Ed told the young man that the departed clerk was dead, and that nothing, no power on earth could bring him back.

'Is that the way to talk? Jesus! Is that any way. . . .'

Eddie ran off to the lavatory to pinch pimples from his hot, raw cheeks. Big Ed considered the word 'laughter'.

SECTION VI: KEGEL AND KLUMPF

Bob Kegel and Rod Klumpf were alike. Often Henry tried to envision some mirror arrangement that would allow him to see, in place of the back of Bob's head in front of him, the back of Rod's head behind him. Clearly the virtual image would be the same.

They were tall, slim and polite, with round heads, round shoulders and long, narrow feet. They wore fashionable clothes and reasonable smiles and neat cowlicks, and they read the same consumer magazine, which prompted them to buy many of the same articles: antifreeze, air conditioners, Ascots, attaché cases, beer mugs, berets, blazers, brandy snifters, cameras, carpeting, cars, cats, deodorants, door chimes, filter cigarettes, golf clubs, hats, LPs, luggage, movie cameras, movie projectors, shavers, silverware, slide projectors, tape recorders, typewriters, television sets, toothbrushes.

At first Henry supposed that he could tell them apart by Rod's freckles and Bob's half-rimmed glasses. But the sun soon brought out freckles on Bob also, and he proved to be quite vain in regard to his glasses, wearing them less and less. At the same time, Rod purchased and began to wear a similar pair of glasses, and since he kept out of the sun, his own freckles began to fade. Being of a size, the two friends loaned one another clothes. Occasionally, for a joke, they would exchange desks. Both spoke in the same modulated tones, and both moved with the grace of bowlers.

It was always Bob or Rod who got up a football pool, who sent out for coffee, who tacked up humorous signs, who started charity drives, who instituted fines for tardiness and swearing, who collected money for flowers whenever anyone fell ill, died or married. Tirelessly and good naturedly, these clean young men organized the life of the office. The others despised them.

SECTION VII: THE COFFEE BREAK

Division A: The idea of coffee break

Coffee break was an old tradition at the Masterson Engineering Company, instituted some years before by Mr Masterson when he read in a management magazine the following advertisement:

UP PRODUCTION WITH A COFFEE BREAK!

Get more out of your workers by giving them a short mid-afternoon rest, with *coffee*, the all-purpose stimulant. Coffee perks up flagging minds and bodies the way fuel injection pumps up the power of an engine. *They* will gladly pay for the coffee – while *you* reap the extra productivity!

His frequent memos on the subject claimed that coffee breaks cost him an enormous amount of money, but that he was determined his clerks should be happy at all costs.

Division B: Coffee break praxis

It was during coffee break that Henry began to learn the peculiar vocabulary of the clerk.

First he heard Clark Markey, the non-lawyer, say, 'I certainly did finalize that item.'

A delighted smile invaded the solemn features of Karl Henkersmahl. 'Finalized it, did you? You do not know the meaning of the word *finalize*. Did you expedite it or ameliorate it? Did you even estimate the final expenditures? Or did you merely correlate the old stabilization programmes? Ha!'

Harold Kelmscott stirred his coffee with a peculiar new kind of pencil. Laughter hissing in his blue eyes, he said, 'Quit it, Karl. We all know what a poor expediter you are yourself, and you're a non-conservative estimator, unless I miss my guess.'

Karl nipped off his rimless glasses and polished them in aggravated silence. It was hard for him to acknowledge the presence of a superior will, but he did so with his best grace. His tiny, wide-set eyes were on the move, looking for a smile he could challenge.

Karl often let his pride and quick temper draw him into an argument on any subject, especially on the subject of Germany, about which he possessed a number of interesting statistics. Claiming to know the exact reason Germany lost the Second World War, he usually won any arguments simply by shouting the same words over and over until his opponent gave up. The only man who ever won the war argument from Karl was Ed Warner who maintained that Germany had *won* the war.

Division C: False teeth

Karl swallowed his coffee and said, 'I estimate that the productionalized operational format will be up-dated by mid-March at the very earliest.'

Harold smiled. 'But that's hardly a conservative estimate, is it, Karl?' The smile became an orange balloon, orgulous and threatening. Karl stared at its teeth in disbelief.

Modestly swirling his coffee and studying the rainbow in it, Harold said aloud that he had found two discrepancies today.

Two! A low murmur of approval went around the group. Indian, or 'ideal', summer descended on the city, and a new movie came to the Apollo. Hurricane Patty Sue was breaking up. The eyes of Eddie Futch glistened with frank hero-worship, which Harold accepted graciously. Even Bob and Rod paused in their counting of the proceeds of a turkey raffle to make the well-known gesture of 'nice going'.

Karl alone refused to congratulate Harold. 'I hope you itemized them both,' he said testily, 'before you followed a plan of procedure.'

'Of course I itemized them. What did you think I'd do – *standardize* them?' Harold *quipped*. The others *laughed* heartily, as much in glee at Karl's discomfiture as in open admiration of the excellent *bon mot*, or good word, of his inquisitor.

It was hard not to like Harold Kelmscott, for he was a true clerk, descended from a line of clerks that could trace its name back to the twelfth century, to a Benedictine monk who broke his vow of celibacy. Harold once lectured to an orientation class of incoming clerks at a business college. He said:

SECTION VIII: A PRIESTHOOD
My esteemed fellow-clerks:

There have not been so many ways in this world in which a man might earn his daily bread, that the desiderata of clerkdom could invariably vie with more dramatic ways of 'bringing home the bacon' (slide shown of Francis Bacon's *Study for a Portrait*, 1953, or *Head IV*, 1949, or *Painting*, 1946) such as police detection work, mass hypnotism, name any sport.

What, then, is it about clerkdom, that draws so many millions of fine young persons of all levels to dedicate their lives, so to speak, to the world of paper and telephones; to join, if I may be permitted a small jest, the pen and pencil set? (Slide shown of comic figure climbing out of inkwell, copyright by Ub Iwerks. Boos and clatter of neolite soles on Armstrong cork floors. Guards take firmer grip on Smith & Wesson .38 calibre police special revolvers, glance inadvertantly at tough Yale locks on all doors, but H.K. has it under control.)

What is it, we may very well ask, for it is an unanswered and perhaps unanswerable question. Let us unask it, then, and move on to a history of paper. The first clerks, we know, lived in ancient cities where they wrote on stone, clay slabs, wax tablets. But very quickly, they moved into their true capacity as priests. (Mixed hissing, but a general feeling of well-being pervades the auditorium. Guards relax and even light up Camels and Luckies. Wearing a plain black business suit, Foreman and Clark with vest and extra pair of pants at home, Harold spreads his arms in benediction. He is plump and blond, but even so, serious as a nose. He is all-English, black round-rimmed glasses and an unruly lock of hair his trade mark.) Yes, *priests*, a shocking word but oh so true! *You* shall be priests in the tradition, handlers of the lamb, then the lambskin then paper. Your hands will caress no whiter flank than the margin of form 289-XB-1967M. Your rituals are many and important, and you will dedicate your life to preserving their routine, that endless cyclic round that drives the universe. Whether you work in the death, birth or marriage registration bureau, it is your work which moves civilization in its great orbit. God bless you all! (From the front of the hall guards and firemen move in with firehoses, using Townely-Ward $1\frac{1}{2}''$ nozzles and Townely-Ward pumpers to empty the hall and flush it out for the next lecture.)

SECTION IX: JAX TV LOUNGE
Division A: Rod
Henry stood at the bar and began a conversation with Rod or Bob. Around them, clerks murmured a kind of plainsong cadence of complaint, and Henry was pleasantly aware of being a clerk himself. He was one with the two clerks in the corner, arguing about the finalization of finalizations. He was one with the boisterous group of tic-tac-toe players in the corner. He was one with the three clerks at the other end of the bar, their arms about one another's shoulders, who counted off by tens. Nearby another comrade was showing someone how to fold a dollar-bill ring. Henry's hands itched for paper to feel. The bar, foreseeing this, had provided a tiny paper napkin with each drink, which his hands raped as he talked.

Peering into his glass, Bob (or Rod) said, 'Rob gives me a pain in the ass. Today he wanted to hand me a tally index, quadruplicate – and would you believe it? – the stupid bastard had the blue copy on top!'

'No kidding?'

'No, really. Even little Eddie Futch knows the white copy goes on top, for Christ's sake.'

Henry could not help but think of Masterson's childhood:

MEMO: *My childhood.* It has come to the attention of this office that the company personnel in general do not know the details of how I was born and raised. I intend to ameliorate this circumstance.

I was conceived because the contraceptive device my mother was wearing at the moment was not properly fitted. It consisted of a small metal button, to which was attached a long wire coil spring. The end of the coil was to be introduced into the cervix and thence into the womb, and screwed up tight until the button sealed the opening of the cervix. Either due to a malfunction of the device itself or an unwillingness on the part of Mom to undergo the discomfort of a really tight seal, an accidental conception occurred.

I learned of all this only on my twenty-first birthday, from a pretty cousin with whom I dallied, in an after-Sunday-dinner way, in a haymow. My mother I hardly remember, except as a ghostly figure standing silent by the electric kitchen range, almost an aura thrown off by the back burners. She liked to stir things. To my knowledge, she never spoke.

I soon was able to go to college, where, thanks to the leadership of Athelstan Spilhaus, I was persuaded to make my goal the sanctification of mechanical engineering, the elevation of thermodynamics to a sacrament. My studies were interrupted by the birth of a younger sister, or half-sister, whom my impoverished parents could not support. The rest is history.

– Masterson

Bob (or Rod) went on, 'Well, to make a long story short, I expedited them, though I had a damned good notion to let them go the way they were. Old Rob is beginning to make too many little discrepancies, if you ask me. Only last week, I caught him *updating a form*, just because it was in short supply!'

'I can't believe it!' cried Henry, clapping his hands to his ears.

'True, though. And he had the itemization slip attached to the bill, and I couldn't find the authorization for that anywhere!'

'Exactly.' Henry sensed his meaning. Down the bar, the trio counted:

'One hundred forty!'

'One hundred fifty!'

'One hundred sixty!'

They laughed and pounded on the bar, then drew themselves up to count again.

'Yes,' Rod (or Bob) went on in thick accents, 'if you ask me, old Rob is about to get the axe. Too many discrepancies, if you see what I mean. One of these days they'll be calling him on the intercom. . . .'

'Do you mean it?' Henry inadvertently genuflected.

'Off the record, you understand, but the trouble with old Rob is – he drinks.'

'No!' said Henry, not disputing it. He bought a round, then Bob (or Rod) tried to interest him in tickets for a turkey raffle.

'But it's only March.'

'We've already raffled off a ham for Easter. Clark won it, and gave it away to Karl. Then we sold everyone cards for Mother's and Father's Days, flags for Veteran's Day, baby trees for Arbor Day, fireworks for the Fourth and St Christopher medals for the Labor Day weekend. Thanksgiving is the only thing we had left,' explained Bob (or Rod). 'I mean, it's a little early for Christmas trees.'

'What about treats for Hallowe'en?' suggested a stranger.

'Sure, that's it, teach kids to beg. That's the American way, all right. If kids worked for their pennies the way I had to – Gee, it's nearly seven! I've got to get to class. Sorry I can't buy you a round, Henry.' He drank up and lunged quickly towards the door.

Rod (or Bob), less because of the ski-ing instructor with whom he had had a brief flirtation than because of his current interest in Arctic literature, had a well-shaped neck, tapering inward slightly under his small ears, and forming a niche in front, into which was set an *Adam's apple*.

'Wait! What is it you study?' Henry cried, and the answer blew back in a block of November wind:

'IBMs.'

Division B: Bob

Bob (or Rod) moved down the bar to talk to Henry as soon as Rod (or Bob) had left. Henry was able at once to confirm that he drank, as the IBM scholar alleged, *for he now had a drink in his hand, and sipped at it.*

'Was that Dob I saw leaving?' he said. 'Intelligent kid, Dob is.'

'Yes, he tells me he's studying IBMs.'

IBM unknown to either of the speakers, represents not only International Business Machines, but *Yebem*, the seventieth angel quinary of the Zodiac. This angel is usually depicted plucking a quill from the wing of its neighbour, 69 or Raah (who hangs head downward like a bat), with which to make, this legend has it, the first 'pen'.

Like wax, the other's face took a smile. 'The real money isn't in IBMs, it's in ICBMs. I study ICBMs.' After a moment he added, 'Yes, I'm no intellectual like Dob, but I can tell you right now he's getting too smart for his own good. For instance, he thinks the white copy of the tally index quadruplicate form goes on top, in the finalized format. Just for the record, I think old Dob's going to be finalized himself one of these days.'

'For the record?'

'The confidential record, of course. Dob makes too many discrepancies, if you know what I mean.'

'I know what you mean, all right,' said Henry, showing some of his teeth. 'He drinks?'

'Golly, yes. In fact, I saw him drinking here, just a few minutes ago.'

There was nothing either of them could add to this, so they turned to watch the television. As the picture slowly brightened, it became even more painfully clear that the monkeys were not free-standing on the ponies' backs, but strapped on. A hidden orchestra played 'Perpetual Motion'. After trying to interest Henry in the first pick of a lot of Norway pines Bob (or Rod) went off to school.

SECTION X: ED AND EDDIE

The unpleasant marsupiality of Ed Warner's eyes was worsened when he smiled. Little sharp shrew-teeth glittered at the ends of big dead-pale gums, and one knew his tongue would also be black.

'There isn't any boss,' he murmured to Eddie Futch.

There was no need to say more. The panic ripples spread, leaving little Eddie bobbing on the surface of his own consciousness, a writer might presume. He who follows the conceit far enough might even glimpse something like slime boiling in the depths.... 'But I *seen* him. He hired me.'

'You saw someone who said he was the boss. Or did he even say that?'

Little Eddie looked around for help, his eyes full of tears. 'But there just has to be a boss,' his shrillness insisted. 'If there's no boss, how can there be a company?'

The shrew-teeth bared in a grin.

'Leave the lad alone, Ed,' Harold bade. 'You'll have him making discrepancies.'

'This whole company is a discrepancy, Harry. I'm trying to say something, now, listen. Unrectifiable—'

'That'll do!' Harold leapt to his feet, a sword of ignorance glimmering in his fine eyes. Cackling, Big Ed moved behind his own desk to gulp heart pills.

This was his defence. Everyone was terrified of Ed's tender heart, as much as of his black breath. If he were pressed too hard in an argument, he would simply clutch his chest and slump to the floor, remaining there until the argument was forgotten.

Henry envied him the trick. If only it were possible to imitate it without soiling his shirt....

SECTION XI: DIRT

Yes, Henry cried out to cleanliness. He bathed morning and evening, and wore clothes scientifically cleaned and packaged in polythene bags. His shirts were first disinfected and boiled at home, then scrubbed to new whiteness by Chinese slaves. He carried about with him toothpaste, carbolic soap, orange sticks, a safety razor, styptic pencil and Kleenex, while the drawer of his desk was crammed with bandaids, new shirts and underwear, depilatory and cotton swabs.

No, cleanliness answered. His was the dirtiest shirt in the office, and the tartar caked up permanently on his teeth. Strange rashes came and went on his coarse-pored, grainy skin, while his fingernails remained in mourning. It was as if another person were determined to keep him foul.

MEMO: *The history of the Masterson Engineering Company.*

The Masterson Engineering Company was started in 1927 by my father. My mother. He began with one draughtsman and a broken T-square, and plenty of guts and sand. In 1931, the company went broke, but by 1950, he was back in business. I took over that year, under his directorship, and soon killed or replaced him. The original name was retained, though the company moved downtown. Wife and child. I am now Mr.

– Masterson

One day Henry tried a daring experiment. After spreading some newspapers on the floor, he clutched his chest and slumped down carefully on them.

No one paid the least attention, even when he groaned and writhed a few times. After several minutes, Henry got up and went back to work, his neck hot against the grey collar of his shirt.

SECTION XII: CLARK

Clark Markey, the non-lawyer, was unpopular because of his political beliefs, though no one was afraid of him.

'I'm no lawyer,' he would say, 'but it seems to me that twenty-five minutes for lunch is below the legal minimum.' He asked each of the others if they would back him in complaining to the Labor Board.

Willard Bask: 'Don't want to rock the boat.'

Eddie Futch: 'Guess it would be all right.'

Karl Henkersmahl: 'Should think we have no right to complain about anything.'

Henry C. Henry: No comment.

Robert Kegel:'I think we need a bowling team.'

Harold Kelmscott: 'Let us give up lunch of the flesh.'

Rodney Klumpf: 'Let's organize a bowling team.'

Clark Markey: 'Will go along with the others.'

Ed Warner: 'Abolish lunch. Abolish the company . . . '

SECTION XIII: CLARK AND KARL AND EDDIE

Clark was viscerally interested in everyone's problems of justice. When Eddie Futch played loud music on his radio, Clark assured him he was well within his rights. But when Karl complained of the noise, Clark hastened to tell him that he, too, had a legitimate claim.

'I've got a claim, all right. I'm going to smash that goddammed radio,' Karl said quietly. 'Then I'm going to smash its owner. Ha!'

'Oh, no, you mustn't do that; your right to smash ends where Eddie's radio begins. But you do have a right to insist that he turn it down if it bothers you.'

Karl began to shout, his head swelling up out of a thick, Michelin-man neck. 'Turn that fucking radio off, before I come over there and smash it!'

Blinking rapidly, little Eddie switched off the music. Clark's eyes filled with tears of compassion. He rushed to comfort the boy. 'Nevertheless, you have a right to listen.'

'I don't want to listen,' Eddie lied. Red flooded the acne-scarred face: a Martian map. 'If I wanted to listen, I'd listen, all right, no matter what anyone said.'

'That's right! You selfish pig!' Karl screamed. 'You care nothing for the nerves of others. *You* aren't doing precision work, as I am. All *you* do is shuffle papers around. But I'm a precision stapler. I have to get the staple in exactly the same place each time; I can't bend it over or ruin it, because then I'd have to start all over again. But what do you care? What do any of you care?'

MEMO: *Automation*

There will be no automation at the Masterson Engineering Company.

– Masterson

SECTION XIV: CLARK AND KARL

Clark rushed over to placate the hysterical Henkersmahl and offer him a halvah bar.

'What is this supposed to be?'

'Halvah. A kind of candy. Just try it.'

Karl bit into it gingerly and chewed, watching Clark to one side. 'It tastes good. Jewish product, is it?' He finished the bar in two bearish gulps and began turning his fingers over, sucking crumbs from them. 'It tastes damned good.'

Clark began to smile, relieved that he had been able to help Karl so easily. Then the Henkersmahl's red jewels of eyes closed with suspicion.

'Damned clever, you Jews. Now I suppose you're going to overcharge me for that candy bar, eh?'

Clark became aware of a problem in communications research. 'No, Karl, that was a gift,' he said.

'Ha ha, a gift. Very cute little tricks. A gift, eh? A gift? Very cute tricks indeed. A gift with Hebrew strings attached, eh? You've fooled me this time, but I'll remember this. I never get fooled twice, and I always remember anyone who cheats me, Clark.' Karl pulled a dollar from his billfold and threw it on Clark's desk.

'Yes, that's the difference between your kind and mine. I may be fooled by your subtleties, but not for long. I pay my debts sportingly, yes, even gladly, when I'm caught in one of your snares. But your kind never pays up, do they? All right, I don't mind being cheated out of mere money. Go on, take it.'

As he said this last, Karl snatched back the dollar and put it away again. From that day on, he would never lose an opportunity to tell people of how Clark tried to charge him a whole dollar for a candy bar, which Karl always referred to as a 'Bar Mitzvah, or one of those crazy names. It might even have been Jewish dope. I felt funny afterwards. . . .'

SECTION XV: THE SECOND WORLD WAR

The real reason Karl disliked Clark was that Jews had undoubtedly cost Germany the Second World War. There could be no other explanation. Germany had what everyone acknowledged the world's finest fighting men. They had the best planes, the best guns, everything. But the army had so dissipated its efforts by hauling around mewling Jews and killing them that its efficiency had suffered, he told Ed. Karl would never forgive the Jews for that.

'It's the real reason Germany lost. Not the second front, but that Jewish fifth column. Not the American bombers, but the sabotage in Germany's bosom.'

'I know just what you mean,' Willard Bask agreed. 'I spent eighteen months in Stuttgart and believe you and me, there ain't a finer kind of folks anywhere than the Germans. We had some godawful fights in them honkytonks, sure, but I respect a man who fights for what's coming to him. Know what I mean? I mean I respect a man who stands up on his hind legs and comes at you with a broke bottle like a white man, and don't go messing around with Big Knives or razors and stuff.'

Ed Warner scratched a mole. 'I don't get it,' he said. 'Didn't Germany *win* the war?'

Not listening, Karl went on. 'German logistics were all snarled. Instead of troop trains and supply trains, they had carloads of Jews lolling about the countryside. *Getting a free ride, while the world's finest fighting men had to walk.*'

'Know just what you mean,' Willard said, nodding fiercely. 'One night this big German and me started out cuttin' each other up with busted bottles, and before the night was over, we was old pals, swapping stories about women. Next night, it was just the other way round. . . .'

'But Germany won the war, Karl. Look at Germany today. One of the top industrial nations in the world. Two continents are overrun every year with

German tourists. They have one of the biggest, best-equipped armies in Europe. How can you say they lost?'

Karl cocked his head and frowned, realizing something had gone wrong. He had to make Ed understand the truth. Smiling, he began his explanation once again. The light reflected off the octagonal shapes of his lenses, blanking out the eyes.

SECTION XVI: CESSPOOLS

When Harold Kelmscott looked at Clark Markey, what did he see?

He saw the ancestor of Clark Markey performing ritual sacrifice of Christian children. He saw the ancestor of Clark Markey breeding money from money: usury: a sin. He saw the ancestor of Clark Markey cursing Christ as He bore His cross, and telling Him to go faster up Calvary. He saw Christ turn to look at that ancestor, saying, 'I go, but thou shalt wait my return.' He saw the ancestor of Clark Markey buying and selling Christian kings.

What were the five sources of the hatred Harold bore the Jew before him?

Old half-remembered stories from childhood; his parents' anti-Semitism; popular slogans recalled unconsciously; the intense dislike of Karl for Clark, as reflected in his glasses; bitterness because Clark had not offered Harold a candy bar.

From what two-fold reason springs this last bitterness?

From Harold's abstention from candy during Lent: first, he would naturally have taken pleasure in refusing a temptation of Satan; secondly, he would have enjoyed refusing the candy on religious grounds, implying that Clark was cruelly intolerant to offer it, and thus wounding him.

When Clark's name was called over the intercom, he went meekly and quietly upstairs. As soon as he was gone, Harold drew and fired a histrionic sigh. 'Good riddance, good riddance,' he clucked. 'I never could stand Jews, not even when they were my best friends. Do you know why?'

'Because they cheat you?' Karl prompted, hoping for an anecdote.

'No, because, during the Middle Ages, the Jews used to slit open the throats of Christian babies and throw them into cesspools.'

Henry thought about the cesspools. He was becoming compulsively clean in habit if not in fact, and only barely restrained himself from wiping off door knobs and answering the phone with a Kleenex.

'Cesspools, eh?' Karl looked disappointed. 'Well, you've got to expect it. Anyone mean enough to charge a dollar for a candy bar would stoop to just about anything.'

'*Anything.* Their name comes from *Judas*, you know – their secret leader (you recall he killed Christ).'

'That's right. For money, wasn't it?' As he spoke, Karl stared hard at the back of Willard Bask's neck.

MEMO: *Power*

We are fighting for, and we expect to win, a return of power to the hands of the white, Anglo-Saxon, God-fearing, Protestant, not overly-intellectualized citizens of American descent, especially in our Southern states, men of integrity who have kept the old values.

– Masterson

SECTION XVII: OLD VALUES

Willard Bask was about six feet tall, slender, with a fine square-featured face that showed only a trace of weakness around the jaw. His clear eyes were the blue-grey of distance, and the necessary impression of fanaticism they produced was softened by his serious grin. Willard spent his summers on the beach, and used lamps to keep his tan dark all winter. Against it, his teeth seemed even and almost sound. His sculptured hair glistened like the whorls of thumb prints in grease. Like the grin, the nose of Willard twisted slightly to one side: he seemed always about to share a private joke with some invisible audience to his right.

Willard opined that it might not be all the fault of the Jews, things were all screwed up in the papers and they slanted things. He was sure things could be fixed up again, if the Southern coloured people stopped listening to agitators and tended their knitting.

'Let folks be, that's what I always say,' he said often.

MEMO: *Dwelling patterns of the Allendar and Bask families: Patrilocal or matrilocal?* At first the kinship arrangements of the Allendar and Bask families may seem complex and even arbitrary, but a closer inspection reveals many basic formations common to Southern United States tribes. At the heart of this scheme we find, of course, the familiar automobile, usually an older Ford or Mercury equipped with phallic aerial(s), with mammary steering knob (see formation of the form 'guffer's knob' in Frazer, 'Courtship in the Merc') and certainly with twin anal 'tailpipes'. The greater mobility provided by these vehicles has not led, as expected, to a breakup of the old matrilocal dwelling patterns but only extended the range of such patterns from village to county, up to 150 miles.

The seven children of Faron Bask and Maypearl Allendar Bask are a case in point: Selma and Wilma settled in the same village with their spouses, while Travis, Truman, Orman, Willard and J.B. moved on to a city at too great a distance to maintain easy contact. Willard's wife, Nelline Parker, bore him four children between her 13th and 17th years. They were then divorced and he moved back into the county of his birth at his mother's death. He left home again, the following year abandoning Etta Leich, his second wife, shortly before her miscarriage. His younger brother, J.B., followed an exactly similar pattern, while Wilma and Selma followed its opposite, e.g., *leaving* the village at the death of their mother. Travis died, and Orman and Truman had not yet married. The Merc belonging to Travis had fender skirts; but when Truman inherited it, these were removed and a sunshade added. The pattern is self-evident.

– Masterson

SECTION XVIII: PATTERNS

'It's them communists, if you'll excuse the expression,' he said earnestly. 'They come down and stir up the coloured. I can't blame the poor coloured. They see all this white pussy around, agitatin', telling them they're as good. ... Well, you can see what that'll lead to, but what can I do? Live and let live, that's my middle name. But you've got to admit the coloured and white used to get along just fine, just fine, without no outside interference. Well, I'm not going to complain. I know God didn't intend coloured and white to mix any more than a washer woman means to mix up coloured and white clothes – it's the white ones get ruint. But who am I to make trouble?'

He glanced around accusingly. A bitter, nagging note came into his voice. 'I'm not complaining. To each their own, that's my motto. I think birds of a feather *ought* to flock together. Why, when I used to pump gas. . . .'

SECTION XIX: GOING OUT OF STYLE

'The Southern coloured are just different and if I sat around here explaining till Doomsday, you wouldn't understand what I meant unless you lived down there. I mean *different*. Like they don't know the value of a dollar. Soon as they get a nickel in their jeans, they just *got* to spend it, like it was burning a hole in their pocket.'

Lazily, he unstraddled a chair to fish a five-dollar bill out of his watch pocket with two fingers. Willard was buying coffee for everyone. The deliveryman set down the box of lukewarm covered containers and reached for his change, but Willard waved it away. Before he could taste his own coffee, however, his name was called on the intercom.

SECTION XX: GONE BUT NOT FORGOT

'Did you ever notice how Willard just throws money away?' asked Karl when he had left. 'Anyone who does that must have a bit tucked away. It wouldn't surprise me to learn that his background is – Biblical, if you get my meaning.'

'I had the same thought,' said Harold. He took a reflective sip of the coffee Willard had bought him – black, for it was Advent – and asked, 'What sort of name is Willard, anyway? Surely not a *Christian* name.'

Ed Warner finished his own coffee and started on Willard's untouched cup. 'Well, he's gone now. No use talking about the dead,' he said firmly.

'He's not—!'

SECTION XXI: IRREGULARITIES

'He's not!' Karl screamed, his Michelin-tyre head inflating dangerously.

Harold's long celluloid teeth clicked on his paper cup. 'Of course not. He's been fired, I'm sure.' He looked warningly at Ed. 'Caught, I suppose, with his hand in the till.'

'What till?' Ed's yellow cheeks turned the colour of pleasure.

'HE'S NOT DEAD!'

'Prove it.'

Karl seemed about to collapse, but Harold shook his head. 'You should know better than that, Ed. It's up to you to prove that what's-his-name is dead.'

For answer, Ed clutched his chest and crumpled to the floor.

SECTION XXII: FAKE

Karl crowed. 'He's faking! Knows he lost!'

The old man's lips turned blue.

'He's dying!' Eddie snatched up the phone and dialled an emergency number. The number was printed in red ink on a card stuck to one corner of the bulletin board. Any user of the telephone confronted the bulletin board and read its notices without realizing it.

'Join a bowling team now!' 'THIMK', 'THINK', 'We don't make much money but then we don't have ulcers, either.' 'Give generously to Univac.' 'Join and contribute now: AMERICANS FOR PRIVATE ENTERPRISE.' 'We are asking for flowers for Willard Bask, departed this afternoon. Please *sign* name and write amount *clearly*.' 'Good books for starving Asia.'

'Forget it,' said Karl, pressing down the phone cradle. 'Do you want to get us all in trouble with the authorities? I told you, he's faking. He's not really turning blue.'

Eddie flushed, and his chin, raw with fresh pustules, began to tremble. Shoving Karl aside, he began to dial again. At that moment, the intercom sputtered:

'Edwin EEEEEEEEEEEEEEP! Futch.'

He dropped the receiver and threw both hands to his face.

'Go on, kid,' said Karl gently. 'If it will make you feel any better, *I'll* call the hospital for Ed. All right? Now go on.' He spanked Eddie lightly, starting him towards the door that led to the stairs. With a zombie stride the youth marched out.

Karl replaced the telephone receiver and lit a cigarette.

'Ed's just faking,' he announced. 'Let's get back to work and just ignore him.'

Harold licked his lips and glanced towards the door. 'Too bad about young Eddie, though. So young – to go like *that*.'

'Yes, death is a natural thing,' Karl said, blowing a smoke ring.

'We must learn to accept it and live with it. There must be nothing frightening or shameful about dying – it is as natural as pee-pee and poop.'

'Yes, the Lord giveth and the Lord taketh away, as the saying goes.'

The figure on the floor coughed, one sudden explosive noise, then lay still. Using his dirty grey handkerchief, Henry picked up the phone and dialled an emergency number.

SECTION XXIII: REAL

'All right, Ed, keep it up, right to the last minute,' Karl yelled down the hall to the covered basket the ambulance men were removing. 'Keep on faking! You're only fooling yourself!'

His voice was shrill with fury. It excited the professional interest of the intern, who had stayed behind to fill out the death certificate.

'Why don't you sit down for a moment?' he invited. 'I know it's hard to believe in the death of someone else.' He pressed Karl into a chair and asked Henry his name.

'Karl Henkersmahl. He's a stapler.'

'I see. Oh, Mr Henkersmahl? Karl? Would you mind putting a few staples in this form for me? It's the death certificate of Mr Warner.'

Karl moved slowly and reluctantly, but with a great deal of ceremony (*Feierlichkeit*) and precision beautiful to behold. He placed one staple neatly in each corner of the form.

'Say, he really is dead, isn't he?' he murmured then, scratching his head. 'I thought he was just faking.'

'It's too late for that,' said the intern, with a mysterious smile. Though he wore a white uniform, he was a black man.

SECTION XXIV: THE END OF ALL CLERKS

One by one, they were all called. Henry thought of quitting first. He even went so far as to interview with another firm, one specializing in famous information. But that night he dreamed that he was brushing his teeth when the toothbrush began ramming wooden splinters up his gums. It was a warning, perhaps.

In the spring, Bob and Rod left, smiling, asking that no flowers be sent after them, that they be cremated by a reliable firm recommended by a leading consumer magazine, and that their ashes be mingled.

At midsummer, Harold left, crossing himself and making signs to ward off the evil eye.

'Nothing to be afraid of,' Karl assured him with a serene smile. 'It's as natural as wee-wee and grunt.'

But when Karl's own name was called he behaved in a strange, unnatural manner. The sound made him jerk erect, spoiling a staple. He carefully replaced it, tidied his desk, and with a private, one-sided smile lifted from the bottom drawer a heavy object encased in leather. This he carried into the lavatory and shut the door. A shot rang out. Before Henry, who was the only one left, could try the door, his own name was called on the intercom.

PART TWO: MASTERSON

SECTION I: THE FIGURE AT THE HEAD OF THE STAIRS

Masterson, or a bulging, obnoxious, enigmatic person like Masterson, stood at the head of the stairs. Henry saw he would have to squeeze past him to gain the fourth floor. The eyes in their lenses were quiet and horrible as glass, watching him ascend. In his hand, Henry carried the sheet of paper with his motto: 'If you work good, we'll do good by you.' It was folded in neat thirds, and he held it up before him, like a shielding dental chart.

Who was this Masterson if this were indeed he? Was he truly the author of all memos, or a figurehead? Had he killed the real Masterson and assumed his place? The figure above, beetling over Henry, seemed almost like a great cancer that had once totally absorbed a man; now its vague memory of his lineaments served to spew forth an idea of death upon the rest of the world.

As Henry moved closer, however, the cancer cleared its throat and stepped back to let him pass. As it did so, he saw the light had been wrong. This was the face of a fat, weary, self-pitying man, nothing more.

SECTION II: THE FOURTH FLOOR

Masterson explained to Henry that he was closing the third floor department and moving all clerks into the draughting room on this, the fourth, floor.

The old clerk with skin like parchment appeared once more and led Henry into a large room he'd never known existed, where a dozen draughtsmen hunched low over their boards. As he passed them, he saw that each man was working on an entirely different project.

The first draughtsman was drawing large circles and small circles, and dividing them into quadrants. Mandalas, wheels, gunsights? Henry wanted to ask him what he drew, but he seemed preoccupied.

The second was drawing a long, continuous curve on a roll of paper. He might have explained that this represented infinity, but Henry did not pause to hear.

The third drew a histogram showing apparently the sales or consumption of oxen and earthen jars. It seemed too self-evident to inquire about, but was it?

The fourth copied, from the cover of a book of matches, the picture of a girl, labelled DRAW ME but he was copying it upside down and reversed. Intrigued, Henry asked him why, but the draughtsman was, alas, stone deaf.

The fifth copied stylized arrowheads, from a pattern book. Henry was too frightened to ask him what his intention was.

The sixth was beginning a schematic diagram called MOODY'S LATEST SERMONS. He asked Henry to get out of his light.

The seventh had outlined a set of regular polygons, and was now beginning to black them in. 'If you like them,' he said to Henry, 'you might pay. Otherwise please move on and give another a chance to see them.'

The eighth drew a bird's wing, 'Detail 43B.' Henry was struck speechless by the beauty of it.

The ninth drew a 'valve' in 'cross-section'. 'It means,' he explained, 'that "My life has for several years been a theatre of calamity."' Henry did not understand.

The tenth made, or had made, a map of possibly the human brain. But he was not at his drawing board, and Henry was able neither to decipher it alone nor await his return.

The eleventh covered his drawing so that Henry could not see it. It was very likely either a blank sheet or a smeary example of the kind of erotic thing he had been dismissed from another job for sketching:

Two breastlike hills are covered with little figures, archers, shooting crossbows at the sky, or rather at certain objects in the sky. These are dozens of large, vicious-looking sickle shapes, apparently descending to attack the archers or breasts. In the background is a walled city, possibly Nürnberg. It is filth like this that makes me, as a father, wish I could administer the death penalty instead of this five-year sentence.

(from notes of District Judge Ruking.)

The twelfth and last draughtsman seemed only to be doing meaningless doodles. This man later left the Masterson Engineering Company and took a job elsewhere lettering placards. He committed suicide in his room by plunging a French knife (bought for the occasion) into his heart. Impaled on the blade near the hilt the police found a large placard serving as a suicide note. It read:

ACCIDENT

SECTION III: LIPS WHITER THAN TEETH

Past them, at the front corner of the room, were familiar faces in a group. Eddie Futch was eating chocolate noisily. Bob and Rod were tacking up signs saying ACCURASY and SUPPORT IBM. Willard Bask was discussing slavery with Clark Markey. Harold Kelmscott, cowled in an old grey sweater, had turned his back on the others. Only Ed Warner looked up to greet Henry.

'About time,' he said. 'We thought you'd died down there.'

Henry was reminded of the possibly violent death of Karl, which he had forgotten, though it had happened only a few minutes before. Should he report it? he wondered, and if so, to whom? Mr Masterson was inaccessible in his office. The placard on the door, hand-lettered by the last draughtsman, read 'No Personal Conversations. This Means You.'

Karl himself had been against making unnecessary trouble by reporting Ed's death. If Karl was dead, then the sensible thing to do would be to say nothing. Henry had a great respect for the wishes of the dead.

He began to convince himself that the 'shot' was a truck backfiring in the street, and the 'gun' nothing but an electric shaver or electric toothbrush. Karl had always, when alive, enjoyed electrical cleanliness. *And to what end?* thought Henry C. Henry.

He had begun to rejoice in his own teeth, covered as they were with a thick resinous deposit like the gum on old furniture. As he remarked to Willard, who was interested in anything like old furniture, 'What if I went around brushing my teeth twice a day all my life, then got them knocked out of my head by some punk in some alley?'

'Hot damn!' said Willard. 'I know just what you mean. Very same thing happened to me once, in 'Frisco. I sure was peeved, I'll tell the world. Makes a fella want to go back home and open an antique store. Fill it with good old solid traditional things. Whew! Fella'd give his left nut for a chance like that.'

Willard wanted to get into a discussion of the draughting tables and the draughtsmen, some of whom were, or seemed to be, Negroes.

Ed Warner kept asking everyone if they knew why he was declared officially dead. No one knew or wanted to know, least of all Karl, when he showed up freshly shaved some days later. Though for some reason he and Ed were not speaking, Karl said loudly for Ed's benefit: 'If he was declared officially dead, he wouldn't be here, and that's that. They don't make mistakes like that, right, Clark?'

'That's right.' The little non-lawyer had grown a foot taller and vaguely hairy. 'They have no right to hire a dead man all over again, when there are so many living unemployed.'

Masterson was not being a pine cone about it. He hired men of all races and nationalities as draughtsmen, because they could be virtually enslaved, and he especially liked to hire Negroes and South American immigrants.

'They all carry big, mean-lookin' knives,' Willard insisted.

'I can't believe that,' said Clark. 'They wouldn't be allowed to carry knives longer than three inches. It's illegal. Besides, I've never seen one of them with such a knife.'

'You better pray you never do see one,' Willard said, 'They only get them out to use them. I know what I'm talking about, now. I could tell you about one street fight I had in Leningrad. Whewee! Them big bucks come at me with knives like . . . '

To defend himself, Willard began to carry a switch-blade.

SECTION IV: DISAPPEARANCES

'No one is so busy as he who has nothing to do,' read the sign Bob (or Rod) was tacking to the wall. Rod (or Bob) looked on in smiling anguish, the better to see him with; later he took up a hammer and amended the sign to read 'he who has *something* to do'. Easter was approaching, and the two pals were selling Valentines – to everyone but Art, the old clerk with his aureole of dust-coloured hair. No one ever tried to sell anything to Art.

The chthonic draughtsmen kept to their stalls and did not mingle with the clerks. It was as if they feared infection, or that fraternizing with their superiors would cost them their jobs. For some reason the draughtsmen did not last long anyhow. They were fired, one at a time, and their tables broken up and burnt, until the day would come when . . . but that day was far in the future when Art revealed a true side to his face, unlimbering himself of the waste baskets of the past.

MEMO: *My childhood.*

I developed acrophobia, or fear of high places, as soon as I walked. When I was nearly two, my father one day decided to cure me of my irrational fear by making me climb up a tall (12 to 14 foot) stepladder to the top, and there sit until I stopped screaming.

– Masterson

SECTION V: ART SPEAKS

Art was in charge of firing, which consisted of simply filling out a pink slip and putting it into a pay envelope. Henry envied Art this power, the power of dealing effectively with papers. Alone of all the clerks, Art could see the real consequences of his work. He was an old, trusted employee who had been with the firm since its inception.

In fact, as he confided at lunch one day, he was its inceptor, and Masterson's father.

'Does he know you are alive?' asked Henry, incredulous that this harmless, friendly, frail, thin, likeable old man had created both an empire and its frightening emperor.

'Yes,' Art took a small bite of his hamburger and mangled it in the wrinkled depths of his mouth contentedly. With a fine jasper hand he flicked greasy crumbs from his tie. 'Yes, I built the whole shebang, and I nursed it all through the Great Depression, too. It was hard going, let me tell you, but on the other hand, I had all that cheap labour in *long* supply. Ten cents an hour, in the good old days, would buy you an unemployed architect. And I could hit them if I liked, without some damned nosy Labor Board coming around asking questions.'

He shook his wattles wistfully. 'Yes, sir, ten cents an hour. And they were *loyal*, mind you. I had men staying on ten, fifteen years. It was the war ruined all that. I have always been against war, and if you talk at me until you are blue in the face, I'll not change my opinion. War destroys stability. Nowadays, the young men only work for you for a year or so, then they run off to get drafted, with not a care for the future of the firm.'

SECTION VI: MASTERSON ON TOUR

Shortly after lunch was the time when Mr Masterson made his afternoon tour. He paced the aisle, holding his fat, hairless hands carefully away from his sides, fingers together and slightly cupped, thumbs braced, as though he were gripping the wheels of a wheelchair. In the watery glass panels on his face, two pale creatures darted back and forth.

Masterson's finger suddenly stabbed the table of one draughtsman with a sound like a thrown knife. He screamed, 'Arrowheads! I said no arrowheads! Take them out! I distinctly said no arrowheads! When I come back here in an hour, I don't want to see a single arrowhead! No arrowheads! Can't you understand plain English?'

The man did not understand a word he was saying, but he realized erasures were in order, and nodded. He bent lower over his board, and the electric eraser trembled in his hand.

Masterson passed on to the next man. 'What's *that* number?' Stab. 'It looks like a three, for Christ's sake.'

'It is a three, sir.'

'Well, it don't look enough like a three, then. Take it out and do it over.'

Smiling, the man obeyed. Masterson's doughy features began to glow. 'Take out *all* your numbers and do them over. Make them all look like threes.'

He came at last to a deaf-mute, Hrothgar.

'What do you call this? A centreline? And this? If these are centrelines, let's make them look like centrelines, huh?'

Hrothgar looked hurt, but moved to obey.

'And I told you before I wanted more space in there and there. Why don't you *listen* when I'm talking to you?'

'Nggyah-ngg!' protested the victim.

'Don't you talk back to me that way!'

SECTION VII: QUESTIONS
From the office came the sound of a knife being thrown with great force and apparent hate. Perhaps it was as Ed said, that arbitrary power corrupts arbitrarily.

Masterson screamed at the draughtsmen continually, but never at the clerks. He never asked the clerks what it was they were doing because he didn't know what they were doing. It did not suit him to ask a question unless he already knew the answer. Nothing infuriated him more than discovering that someone else knew the answer, too.

'How fast does light travel?' he asked Henry casually one day. Henry did not know.

'I know, naturally. In our measurement system, 186,000 miles per second,' said Karl.

'Who asked you?' said Masterson's right eye. Somewhere inside Karl another eye was closed forever by a foot squashing it; it spewed forth a grapey eye-seed.

The unpleasant marsupiality of Karl's eyes was worsened when he smiled. Little sharp shrew-teeth glittered at the ends of big dead-pale gums, and one knew his tongue would also be black. He looked like someone Henry had met before, somewhere, and Karl had changed. He was a spoiled bear, a bear gone finicky – yet how had he got these teeth?

SECTION VIII: MORE QUESTIONS

Masterson slapped Harold on the shoulder and asked if he could borrow ten till payday. 'I'm a little short, heh heh.' Assuming the boss was joking, Harold began to chuckle.

'No, I'm serious. Had a big weekend with a doll in Boston. I'm flat broke. You know how it is. I could always pay myself my own salary early, but I hate to screw up the book-keeping, see?' Reluctantly Harold saw. He loaned the ten.

'You'll never see that again,' whispered Big Ed, his face a complete blank. Harold pretended to be unaware of the old man's existence.

Henry noticed how blank Ed was actually becoming, as if someone were slowly erasing him. He was not just blurry, like Clark (who was growing a great mouth-devouring beard), but less definitely there at all.

On the following payday when Art passed around the pay envelopes, Harold did not get his ten. He tried to catch the flickering eye of Masterson when he stalked through the room, but the boss pretended to be unaware of Harold's existence.

'In the good old days,' Art said to Henry, 'I never had to take crap from anybody. Good feeling, being your own boss.

'Why, I used to walk down that aisle and I never even looked at what was on their boards. I just stared real hard at the back of each draughtsman's neck, stared until he thought he was going to get hit. If he flinched, my rule was, I got to hit him twenty times on the arm. Hee hee, they nearly always flinched.'

The two men sat in the warm diner speaking to one another through pale yellow clouds of steam from the french fryer: mists of the distant present. On the previous day, window cleaners had appeared at the office and wiped away the winter's grime. An hour after they had left, a dirty rain began.

'I notice everyone smokes around the office,' Art said. 'Not in my day. I never let anyone smoke, and I'd walk around the office all day puffing fifty-cent cigars and blowing the smoke at them. Drove 'em crazy, especially when I'd dump hot ashes on their drawings. Yes, sir, I ran a tight office in those days.

'If anyone ever sneaked off to the can for a smoke, I'd lock him in there for the rest of the day, then fire him. "Enjoy your smoke," I'd say as I turned the key. "You got all day, bright boy."

'Whee, one time a new kid ran in there for a smoke at about nine in the morning. I locked him in till six. Hee hee, the rest of them didn't like that, I can tell you, working all day without a biff.

'Well, came six o'clock and I opened to let him out, and what do you think that young bastard had done? Hanged himself! Yep, he had that old chain right around his neck and he was stone cold, and the toilet running gallons and gallons. You should have seen my water bill that month.'

His eyes crinkled with amusement. 'Yes, sir, that's the only time anyone put anything over on old Art. Hee hee.' He hugged his new coat around him gleefully, while some of his coffee dribbled off the point of his chin.

SECTION IX: THE THEOLOGICAL VIRTUES
Division A: Faith
It soon became apparent to all that Harold was going to get the shitty end of the stick.

'Did you even ask him for the money?' asked Ed.

'Well – no. How can I? He'll think I don't trust him.'

'Do you trust him?'

'Of course I do. Heck, he's the *boss*. Our lives are in his keeping, so to speak. Our names are in his book. He gives us each payday our wages. How can we turn against him? The pen is mightier than the sword.'

'But if you trust him, what have you got to gripe about?'

Harold, descended of a flawed monk, pondered this point of faith. 'It isn't the money, you understand. Heck, I don't care if I never see that ten again.'

'What is it, then?'

'It's just that I trust him, and now he's going to betray that trust. He's going to welsh on me.'

'Maybe he just forgot,' Karl purred, showing his little nasty teeth.

'Oh sure. He forgets, and I never see my money again. You can be sure *he* wouldn't forget it if *I* owed *him* ten dollars.'

Clark made a diplomatic suggestion. 'Look, just ask him if you can borrow ten from him. If he's forgotten about the loan, it'll remind him of it, and if he's planned on welshing, he'll be caught out ashamed. Besides, this way he'll know you need the money right away.'

Division B: Hope
Harold accosted Mr Masterson. 'Sir, could I borrow ten from you till payday? Heh, heh, I'm a little short, at the moment.'

The bulging figure turned slowly with the dignity of a wagon train, and faced him. For over a minute, Masterson subjected Harold to an intense stare of scorn and disbelief. Then he sighed and pulled out his billfold. Harold sighed, too.

'I wish you'd learn to live within your means, Kelmscott. I'm not a loan company. Now I'm going to loan you this, but it's the last time, understand?' The hinged glasses beetled over him.

'But I do live within my means, sir,' Harold stammered. 'It's not me who has weekends in Boston with a girl.'

The pale eyes did not register anything. Masterson sighed again, heaving his big, flabby shoulders. 'I'm not interested in nasty details of your personal life, Kelmscott. If you can't live on what I pay you, maybe you'd better look elsewhere for a job.' With a snort of disgust, he peeled a ten from his thick bundle of large bills and slapped it on Harold's desk. Then he stalked off to his office to throw, presumably, knives.

Division C: Charity

Every time an object hit the wall, Willard jumped. 'Oh God,' he moaned. 'I just know he's got some big, mean-lookin' knives in there.'

From time to time, Willard got out his own knife and tested the action. It was never fast enough to suit him.

At lunch, Henry asked Art about the pink slips. Did he ever warn anyone they were about to be fired?

The old man stopped masticating. 'Sir, watch your tongue. The job of firing is a sacred trust. My son, Mr Masterson, has entrusted me with the care of and disbursement of those pink slips, and of the persons they represent. Do you think I could let him down? My own son?'

Drawing himself up, Art for the moment resembled a famous general, and his thin chest seemed even to fill out the folds of his new coat.

'Besides,' he added with a wheeze. 'I like to watch a man's face when he opens his envelope. Boy, he sees those streets, those employment offices, even soup lines, hee hee hee. . . .' His laughter turned to a fit of dry coughing.

SECTION X: A HIGH OFFICE

That afternoon, Mr Masterson called Henry into his office. None of the clerks but Art had ever been there before, and Art had forgotten what it was like. Rod and Bob looked envious of Henry, but Karl smirkingly assumed he was being *given the axe*.

'If you want my opinion,' he said, 'I think you're going to be quietly *axed* to leave. Ha!'

Willard drew him aside and said, 'Play it cool, boy. If he pulls a knife, just you give me a holler.'

Henry pushed open the door with the placard and entered a plain, drab room. On one wall was a peculiar dart board, and on the floor beneath it a huge pile of darts with plastic fins. Near the opposite wall was a long desk behind which was visible the upper half of Mr Masterson. In his hands was a dart with green plastic fins. Nothing else in the room was describable.

The boss half-rose and hurled the dart; it hit a spot near the baseboard with a sound like a thrown knife, hung for an instant, then fell to the heap.

'So it goes,' sighed Masterson, or maybe, 'How would you like a raise?'

'Fine, sir.'

'Here's the set-up. We may have a new contract or two. Already we have a new contact or two. It's the big chance. All the candy companies on the coast are changing over to dynamometers. They'll need a lot of records and stuff switched over, too, and that's where we come in. If we can handle the changeover for one company, we can do good. Then all the other companies will want us to do good for them, too. Get it? Then later on, when the armed forces change from telephones to radios, we'll be set, see?

'But we'll need some extra help, and I'll need your help. You could be my right hand, and it'll mean a lot of extra money for the company, o.k.?'

SECTION XI: THE MYSTERIOUS MOTTO

Henry remembered his motto, the words spoken to him by the boss the day he'd hired him. As they had occurred to him, Henry had added interpretations, until now the sheet was covered; but which had the boss actually said?

If you work good, we'll do good by you.
If few work good, we'll do good by you.
If you were good, we'll do good by you.
If few were good, we'll do good by you.
If you work good weal, do good by you.
If few work good weal, do good by you.
If you were good weal, do good by you.
If few were good weal, do good by you.

In addition to these, there were the 24 combinations possible by replacing 'good by you' by 'good buy you', 'goodbye, you', and finally 'good bayou'. Though it was unlikely that he said 'If few were good weal, do good bayou,' that possibility could not be overlooked, Henry thought as he shook hands and prepared to leave.

'One thing, though,' said Masterson, counting that thing on his forefinger. 'Of course you'll make a lot of dough eventually, after our contacts become contracts, but you'll have to take a little pay cut for now, o.k.?'

They shook hands once more, and Henry started to leave. The boss held up two fingers. 'Secondly, now that you're a boss, you'll have to do a little informing on your pals. Remember, a boss has no real pals, and the great are always lonely.

'So I want you to tell me who hates me and who likes me. Let me know everything they say about me, understand?' He brought out another dart and threw it at the strange dart board.

'When the times comes – ' the dart stuck weakly in the edge of the board and dropped. 'You'll get your reward.' The dart fell quietly to the floor.

'Especially I want to know what my father says about me. You eat with him, don't you?'

'How did you know?'

Masterson wagged his fat forefinger. 'I have my spies, I have my spies,' he said archly. 'But tell me, does he talk about me a lot?'

'No.'

'Don't you lie to me! I know he talks about me all the time. All right, get out of here, then, and forget about that swell job.'

Henry waited for a pink slip, but it never came. Indeed, he seemed to receive the promotion after all, for he took a pay cut.

SECTION XII: A HAZARD OF NEW FORTUNES

All that week they worked on the bid. Masterson never left the aisle, but stamped, screamed, pounded on tables, and chewed to pieces dozens of dart-fins. He directed his father to hand out pink slips to anyone who got in his way, or to anyone who sneaked around behind him.

MEMO: *Is there life on other planets?*

This question is of the utmost importance to all of us, whether or not we are actually located in the aerospace industries, for it is a restatement of another, all-inclusive question: *Are we alone in the universe?* And if not, *who else is there?* These questions pose problems as yet unanswered; we can only wonder and hope and pray. But whether or not we ever find life on other planets, I feel confident that each and every one of us will want to give this question our full and careful consideration.

– Masterson

The first real crisis was paper. Masterson decided that ordinary tracing vellum was too expensive, and substituted newsprint. This rough, absorbent stuff made spiderwebs of ink lines and spiders of lettering. Masterson began to scream at the draughtsmen, sometimes with eloquence, sometimes wordlessly.

'Why can't you make neat, black lines and letters?' he demanded, and held up a newspaper. Pointing to a story about Hurricane Patty Sue, he said: 'Take a look at this. *They* don't have any trouble making neat lines and letters. Just look at this neat work.'

They tried again, again complaining of the paper, until Masterson, with a martyred smile, said, 'All right, all right. I'll get you some fancy, expensive paper. But *then*—'

He left, and returned an hour later with what appeared to be a roll of wide, slick toilet paper. Along one border ran the tiny green works: 'Deutsches Bundesbahn'.

In Austria, a fat Mercedes-Benz rolled on fat tyres into a filling station. The attendant saluted and began to fill the tank, while from behind the wheel a fat man rolled out, hitched up his belt and moved towards the toilet like a file of elephants going to the river. The sunlight gleamed on him, on his damp hair and his white shirt of miracle fibres. In one pocket of it was a leather liner containing a matching ballpoint pen and mechanical pencil and a steel scale, marked off both in centimetres and inches. In the other pocket was a package of Roth Handel cigarettes and a roll of hard candy liqueurs. The man stood a moment in the sun, gazing at four brown cows in the field nearby; in this town lived the engineer who designed the oven at Dachau; the traveller thought of all this and then went in to shit. He, too, was an engineer. Once he had written to an American magazine, asking for the names of engineering firms, of the particular type which included the Masterson Engineering Company. Due to an oversight, however, the engineer did not receive that name.

The draughtsmen tried again and again, but still their work did not satisfy Masterson. Finally, the eyes swelling behind his huge lenses, he screamed, 'Stop! I want you to stop. Erase everything. I want you to erase everything.'

For an hour, the only sound was the hum of electric erasers. One or two people erased holes in the fragile paper; they were given pink slips at once. Finally Masterson collected the twenty blank sheets, touched them up with an artgum eraser, wrapped them carefully and sent them out.

'We've got the contract sewed up,' he joyfully confided to the clerks. 'No one else could turn out work as neat as that, ever. Not one single mistake!'

Yet the next day, even while Rod and Bob were collecting money to buy flowers for the departed package, it came back. His thick hands fumbled at the bale of tattered tissue; Masterson read the accompanying letter aloud, and sobs hung quivering from his voice like drops of water from a tap.

'Dear Sirs:

Re yours of the thirteenth inst., we have no specific need for railroad station toilet tissue at present.

Thank you for keeping us in mind.'

SECTION XIII: ALL'S WELL IN THE END
Masterson removed his glasses and began cleaning them on a scrap of the

tissue. He turned his back modestly so that no one could glimpse his naked eyes. As he settled the frames once more on his cheeks, he cleared his throat with an oddly familiar sound. Henry leaned over and asked Ed, 'Will you tell me why you were declared officially dead?'

Ed pretended not to hear, and gazed steadily at the boss, who moved now on ponderous tiptoes to Art's desk. 'Give yourself a pink slip,' he sighed, and ran away to his office. The little old man nodded eagerly and began filling out a pink slip at once.

The next day was payday, and all watched Art closely as he passed out the envelopes. Smirking as usual, he sat down to open his own. The money he'd sealed into it and the pink slip he'd signed slid out together, and Art's face seemed to fold in thirds, like a business letter.

Clark Markey, always the barometer of another's mood, began to weep for him. Art himself merely sat there, staring at the slip lying flat on his desk.

'No,' he said in a small voice. 'They can't do this to me. Not to old Art.' He said it like a speech of condolence.

'It isn't fair,' said Clark with feeling. 'They can't make a man fire himself.'

Art walked slowly to the office, pounded on the placard, waited. The sound of darts within ceased.

'Let me in,' he cried. 'You've got to talk to me, Mr Masterson.'

'Go away, Dad,' said a muffled voice. Art trudged to the coat rack, slipped on his old, worn coat, and left.

A moment or two later, the dart game resumed.

PART THREE: THE DISMANTLING

MEMO: *My childhood.*

My father was a large cheque drawn on First National City Bank, and my mother was very tired.

– Masterson

SECTION I: IMPROVEMENTS

Things were looking up. Business seemed much improved, for everyone took enormous pay cuts. Karl was promoted to Art's old job. In addition to precision stapling, he now made out pink slips and took charge of office supplies. He began to detect and eliminate sources of waste.

Bob and Rod were promoted to informers. They blamed Masterson's father for everything, so their pay was not cut.

Clark Markey had begun to study law. Too many questions of justice now tormented him. How could a dead man be rehired? How could a man be forced to fire himself? At lunch hour he sat hunched over a large volume of labour laws, dropping crumbs (larger than whole words of the fine print) from his cream cheese sandwich. He was not a lawyer, and many of the long paragraphs were unintelligible to him. He began to suspect that in these lay the very answers he was seeking.

Masterson began looking fresh and fit. His death-colour skin took on a pink tinge, as if he daily gorged on blood. He bulged less, and began to walk around the office on new ripple-soled shoes, smacking his fist in his palm and saying, 'Now that the dead wood is cleared away, we can really *move*.' He made a progress chart.

Karl moved to eliminate the shocking waste of forms around the office. 'Look,' he explained to the group. 'We always have old, used forms around. Why don't we just eradicate the ink from them and re-use them?'

SECTION II: A FAST

After Christmas, Harold Kelmscott began a fast. It was, he said, in protest of his not being repaid the ten dollars the boss had borrowed; it was a form of sitting in dharna. Karl, who handled the pay envelopes, knew better. Masterson had garnished all of Harold's wages against the twenty he claimed Harold owed him.

'You can have your pay,' Karl explained, 'when the boss gets his twenty back.'

'Twenty! But I only borrowed ten, and that he had already borrowed from me.'

'If he borrowed it from you, how come you had to borrow it back? Come on, Harold, don't be a welsher. You're too nice a guy. Pay him his twenty, will you?'

'How can I, as long as I'm not getting paid myself? This is worse than debtor's prison, isn't it, Clark?' Harold looked to the non-lawyer for sympathy.

'What? Who knows? I'd have to check with English Civil Law,' said Clark testily, not looking up from his perusal of the New York Code.

Karl wagged his close-cropped head. 'Harold, you're a case, the worst I've ever seen. You know very well the boss isn't trying to cheat you. In fact, I begged him – I *begged* him to fire you and haul you into court. God knows you deserve it.

'But no, he said he wouldn't even stop the money out of your wages. He said if you didn't want to pay him, that was between you and your conscience. "I'm worried about Harold," he said to me. "I think I'll just garnishee his wages until he pays me back."

'You see, he knows you've got this shack-job in Boston, and he figures it ain't doing your character any good. But by the time you get squared away on your debt, she'll have forgotten all about you. Not only that, but you'll get all your pay at once, a real pile.'

'I'm starving,' Harold announced humbly. 'To death.'

Karl continued counting paper clips. 'You're a real case,' he muttered.

SECTION III: FURTHER PROGRESS

Having devised a method for rebending and re-using old paper clips, Karl saw a further short cut. Rather than eradicate the ink from old forms, he encouraged the others to use disappearing ink in the first place.

Willard kept his knife in his hand at all times, now, and feared everyone who moved suddenly or talked loudly. He took up whittling, to give himself an excuse for holding a knife. One day Masterson, jogging by, asked him if he could make a table, since he was so clever with his hands.

One week later, Willard presented him with a perfect matchbox-size Louis Quinze table, painted and gilded. Lifting it from his calloused palm, Willard set it carefully in the centre of the boss's desk.

'Idiot!' Masterson screamed, and brought his fist down on it. 'I meant a *real* table. A table of our progress.'

'Wait,' said Karl. 'If he can do this, Willard here can make big tables for all the clerks. Then we could sell off all the desks.'

Masterson had taken down and discarded the dart board, and now his walls were covered with charts. He and Karl planned many new charts and tables, and Harold executed them.

There was a chart of business volume compared to paper-clip expenditure, one of volume of work versus man-hours, one of level of water in the water cooler versus work output and one of Mr Masterson's weight versus the strength of his grip. They were inversely proportional, so that, had his weight been zero, his grip would have been a thousand pounds.

Three times a day he lifted weights in his office, rising on the toes and exploding breath through clenched teeth. At lunch hour, he ran three laps around the block, showered and gulped quantities of natural foods. Most mornings he came in with skinned knuckles and stories of brawls that frightened Willard. Masterson was no longer a shapeless bulgy man of indeterminate age, but a handsome, powerful man of about twenty-five.

'He's getting in shape to die,' Ed 'opined'.

Masterson had Harold post charts of his progress. There were graphs of his biceps and triceps, and a phrenological chart of his head. The boss began to talk about what great shape the company was in, squeezing grip developers as he talked.

'As soon as we trim off a little fat here and there, as soon as we fire the draughtsmen, we'll be in great shape.' He fired the draughtsmen next day, *en masse*, owing them three weeks' wages, and Henry complained to Clark about it.

Clark was getting jowly and near-sighted from cream cheese and law, and his temper was noticeably shorter. 'What am I supposed to do?' he said. '*Caveat emptor*. Why come to me with your problems? All I want is to be left alone with Law.'

Henry scooped up some dirty, tattered forms from the floor and began filling them out, in invisible ink. For several weeks, no work had left the office. Messengers who called to pick up work were sent out to get more natural food for Mr Masterson. Karl sent them on errands for invisible carbon paper, or to sell the desks that were slowly being replaced by Willard's tables.

Great bales of papers piled up, collecting dust. They grew greasy and black from handling, and Henry grew greasy and black from handling them. He washed and brushed his teeth often, but one cannot hold in the heart what is not bred in the bone: he stank.

Bob and Rod organized a clean-up campaign. They collected all the dirty forms in the office and laundered them. Karl was so pleased with their efforts that he even permitted them to sew patches on worn-out forms, though common practice did not permit this. Even so, after the windows came out, they could not keep up with the dirt.

No one but Henry and Ed and Eddie were working full-time on clerical duties. Clark was reading law full-time now, and Masterson had come to approve this. 'You never can tell when you'll need a good mouthpiece,' he said, and began calling Clark 'the mouthpiece'. The mouthpiece never spoke to anyone.

Harold was making charts of the company and of Mr Masterson full time. They overflowed the walls of his office and began to cover the corridor.

There was a chart showing the chain of command and another showing the flow of work. There was a chart showing weight of forms handled per clerk per day; a chart showing all the muscles of Mr Masterson's body (with the Latin labels lettered by Harold in half-uncials); a chart of company work-output vs. world population, and a fishing map of Northern Minnesota, which Mr Masterson planned to visit some day. There was a graph showing the monthly number of accidents, fatal, and accidents, non-fatal, per clerk.

Karl's job included researching the data for all of these. He counted paper clips, measured the level of water in the cooler, taped Mr Masterson's biceps, weighed forms, and estimated the world population. His estimates, Harold chuckled, were not conservative enough.

But Masterson pointed out how efficient Karl was. Who else would have realized the wasteful duplication in using both pink and blue copies of the same form? Karl had purchased a new single form printed on litmus paper, which was either blue or pink, depending on the weather. Ed seemed to grow a beard, which had the appearance of frightening Masterson. Clark wore rimless glasses.

The janitor service was cut off because the rent had not been paid. Karl had estimated the company could survive one year without it, saving several thousand dollars.

On the stage of a nearby theatre, two girls, one dressed as a man, were singing a song about making little gifts. One of the girls was sincere, but it was never clear which. Bob and Rod explained to the boss his father had sabotaged the janitor service.

'He sees what a good thing the company is getting to be,' one of them said. 'He wants to muscle in on you.'

'Well, I'm ready for him,' said Masterson. 'Let him try something.' Grinning, he flexed his forearm and watched the sinew lumps move in it as characters move about on a stage. Rod and Bob, or as they preferred being called, Dob and Rob, began doing janitor work around the office. They refused service to anyone who would not contribute to their list of charities: CORE, CARE, KKK, CCC, the Better Business Bureau, AAA and Minnesota Mining and Manufacturing Company. Only Harold did not give.

They cornered him one day. 'What's the matter? Don't you care that millions of Asians are starving while you sit here well-fed and complacent?' Harold did not deign to reply, or perhaps had not the strength. His skeletal face showed odd emotions, but he did not look up from his chart. Steadying a hunger-quaking hand, he went on with his beautiful, flowing uncials.

Living on the scraps of other clerk's lunches, and on the crumbs of cream cheese in Clark's law books, Harold was under a hundred pounds. He gulped water from the cooler, until Karl stopped him, saying that it ruined the line on the water-consumption estimates.

Once Harold fainted, and Mr Masterson revived him with a little natural soya meal. Harold gulped it down until Karl, alarmed at the way the expensive stuff was disappearing, grabbed the canister away. 'Easy does it, now,' he said. 'Not good to take too much at once.'

Willard made tables to replace all desks, but more tables were required. The volume of business, as Karl explained it, was steadily increasing. Consulting a table of Willard's table-making progress, he was not satisfied. 'Why don't you make tables out of the doors? It might be faster.'

'Or make coffins,' whispered Ed.

Willard converted all the doors into tables. When still more were needed, he unputtied window-panes and began using them for table-tops. The windows were grimy, and nearly everyone appreciated the increase in light.

Clark's sight was failing. Eddie Futch now read Law to him. Clark's sedentary life had made him gouty, and he began to walk about with a stick. From time to time, he would take a turn about the room, flicking with his stick at the dead forms that lay everywhere like leaves, like history. He would mutter legal phrases to himself through gritted teeth.

It was spring again, and a chill, dirty wind whipped through the office, whirling drawings and forms in a constant flux. To keep some of them in place, Henry borrowed weights from Mr Masterson's office.

The boss was rarely there these days. He worked out at a gym most of the week, and only bounced in occasionally to assure them that the company was recouping its losses at a truly fantastic rate. The litter of dirty forms was now ankle deep.

MEMO: *Dreams*

I dreamed of finding pieces of hate.

I dreamed an obscure dream: part of it was talking with a psychiatrist who looked something like Hemingway and something like Jung, and showing him my written-down dreams. It seems that I had never remembered the important parts. I forget the rest.

I dreamed of loving the princess of the glass house, Geopatra, full of mirrors and swimming pools.

– Masterson

No one talked, except Eddie Futch, droning periods of Law. Whenever the youngster stumbled, Clark caned him across the back, screaming epithets. Once the non-lawyer grew so excited that he had to take a turn around the room, limping and muttering, ' . . . ergo sum . . . ignoratio elenchi . . . petitio principii . . . non compos mentis . . . mons veneris . . . '

'Ed' nudged Henry, pointed to the ponderous figure and laughed. 'They're fattening him up for the kill,' he said.

'Who is?' Henry's ass felt a chill.

'Who knows? Maybe no one. Maybe "they" is just a figure of speech . . . but then maybe, you know, maybe *we're* just figures of speech, eh?'

MEMO: *Park conditions today*

Thick pink balloons were drifting over the park from some unknown source. They reminded the boy and the girl of giant drops of rosy sperm. Flowers seemed to be exploding at their feet as the boy took out his gold-filled ballpoint pen and wrote, in an unpretentious, sturdy, masculine hand, a love poem.

The poem spoke of fire-trucks and other excitements, of televisable passions, of a love nest made of food, wherein they settle:

No car honks madly;

The mayor gives the death penalty for honking tonight;

And cars have nightingales in place of horns.

The girl placed a drop of perfume on the pulse of her throat, and began to curve the soft inner part of her arm through the boy's writing hand. Inside every pink balloon was a hundred-dollar bill. A passing policeman thrust his nightstick at the polka-dot sky and laughed out of pure joy. The flowers made a noise like distant target practice. The boy leaped and the girl laughed. The policeman's gun belt shook with laughter, while overhead the opalescences bumped one another silently.

– Masterson

'You want to know why I was declared offically dead?' Ed asked. Henry shook his head and pointed to a sign affixed to his table: 'No Personal Conversations. This Means You.'

'I was declared officially dead because Karl put four staples in my death certificate.' The water was cut off. Henry seized Ed by the throat and tried to strangle him, as one might strangle an empty faucet, not to choke it off, but to make it flow again.

'Art's cut off the water, now,' Rob and Dob reported to Art's son.

'Oh, trying to starve us out, is he?' His heavy handsome jaw took a stern set. 'We'll just see about that.'

Harold showed him his latest, indeed his last effort, a chart of the basic natural foods and their constituents, arranged in a segmented circle. Heavy with gold-and-red illumination, the chart was called: 'THE WHEEL OF LIFE'.

'Very nice indeed, Harold,' said the boss, reaching for it. A ripple of muscle was visible through his specially-tailored suit. 'But you seem to be losing weight. Why is that? Dieting to improve the strength of your grip? I tried that, and it worked wonders.

'By the way, I hate to ask you for it, Harold, but when are you going to pay me that twenty you owe me? I really need it – got a big week-end in Boston coming up. You know what I mean.' He winked, and winked again at Clark.

'Well, now, mouthpiece, say something legal,' boomed the boss. A voice croaked from the tangled depths of Clark's beard. Holding his cane to the sky, he said, '*Mens sana in*—' he belched painfully, '—*in corpore sano*.'

'Fine, fine,' said Masterson, not hearing him. His powerful calves waded through the knee-deep debris effortlessly and carried him to his office.

MEMO: *On Communication*

_____

_____

_____

– Jqw534w9h

From the office came the clink and chunk of weights, and breath hissing through clenched teeth. Suddenly, as he lettered the words 'The Form Divine', Harold collapsed. Henry reached him first and held up his head. Harold cast a rueful look on his unfinished work, murmured, 'I go . . . I go to the Death Registration Office,' and died.

'Now where,' said Karl, 'did I put that fatal accidents chart?'

There came a deep reverberation, not Masterson. He came bounding from his office in sweatpants, his chest gleaming with perspiration. 'What the hell is going on?' he demanded. 'Is someone else lifting weights around here? He's fucking up my timing.'

The crew made its way down the stairs after him, to see the other weightlifter. Eddie led Clark down last, a step at a time. Naturally Ed and Harold remained behind.

The offices all the way down were empty. When they reached the sidewalk, the clerks found a derrick smashing at their building with a steel ball.

Masterson walked over to have a word with the foreman, who held up the destruction for the moment.

'We're tearing it down.'

'Why?'

'Abandoned.'

' . . . some mistake, or . . . '

'But nobody works there.'

Masterson said something else as the foreman gave a signal and the derrick engine roared. The tall tower turned awkwardly, like a hand puppet, setting the ball into motion.

The man shook his pink helmet. 'I don't know nothing about no father,' he shouted. 'All I know is, we got *work* to do.' He signalled the derrick operator, who swung the moving ball far back, then towards the wall.

Mr Masterson ran headlong towards it, springing with the grace of a dancer on his ripple soles. For a moment, it looked as if the steel ball would bounce harmlessly off his great chest.

Multi-value Motorway

BRIAN W. ALDISS

She too was obsessed with pelting images. Phil Brasher, her husband, was growing more and more violent with Charteris, as if he knew the power was passing from him to the foreigner. Charteris had the absolute certainty Phil lacked, the *gestalt*. He was himself; also, perhaps, a saint. Two weeks here, and he had spoken and the drugged crowds had listened to him in a way they never did to her husband. She could not understand his message, but then she had not been sprayed. She understood his power.

Nerves on edge. Burton, who ran a pop group, passed through her mind, saying, 'We are going to have a crusade.' She could not listen to the two men for, as they walked over the withdrawn meaning of the wet and broken pavement, the hurtling traffic almost tore at their elbows. That other vision, too, held her near screaming pitch; she kept hearing the wheels of a lorry squeal as it crashed into her husband's body, could see it so clear she knew by its name-boards it was travelling from Glasgow down to Naples. Over and over again it hit him and he fell backwards, disintegrating, quite washing away his discussion, savage discussion of multi-value logic, with Charteris. Also, she was troubled because she thought she saw a dog scuttle by wearing a red and black tie. Bombardment of images. They stood in a web of alternatives.

Phil Brasher said, 'I ought to kill Charteris.' Charteris was eating up his possible future at an enormous pace. Brasher saw himself spent, like that little rat Robbins, who had stood as saint and had not been elected. This new man, whom he had at first welcomed as a disciple, was as powerful as the rising sun, blanking Brasher's mind. He no longer got the good images from the future. It was dead, there was a dead area, all he saw was that damned Christmas cactus which he loathed for its meaninglessness, like flowers on a grave. So he generated hate and said powerfully and confusedly to Charteris, 'I ought to kill Charteris.'

'Wait, first wait,' said Colin Charteris, in his slightly accented and perfect English. 'Think of Ouspensky's personality photographs. You have many alternatives. We are all rich in alternatives.' He had been saying that all afternoon, during this confused walk, as he knew. The damp smudged crowded city, matured to the brown nearest black, gave off this rich aura of possibilities, which Brasher clearly was not getting. Charteris had glimpsed the world-plan, the tides of the future, carried them within him, was not so much superior to as remote from the dogged Brasher and Brasher's pale-thighed wife, Angeline. There were many alternatives; that was what he would say when next he addressed the crowds. A power was growing in him; he stood back modest and amazed to see it and recognize its sanctity. Brasher grabbed his wet coat and waved a fist in his face, an empty violent man saying, 'I ought to kill you!' Traffic roared by them, vehicles driven by drivers seeing visions, on something called Inner Relief Road.

The irrelevant fist in his face; in his head, the next oration. You people – you midland people are special, chosen. I have come from the south of Italy to tell you so. The roads are built, we die on them and live on them, neural paths made actual. The Midlands of England is a special region; you must rise and lead Europe. Less blankly put than that, but the ripeness of the moment would provide the right words, and there would be a song, Charteris we cry! He could hear it although it was not yet written. Not lead but deliver Europe. Europe is laid low by the psychedelic bombs; even neutral France cannot help, because France clings to old nationalist values. I was an empty man, a materialist, waiting for this time. You have the alternatives now.

You can think in new multi-value logics, because that is the pattern of your environment. The fist swung at him. Angeline's face was taking in the future, traffic-framed. It seemed to me I was travelling aimlessly until I got here.

'I was just passing through on my way to Scotland, belting up the motorway. But I stopped here because here is my destiny. Think in fuzzy sets. There is no either-or, black-white dichotomy any more. There is only a spectrum of partiallys. Live by this, as I do – you will win. We have to think new. It's easy in this partially country.'

But Brasher was hitting him. He looked at the fist, saw all its lines and tensions as Brasher had never seen it, a fist less human than many of the natural features of the man-formed landscape in this wonderful traffic-tormented area. A fist struck him on the jaw.

Even in this extreme situation, Charteris thought, multi-value logic is the Way. I am choosing something between being hit and not being hit; I am not being hit very much.

He heard Angeline screaming to her husband to stop. She seemed not to have been affected by the PCA Bomb, the Psycho-Chemical Aerosols that had sprayed most of Europe, including Britain, in the Acid Head War. But it was difficult to tell; the effects were so intricate. Charteris had a theory that women were less affected than men. He liked Angeline, but disliked her screaming. Bombardment of images, linked to her scream – theory of recurrence? – especially toads and the new animal in the dead trees at home.

There was a way to stop the screaming without committing oneself to asking her to cease. Charteris clutched at Brasher's ancient blue coat, just as the older man was about to land another blow. Behind Brasher, on the other side of Inner Relief, was an old building of the drab ginger stone of Leicestershire, to which a modern glass-and-steel porch had been tacked. A woman was watering a potted plant in it. All was distinct to Charteris as he pulled Brasher forward and then heaved him backward into Inner Relief.

The lorry coming from the north swerved out. The old Cortina blazing along towards it spun across the narrow verge, swept away the glass-and-steel porch, and was itself hit by a post office van which had driven out to avoid the lorry. The lorry, still bucking across the road, hit another oncoming car which could not stop in time. Another vehicle, its brakes squealing, ran into the wall within feet of where Charteris and Angeline stood, and crumpled up. A series of photographs, potentialities multiplying or cancelling.

'So many alternatives,' Charteris said wonderingly. He was interested to see that Brasher had disappeared, bits of him distributed somewhere among the wreckage. He remembered a multiple crash he had seen on the autostrada near Milano. This was much richer, and he saw a tremendous rightness in the shape of wreckage; it was like a marvellous – he said it to the girl, 'It is like a marvellous complex work of sculpture, where to the rigorous man-formed shapes is added chance. The art of the fortuitous.'

She was green and drab, swaying on her heels. He tried looking closely at the aesthetic effect of this colour-change, and recalled from somewhere in his being a sense of pity. She was hurt, shocked, although he saw a better future for her. He must perform a definite action of some sort: remove her from the scene.

She went unprotestingly with him.

'I think Charteris is a saint. He has spoken with great success in Rugby and Leicester,' Burton said.

'He has spoken with great success in Rugby and Leicester,' Robbins said, thinking it over. Robbins was nineteen, his hair very long and dirty; he had been an art student; his psychedelic-disposed personality had disintegrated under the effect of being surrounded by acid heads, although he was not personally caught by the chemicals. Burton had been a third-yearer, had turned agent, ran the pop group, the Escalation, operated various happenings; he had run Robbins as a saint with some reward, until Robbins had deflated one morning into the rôle of disciple. They lived with a couple of moronic girls in old housing in the middle of Loughborough, overlooking the rear of F. W. Woolworth's. All round the town was new building, designed to cope with the fast-growing population; but the many conflicting eddies of society had sent people gravitating towards the old core. The straggle of universities and technical colleges stood in marshy fields. It was February.

'Well, he spoke with great success in Leicester,' Burton said.

'Ay, he did that. Mind you, I was a success in Leicester,' Robbins said.

'Don't run down Leicester,' Greta said. 'I came from there. At least, my uncle did. Did I ever tell you my Dad was a Risparian? An Early Risparian. My Mum would not join.'

Burton dismissed all reminiscence with a sweep of his hand. He lit a reefer and said, 'We are going to have a crusade.'

He could see it. Charteris was good. He was foreign and people were ready for foreigners. Foreigners were exotic. And Charteris had this whole thing he believed in. People could take it in. Charteris was writing a book.

The followers were already there. Brasher's following. Charteris beat Brasher at any meeting. You'd have to watch Brasher. The man thought he was Jesus Christ. Even if he is Jesus Christ, my money's on Charteris. Colin Charteris. Funny name for a Jugoslav!

'Let's make a few notes about it,' he said. 'Robbins, and you Gloria.'

'Greta.'

'Greta, then. A sense of place is what people want – something tangible among all the metaphysics. Charteris actually likes this bloody dump. I suppose it's new to him. We'll take him round, tape-record him. Where's the tape-recorder?' He was troubled by images and a presentiment that they would soon be driving down the autobahns of Europe. He saw the sign to Frankfurt.

'I'll show him my paintings,' Robbins said. 'And he'll be interested about the birds.'

'What about the birds?'

'A sense of place. What they do, you know, like the city.' They liked the city, the birds. He had watched, down where the tractor was bogged down in the muddy plough, the landscape the brown nearest black under the thick light. It was the sparrows and starlings, mainly. There were more of them in the towns. They nested behind the neon signs, over the fish and chip shops, near the Chinese restaurants, for warmth, and produced more babies than the ones in the country, learning a new language. The seagulls covered the ploughed field. They were always inland. You could watch them, and the lines of the grid pencilled on the sky. They were evolving, giving up the sea. Or maybe the sea had shrivelled up and gone. God knows what the birds are up to, acid-headed like everything else.

'What are you talking about?' She loved him really, but you had to laugh.

'We aren't the only ones with a population explosion. The birds too. Remember that series of paintings I did of birds, Burton? Flowers and weeds, too. Like a tide. Pollination explosion.'

'Just keep it practical, sonnie. Stick to buildings, eh?' Maybe he could unzip his skull, remove the top like a wig, and pull that distracting Frankfurt sign out of his brain.

'The pollination explosion,' Charteris said. 'That's a good title. I write a poem called The Pollination Explosion. The idea just came into my head. And the time will come when, like Judas, you try to betray me.'

Angeline was walking resting on his arm, saying nothing. He had forgotten where he had left his red Banshee; it was a pleasure walking through the wet, looking for it. They strolled through the new arcade, where one or two shops functioned on dwindling supplies. A chemist's; Get Your Inner Relief Here; a handbill for the Escalation, Sensational and Smelly. Empty shells where the spec builder had not managed to sell shop frontage, all crude concrete, marked by the fossil-imprints of wooden battens. Messages in pencil or blue crayon. YOUNG IVE SNOGED HERE, BILL HOPKINS ONLY LOVES ME, CUNT SCRUBBER. What was a cunt scrubber? Something like a loofah, or a person? Good opening for bright lad!

The Banshee waited in the rain by a portly group of dustbins. It was not locked. They turned out an old man sheltering inside it.

'You killed my husband,' Angeline said, as the engine started. The garage up the road gave you quintuple Green Shields on four gallons. Nothing ever changed except thought. Thought was new every generation, and she heard wild music playing.

'The future lies fainting in the arms of the present.'

'Why don't you listen to what I'm saying, Colin? You're not bloody mad, are you? You killed my husband and I want to know what you're going to do about it!'

'Take you home.' They were moving now. Although his face ached, he felt in a rare joking mood.

'I don't live out this direction.'

'Take you to my home. My place. I've started making a new model for thought. You came once, didn't you? It's not town, not country. You can't say which it is; that's why I like it – it stands for all I stand for. Things like art and science have just spewed forth and swallowed up everything else. There's nothing now left that's non-art or non-science. My place is neither urban nor non-urban. Fuzzy set. Look outwards, Angeline! Wonderful!'

'You Serbian bastard! There may have been a war, the country may be ruined, but you can't get away with murder! You'll die, they'll shoot you.' There was no conviction in her voice; his sainthood was drowning her old self.

'No, I shall live. I haven't fulfilled my purpose yet.' They were easing on to the Inner Relief. Behind them, ambulances and a fire engine and police cars and breakdown vans were nuzzling the debris. 'I've seen reality, Angeline. And I myself have materialized into the inorganic, and so am indestructible.'

The words astonished him. Since he had come to England, the psychedelic effect had gained on him. He had ceased to think what he was saying; the result was he surprised himself, and this elation fed back into the system. Every thought multiplied into a thousand. He pursued them all on deep levels, struggling with them as they propagated in their deep burrows away from the surface. Another poem: On the Spontaneous Generation of Ideas During Conversation. Spontagions Ideal Convertagion. The Conflation of Spontagion in Idations. Agenbite of Auschwitz.

'Inwit, the dimlight of my deep Loughburrows. That's how I materialized, love! Loughborough is me, my brain, here – we are in my brain, it's all me. I am projecting Loughborough. All its thoughts are mine.' It was true. He knew what other people were thinking, or at least shared their bombardment of images.

'Don't be daft – it's raining again!' But she sounded frightened.

They swerved past concrete factories, long drab walls, filling stations. Ratty little shops now giving up; no more *News of the World*. Grey stucco urinal. A railway bridge, iron painted yellow, advertising Ind Coope, sinister words to him. Then rows of terrace houses, time-devoured. A complete sentence yet to be written into his book; he saw his hand writing the truth is in static instants. Then the semis. More bridges, side roads, iron railings, the Inner Relief yielding to fast dual-carriage out on to the motorway, endless roads crossed over it on primitive pillars. Railways, some closed, canals, some sedge-filled, a poor sod pushing a sack of potatoes across a drowning allotment on the handlebars of his bike, footpaths, cyclepaths.

Geology. Strata of different man-times. Each decade of the past still preserved in some gaunt monument. Even the motorway itself yielded clues to the enormous epochs of antepsychedelic time: bridges cruder, more massive in earliest epoch, becoming almost graceful later, less sick-yellow; later still, metal; different abutment planes, different patterns of drainage in the under-flyover bank, bifurcated like enormous Jurassic fern-trees. Here we distinguish by the characteristic of this mediumweight aggregate the Wimpey stratum; while, a little further along, in the shade of these cantilevers, we distinguish the beginning of the McAlpine seam. The spread of that service area, of course, belongs characteristically to the Taylor Woodrow Inter-Glacial. Further was an early electric generating station with a mock-turkish dome, desolate in a field. All art. Pylons, endlessly, too ornate for the cumbersome land.

The skies were lumped and flaky with cloud, Loughborough skies. Squirting rain and diffused lighting. No green yet in the hedges. The brown nearest black. Beautiful. . . .

'We will abolish that word beautiful. It implies ugliness in an Aristotelian way. There are only gradations in between. No ugliness.'

'There's the word "ugliness", so there must be something to attach it to, mustn't there?'

'Stop quoting Lewis Carroll at me!'

'I'm not!'

'You should have allowed me to give you the benefit of the doubt.'

He flicked away back on to his own side of the motorway, narrowly missing an op-art Jag, its driver screaming over the wheel. I drive by fuzzy sets, he thought admiringly. The two cars had actually brushed; between hitting and not-hitting were many degrees. He had sampled most of them. It was impossible to be safe – watering your potted plant, which was really doing well. A Christmas cactus it could be, you were so proud of it. The Cortina, Consortina, buckling against – you'd not even seen it, blazing in a moment's sun, Christ, just sweeping the poor woman and her pathetic little porch right away in limbo!

'Never live on Inner Relief.' Suddenly light-hearted and joking.

'Stop getting at me! You're really rather cruel, aren't you?'

'*Jebem te sunce!* Look, Natrina – I mean, Angelina, I love you.'

'You don't know what it means!'

'So? I'm not omniscient yet. I don't have to know what it is to do it, do I? I'm just beginning. Burton's group, Escalation Limited, I'll write songs for them. How about Truth Lies in Static Instants? Or When We're Intimate in the Taylor Woodrow Inter-Glacial. No, no – Accidents and Aerodynamics Accrete into Art. No, no, sorry! Then how about . . . ha, I Do My Personal Thinking In Pounds Sterling? Or Ouspensky Ran Away With My Baby. Good job I gave up my NUNSACS job. Too busy. Look – *zbogom*, missed him! Maybe get him tomorrow! Must forget these trivialities, which others can perform. I'm just so creative at present, look, Angelina—'

'It's Angeline. Rhymes with "mean".'

'My lean angel mean, Meangeline. I'm so creative. And I feel the gift in you too as you struggle out of old modes towards areas of denser feeling. Anyhow, see that church of green stone? We're there. Partially there.'

And this partial country was neither inhabitable nor uninhabitable. It functioned chiefly as an area to move through; it was a dimensional passage, scored, chopped up by all the means the centuries had uncovered of annihilating the distance between Loughborough and the rest of Europe, rivers, roads, rails, canals, dykes, lanes, bridges, viaducts. The Banshee bumped over a hump-backed bridge, nosed along by the municipal dump, and rolled to a stop in front of a solitary skinned house. A squadron of diabolical lead birds sprang up to the roof, from instant immobility to instant immobility, on passage from wood to city. The slates were broken by wind and birds. Sheer blindness had built this worthy middle-class house here, very proper and some expense spared in the days before the currency had gone decimal. It stood in its English exterior plumbing as if in scaffolding. A land dispute perhaps. No one knew. The proud owner had gone, leaving the local council easy winners, to celebrate their triumph in a grand flurry of rubbish which now lapped into the front garden, eroded, rotting intricate under the creative powers of decay. Caught by the fervour of it, the Snowcem had fallen off the brick, leaving a leprous dwelling, blowing like dandruff round the porch. And she looked up from the lovely cactus – he had admired it so much, bless him, a good husband – just in time to see the lorry sliding across the road towards her. And then, from behind, the glittering missile of the north-bound car. . . .

Charteris leant against the porch, covering his eyes to escape the repetitive image.

'It was a conflux of alternatives in which I was trapped. I so love the British – you don't understand! I wouldn't hurt anyone. . . . I'm going to rule by—'

'You can't bring him back by being sorry.'

'Her, the woman with the cactus! Her! Her! Who was she?'

The Escalation had taken over the old Army Recruiting Office in Ashby Road. Their surroundings had influenced two of their most successful songs, 'Braid on the Inside of Your Britches' and 'A Platoon of One'. There were four of them, four shabby young men, sensational and smelly, called, for professional purposes, Phil, Bill, Ruby and Featherstone-Haugh; also Barnaby, who worked the background tapes to make supplementary noise or chorus. They were doing the new one. They could hear the ambulances still squealing in the distance, and improvised a number embodying the noise called 'Lost My Ring In the Ring Road'. Bill thought they should play it below, or preferably on top of, 'Sanctions, Sanctions'; they decided to keep it for a flip side.

They began to rehearse the new one.

Bank all my money in slot machines
These new coins are strictly for spending
Old sun goes on its rounds
Now since we got the metric currency
I do my personal thinking in pounds
We haven't associated
Since twelve and a half cents of this new money
Took over from the half-crowns
Life's supposed to be negotiable, ain't it?
But I do my personal thinking in pounds

Greta and Flo came in, with Robbins and Burton following. Burton had lost his lovely new tie, first one he ever had. He was arguing that Charteris should speak publicly as soon as possible – with the group at Nottingham on the following night; Robbins was arguing that there had been a girl at the art college called Hyperthermia. Greta was saying she was going home.

'Great, boys, great, break it up! You've escalated, like I mean you are now a choir, not just a group, okay? At Nottingham tomorrow night, you're a choir, see? So we hitch our fortunes to Colin Charteris, tomorrow's saint, the author of *Fuzzy Sets*.'

'Oh, he's on about sex again! I'm going home,' said Greta, and went. Her mum lived only just down the road in a little house on the Inner Relief; Greta didn't live there any more, but they had not quarrelled, just drifted gently apart on the life-death stream. Greta liked squalor. What she could not take was the clutter of indoor plants with which her mother hedged her life.

Sister, they've decimalized us
All of the values are new
Bet you the twenty-cent piece in my hip
When I was a child on that old £.s.d.
There was a picture of a pretty sailing ship
Sailing on every ha'penny. . . .

They were used to Burton's madness. He had got them the crowds. They needed the faces there, the noise, the interference, the phalanx of decibels the audience threw back at them in self-defence, needed it all, and the stink and empathy, really to give out. In the last verse, The goods you buy with this new coinage, they could have talk-chant as counterpoint instead of instrument between lines. Maybe even Saint Charteris would go for that. Saint Loughborough? Some people said he was a communist, but he was all the things they needed. He could even give them songs. They looked back too much. The future and its thoughts they needed. Lips close, New pose, Truth lies in static instants. Well, it had possibilities.

As Charteris laboured at his masterwork, cutting, super-imposing, annotating, Angeline wandered about the house. A tramp lived upstairs in the back room. She avoided him. The front room upstairs was empty because it was so damp where the rain poured in. She stood on the bare boards staring out at the sullen dead sea with shores of city rubbish, poor quality rubbish, supporting flocks of gulls, their beaks as cynical as the smile of the serpent from which they had originated. The land so wet, so dark, the brown nearest black, late February and the trains all running late with the poor acid-head drivers forgetting their duties, chasing their private cobwebs. Nobody was human any more. She would be better advised to take LSD and join the majority, forget the old guilt theories. Charteris gave her hope because he thought the situation was good and could be improved within fuzzy limits.

Wait till you read *Man the Driver*, he told Phil Brasher. You will see. No more conflict in society once man recognizes that he always was a hunter. The modern hunter has become a driver. His main efforts do not go towards improving his lot, but towards complicating ways of travel. In his head is a multi-value motorway. Now, in the post-war period, he is free to drive down any lane he wants. No external frictions or restrictions any more. Thus spake Charteris. She had felt compelled to listen, thus possibly accomplishing Phil's death. There had been a rival group setting up in the cellars of Loughborough, the Mellow Bellows. They had taken one title out of thin air: There's a fairy with an Areopagitica, No external frictions or restrictions, We don't need law or war or comfort or that bourgeois stuff, No external frictions or restrictions. Of course, they did say he was a communist or something. What we needed was freedom to drive along our life lines where we would, give or take the odd Brasher. More irrational fragments of the future hit her: through him, of course; a weeping girl, a – a baked bean standing like a minute scruple in the way of self-fulfilment.

She wanted him to have her, if she could square her conscience about Phil. He was okay, but – yes, a change was so, so welcome. Sex, too, yes, if he didn't want too much of it. He was clean-looking; good opening for bright young lad – where had she overheard that?! Well, it was self-defence.

The gulls rose up from the mounds of rotting refuse. There was a dog down there, running, free, so free, companion of man. Perhaps now man was going to be as free as his companion.

Tears trickling down her cheek. Even if it proved a better way of life, good things would be lost. Sorry, Phil, I loved you all I could for six years, but I'm going to bed with him if he wants me. It's you I'm going to betray, not him, if I can make it, because he really has something. I don't know if he is Loughborough, but he is a sort of saint. And you did hit him first. You always were free with your fists. She went downstairs. Either that running dog wore a tie or she was going acid head like the others.

'It's a bastard work, a mongrel,' he said. He was eating something out of a can; that was his way, no meals, only snack, the fuzzy feeder. 'I'm a mongrel, aren't I? Some Gurdjieff, more Ouspensky, less Marshall McLuchan, time-obsessed passages from the Great Chain of Being, no zen or all that – no Englishmen, but it's going to spread from England out, we'll all take it, unite all Europe at last. America's ready, too. The readiest place, always.'

'If you're happy.' She touched him. He had dropped a baked bean on to the masterwork. It almost covered a word that might be 'self-fulfilment'.

'See those things crawling in the bare trees out there? Elms, are they? Birds as big as turkeys crawling in the trees, and toads and that new animal. I often see it. There is an intention moving them, as there is in us. They seem to keep their distance.'

'Darling, you're in ruins, your mind, you should rest!'

'Yes. Happiness is an out-moded concept. Say, think, "tension-release", maintain a sliding scale, and so you do away with sorrow. Get me, you just have a relief from tension, and that's all you need. Nothing so time-consuming as happiness. If you have sorrow, you are forced to seek its opposite, and vice versa, so you should try to abolish both. I must speak to people, address them. You have some gift I need. Come around with me, Angelina?'

She put her arms about him. There was some stale bread on the table, crumbs among the books he was breaking up and crayoning. Activity all the time. 'Darling.'

When the Escalation came along, the two of them were lying on the camp-bed, limbs entangled, not actually copulating.

Greta wept, supported by two of the group. Featherstone-Haugh touched a chord on his balalaika and sang, 'Her mother was killed by a sunlit Ford Cortina.'

'Man the Driver,' Chapter Three. Literature of the Future Affecting Feeling of the Future. Ouspensky's concept of mental photographs postulates many photographs of the personality taken at characteristic moments; viewed together, these photographs will form a record by which man sees himself to be different from his common conception of himself – and truer. So, they will suggest the route of life without themselves having motion. The truth is in static instants; it is arrived at through motion. There are many alternatives.

Fiction to be mental photographs, motion to be supplied purely by reader. Action a blemish as already in existence. Truth thus like a pile of photos, self-cancelling for self-fulfilment, multi-valued. Impurity of decision one of the drives towards such truth-piles; the Ouspenskian event of a multiple crash on a modern motorway is an extreme example of such impurities.

Wish for truth involved here. Man and landscape interfuse, science presides.

Charteris stood at the window listening to the noise of the group, looking out at the highly carved landscape. Hedges and trees had no hint of green, were cut from iron, their edges jagged, ungleaming with the brown nearest black, although the winds drove rain shining across the panorama. Vehicles scouring down the roads trailed spume. The earlier nonsense about the terrors of the population explosion; one learned to live with it. But mistakes were still being made. The unemployed were occupied, black Midland figures like animated sacks, planting young trees in groupings along the grand synclines and barrows of the embankments and cuttings and underpasses, thereby destroying the geometry, mistakenly interfusing an abstract of nature back into the grand equation. But the monstrous sky, squelching light out of its darkest corners, counteracted this regressive step towards out-dated reality moulds. The PCA Bombs had squirted from the skies; it was their region.

There was a picture of a pretty sailing ship
Sailing every ha'penny

The goods you buy with this new coinage
Weren't made any place I heard of
They give out the meagrest sounds
But I don't hear a thing any longer
Since I did my personal thinking in pounds

I had a good family life and a loving girl
But I had to trade them in for pounds

The damned birds were coming back, too, booking their saplings, ready to squirt eggs into the first nests at the first opportunity. They moved in squadrons, heavy as lead, settled over the mounds of rubbish, picking out the gaudy Omo packets. They had something planned, they were motion without truth, to be hated. He had heard them calling to each other in nervous excitement, 'Omo, Omo'. Down by the shores of the dead sea, they were learning to read, a hostile art. And the new animal was among them by the dead elms.

Angeline was comforting Greta, Burton was turning the pages of *Man the Driver*, thinking of a black and red tie he had worn, his only tie. Words conveyed truth, he had to admit, but that damned tie had really sent him. He thought he had tied it round the neck of a black dog proceeding down Ashby Road. Spread the message.

'Greet, you didn't hear of a dog involved in this pile-up?'

'Leave her alone,' Angeline said. 'Let her cry it out.'

'He did it, you know,' Greta wept. 'You can't have secrets in this city any more. Well, it's more of an urban aggregation than a city, really, I suppose. He pushed the whole chain of events into being, piled up all them lorries, killed my mum and everything.'

'I know,' Angeline said. The heart always so laden.

Great crowds in Nottingham to greet the Escalation, teenagers blurry in the streets, hardly whispering, the middle-aged, the old, the crippled and the halt, all those who had not died from falling into fires or ditches or roads, all those who had not wandered away after the aerosols drifted down, all those who had not opened their spongy skulls with can-openers to let out the ghosts and the rats. All were hot for the Escalation.

At half-term, the boys, sensational and smelly, had the crowds throwing noise back at them. Burton stood up, announced Saint Charteris, asked if anyone had seen a stray dog wearing a red and black tie. The Escalation howled their new anthem.

Adsolescent Loughborough
With slumthing to live through
Charteris we cry
Is something to live by

He had scarcely thought out what he was going to say. It seemed so apparent that he felt it did not need uttering. The slav dreamers, Ouspensky and the rest, sent him travelling with his message through to this outpost of Europe. Obviously, if the message had validity, it was shaped by the journey and the arrival. In Metz, in France, he had realized the world was a web of forces. Their minds, their special Midland minds had to become repositories of thinking also web-like, clear but indefinite. If they wanted exterior models, the space-time pattern of communication-ways with which their landscape was riddled functioned as a valuable master plan. All the incoherent aspirations that filled their lives would then fall into place. The empty old nineteenth-century houses built by new classes which now stood rotting in ginger stone on hillsides, while carriageways either approached or receded like levels of old lakes, were not wasted; they functioned as landmarks. Nothing should be discarded; but the New Thought would re-orient everything, as the ginger stone mansions or the green stone churches were re-oriented by the changing dynamic of the landscape. He was the Aristotle of the New Thought. The Fourth World System, Man the Driver, would appear soon.

Greta stood up and screamed, 'He killed my mother! He caused the multiple accident on the Inner Relief. Kill him!'

White-faced Angeline said from the platform for all to hear, 'And he killed my husband, Phil Brasher.' But it was sin whether she spoke or not; she worked by old moralities, where someone was always betrayed.

Their faces all turned to his face, seeking meaning.

'It's true! The lorry was sweeping along the great artery from Glasgow down to Naples. In Naples, they will also mourn. We are all one people now, and although this massive region of yours is as special as the Adriatic Coast or the Dutch Lowlands, or the Steppes of central Asia, the similarity is also in the differences. You know of my life, that I was a communist, coming from Montenegro in Jugoslavia, that I lived long in the south of Italy, that I dreamed all my life of England. Now I arrive here and fatal events begin, spreading back along my trail. See how in this context even death is multi-valued, the black nearest brown. Brasher falling back into the traffic was a complex event from which the effects still radiate. We shall all follow that impulse. The Escalation and I are now setting out on a motor-crusade down through our Europe, the autobahns. All of you come too, a moving event to seize the static instant of truth! Come too! There are many alternatives.'

They were crying and cheering. It would take on truth, be a new legend, a new communication in the ceaseless dialogue. Even Angeline thought, Perhaps he will really give us something to live by. It surely can't really matter, can it, whether there was a dog with a tie or not; the essential thing was that I saw it and stand by that. So it doesn't matter whether he is right or not; just stay in the Banshee with him.

He was talking again, the audience were cheering, the group were improvising a driving song about a Midland-minded girl at the wheel of a sunlit automobile. An ambiguity about whether they meant the steering or the driving wheel.

Traveller's Rest

DAVID I. MASSON

It was an apocalyptic sector. Out of the red-black curtain of the forward sight-barrier, which at this distance from the Frontier shut down a mere twenty metres north, came every sort of meteoric horror: fission and fusion explosions, chemical detonations, a super-hail of projectiles of all sizes and basic velocities, sprays of nerve-paralysants and thalamic dopes. The impact devices burst on the barren rock of the slopes or the concrete of the forward stations, some of which were disintegrated or eviscerated every other minute. The surviving installations kept up an equally intense and nearly vertical fire of rockets and shells. Here and there a protectivized figure could be seen 'sprinting' up, down or along the slopes in its mechanical 'walker' like a frantic ant from an anthill attacked by flame-throwers. Some of the visible oncoming trajectories could be seen snaking overhead into the indigo gloom of the rear sight-curtain, perhaps fifty metres south, which met the steep-falling rock surface forty-odd metres below the observer's eye. East and west, as far as the eye could see, perhaps some forty miles in this clear mountain air despite the debris of explosion (but cut off to west by a spur from the range) the visibility-corridor witnessed a continual onslaught and counter-onslaught of devices. The audibility-corridor was vastly wider that that of sight; the many-pitched din, even through left ear in helm, was considerable.

'Computer-sent, must be,' said H's transceiver into his right ear. No sigil preceded this statement, but H knew the tones of B, his next-up, who in any case could be seen a metre away saying it, in the large concrete bubble whence they watched, using a plaspex window and an infra-red northviewer with a range of some hundreds of metres forward. His next-up had been in the bunker for three minutes, apparently overchecking, probably for an appreciation to two-up who might be in station VV now.

'Else how can they get minute-ly impacts here, you mean?' said H.

'Well, of course it could be long-range low-frequency – we don't really know how Time works over There.'

'But if the conceleration runs asymptotically to the Frontier, as it should if Their Time works in mirror-image, would anything ever have got over?'

'Doesn't have to, far's I can see – maybe it steepens a lot, then just falls back at the same angle the other Side,' said B's voice; 'anyway, I didn't come to talk science: I've news for you, if we hold out the next few seconds here: you're Relieved.'

H felt a black inner sight-barrier beginning to engulf him, and a roaring in his ears swallowed up the noise of the bombardment. He bent double as his knees began to buckle, and regained full consciousness. He could see his replacement now, an uncertain-looking figure in prot-suit (like everybody else up here) at the far side of the bunker.

'XN 3, what orders then?' he said crisply, his pulse accelerating.

'XN 2: pick em-kit now, repeat now, rockets 3333 to VV, present tag' – holding out a luminous orange label printed with a few coarse black characters – 'and proceed as ordered thence.'

H stuck up his right thumb from his fist held sideways at elbow length, in salute. It was no situation for facial gestures or unnecessary speech. 'XN 3, yes, em-kit, 3333 rocket, tag' (he had taken it in his left glove) 'and VV orders; parting!'

He missed B's nod as he skimmed on soles to the exit, grabbed a small bundle hanging (one of fifteen) from the fourth hook along, slid down the greasy slide under ground ten metres to a fuel-cell-lit cavern, pressed a luminous button in the wall, watched a lit symbol passing a series of marks, jumped into the low 'car' as it ground round the corner, and curled up foetuswise. His weight having set off the car-door mechanism, the car shut, slipped down and (its clamps settling on H's body) roared off down the chute.

Twenty-five seconds after his 'parting' word H uncurled at the forward receiver cell of station VV nearly half a mile downslope. He crawled out as the rocket ground off again, walked ten steps onward in this larger version of his northward habitat, saluted thumb-up and presented his tag to two-up (recognized from helm-tint and helm-sign), saying simultaneously, 'XN 3 rep, Relieved.'

'XN 1 to XN 3: take this' (holding out a similar orange tag plucked from his pocket) 'and take rocktrain down, in – 70 seconds. By the way, ever seen a prehis?'

'No, sir.'

'Spot through here, then; look like pteros but more primitive.'

The infra-red telescopic viewer looking northwest passed through the forward sight-barrier which due north was about forty metres away here; well upslope yet still well clear of the dark infra-red-radiation barrier could be seen, soundlessly screaming and yammering, two scaly animals about the size of large dogs, but with two legs and heavy wings, flopping around a hump or boulder on the rock. They might have been hit on their way along, and could hardly have had any business on that barren spot, H thought.

'Thanks; odd,' he said. Seven seconds of the seventy had gone. He pulled out a squirter-cup from the wall and took a drink from the machine, through his helm. Seventeen seconds gone, fifty-three to go.

'XN 1 to XN 3: how are things up there?'

Naturally a report was called for: XN 2 might never return, and communication up-time and down-time was nearly impossible at these latitudes over more than a few metres.

'XN 3. Things have been hotting up all day; I'm afraid a burst through may be attempted in the next hour or so – only my guess, of course. But I've never seen anything like it all this time up here. I suppose you'll have noticed it in VV too?'

'XN 1, thanks for report,' was all the answer he got. But he could hear for himself that the blitz was much more intense than any he had known at this level either.

Only twenty-seven seconds remained. He saluted and strode off across the bunker with his em-kit and the new tag. He showed the tag to the guard, who stamped it and pointed wordlessly down a corridor. H ran down this, arriving many metres down the far end at a little gallery. An underslung rail-guided vehicle with slide-doors opening into cubicles glided quietly alongside. A gallery-guard waved as H and two others waiting opened doors whose indicators were unlit, the doors slid to, and H found himself gently clamped in on a back-tilted seat as the rocktrain accelerated downhill. After ten seconds it stopped at the next checkhalt, a panel in the cubicle ceiling lit up to state 'DIVERSION, LEFT', presumably because the direct route had been destroyed. The train now appeared to accelerate but more gently, swung away to left (as H could feel), and stopped at two more checkhalts before swinging back to right and finally decelerating, coming to rest and opening some 480 seconds after its start, by Had's personal chronograph, instead of the 200 he had expected.

At this point daylight could again be seen. From the top bunker where XN 2 had discharged him, Had had now gone some ten miles south and nearly three thousand metres down, not counting detours. The forward sight-barrier here was hidden by a shoulder of mountain covered in giant lichen, but the southern barrier was evident as a violet-black fog-wall a quarter of a mile off. Lichens and some sort of grass-like vegetation covered much of the neighbouring landscape, a series of hollows and ravines. Noise of war was still audible, mingled with that of a storm, but nearby crashes were not frequent and comparatively little damage could be seen. The sky overhead was turbulent. Some very odd-looking animals, perhaps between a lizard and a stoat in general appearance, were swarming up and down a tree-fern near by. Six men in all got out of the rocktrain, besides Had. Two and three marched off in two groups down a track eastward. One (not one of those who had got in at VV) stayed with Had.

'I'm going down to the Great Valley; haven't seen it for twenty days; everything'll be changed. Are you sent far?' said the other man's voice in Had's right ear through the transceiver.

'I – I – I'm Relieved,' tried Had uncertainly.

'Well I'm ... disintegrated!' was all the other man could manage. Then, after a minute, 'Where will you go?'

'Set up a business way south, I think. Heat is what suits me, heat and vegetation. I have a few techniques I could put to good use in management of one sort or another. I'm sorry – I never meant to plume it over you with this – but you did ask me.'

'That's all right. You certainly must have Luck, though. I never met a man who was Relieved. Make good use of it, won't you. It helps to make the Game worth while, up here – I mean, to have met a man who is joining all those others we're supposed to be protecting – it makes them real to us in a way.'

'Very fine of you to take it that way,' said Had.

'No – I mean it. Otherwise we'd wonder if there *was* any people to hold the Front for.'

'Well, if there weren't, how'd the techniques have developed for holding on up here?' put in Had.

'Some of the Teccols I remember in the Great Valley might have developed enough techniques for that.'

'Yes, but think of all the pure science you need to work up the techniques from; I doubt if that could have been studied inside the Valley Teccols.'

'Possibly not – that's a bit beyond me,' said the other's voice a trifle huffily, and they stood on in silence till the next cable-car came up and round at the foot of the station. Had let the man get in it – he felt he owed him that – and a minute later (five seconds only, up in his first bunker, he suddenly thought ironically and parenthetically) the next car appeared. He swung himself in just as a very queer-looking purple bird with a long bare neck alighted on the stoat-lizards' tree-fern. The cable-car sped down above the ravines and hollows, the violet southern curtain backing still more swiftly away from it. As the time-gradient became less steep his brain began to function better and a sense of well-being and meaningfulness grew in him. The car's speed slackened.

Had was glad he still wore his prot-suit when a couple of chemical explosions burst close to the cable line, presumably by chance, only fifty metres below him. He was even more glad of it when flying material from a third broke the cable itself well downslope and the emergency cable stopped him at the next pylon. He slid down the pylon's lift and spoke with his transceiver close to the telephone at the foot. He was told to make west two miles to the next cable-car line. His interlocutor, he supposed, must be speaking from an exchange more or less on the same latitude as that of his pylon, since communication even here was still almost impossible north-south except at ranges of some metres. Even so, there was a squeaky sound about the other voice and its speech came out clipped and rapid. He supposed his own voice would sound gruff and drawled to the other.

Using his 'walker', he picked his way across ravines and gullies, steering by compass and watching the sight-barriers and the Doppler tint-equator ahead for yawing. 'All very well for that man to talk about Teccols,' he thought, 'but he must realize that no civilization could have evolved from anywhere as far north as the Great Valley: it's far too young to have even evolved Men by itself – at least at this end; I'm not sure how far south the eastern end goes.'

The journey was not without its hazards: there were several nearby explosions, and what looked like a suspicious artificial miasma, easily overlooked, lay in two hollows which he decided to go round. Moreover, an enraged giant bear-sloth came at him in a mauve shrub-thicket and had to be eliminated with his quick-gun. But to one who had just come down from that mountain-hell all this seemed like a pleasant stroll.

Finally he came upon the line of pylons and pressed the telephone button at the foot of the nearest, after checking that its latitude-number was nearly right. The same voice, a little less outlandish and rapid, told him a car would arrive in three-quarters of a minute and would be arranged to stop at his pylon; if it did not, he was to press the emergency button near by. Despite his 'walker', nearly an hour had gone by since he set out by it. Perhaps ninety minutes had passed since he first left the top bunker – well over a minute and a half of their time there.

The car came and stopped, he scrambled up and in, and this time the journey passed without incident, except for occasional sudden squalls, and the passage of flocks of nervous crows, until the car arrived at its terminus, a squat tower on the heathy slopes. The car below was coming up, and a man in it called through his transceiver as they crept past each other. 'First of a bunch!' Sure enough the terminus interior was filled with some twenty men all equipped – almost enough to have warranted sending them up by polyheli, thought Hadol, rather than wait for cars at long intervals. They looked excited and not at all cast down, but Hadol refrained from giving away his future. He passed on to the ratchet-car way and found himself one of a group of men more curious about the landscape than about their fellows. A deep reddish curtain of indeterminate thickness absorbed the shoulders of the heights about a quarter-mile northward, and the bluish fog terminated the view over the valley at nearly half a mile southward, but between the two the latitudinal zone was tolerably clear and devoid of obvious signs of war. Forests of pine and lower down of oak and ash covered the slopes, until finally these disappeared in the steepening edge of the Great Valley, whose meadows could however be glimpsed past the bluff. Swirling cloud-shadows played over the ground, skirts and tassels of rain and hail swept across it, and there was the occasional flash and rumble of a storm. Deer could be seen briefly here and there, and dense clouds of gnats danced above the trees.

A journey of some fifty minutes took them down, past two empty stations, through two looped tunnels and among waterfalls and under cliffs where squirrels leapt across from dangling root to root, through a steadily warmer and warmer air to the pastures and cornfields of the Great Valley, where a narrow village of concrete huts and wooden cabins, Emmel, nestled on a knoll above the winding river, and a great road ran straight to the east, parallel to a railway. The river was not, indeed, large here – a shallow, stony but attractive stream, and the Great Valley (all of whose breadth could now be seen) was at this western point no more than a third of a mile across. The southward slopes terminating the North-Western Plateau, now themselves visible, were rich in shrubland.

The utter contrast with what was going on above and, in top bunker time, perhaps four minutes ago, made Hadolar nearly drunk with enjoyment. However, he presented his luminous tag and had it (and his permanent checktab) checked for radiation, countersigned and stamped by the guard commander at the military terminal. The detachable piece at the end of the tag was given back to him to be slipped into the identity disc which was, as always, let into a slot in one of his ribs; the other portion was filed away. He got out of his prot-suit and 'walker', gave up his gun, ammunition and em-kit, was given two wallets of one thousand credit tokens each and a temporary civsuit. An orderly achieved the identity-disc operation. The whole ceremony from his arrival took 250 seconds flat – two seconds up in the top bunker. He walked out like an heir to the earth.

The air was full of scents of hay, berries, flowers, manure. He took intoxicated gulps of it. At the freshouse he ordered, paid for, and drank four decis of light ale, then ordered a sandwich and an apple, paid and ate. The next train east, he was told, would be in a quarter of an hour. He had been in the place perhaps half an hour. No time to spend watching the stream, but he walked to the railhead, asked for a ticket to Veruam by the Sea some 400 miles east and, as the detailed station map showed him, about 30 miles south, paid, and selected a compartment when the train arrived from its shed.

A farm girl and a sleepy-looking male civilian, probably an army contractor, got in one after the other close behind Hadolar, and the compartment contained just these three when the train left. He looked at the farm girl with interest – she was blonde and placid – as the first female he had seen for a hundred days. Fashions had not changed radically in thirty-odd years, at least among Emmel farm-girls. After a while he averted his gaze and considered the landscape. The valley was edged by bluffs of yellowish stone now to north and now to south. Even here their difference in hue was perceptible – the valley had broadened slightly; or perhaps he was being fanciful and the difference was due solely to normal light-effects. The river meandered gracefully from side to side and from cliff to cliff, with occasional islands, small and crowned with hazel. Here and there a fisher could be seen by the bank, or wading in the stream. Farm houses passed at intervals. North above the valley rose the great slopes, apparently devoid of signs of human life except for funicular stations and the occasional heliport, until they vanished into the vast crimson-bronze curtain of nothingness which grew insensibly out of a half cloud-covered green sky near the zenith. Swirls of whirlwind among the clouds told of the effects of the time-gradient on weather, and odd lightning-streaks, unnoticed further north amid the war, appeared to pirouette among them. To the south the plateau was still hidden by the height of the bluffs, but the beginnings of the dark blue haze grew out of the sky above the valley skyline. The train stopped at a station and the girl, Hadolar saw with a pang, got out. Two soldiers got in in light dress and swapped minor reminiscences: they were on short-term leave to the next stop, a small town, Granev, and eyed Hadolar's temporary suit but said nothing.

Granev was mostly built of steel and glass: not an exciting place. It made a one-block twenty-storey five-mile strip on either side of the road, with over-pass-canopy. (How lucky, thought Hadolar, that speech and travel could go so far down this Great Valley without interlatitude problems: virtually the whole 450 miles.) Industry and some of the Teccols now appeared. The valley had broadened until, from the line, its southern cliffs began to drown in the blue haze half a mile off. Soon the northern slopes loomed a smoky ruddy brown before they, too, were swallowed up. The river, swollen by tributaries, was a few hundred metres across now and deep whenever the line crossed it. So far they had only gone fifty-odd miles. The air was warmer again and the vegetation more lush. Almost all the passengers were civilians now, and some noted Hadolar's temporary suit ironically. He would buy himself a wardrobe at Veruam at the first opportunity, he decided. But at the moment he wished to put as many miles as possible between himself and that bunker in the shortest personal time.

*

Some hours later the train arrived at Veruam by the North-Eastern Sea. Thirty miles long, forty storeys high, and five hundred metres broad north-south, it was an imposing city. Nothing but plain was to be seen in the outskirts, for the reddish fog still obliterated everything about four miles to the north, and the bluish one smothered the view southward some seven. A well-fed Hadolaris visited one of the city's Rehabilitation Advisors, for civilian techniques and material resources had advanced enormously since his last acquaintance with them, and idioms and speech-sounds had changed bewilderingly, while the whole code of social behaviour was terrifyingly different. Armed with some manuals, a pocket recorder, and some standard speechform and folkway tapes, he rapidly purchased thin clothing, storm-wear, writing implements, further recording tools, lugbags and other personal gear. After a night at a good guestery, Hadolaris sought interviews with the employing offices of seven sub-tropical development agencies, was tested and, armed with seven letters of introduction, boarded the night liner rocktrain for the south past the shore of the North-Eastern Sea and to Oluluetang some 360 miles south. One of the tailors who had fitted him up had revealed that on quiet nights very low-pitched rumblings were to be heard from, presumably, the mountains northward. Hadolaris wanted to get as far from that North as he conveniently could.

He awoke among palms and savannah-reeds. There was no sign of either sight-barrier down here. The city was dispersed into compact blocks of multistorey buildings, blocks separated by belts of rich woodland and drive-like roadways and monorails. Unlike the towns of the Great Valley, it was not arranged on an east-west strip, though its north-south axis was still relatively short. Hadolarisóndamo found himself a small guestery, studied a plan of the city and its factory areas, bought a guide to the district and settled down to several days of exploration and inquiry before visiting the seven agencies themselves. His evenings were spent in adult classes, his night absorbing the speech-form recordings unconsciously in sleep. In the end after nineteen days (about four hours at Veruam's latitude, four minutes at that of Emmel, less than two seconds at the higher bunker, he reflected) he obtained employment as a minor sales manager of vegetable products in one of the organizations.

Communication north and south, he found, was possible verbally for quite a number of miles, provided one knew the rules. In consequence the zoning here was far from severe and travel and social facilities covered a very wide area. One rarely saw the military here. Hadolarisóndamo bought an automob and, as he rose in the organization's hierarchy, a second one for pleasure. He found himself well liked and soon had a circle of friends and a number of hobbies. After a number of love-affairs he married a girl whose father was higher up in the organization, and, some five years after his arrival in the city, became the father of a boy.

'Arison!' called his wife from the boat. Their son, aged five, was puttering at the warm surface of the lake with his fists over the gunwale. Hadolarisón-damo was painting on the little island, quick lines and sweeps across the easelled canvas, a pattern of light and shade bursting out of the swamp trees over a little bay. 'Arison! I can't get this thing to start. Could you swim over and try?'

'Five minutes more, Mihányo. Must get this down.'

Sighing, Karamihanyolàsve continued, but without much hope, to fish from the bows with her horizontal yo-yo gadget. Too quiet round here for a bite. A parakeet flashed in the branches to right. Deresto, the boy, stopped hitting the water, and pulled over the tube-windows, let it into the lake and got Mihányo to slide on its lightswitch. Then he peered this way and that under the surface, giving little exclamations as tiny fish of various shapes and hues shot across. Presently Arison called over, folded up his easel, pulled off his trousers, propped paints and canvas on top of everything, and swam over. There were no crocs in this lake, hippo were far off, filariasis and bilharzia had been eliminated here. Twenty minutes' rather tense tinkering got things going, and the silent fuel-cell driven screw was ready to pilot them over to the painting island and thence across the lake to where a little stream's current pushed out into the expanse. They caught four. Presently back under the westering sun to the jetty, tie-up and home in the automob.

By the time Deresto was eight and ready to be formally named Lafondere-stónami, he had a sister of three and a baby brother of one. He was a keen swimmer and boatman, and was developing into a minor organizer, both at home and in school. Arison was now third in the firm, but kept his balance. Holidays were spent either in the deep tropics (where one could gain on the time-exchange) or among the promontories on the southern shore of the North-Eastern Sea (where one had to lose), or, increasingly, in the agricultural stream-scored western uplands, where a wide vista of the world could in many areas be seen and the cloudscapes had full play. Even there the sight-barriers were a mere fogginess near the north and south horizons, backed by a darkness in the sky.

Now and then, during a bad night, Arison thought about the 'past'. He generally concluded that, even if a breakthrough had been imminent in, say, half an hour from his departure, this could hardly affect the lives of himself and his wife, or even of their children, down here in the south, in view of the time-contraction southwards. Also, he reflected, since nothing ever struck further south than a point north of Emmel's latitude, the ballistic attacks must be mounted close to the Frontier; or if they were not, then the Enemy must lack all knowledge of either southern time-gradients or southern geography, so that the launching of missiles from well north of the Frontier to pass well south of it would not be worth while. And even the fastest heli which could be piloted against time conceleration would, he supposed, never get through.

Always adaptable, Arison had never suffered long from the disabilities incident on having returned after a time at the Front. Rocktrain travel and other communications had tended to unify the speech and the ethos, though naturally the upper reaches of the Great Valley and the military zone in the mountains of the North were linguistically and sociologically somewhat isolated. In the western uplands, too, pockets of older linguistic forms and old-fashioned attitudes still remained, as the family found on its holidays. By and large, however, the whole land spoke the tongue of the 'contemporary' subtropical lowlands, inevitably modified of course by the onomatosyntomy or 'shortmouth' of latitude. A 'contemporary' ethical and social code had also spread. The southern present may be said to have colonized the northern past, even geological past, somewhat as the birds and other travelling animals had done, but with the greater resources of human wits, flexibility, traditions and techniques.

Ordinary people bothered little about the war. Time conceleration was on their side. Their spare mental energies were spent in a vast selection of plays and ploys, making, representing, creating, relishing, criticizing, theorizing, discussing, arranging, organizing, co-operating, but not so often out of their own zone. Arison found himself the member of a dozen interweaving circles, and Mihányo was even more involved. Not that they were never alone: the easy tempo of work and life with double 'week' of five days' work, two days free, seven days' work and six days free, the whole staggered across the population and in the organizations, left much leisure time which could be spent on their own selves. Arison took up texture-sculpting, then returned after two years to painting, but with magneto-brush instead of spraypen; purified by his texture-sculpting period, he achieved a powerful area control and won something of a name for himself. Mihányo, on the other hand, became a musician. Deresto, it was evident, was going to be a handler of men and societies, besides having, at thirteen, entered the athletic age. His sister of eight was a great talker and arguer. The boy of six was, they hoped, going to be a writer, at least in his spare time: he had a keen eye for things, and a keen interesting in telling about them. Arison was content to remain, when he had reached it, second in the firm: a chiefship would have told on him too much. He occasionally lent his voice to the administration of local affairs, but took no major part.

Mihányo and Arison were watching a firework festival on the North-Eastern Sea from their launch, off one of the southern promontories. Up here, a fine velvety backdrop for the display was made by the inky black of the northern sight-barrier, which cut off the stars in a gigantic arc. Fortunately the weather was fine. The silhouettes of the firework boats could just be discerned. In a world which knew no moon the pleasures of a 'white night' were often only to be got by such displays. The girl and Deresto were swimming round and round the launch. Even the small boy had been brought out, and was rather blearily staring northward. Eventually the triple green star went up and the exhibition was over; at the firework boats a midnight had been reached. Deresto and Venoyyè were called in, located by a flare, and ultimately prevailed on to climb in, shivering slightly, and dry off in the hot-air blaster, dancing about like two imps. Arison turned the launch for the shore and Silarrè was found to be asleep. So was Venoyyè when they touched the jetty. Their parents had each to carry one in and up to the beach-house.

Next morning they packed and set out in the automob for home. Their twenty days' holiday had cost 160 days of Oluluetang time. Heavy rain was falling when they reached the city. Mihányo, when the children were settled in, had a long talk on the opsiphone with her friend across the breadth of Oluluetang: she (the friend) had been with her husband badger-watching in the western uplands. Finally Arison chipped in and, after general conversation, exchanged some views with the husband on developments in local politics.

'Pity one grows old so fast down here,' lamented Mihányo that evening; 'if only life could go on for ever!'

'For ever is a big word. Besides, being down here makes no difference to the feeling – you don't feel it any slower up on the Sea, do you, now?'

'I suppose not. But if only ... '

To switch her mood, Arison began to talk about Deresto and his future. Soon they were planning their children's lives for them in the way parents cannot resist doing. With his salary and investments in the firm they would set up the boy for a great administrator, and still have enough to give the others every opportunity.

Next morning it was still in something of a glow that Arison bade farewell to his wife and went off to take up his work in the offices. He had an extremely busy day and was coming out of the gates in the waning light to his automob in its stall, when he found standing round it three of the military. He looked inquiringly at them as he approached with his personal pulse-key in hand.

'You are VSQ 389 MLD 194 RV 27 XN 3, known as Hadolarisóndamo, resident at' (naming the address) 'and subpresident today in this firm.' The cold tones of the leader were a statement, not a question.

'Yes,' whispered Arison as soon as he could speak.

'I have a warrant for your immediate re-employment with our forces in the place at which you first received your order for Release. You must come with us forthwith.' The leader produced a luminous orange tag with black markings.

'But my wife and family!'

'They are being informed. We have no time.'

'My firm?'

'Your chief is being informed. Come now.'

'I – I – I must set my affairs in order.'

'Impossible. No time. Urgent situation. Your family and firm must do all that between them. Our orders override everything.'

'Wh – wh – what is your authority? Can I see it please?'

'This tag should suffice. It corresponds to the tagend which I hope you still have in your identity disc – we will check all that en route. Come on now.'

'But I *must* see your authority, how do I know, for instance, that you are not trying to rob me, or something?'

'If you know the code you'll realize that these symbols can only fit one situation. But I'll stretch a point: you may look at this warrant, but don't touch it.'

The other two closed in. Arison saw that they had their quickguns trained on him. The leader pulled out a broad screed. Arison, as well as the dancing characters would let him, resolved them in the light of the leader's torch into an order to collect him, Arison, by today at such and such a time, local Time, if possible immediately on his leaving his place of work (specified); and below, that one man be detailed to call Mihányo by opsiphone simultaneously, and another to call the president of the organization. The Remployee and escort to join the military rocktrain to Veruam (which was leaving within about fifteen minutes). The Remployee to be taken as expeditiously as possible to the bunker (VV) and thence to the higher bunker (from which he had come some twenty years before, but only about ten minutes in the Time of that bunker, it flashed through Arison's brain – apart from six or seven minutes corresponding to his journey south).

'How do they know I'm fit enough for this job after all these years?'

'They've kept checks on you, no doubt.'

Arison thought of tripping one and slugging two and doing a bolt, but the quickguns of the two were certainly trained upon him. Besides, what would that gain him? A few hours' start, with unnecessary pain, disgrace and ruin on Mihányo, his children and himself, for he was sure to be caught.

'The automob,' he said ridiculously.

'A small matter. Your firm will deal with that.'

'How can I settle my children's future?'

'Come on, no use arguing. You are coming now, alive or dead, fit or unfit.'

Speechless, Arison let himself be marched off to a light military vehicle.

In five minutes he was in the rocktrain, an armoured affair with strong windows. In ten more minutes, with the train moving off, he was stripped of his civilian clothes and possessions (to be returned later to his wife, he learnt), had his identity disc extracted and checked and its Relief tagend removed, and a medical checkup was begun on him. Apparently this was satisfactory to the military authorities. He was given military clothing.

He spent a sleepless night in the train trying to work out what he had done with *this*, what would be made of *that*, who Mihányo could call upon in need, who would be likely to help her, how she would manage with the children, what (as nearly as he could work it out) they would get from a pension which he was led to understand would be forthcoming from his firm, how far they could carry on with their expected future.

A grey pre-dawn saw the train's arrival at Veruam. Foodless (he had been unable to eat any of the rations) and without sleep, he gazed vacantly at the marshalling-yards. The body of men travelling on the train (apparently only a few were Remployees) were got into closed trucks and the long convoy set out for Emmel.

At this moment Hadolaris' brain began to re-register the conceleration situation. About half a minute must have passed since his departure from Oluluetang, he supposed, in the Time of his top bunker. The journey to Emmel might take up another two minutes. The route from Emmel to that bunker might take a further two and a half minutes there, as far as one could work out the calculus. Add the twenty-years' (and southward journey's) sixteen to seventeen minutes, and he would find himself in that bunker not more than some twenty-two minutes after he had left it. (Mihan, Deres and the other two would all be nearly ten years older and the children would have begun to forget him). The blitz was unprecedentedly intense when he had left, and he could recall (indeed it had figured in several nightmares since) his prophecy to XN 1 that a breakthrough might be expected within the hour. If he survived the blitz, he was unlikely to survive a breakthrough; and a breakthrough of what? No one had ever seen the Enemy, this Enemy that for Time immemorial had been striving to get across the Frontier. If it got right over, the twilight of the race was at hand. No horror, it was believed at the Front, could equal the horror of that moment. After a hundred miles or so he slept, from pure exhaustion, sitting up in a cramped position, wedged against the next man. Stops and starts and swerves woke him at intervals. The convoy was driving at maximum speeds.

At Emmel he stumbled out to find a storm lashing down. The river was in spate. The column was marched to the depot. Hadolar was separated out and taken in to the terminal building where he was given inoculations, issued with 'walker', quickgun, em-kit, prot-suit and other impedimenta, and in a quarter of an hour (perhaps seven or eight seconds up at the top bunker) found himself entering a polyheli with thirty other men. This had barely topped the first rise and into sunlight when explosions and flarings were visible on all sides. The machine forged on, the sight-curtains gradually closing up behind and retreating grudgingly before it. The old Northern vertigo and somnambulism re-engulfed Had. To think of Kar and their offspring now as to tap the agony of a ghost who shared his brain and body. After twenty-five minutes they landed close to the foot of a rocktrain line. The top-bunker lapse of 'twenty-two minutes' was going, Had saw, to be something less. He was the third to be bundled into the rocktrain compartments, and 190 seconds saw him emerging at the top and heading for bunker VN. XN 1 greeted his salute merely with a curt command to proceed by rocket to the top bunker. A few moments more and he was facing XN 2.

'Ah, here you are. Your Relief was killed so we sent back for you. You'd only left a few seconds.' A ragged hole in the bunker wall testified to the incident. The relief's cadaver, stripped, was being carted off to the disposal machine.

'XN 2. Things are livelier than ever. They certainly are hot stuff. Every new offensive from here is pitched back at us in the same style within minutes, I notice. That new cannon had only just started up when back came the same shells – I never knew They had them. Tit for tat.'

Into H's brain, seemingly clarified by hunger and exhaustion and much emotion, flashed an unspeakable suspicion, one that he could never prove or disprove, having too little knowledge and experience, too little overall view. No one had ever seen the Enemy. No one knew how or when the War had begun. Information and communication were paralysingly difficult up here. No one knew what really happened to Time as one came close to the Frontier, or beyond it. Could it be that the conceleration there became infinite and that there was nothing beyond the Frontier? Could all the supposed missiles of the Enemy be their own, somehow returning? Perhaps the war had started with a peasant explorer light-heartedly flinging a stone northwards, which returned and struck him? Perhaps there was, then, no Enemy?

'XN 3. Couldn't that gun's own shells be reflected back *from* the Frontier, then?'

'XN 2. Impossible. Now you are to try to reach that forward missile post by the surface – our tunnel is destroyed – at 15° 40′ East – you can just see the hump near the edge of the I/R viewer's limit – with this message; and tell him verbally to treble output.'

The ragged hole was too small. H left by the forward port. He ran, on his 'walker', into a ribbon of landscape which became a thicket of fire, a porcupine of fire, a Nessus-shirt to the Earth, as in a dream. Into an unbelievable supercrescendo of sound, light, heat, pressure and impacts he ran, on and on up the now almost invisible slope....

A Landscape of Shallows
CHRISTOPHER FINCH

The casa-media complex spreads over hundreds of square miles – a low density spread of sun-bleached suburbs and neon boulevards, the whole fringed with surf and mountains, studded with sub-tropical vegetation and knit together by a system of freeways as elaborate as a computer circuit. Motels, lidos, campuses and space projects co-exist in an atmosphere of faintly menacing nostalgia. Already the Arabs have proliferated more than 200 names to describe the smog which fuses with the drifting spray blown off Atlantic breakers: euphoric emptiness/the dreamer/moist fatigue-gilded promenade – these are a few that I have noted.

Submerged meanings proliferate in this city which is a landscape of shadows.

Drover woke from a dream in which he had loved a dead (and minor) goddess of the screen. Shadows moved across the façades of the white towers that encircled the sea. Already, in the morning light, surfers in transparent wet-suits crouched on their glinting boards, shifting direction along translucent crests. At frequent intervals the big jets skimmed in across the mist like the phantoms of some lost Homeric race.

The room was large and cool: a late exercise – like the entire hotel – in Moorish art nouveau. The floor was tiled and a tall window (capped with elaborate stucco work) opened on to a stone balcony. Once this hotel had been the city's star establishment – outside, that is, of the *quartier reservé*. An earlier visitor had described its corridors as being full of perfume as a Caid's palace; in those days ash trays packed with cedar shavings had been placed in these corridors and the smouldering wood had been responsible for that aromatic sub-climate. Now the main arteries of the hotel smelled faintly, but not offensively, of disinfectant. The furnishings were of painted steel and chrome tubing in a Hollywood colonial style. The bedside lamp was an elegant Brancusi mutation. The room faced out across Place Mahommed, overlooking the old medina and the docks. Above the rooftops a narrow strip of ocean (swarming with restless hammerheads) could be seen, cut into segments by a network of minarets and cranes. It was autumn but the rickety balconies of the medina and its lines of washing were distorted by heat haze. Immediately below the window a taxi rank obeyed the laws of Heraclitus –

seeming to be always the same synthesis of obsolescent Cadillacs but in fact constantly changing, subject (like the whole city) to the chemistry of urban metabolism. A colony of scarabs shared the room with Drover and at dusk thousands of tiny birds threw themselves into a frenzy among the trees outside his window. Beyond the trees – on a huge hoarding – a gauntlet of prismatic gas singled out the masked figure of a young woman.

Drover strolled along a pavement lined with date palms: the smog was luminous today. Five minutes brought him to the intersection at which his car – an old black Chrysler, caked with dust – was parked. He headed out through the neo-Egyptian masonry of the inner suburbs, then the Chrysler, like some heraldic beast, sped among the mansions of Anfa, where orchids and bougain villaea turned the roofs into efflorescent domes. At the crest of the hill Drover caught a glimpse of sea, sparkling through the bluish vapour. The news bulletin informed him it was eleven-thirty.

Hitting the coast at Ain Diab, Drover pulled into the nearest filling station.

AMARYLLIS

Six foot plus of nickeled grille and fender reflecting sky and coloured slogans. Between sets of twin headlamps and following the vee of the radiator profile, a red fluted bar terminating in the legend *Gran Sport*. Red-wall tyres; crimson rally-stripes and hood-scoops laid on blue-metallic trim. This much Drover could make out as the water was wiped from the windscreen in front of him. A semi-customised Buick. The girl beside the car was tall, dressed in a shift of translucent silk, bending towards the wing-mirror critically. Nice legs that could be seen from near the stocking tops and small feet pushed into 300 francs worth of cobra skin. A chauffeur sat behind the wheel – low in a black shiny bucket-seat. He wore a red linen jacket cut like a blazer with white buttons; blue tinted glasses shaded by a red peaked cap. Drover lit a cigarette. It was cool there in the car-wash bay but out beyond the autoroute a ribbon of suburban villas shimmered through the heat haze. As girls in blue bikinis polished Drover's Chrysler a mechanic moved round to the other side of the Buick; the chauffeur handed him some coins and started the motor. The tall girl climbed in, showing a good deal more leg. The motor idled for a few seconds while the girl checked her eyes once more in the driving mirror, then the Buick nosed off the forecourt and on to the autoroute. There was not much traffic about and Drover was soon able to pull within a hundred yards of the Buick; he followed it up a cloverleaf on to the overhead freeway that ran parallel with the old coast highway towards El Jadida.

(Styling details vary a good deal, but taking automobile design as a whole there is a marked trend towards longer, lower, sportier lines. Cars will feature concealed headlights and some will sport racy, bubble-like flares in the fenders around the wheels. Much of the excitement will be induced by three brand-new name-plates scheduled for introduction during the coming model year.

A preliminary finding: nothing less than an electrical force 400,000 times greater than the Earth's magnetic field will stall a car.)

The sea was blue, shifting to indigo. Below Drover now, spreading along the 200-yard strip that separated the freeway from the ocean's edge, was a bidonville – an Arab shanty town built from oil-cans, driftwood, corrugated iron. The entire population of the settlement seemed to be gathered on the shore, looking out to sea. This had caught the attention of the occupants of the Buick. Their coupé – glinting in the sunlight – turned off at the next feeder road and doubled back along the coast, following the old highway. Drover pulled up alongside it. 'What's happened?' she asked. Drover shrugged. The chauffeur stayed in the Buick, lighting a cheroot; he didn't seem too interested.

Names were exchanged. Drover. Amaryllis.

Two police officers in white caps and tunics leaned against the bonnet of their patrol car.

'What's happened?'

The nearest officer looked at Drover for several seconds through black lenses.

'Just a drowning.'

The corpse was bobbing in the surf which broke over jagged rocks a hundred yards away. The white robes acted as camouflage. The Arab crowd was quite silent.

'Let's go away from here,' said Amaryllis.

As Drover started the Chrysler's motor a police siren wailed. A van drew up and half a dozen uniformed men leapt out, two of them dragging a heavy net.

CONTACTS
We will at this stage say something about one or two of the ways in which the writer's view on the logic of deduction and the logic of natural science were put together in their complete form.

Drover followed the Buick back on to the freeway and they headed south for half an hour. Ahead of them a chain of snow-capped peaks came into view. Down to the right, along the water's edge, was a line of high-rise apartment blocks. The Buick headed down a cloverleaf on to the old coast road once more, cruising along beside the buildings. Amaryllis signalled for Drover to turn into a parking lot.

Amaryllis lived in a large apartment on the 23rd and 24th floors. The living-room was two storeys high, running from front to back of the building. A mezzanine floor rose from one side of the room. The apartment was furnished with reproduction 'twenties furniture.

An Arab maid brought drinks. Drover sat beside Amaryllis on a white leather sofa.

'What are you doing in Casa?' she asked.

'I'm at the studios.'

'At the studios' . . .

'Delta Studios. Mounting a new campaign.'

Drover pulled a sheaf of papers from his inside pocket and handed them to Amaryllis.

THE ART OF FICTION:
YESTERDAY AND TODAY

PROGRAMME: OZARKS. Flickers. Out of Sight. MEXICO. CASCADE. Photographs & Photographs. Great Errors. KORZYBOKY. Claridges. Encephalograms. Create AN ALTERATION. Maybe the Last Time. 13 Children. Excuse me, there is no accurate description. – it's always imaginary—. Try me.

                            OZARKS: Since we are here concerned/and chiefly with the frontal lobes/ – the lamps, the bridges/and the golden light – /descend therefore/ (to reconstruct that Westward Arkadia/ – ring road to happiness – sculpted by the White and Arkansas/but lost to sight;/above the budding trees/and groves of masonry/the viaduct extends./ Bridges and lamps;/the sky with golden reinforcements./Golden too those shuttered stalls whence steamers connect with Western Isles/and yards/ elaborate/refuse the road) – step down, therefore. . . .

Contact: with a drive through a prolonged winter dusk. Among shadowy trees the melancholy classical echoes of chapels and factories. A red glow of neon across darkening fields.

Contact: with another coast line. Gentle surf breaking against the wind. Ribbons of purple and green water. Ridges of cloud driven across the sky. Long patches of sunlight. Rip tides pulling along the sandbars. A kite. A dog in the shallows. Pavilions and chimneys in the distance.

At some time while he had been unconscious the girl had removed his jacket. Now her hand had slipped inside his shirt; he pulled her head down to him. The girl responded with a low crooning noise. Then she uncovered the aerial belt which he always wore next to his skin. (The feedback principle – as Von Neuman has noted – while it has the appearance of a device for solving implicit relationships is in reality a particularly elegant short-circuited iteration and successive approximation scheme.)

Drover and Amaryllis sat on the cantilevered balcony smoking kif. A blue-grey shadow spread into the sky. The sea shimmered in the after-light. Beyond the breakers a coast-guard helicopter cruised past a few feet above the surface of the water – the sky about to shatter into stars. Familiarising himself once more with this jewelled twilight world, Drover strayed from the old centres of motor activity. Filament of gas traced incandescent patterns through his skull. The girl's appearance changed as he watched her, but that made little difference. She was in place because here she alludes to the bliss of life on Olympus. The floral capitals allude to her as the goddess of all vegetation and as the guarantor of immortality. Finally the superb mixed floral ornament is in place because Virgil tells us that in an era of peace the earth without cultivation will blossom with ivy, valerian, lilies, akanthos and vines. (The desires and courage of the birds engaged in the quest are not equal. The nightingale would content himself with the love of the perishable rose; the parrot only searches for the water of immortality, the peacock only desires the joys of Paradise. The hoopoe always proclaims that the real end is beyond.)

It was 5 a.m. when Drover left the apartment. The streets were deserted except for a girl dressed all in black; the silver zip of her jeans was echoed by a crucifix slung around her neck as she walked through the dawn, hugging herself against the chill breeze. An airline glowed above the low façades over to Drover's right. Palm trees and drooping lamp-standards rose against the curtain-walling of the apartment blocks. Drover reached his car and started the motor, drowning the rhythmic crash of the invisible surf. As he drove north along the freeway the sun rose above the hills and it was soon quite warm. Back at the hotel he slept for two hours, then he dressed, packed and checked out. He loaded his bags into the Chrysler and headed south again, booking into a motel at Clichy Plage. Here he would be within thirty minutes' drive of the town centre, the studios and of Amaryllis. He was given a chalet right on the beach and spent what remained of the morning at his typewriter. A long natural breakwater kept the surf out of Clichy Plage. After lunch Drover swam out as far as the lifeguard station on the point and would have ventured farther, but he was turned back. He returned to the shore, dressed and checked the time. Heading towards the mountains Drover switched the car radio to YBM*Sonic, which, in the interests of safer driving, transmits a 24-hour programme of shifting electronic patterns. (YBM*Sonic provides an axis of stability in the open-plan programme patterns of the radio/TV networks. On other channels audience response is monitored through computerised control points to the studio hardware; the broadcaster thrives on electronic empathy. Instant news is a speciality – select your own world-shattering event and it will be bounced to you off an orbiting satellite. Inert viewers can have their scanning patterns respond to encephalogram readings. Situation comedies are computed from life while law-breaking and enforcement are integral with the communications system. The broadcaster serves as a prism.) Drover headed towards the mountains in this landscape where transport was a recognised art form. A sign warned him that he was approaching Faubourg Castaly. He swung down the cloverleaf towards the already familiar ribbon of apartments blocks.

Amaryllis was waiting. She wore a shorts suit of yellow satin with a long white zip fastening. She looked sixteen.

'Ready?' asked Drover. 'We'll head straight for the studios.'

Amaryllis spoke of the future – her voice like snow on a summer day.

DAWNS OF PLASTIC MEMORY

Delta Studios occupies several thousand acres of semi-desert on the eastern edge of the city. Around a tight complex of administration buildings, huge pneumatic tents – translucent and resembling giant conservatories – house film-sets, live studios and computer installations.

The Hip Young Scientist slid out of his Orgone Accumulator.

'Call from Monsieur Drovair,' whispered his beautiful French-Lithuanian assistant, sauntering in from the Sauna Bath pavilion. Beneath the nylon overall she was naked. With studied disinterest THYS flicked the switch of a tape machine linked to the telephone. Drover's recorded voice was heard.

'I've been checking the programme. . . . We've been playing it too straight . . . Not getting through those fences. . . . I have a special project in mind. . . . I'm counting on you to accelerate progress.'

The tape machine clicked off. THYS watched flesh move beneath tight nylon.

'Alors?' demanded HBF-LA.

'All right,' shrugged THYS, 'we'll put some skates under his digit pickin' arse.'

He tore a bunch of plugs from a pin-board and replaced them at random.

'Fresh air. That's all he needs.'

To get things moving he fed in some Riemannian equations, then switched the processor on to sense data.

'Now for the narcissistic routine.'

THYS detached the sense data console from its cage and lifted it on to a metal table-top. Lenses and antennae were directed towards a bank of monitors where violet wave patterns already flickered. Watching themselves they became more agitated.

HBF-LA laughed.

Grey codes crackled through jungles of matrix and memory. Undreamed-of emotions built up at buffers, then exploded across the screens in jewelled anarchy.

Life without eyelids.

THYS watched flesh move beneath taut nylon.

Framed by an unwinking monitor, a tiny rag of blue was torn to black nothingness.

'The dawns are heartbreaking.'

Filtered through a bed of silica, new perfumes reached their minds: odours of vine, odours of beer. Grey codes crackled in the skyless jungles of memory. Sauna flesh beneath tight nylon. Orgone explosions monitor THYS.

The overall is fastened by a single narrow zip of colourless plastic. HBF-LA touches the neck. The violet waves dissolve. Magnetic reels click in skyless jungles, releasing zones of semantic melancholy – patterns of colourless vegetation – dawns of plastic memory.

'Filter the routine?'

'No. Scramble it.'

Fastened by a single zip, the overall opens. Odours of vines, odours of sauna flesh advancing through the magnetic jungles. HBF-LA reached for the pinboard – replaced plugs at random. Filtering through undreamed-of buffers THYS watches the colourless vegetation explode across the screens along with balconies and terraces of the machine, releasing dawns of plastic memory. Magnetic reels – magnetic drums – click beneath the taut nylon. Odours of vines, odours of memory advancing through the blue dawns.

'All right ... lay down some more signals.'

Beneath the crisp nylon, odours of Sauna flesh reach their minds. THYS touched the neck. The waves dissolve in zones of colourless memory. Magnetic reels – magnetic drums. The waves dissolve. Odours of Sauna flesh click in skyless jungles. THYS slid his hand beneath the taut nylon. Along the terraces and balconies of the machine unwinking codes tore through jungles of memory and matrix. Semantic anarchy built up at buffers, then exploded in patterns of colourless vegetation.

'Click. Click. Click. Click.'

The girl's stomach curved forward beneath his fingers and as she responded THYS reached out for the console – tapped an elliptic message. Paper tape looped towards memory. Data transformed to uncharted channels, clicked through unfastened memory and returned to the monitors. Orchids of blood flood the screens. Music in the lowest common denominator of modes. Crimson flowers. Operetta of sinister comedy.

A physical necessity along the balconies and terraces.

'Click. Click. Click.'

Crisp nylon crushed against polished console housing. The algebra of memory unfastened. Crimson necessity transferred to uncharted channels.

'Click. Click. Click.'

Orchids of Sauna flesh explode across the screens. Odours of vines, odours of necessity. . . .

CHALCEDON

Then it was time for Amaryllis to ride the waves of the machine. Odours of vine, odours of memory reached her as she paddled out towards the translucent crests of her torpedo of polyurethane, golden shoulders glistening. Then she slid into the gleaming tunnel. The big wipe-out came and darkness cascaded her towards the sandy bottom. She held her breath until she was sure that the rocketing board had hit the water once more. When she reached the surface she found herself in the shallows of a calm sea.

The following morning they sat on the terrace of the Patrice Lumumba café; Amaryllis alert, Drover silent – as though waiting for a message. The white and blue walls of Chalcedon fluttered in the Mediterranean light. They walked to the edge of the town – a no-man's-land where the wilderness began. Streets had been laid out with lamp posts and flowering shrubs but nothing had been built except for a solitary apartment block on a corner here, a church there, a cinema there. Over to their left – towards the beach – the eastern autoroute circled a small filling station, on the forecourt of which half a dozen Arabs watched two others playing chess. Drover and Amaryllis crossed the autoroute where it ran by an overgrown village, then headed north towards the headland on which Al Qasaba stood. Towers of cumulus were building up over to the west. Soon Drover and Amaryllis arrived beneath the crenellated walls of the fortress. A gateway of carved cedar-wood swung open and they entered the gardens. They walked beside a channel of running water edged with orange trees and myrtles. Elsewhere jets arched up from pierced brick paths. St Germain and Mercedes greeted them from a window; an Arab boy led the way through tiled rooms and courtyards to the large reception chamber, which they entered just as the storm broke.

'It won't last.'

St Germain dismissed in advance any suggestion that might be made to the contrary. Bolts of lightning travelled the length of the horizon but, an hour later, the rain had stopped. Amaryllis made her way down to the gardens – where already the paving stones beside the fountains were almost dry. Drover

– alone – found himself in a part of the fortress that had not been rebuilt. A sizeable terrace partially overgrown with scrub, extended to a low wall where Roman pillars supported the remains of delicate moorish arches to which clung a few scraps of intricate stucco-work. Beyond these skeletal windows olive-clad slopes fell away towards rocks which, in turn, dropped sheer to the sea. The horizon was lost in haze. The sun, beating on the back of Drover's skull, became uncomfortable; he retired to the shade of a wall overgrown with wisteria and winter jasmine. He lay down – his body in the sunlight, his head in the shade and cushioned by the soft bulk of some nomadic shrub – the smell of the sea and the acrid odour of crushed vegetation drifting against the walls of consciousness.

'I was awakened in the cool of the evening just before twilight by a voice calling, "Equal is not contrary" ... '

Xavier Malebranche had written those words in his Black Diary during his stay at Al Qasaba almost a century previously.

' ... A handsome servant girl, barefoot and of Ethiopian blood, had been seen sent to me, bringing a bowl of curds which, kneeling, she offered me as I lay on the terrace surrounded by satin cushions.

'"Equal cannot be opposite," I replied – a polite common phrase of thanks. A short skirt, bravely embroidered, made her almost a beauty and in the African dusk she watched me – her big green eyes flecked with golden contradiction. Palm trees and pomegranates were predicated by the shadows. Among substance and shadow a nightingale was singing and the little river nearby murmured, innate like the sense. "Time to seek the principles and causes of existing things," I reflected.'

Drover's mind drifted on to other images: moths/swallows/voile/cranes/ strange Hong Kongs of mist and pantomime/silk/blue look of sea/cotton flowers/richly laden camels ... then back to Malebranche.

'In the high guest chamber which I occupied were two visible heavens and other civilised conveniences. A nightingale still sang in the garden beneath my window as the countess entered, clad only in stockings of green silk and ribbons of ruched purple satin. She was accompanied by that same negro child which had brought me my curds and a huge Turk (known in the household as the Prime Mover). The countess joined me upon the brass four-poster and ordered the Turk to thrash the negress for some imagined crime. The Turk, however, was drunk through intemperance of pleasure and pain and soon was snoring in a corner. I too was weary – exhausted through the receipt of sacrifices – and slid into a languorous coma, ignoring the catatonic advances of the countess. In sleep my consciousness was flooded with sweet images.

'Somewhere in the distance a gong sounded, penetrating my strangely chaste dream. The countess had left my side. Her hands now idle among the velvet folds of the sleeping Turk's voluminous trousers; her eyes, daubed with viridian, were mirrored in the sweat that drenched the vast convexities of the creature's torso. The young negress? Perhaps escaping from the richly laded atmosphere of the room, she leaned on the railings of the balcony. Glass beads dangled from the points of her scarcely formed breasts (an unlikely remnant of I forget which Hellenic custom). Down in the gardens – among the fountains and palms – buttocks flashed in the moonlight; plebian sighs and the smack of colliding flesh mingled with the eternal melodies of water and cicadas. The girl explained that it was the kitchen-maid's night off and indicated her father – an athletic figure – one of a group of men who clustered beneath an ambiguous knot of statuary, amusing themselves while awaiting their respective turns.

'"Extremely handsome," I was able to concede.

'That she appreciated this remark I was able to judge by the sensible evidence which she afforded. Below, among the heaving vegetation, the kitchen-maid sobbed with sudden pleasure. One assailant withdrew and – edged by the crimson frills of an Andaluzian petticoat – I glimpsed a wedge of sable as another body replaced the first. The negress smiled. Apart from the glass beads she wore now only shorts of white cambric; I unfastened these and they slipped down about her thighs. She trembled a little as I touched her.

'"Duende. . . ." she breathed, and I too sighed – though not for pleasure but in recognition of those dark groves of fatalism that surround us (always, since early youth, ethics have been known to invade me in this manner).

'The sounds and odours of the African night restored me to the empirical.

'I asked the girl her name.

'"Noisette . . . " she replied.

'"A pretty name," I murmured, confident that my nakedness did not rob me of an air of breeding. Noisette knelt at my feet and attended to the spectrum of pleasure while I gazed out into the night where my spirit sailed among the spangled galaxies of ontology. My palms rested upon the girl's shaven head. Another sob beside the fountain and a new contender detached himself from the group beneath the statuary – it was the girl's father. The tall, ebony figure – lithe with anticipation – crossed to the panting servant and rolled the plump body over. Noisette watched, leaning on the railings – her back arched, her legs slightly parted. The kitchen-maid uttered brief cries in Spanish and Arabic and Noisette laughed, pulling me towards her.

'The night, the odour of the sea, began to poach upon my consciousness. A final thought drifted into my mind from some vanishing continent of curiosity. What chain of cause and effect ... what ritual of custom carried me to this pitch of inflorescent warmth? Cremorne flares falling through my skull! Induction/inference/syllogisms of identity? Substance/beauty/universals? Noisette's eyes were fixed to the spot where her father's buttocks thrashed rhythmically in the darkness. I abandoned myself to the gardens and the sky, the girl cooed and bucked more violently so that her father and I were both paralysed at the same moment by the silent ecstasy of true poetry (Ah Sappho! Ah Catullus!).

'Noisette watched her father as he washed himself in a fountain; she called out to him and waved naïvely before joining me in the room where the countess was violently at work upon the epic member of the sleeping Turk. Just then the Ottoman's dream achieved an unparalleled peak of infamy and he sent a gleaming jet of yellowish sperm flying towards a crystal chandelier, from which it dripped for some hours to come.'

When he awoke, Drover found himself completely in shadow. There was a slight chill in the air. Somewhere he could hear voices. Drover lay there for a few seconds, shivering, then rose to his feet and stepped into the evening sunlight. The change in temperature was marked. He walked to a projecting part of the terrace – once, no doubt, the site of a look-out tower – which commanded a view westward towards the town and southward into the gardens. Out at sea the haze had cleared; the Mediterranean lay flat and silver. Beyond the town the ruins of Albus could be seen clearly and beyond them the mountains running down to the coast – a flash of pink snow just visible beyond the nearer peaks.

Behind him peacocks strutted on green tiles.

'So – you're awake,' said Mercedes.

Drover turned and followed her into the building.

Dinner was served in a long chamber – smoke rising from candles to the coffered ceiling. A row of cusped windows opened on to the sea and part of the town. Date palms flapped in silhouette against the sodium lamps of the Corniche. At one end of the room was a raised platform. It was on this that they ate. St Germain explained that in the past he had sat with the Emir on this dais while the well of the room was flooded with entertainments.

'It was last put to these uses in the time of Malebranche.'

Now the area was occupied by a mature chaise-longue and a mass of potted vegetation.

St Germain looked into this pleasure area with a trace of nostalgia.

'Pointless to regret the Golden Age,' he sighed. 'Drained of the present any period can be offered as the Golden Age. An historian may point to the slops thrown from windows into gutters choking with rotting garbage – or of the pressures of expansion; but for the favoured mind an Age is the sum of its genius. The inhabitants of Periclean Athens placed the Golden Age centuries before their own time, but for us the Athens of Pericles has become an authentic part of the Golden Age. The genius of Socrates and Aristophanes has survived, whereas the system of slavery and the absurd feuds between Polis and Polis have been committed to oblivion. Can we discuss the genius as fiction? Then there is the genius of childhood – the genius of anonymity – the genius of the future. All these are fragments of the Golden Age. And the Present? Are we to understand the Present as a finger moving through the Universe turning everything it touches – and the substance of the Universe is genius – to matter? Time is concerned only with that which is transitory – that is to say, with *matter* ... with extended matter ... with substance in a state of decay. The Golden Age exists outside of time – it surrounds us and we can choose to live in it by adjusting our attitude to time.'

Depressed by his own speech, St Germain left the room.

At midnight Drover stood on the tiled balcony. The words of Malebranche and St Germain drifted through his mind, their patterns mingling with the chorus of insects in the orange trees. He heard his name called, softly, and looked down to see Mercedes seated in an open car directly below the balcony. Drover descended to the garden and approached the car. Mercedes moved over to let him sit at the wheel. Drover released the handbrake and let the car coast down the gravel drive towards the open gate and the highway beyond.

The Disaster Story
CHARLES PLATT

This is an attempt to isolate and express the ingredients which endow a distinct type of science fiction with unusual appeal.

ESCAPE

So long as I am left free and unharmed in an emptied world, I don't mind what my disaster is. Bacteriological pestilence against which I possess chance immunity ... Armageddon while I cower deep underground ... anything will suffice. My wants are simple: to be free, alone with the world, and no longer trapped in the crawling assembly lines, stagnation where there is no time and every month is identical, where the operations are coded and lack purpose or meaning, and the hot sun slants in and bakes the dark room that has no ceiling, silver light streaming through a vast dusty window and glinting on polished desk tops laid out in military lines.

I will be freed from this, they will not be able to touch me – they, unimaginable, unapproachable, will be gone – and I will find the freedom that men talked of before the disaster.

IMAGES

I will join maggots crawling through tarnished supermarkets and I will feed parasitically on the remains of the Welfare State. In a damaged helicopter I will fly, like some grotesque leather-winged prehistoric bird, over the broken faces of decaying cities: traffic jammed in Paris and rusting into the ground, weathered concrete teeth of New York striking up through grey morning mist. Taking giant steps over the global museum of civilization, halted at the instant of disaster in its inexorable progression and left to die, the images of a previous way of life will fall in on me like melting synthetic snowflakes.

Standing under one corner of the Rockfeller Center, the sweating heat will shimmer and rise around me into the vertical columns of drifting sunlight; the dust on the uneven road surface will be thick around my shoes; cars with faded paint slumped down on flattened tyres, looted stores with their rotting contents strewn on the cracked sidewalks ... Throwing an empty bottle at a plate glass window, I will see its surface split and crash into a background of enveloping, tomb-like silence.

Jumping over rusting automobiles in Detroit, I'll be the only man left, laughing, breaking up the remains of the machinery of technological culture. In a red-plastic-lined restaurant, robot waiters will serve up radioactive food. I will exist and feed on the remnants of the civilization I used to imagine as hanging, ponderous and immense, ready to crush me like a speck of dust.

YESTERDAY'S LOVE

Tuning a plastic-cased transistor radio catches distorted sound from a radio station still powered by dying generators; over a turntable left running the needle jumps and jumps again in the chipped groove of a pop record, broadcasting. 'Treat me like you did the night before,' endlessly repeated over the face of a dead world. The meaning is lost; love's vanished hungers and fears and suspicions are wiped clean by Armageddon. Sex is suppressed; the feeling is gone.

WANDERING, SEARCHING

Freed of my past and my position in the suffocating mass of crawling people, I will become a breathing, moving, living fantasy figure, skimming a white desert in a fast flame-red sportscar, chrome dazzling in the eternal baking sunlight. Cities will recede behind me: mass-made complexes of wires and concrete all decomposing into dust.

Travel: I will travel free, at liberty to see the world. Peace everywhere: final peace, from cold, wet blue-green Scottish hills to the white slopes of chisel-faced Swiss mountainsides spanned by black threads of broken, rusting cable cars. The glaciers will crawl on unchanged, rivers of green ice slipping through time down into the valleys below.

THE DREAM WILL HAPPEN

The wandering will cease. having seen what I want to see of civilization's dead, hollow carcase, I will find true happiness, true love and true life, adjusted completely and at peace with my environment, in a world of all the good things and none of the bad.

When the disaster has occurred, this will be possible. The dream will happen. I will meet the last woman on Earth. She will be young and physically attractive and she will love me and serve me unquestioningly. She will be the last symbol I need.

I will still remain the only person existing, for I shall certainly not treat her like one. In my world, I am the centre. She shall be made happy, but she is to serve me obediently and love me and answer my whims of passion.

The picture is compelling . . . Down in the valley under a vast heap of refuse lies the empty shell of a city, symbol of the past. Up above it, looking over it, free of it and of all it used to mean, I sit at ease with life, reading books I never had time to read before, eating food I have cultivated myself, breathing cold, clean air, now-and-then tainted with wood smoke . . . Hands hardened through honest work, face tanned, happy through my closeness to the soil and to nature, in a way that city dwellers used to dream of, before the disaster.

THE ESCAPIST SICKNESS

The feeling of *lacking* I used to feel – or used to imagine I felt – in the old time, will be satisfied. I will discharge the deepest fears and neuroses of men. I will find myself. I will be me.

Because this is what I want now. This is what I want to be able to believe, what I think I need, what I think I lack and wish to find. I have the escapist sickness, whose cure is the world always just around the corner – the dream which, after the disaster, I imagine could become real. My disaster can be anything; so long as I am left free and unharmed in an emptied world, I will be able to see myself as being happy.

Conversations at Ma Maia Metron

ROBERT MEADLEY

Faugh! Autumn barely and the corpses already shrivelling on the gibbets by the road. I stood in the frost before the two-towered gate. There was heavy rime on my moustache, and the smoky fret of my horses' breath splayed in long, dissolving cones that curved as their heads moved. At frequent intervals I struck the gong before the gate; not impatiently, but with the imperative tone proper to my office. After an hour the keeper, surly and perhaps a little drunk, opened the gate and let me through.

According to this keeper, a steep range of mountains obstructed the way to the next gate and the road was uncertain. For a fee, however, two ingots of tin, he procured for me the services of a guide, a dismal young man of great height and little breadth who walked before me brandishing a scythe blade lashed to a stout pole and droning dull hymns extolling the current theogeny of the province. On his advice I left my horses and proceeded on foot, leading a pack ass. Further horses, he assured me, would be available beyond the mountains. It was not a comfortable walk.

The gate keeper, presumably through ignorance, had not exaggerated. The mountains were steep and craggy, and so thickly foliated that the wind, even among the heights, sounded far off, as if it were being carried, buffeting in a bag, by someone with large feet walking some distance ahead along the undecipherable path. After struggling through an interminable maze of fallen rocks, the roots of invisible trees and ravines choked with dense thickets, I followed my guide out of the undergrowth on to the sudden banks of a river in spate. Only two humped smears of foam showed where the pillars of the bridge remained.

The noise of the river, resounding among the mountains, rendered all other sounds inaudible, but by retreating a short distance into the squat jungle behind us, the guide was able to explain that, although the overwhelming of the bridge made progress impossible until the flood subsided, there was a monastery higher up the river where we might be offered hospitality while we waited. Which monastery we found, rather startlingly, suspended from one wall of a chasm at a point where, the mountain falling away abruptly in a sheer crag, the water shot out into the air with immense force in an arc whose radius stretched several men's height from the cliff; the whole scene misted with blurry traces of a rainbow despite the greyness of the day. Access to the monastery, by basket and tilting spiral stair, proved less perilous than one might have feared.

We were immediately accommodated by the monks, and offered as great a variety of quarters as the monotony of the view allowed. Hot water for a bath was brought to me as I changed, with afterwards a steaming dumpling plumped with prunes and walnuts, a whole honeycomb to break over it, and a quart jug of beer. It all seemed very civilised after the bitter exigencies of war and brutal taps of provincial caravanserai.

For dinner I was the guest of the abbot and senior monks at high table. My accountrements and scars having already caused some comment when I arrived, I was now required by courtesy to give some recital of the seige at K——, my conduct of the defence, and the death of my daughter and expected grandchild through her conviction that both city and defence were illusory. This latter particularly excited more than polite amazement.

It was after dinner, when asked why he had earlier murmured abstractedly 'Although out of whose anus the river originally ran will not be resolved, some progress will be presumed in extending the enigmatic way', that the abbot affably invited us to join him in imagining a culture, stemming from a river valley, the first principle of whose mysteries is that the river, the source of arbitrary and absolute Life, first flowed from the anus of one of the gods. At an assumed point in time, the favourite candidate for this honour is the Serpent, whose popularity rests largely on a mystical poem, the *Colon* of Xnath Lora, in which the author avers that he has been swallowed by the Serpent and seen through the divine intestine into the future.

Among the intelligentsia of this culture a game is known in which two players attempt to construct symbolic heptagrams by placing variously inscribed tiles on an eleven-lined board, the top lines of the two heptagrams thus overlapping. As each tile is placed on the board its player ascribes to it a metaphysical value appropriate to its inscription. A tile may be taken off the board by its player's opponent, but only if its value is mutually agreed to be less than that of the tile with which the taker must replace it, hence the name of the game which is Thetnol, or Honest Men.

An instance of this game is postulated in which, by skilful play, the two heptagrams have been so interwoven that only the space of one tile remains to be contended. The first player, Mohr Yllamn, completes his heptagram by playing *S*, apparently the strongest piece, with the value 'The Serpent and the River'. His opponent, Toor Hcern, refusing to acknowledge defeat, still appears unable to win. He must play *R* to complete his heptagram, but has only *O* which he plays with the value 'The Jaws of the Jaguar', covering the previously omnipotent S. When challenged he argues that the power of Mohr Yllamn's S depends wholly on a literal acceptance of

'Within the Serpent, Beyond the Gate of Fangs,
The Way Before Me endless as the Road to the Horizon.'

the opening lines of Xnath Lora's *Colon*. An alternative interpretation could run thus:

Xnath Lora at the Gate of Fangs did not find himself facing the jaws of the Serpent but saw in fact those of the Jaguar reflected in the translucent petals of the Flower. The 1037 scales that Xnath Lora counted between the Serpent's eyes were actually those facets of the focal petal visible from where Xnath Lora stood at the time. In support of this, Halt Rume's argument that the 1037 scales were those which Xnath Lora was allowed to see, not those which *were*, could be extended to assert the necessity for a reflected image, an immediate and complete perception being inconsistent with the primary principles of divinity, eternity and accident. Xnath's subsequent elision of the two experiences (the Flower and the Jaguar) into one (the Serpent), may be ascribed to temporal parallax if Xnath's simple analism is translated into Perspective Time by applying the 5th Extraordinary Proposition in Piat Thlugh's *Light and Time, Parallels of Pragmatic Function*.

Mohr Yllamn accepts Toor's argument but reminds him of that rule which insists that any tile placed on the board must be consistent with the definition of the intended heptagram. O, having been accepted as stronger than S, must now be shown to be R. Though they are friends, Mohr Yllamn permits himself a short laugh at Toor's expense. Is this laugh justified?

'No,' I cried, rather too loudly, having become excited by the abbot's game. 'If I understand the thing correctly, we may assume for this society at least a simple prosody. If to this we apply the notions of perspective contained in Piat's Extraordinary Proposition, Toor Hcern could argue the following formula:

Is jaguar
is aguar
is guar
is uar
is ar
is R.'

The abbot seemed greatly pleased with this. His own solutions had been to argue that R as the Pregnant Woman, a common value for R, was thus an infinite series and therefore The Way Before Me which, it follows from Toor's first argument, is included in the Jaguar and a logical extension of its jaws, or that O as the Philosopher's Stone, might be jaws or R or what it chose.

But my solution, he felt, was more in accordance with Toor's dialectic of disparates and displayed a superior understanding. I was duly flattered, of course, but equally dismayed when the abbot went on to say that in the presence of so superior a philosopher (myself!) he felt he must abdicate his abbatial chair to me. I was too soured with wine to suspect a pleasantry and explained stupidly that I was even now on my way to the capital to plead for the extirpation of philosophy; that this was my duty, the proper response to the dissolution of my daughter.

At breakfast the next day the abbot again placed me beside him and suggested, with reference to the purpose of my journey, that we might usefully consider the hypothetical but still illuminating case of Piat Thlugh, the fictive physicist whose theories we had touched on previously.

'Piat, having achieved fame early, settles into middle age as a landowner in a small way, with a wife and as many children as is seemly, ambitious now only for a quiet life and quieter death. One evening, however, having retired to share a bottle and a pipe in convivial silence with Halt Rume, a close friend, his peace is abruptly ended: the door of the library bursts open and a dozen troopers rush into the room, seizing and binding its two incumbents. Piat's wife, it transpires, has reported having seen through the library window the reflection in the mirror of her husband being stabbed to death by Halt Rume, using the sabre that had always and still hung beside the mirror. Her affidavit to this effect is produced.

'Piat naturally assumes that his presence alive and hale, confirmed by his wife's subsequent identification, will suffice to correct the misunderstanding. Herein he errs. Sufficient time has elapsed for the traces of any crime to be disguised, and the officer cannot dismiss the matter so lightly.'

By this time I was having difficulty in refraining from fidgeting. The abbot had not touched his breakfast and it was not for me to be his example, but the kidneys before me were becoming spangled with congealing fat and would soon be uneatable. And this after a bad night and a stiff walk on a crisp morning. The abbot:

'A committee of philosophers is assumed, which first asks: Had any action been performed which might be construed as a mime of the supposed event? No, the two of them had remained seated since entering the room. At this discovery gloom settles over the philosophers, until one of them thoughtfully suggests that they need not be bound by Madame Piat's identification of her husband – that Piat minutely resembles himself does not prove that he is himself, two identical objects are not the same object. If the assumption of Piat's identity were suspended, the rest of the evidence might be more successfully considered. With such renewed optimism as this bridging of the hiatus allows, one of the other philosophers demands an inspection of the supposed murder weapon and, the sabre being drawn, its scabbard is found to be full of blood. A further philosopher then demands, since the murder had been reported as seen in or through the mirror, that the mirror be removed from the wall, whereon a large fresh bloodstain is revealed on the crumbling plaster behind. Obviously, by some alchemy (and it is generally felt that Piat's own theories of light and time could assist here if properly applied), the murder was committed *within* the mirror.'

I was strongly moved to protest: the state of my breakfast had long banished appetite, but even allowing for my state of mind the abbot's fable was getting too wild. My face must have shown at least a part of my feelings, for the abbot suddenly and apologetically broke off his monologue and bade me eat. I replied, gratefully, that I would eat when he had finished talking, that etiquette could bow to neither whim nor compass. A subsequent brief dialogue produced the removal of the distressing kidneys and the promise of something fresh shortly. 'Conceive,' the abbot measured himself a little rhetoric, 'conceive the emotions of poor Piat, torn so abruptly from bland success and dashed into the abyss of sudden philosophy! His reaction is vigorous and original: he suggests to the committee that the denial of his identity must imply doubt as to that of the persons and authority of all present. It would be more constructive to consider the factor Time. Was it not possible that in some way he had been murdered but was subsequently alive, in which case Halt Rume perhaps had been guilty but could be so no longer? The philosophers cannot accept the conclusion of this argument, so Piat turns to the implications of the mirror. If any intra-speculary crime has taken place, a murder within the mirror, then surely an intra-speculary solution is required. Could a murder have taken place within the mirror and not without? Could some or all of the events within the library be ab-speculary projections, images of a reality within the mirror? Could the room be shown to contain simultaneously both ab-speculary and extra-speculary phenomena?'

Despite the abbot's excitement, I was hard put to contain my impatience.

'Surely,' I demanded, 'the solution proper to the terms of the problem is that Halt Rume, if his image is found guilty, should be punished only within the mirror; that he be hanged in such a way that a rope suspended over the mirror should be stretched appropriate to his weight and the excreta which accompany hanging be found behind the mirror, the man himself remaining unharmed.'

The abbot frowned, perhaps offended by the brutality of my tone, then his fingers flew up suddenly as if to press back the expressive furrows above his eyes.

'I had in mind something subtler,' he frowned again at the implication of this, and shrugged as though declaring a truce to social niceties, 'something of wider application; to have Piat develop his argument so multiplying and intricating the parameters of the problem that he constructs an ineluctable kaleidoscope of possibility. It is arguable, for instance, that a murder within the mirror is properly the province of authorities within the mirror; or that image of the murder was premonitary, not actual, and that perhaps time was in reverse, that this was a symptom of incipient entropy. Or what follows from the discovery that the shape of the bloodstain behind the mirror was that of a horizontal, not a vertical stain? By rendering each discrete fact into a divergent series of possibilites, I had hoped to have Piat confound the speculative philosophers into a recognition of reality.'

I appreciated the principle but doubted its efficacy, after all the sophistication of fire-power correlates very closely to the increase in population. I said so, but before the abbot could reply I was served with kidneys and baked eggs in a basket of mushrooms and the abbot insisted I eat. While I ate the abbot remained shrunk in meditation, but as my plate was removed he sighed. He could not, he said, absolve himself from adding to my already opulent distrust of philosophers. The improbability of his initial problem, he saw, debased the value of his intended solution. He had hoped to offer some constructive, non-violent form to my campaign against philosophers, but alas . . . He was evidently one of those who imagine soldiers settle all their differences with shrapnel and bayonet, and was working himself up into a state of self-mortification that I was now too well fed to permit.

'We are all liable to err,' I soothed. 'The general stupidity of the species does not allow the exception of ourselves.'

The abbot looked at me curiously, but only nodded by way of comment.

I spent the rest of the day in my quarters with a gallon of beer and a sketching block, devising possible new bridges for the lower pass. I had made some preliminary drawings of the scene on my early morning walk, so the rain, which blew up in mid-morning and was well established by noon, did not deprive me wholly of useful amusement, and I was glad to be able to present these plans and sketches to the abbot at dinner as a token of gratitude for the hospitality he had so readily provided.

It was during the late afternoon, when I had paused to stretch my legs and sit mellowed over a cigar, that I remembered my earlier assurance to the abbot that we are all more or less fools. The devil of the thing, which these admissions good food or fine weather cheat from us, is that they return to haunt one so. My own plans suddenly appeared asinine. What had seemed so vital in the immediate and bitter aftermath of the seige now manifested itself to my revived reflection as silly and demeaning. One has to lose sometimes to accident and war, and even in sorrow one can behave with dignity. Who was I to scald all philosophers for the faults of the fools among them? I, it struck me, could in no way countenance the abolition of the army, despite the flagrant inanity of many senior officers. Obviously the sooner I returned to the rigours of regimental life the better.

I mentioned this change in my plans to the abbot that evening and he seemed greatly relieved. He would, I suspect, have liked to dissuade me from returning to my military career, but was too shrewd to press the point and turned the conversation to a discussion of modern theories of education. It was my contention, derived partly from gentle malice, that the only disciplines necessary to any man were mathematics, for understanding trajectory and logistics, and music, to imbue a sense of tactical harmony in movement; for the rest, there is no discipline guaranteed to improve one's native wit and a boy can glean all the culture he needs from browsing in his father's library on wet days. The abbot vigorously defended the proper study of history as essential to any responsible social activity, and this I was forced to concede, though I like to think I held my own against metaphysics and philology.

Over the last dozen of wine the abbot asked us all to consider the proposition: If the relationship XY must be temporally represented by that number of typefaces whose permutations are infinite, how should we restructure simple logic to accommodate this? But I was too fuddled from my day's labours at pen and bottle to cope with steep matter of this sort and mumbled myself off to bed.

The following day, the river having fallen, we went down to review the bridge. It was a remarkable contrivance; low in profile and set on buttresses so massive as almost to dam the ravine through which the river roared, it seemed built not to override any inflation of the torrent but bluntly to withstand whatever weight of water might try to overwhelm it, as if the engineer knew or approved only one design of bridge and would alter only the length of the arches, and that minimally, to accommodate variations in the terrain.

I was pleased as well as amused to see it, however, and immediately made arrangements to depart, if possible, before noon. The abbot was concerned that I should stay at least to lunch, but I put him off, pleading soldier's haste and the need to be out of the mountains before dark. Convivial and instructive as his hospitality had been, I dislike enforced idleness and his conversation, of which he offered more as bait to keep me, seemed liable to prove oppressive if indulged too long.

No Direction Home

NORMAN SPINRAD

> How does it feel
> To be on your own?
> With no direction home . . .
> Like a complete unknown.
> Like a rolling stone.
>
> — Bob Dylan, *Like A Rolling Stone*

'But I once *did* succeed in stuffing it all back in Pandora's box,' Richardson said, taking another hit. 'You remember Pandora Deutchman, don't you, Will? Everybody in the biochemistry department stuffed it all in Pandora's box at one time or another. I seem to vaguely remember one party when you did it yourself.'

'Oh you're a real comedian, Dave,' Goldberg said, stubbing out his roach and jamming a cork into the glass vial which he had been filling from the petcock at the end of the apparatus' run. 'Any day now, I expect you to start slipping strychnine into the goods. That'd be pretty good for a yock, too.'

'You know, I never thought of that before. Maybe you got something there. Let a few people go out with a smile, satisfaction guaranteed. Christ Will, we could tell them exactly what it was and still sell some of the stuff.'

'That's not funny, man,' Goldberg said, handing the vial to Richardson, who carefully snugged it away with the others in the excelsior-packed box. 'It's not funny because it's true.'

'Hey, you're not getting an attack of morals, are you? Don't move, I'll be right back with some methalin – that oughta get your head straight.'

'My head is straight already. Canabinolic acid, our own invention.'

'*Canabinolic acid?* Where did you get that, in a drugstore? We haven't bothered with it for three years.'

Goldberg placed another empty vial in the rack under the petcock and opened the valve. 'Bought it on the street for kicks,' he said. 'Kids are brewing it in their bathtubs now.' He shook his head, almost a random gesture. 'Remember what a bitch the original synthesis was?'

'Science marches on!'

'Too bad we couldn't have patented the stuff,' Goldberg said as he contemplated the thin stream of clear green liquid entering the open mouth of the glass vial. 'We could've retired off the royalties by now.'

'If we had the Mafia to collect for us.'

'That might be arranged.'

'Yeah, well maybe I should look into it,' Richardson said as Goldberg handed him another full vial. 'We shouldn't be pigs about it, though. Just about ten per cent off the top at the manufacturing end. I don't believe in stifling private enterprise.'

'No really, Dave,' Goldberg said, 'maybe we made a mistake in not trying to patent the stuff. People *do* patent combo psychedelics, you know.'

'You don't mean *people*, man, you mean outfits like American Marijuana and Psychedelics, Inc. They can afford the lawyers and grease. They can work the FDA's head. We can't.'

Goldberg opened the petcock valve. 'Yeah, well at least it'll be six months or so before the Dope Industry or anyone else figures out how to synthesize the new crap, and by that time I think I'll have just about licked the decay problem in the cocanol extraction process. We should be one step ahead of the squares for at least another year.'

'You know what I think, Will?' Richardson said, patting the side of the half-filled box of vials. 'I think we got a holy mission, is what. I think we're servants of the evolutionary process. Every time we come up with a new psychedelic, we're advancing the evolution of human consciousness. We develop the stuff and make our bread off it for a while, and then the Dope Industry comes up with our synthesis and mass produces it, and then we gotta come up with the next drug out so we can still set our tables in style. If it weren't for the Dope Industry and the way the drug laws are set up, we could stand still and become bloated plutocrats just by putting out the same old dope year after year. This way, we're doing some good in the world, we're doing something to further human evolution.'

Goldberg handed him another full vial. 'Screw human evolution,' he said. 'What has human evolution ever done for us?'

'As you know, Dr Taller, we're having some unforeseen side-effects with eucomorfamine,' General Carlyle said, stuffing his favourite Dunhill with rough-cut burley. Taller took out a pack of Golds, extracted a joint, and lit it with a lighter bearing an Air Force rather than a Psychedelics, Inc. insignia. Perhaps this had been a deliberate gesture, perhaps not.

'With a psychedelic as new as eucomorfamine, General,' Taller said, 'no side-effects can quite be called "unforeseen". After all, even Project Groundhog itself is an experiment.'

Carlyle lit his pipe and sucked in a mouthful of smoke which was good and carcinogenic; the General believed that a good soldier should cultivate at least one foolhardy minor vice. 'No word-games, please doctor,' he said. 'Eucomorfamine is supposed to help our men in the Groundhog moonbase deal with the claustrophobic conditions; it is not supposed to promote faggotry in the ranks. The reports I've been getting indicate that the drug is doing both. The Air Force does not want it to do both. Therefore, by definition, eucomorfamine has an undesirable side-effect. Therefore, your contract is up for review.'

'General, General, psychedelics are not uniforms, after all. You can't expect us to tailor them to order. You asked for a drug that would combat claustrophobia without impairing alertness or the sleep cycle or attention-span or initiative. You think this is easy? Eucomorfamine produces claustrophilia without any side-effect but a raising of the level of sexual energy. As such, I consider it one of the minor miracles of psychedelic science.'

'That's all very well, Taller, but surely you can see that we simply cannot tolerate violent homosexual behaviour among our men in the moonbase.'

Taller smiled, perhaps somewhat fatuously. 'But you can't very well tolerate a high rate of claustrophobic breakdown, either,' he said. 'You have only four obvious alternatives, General Carlyle: continue to use eucomorfamine and accept a certain level of homosexual incidents, discontinue eucomorfamine and accept a very high level of claustrophobic breakdown, or cancel Project Groundhog. *Or . . .*'

It dawned upon the General that he had been the object of a rather sophisticated sales pitch. 'Or go to a drug that would cancel out the side-effect of eucomorfamine,' he said. 'Your company just wouldn't happen to have such a drug in the works, would it?'

Dr Taller gave him a we're-all-men-of-the-world-grin. 'Psychedelics, Inc. *has* been working on a sexual suppressant,' he admitted none too grudgingly. 'Not an easy psychic spec to fill. The problem is that if you actually decrease sexual energy, you tend to get impaired performance in the higher cerebral centres, which is all very well in penal institutions, but hardly acceptable in Project Groundhog's case. The trick is to channel the excess energy elsewhere. We decided that the only viable alternative was to siphon it off into mystical fugue-states. Once we worked it out, the biochemistry became merely a matter of detail. We're about ready to bring the drug we've developed – trade name nadabrin – into the production stage.'

The General's pipe had gone out. He did not bother to relight it. Instead, he took 5 mg. of lebemil, which seemed more to the point at the moment. 'This nadabrin,' he said very deliberately, 'it bleeds off the excess sexuality into *what?* Fugue-states? Trances? We certainly don't need a drug that makes our men psychotic.'

'Of course not. About three hundred micrograms of nadabrin will give a man a mystical experience that lasts less than four hours. He won't be much good to you during that time, to be sure, but his sexual energy level will be severely depressed for about a week. Three hundred micrograms to each man on eucomorfamine, say every five days, to be on the safe side.'

General Carlyle relit his pipe and ruminated. Things seemed to be looking up. 'Sounds pretty good,' he finally admitted. 'But what about the content of the mystical experiences? Nothing that would impair devotion to duty?'

Taller snubbed out his roach. 'I've taken nadabrin myself,' he said. 'No problems.'

'What was it like?'

Taller once again put on his fatuous smile. 'That's the best part of nadabrin,' he said. 'I don't remember what it was like. You don't retain any memories of what happens to you under nadabrin. Genuine fugue-state. So you can be sure the mystical experiences don't have any undesirable content, can't you? Or at any rate, you can be sure that the experiences can't impair a man's military performance.'

'What the men don't remember can't hurt them, eh?' Carlyle muttered into his pipestem.

'What was that, General?'

'I said I'd recommend that we give it a try.'

They sat together in a corner booth back in the smoke, sizing each other up while the crowd in the joint yammered and swirled around them in some other reality, like a Bavarian merryground.

'What are you on?' he said, noticing that her hair seemed black and seamless like a beetle's carapace, a dark metal helmet framing her pale face in glory. Wow.

'Peyotadrene,' she said, her lips moving like incredibly jeweled and articulated metal flower-petals. 'Been up for about three hours. What's your trip?'

'Canabinolic acid,' he said, the distortion of his mouth's movement casting his face into an ideogramic pattern which was barely decipherable to her perception as a foreshadowing of energy release. Maybe they would make it.

'I haven't tried any of that stuff for months,' she said. 'I hardly remember what that reality feels like.' Her skin luminesced from within, a translucent white china mask over a yellow candle-flame. She was a magnificent artifact, a creation of jaded and sophisticated gods.

'It feels good,' he said, his eyebrows forming a set of curves which, when considered as part of a pattern containing the movement of his lips against his teeth, indicated a clear desire to donate energy to the filling of her void. They *would* make it. 'Call me old-fashioned maybe, but I still think canabinolic acid is groovy stuff.'

'Do you think you could go on a sex-trip behind it?' she asked. The folds and wrinkles of her ears had been carved with microprecision out of pink ivory.

'Well, I suppose so, in a peculiar kind of way,' he said, hunching his shoulders forward in a clear gesture of offering, an alignment with the pattern of her movement through space-time that she could clearly perceive as intersecting her trajectory. 'I mean, if you want me to ball you, I think I can make it.'

The tiny gold hairs on her face were a microscopic field of wheat shimmering in a shifting summer breeze as she said: 'That's the most meaningful thing anyone has said to me in hours.'

The convergence of every energy configuration in the entire universe toward complete identity with the standing wave pattern of its maximum ideal structure was brightly mirrored for the world to see in the angle between the curves of his lips as he spoke.

Cardinal McGavin took a peyotadrene-mescamil combo and 5mg. of metadrene an hour and a half before his meeting with Cardinal Rillo; he had decided to try to deal with Rome on a mystical rather than a political level, and that particular prescription made him feel most deeply Christian. And the Good Lord knew that it could become very difficult to feel deeply Christian when dealing with a representative of the Pope.

Cardinal Rillo arrived punctually at three, just as Cardinal McGavin was approaching his mystical peak; the man's punctuality was legend. Cardinal McGavin felt pathos in that: the sadness of a Prince of the Church whose major impact on the souls of his fellows lay in his slavery to the hands of a clock. Because the ascetic-looking old man, with his colourless eyes and pencil-thin lips, was so thoroughly unlovable. Cardinal McGavin found himself cherishing the man for this very existential hopelessness. He sent forth a silent prayer that he, or if not he then at least someone, might be chosen as an instrument through which this poor cold creature might be granted a measure of Divine Grace.

Cardinal Rillo accepted the amenities with cold formality, and in the same spirit agreed to share some claret. Cardinal McGavin knew better than to offer a joint; Cardinal Rillo had been in the forefront of the opposition which had caused the Pope to delay his inevitable encyclical on marijuana for long ludicrous years. That the Pope had chosen such an emissary in this matter was not a good sign.

Cardinal Rillo sipped at his wine in sour silence for long moments while Cardinal McGavin was nearly overcome with sorrow at the thought of the loneliness of the soul of this man, who could not even break the solemnity of his persona to share some Vatican gossip over a little wine with a fellow Cardinal. Finally, the Papal emissary cleared his throat – a dry, archaic gesture – and got right to the point.

'The Pontiff has instructed me to convey his concern at the addition of psychedelics to the composition of the communion host in the Archdiocese of New York,' he said, the tone of his voice making it perfectly clear that he wished the Holy Father had given him a much less cautious warning to deliver. But if the Pope had learned anything at all from the realities of this schismatic era, it was caution. Especially when dealing with the American hierarchy, whose allegiance to Rome was based on nothing firmer than nostalgia and symbolic convenience. The Pope had been the last to be convinced of his own fallibility, but in the last few years events seemed to have finally brought the new refinement of Divine Truth home.

'I acknowledge and respect the Holy Father's concern,' Cardinal McGavin said. 'I shall pray for divine resolution of his doubt.'

'I didn't say anything about doubt!' Cardinal Rillo snapped, his lips moving with the crispness of pincers. 'How can you impute doubt to the Holy Father?'

Cardinal McGavin's spirit soared over a momentary spark of anger at the man's pigheadedness; he tried to give Cardinal Rillo's soul a portion of peace. 'I stand corrected,' he said. 'I shall pray for the alleviation of the Holy Father's concern.'

But Cardinall Rillo was implacable and inconsolable; his face was a membrane of control over a musculature of rage. 'You can more easily relieve the Holy Father's concern by removing the peyotadrene from your hosts!' he said.

'Are those the words of the Holy Father?' Cardinal McGavin asked, knowing the answer.

'Those are my words, Cardinal McGavin,' Cardinal Rillo said, 'and you would do well to heed them. The fate of your immortal soul may be at stake.'

A flash of insight, a sudden small satori, rippled through Cardinal McGavin: Rillo was sincere. For him, the question of a chemically-augmented host was not a matter of Church politics, as it probably was to the Pope; it touched on an area of deep religious conviction. Cardinal Rillo was indeed concerned for the state of his soul and it behoved him, both as a

Cardinal and as a Catholic, to treat the matter seriously on that level. For after all, chemically-augmented communion was a matter of deep religious conviction for him as well. He and Cardinal Rillo faced each other across a gap of existentially-meaningful theological disagreement.

'Perhaps the fate of yours as well, Cardinal Rillo,' he said.

'I didn't come here all the way from Rome to seek spiritual guidance from a man who is skating on the edge of heresy, Cardinal McGavin. I came here to deliver the Holy Father's warning that an encyclical may be issued against your position. Need I remind you that if you disobey such an encyclical, you may be excommunicated?'

'Would you be genuinely sorry to see that happen?' Cardinal McGavin asked, wondering how much of the threat was Rillo's wishful thinking, and how much the instructions of the Pope. 'Or would you simply feel that the Church had defended itself properly?'

'Both,' Cardinal Rillo said without hesitation.

'I like that answer,' Cardinal McGavin said, tossing down the rest of his glass of claret. It was a good answer – sincere on both counts. Cardinal Rillo feared both for the Church and for the soul of the Archbishop of New York, and there was no doubt that he quite properly put the Church first. His sincerity was spiritually refreshing, even though he was thoroughly wrong all round. 'But you see, part of the gift of Grace that comes with a scientifically-sound chemical augmentation of communion is a certainty that no one, not even the Pope, can do anything to cut you off from communion with God. In psychedelic communion, one experiences the love of God directly. It's always just a host away; faith is no longer even necessary.'

Cardinal Rillo grew sombre. 'It is my duty to report that to the Pope,' he said. 'I trust you realize that.'

'Who am I talking to, Cardinal Rillo, you or the Pope?'

'You are talking to the Catholic Church, Cardinal McGavin,' Rillo said. 'I am an emissary of the Holy Father.' Cardinal McGavin felt an instant pang of guilt: his sharpness had caused Cardinal Rillo to imply an untruth out of anger, for surely his Papal mission was far more limited than he had tried to intimate. The Pope was too much of a realist to make the empty threat of excommunication against a Prince of the Church who believed that his power of excommunication was itself meaningless.

But again, a sudden flash of insight illuminated the Cardinal's mind with truth: in the eyes of Cardinal Rillo, in the eyes of an important segment of the Church hierarchy, the threat of excommunication still held real meaning. To accept their position on chemically augmented communion was to accept the notion that the word of the Pope could withdraw a man from Divine

Grace. To accept the sanctity and validity of psychedelic communion was to deny the validity of excommunication.

'You know, Cardinal Rillo,' he said, 'I firmly believe that if I am excommunicated by the Pope, it will threaten my soul not one iota.'

'That's merely cheap blasphemy!'

'I'm sorry,' Cardinal McGavin said sincerely, 'I meant to be neither cheap nor blasphemous. All I was trying to do was explain that excommunication can hardly be meaningful when God through the psychedelic sciences has seen fit to grant us a means of certain direct experience of His countenance. I believe with all my heart that this is true. You believe with all your heart that it is not.'

'I believe that what you experience in your psychedelic communion is nothing less than a masterstroke of Satan, Cardinal McGavin. Evil is infinitely subtle; might not it finally masquerade as the ultimate good? The Devil is not known as the Prince of Liars without reason. I believe that you are serving Satan in what you sincerely believe is the service of God. Is there any way that you can be sure that I am wrong?'

'Can you be sure that *I'm* not right?' Cardinal McGavin said. 'If I am, you are attempting to stifle the will of God and wilfully removing yourself from His Grace.'

'We cannot both be right . . . ' Cardinal Rillo said.

And the burning glare of a terrible and dark mystical insight filled Cardinal McGavin's soul with terror, a harsh illumination of his existential relationship to the Church and to God: they both couldn't be right, but there was no reason why they both couldn't be wrong. Apart from both God and Satan, existed the Void.

Dr Braden gave Johnny a pat-on-the-head smile and handed him a mango-flavoured lollypop from the supply of goodies in his lower-left desk drawer. Johnny took the lollypop, unwrapped it quickly, popped it into his mouth, leaned back in his chair, and began to suck the sweet avidly, oblivious to the rest of the world. It was a good sign – a preschooler with a proper reaction to a proper basic prescription should focus strongly and completely on the most interesting element in its environment, should be fond of unusual flavours. In the first four years of its life, a child's sensorium should be tuned to accept the widest possible spectrum of sensual stimulation.

Braden turned his attention to the boy's mother, who sat rather nervously on the edge of her chair smoking a joint. 'Now, now, Mrs Lindstrom, there's nothing to worry about,' he said. 'Johnny has been responding quite normally to his prescription. His attention-span is suitably short for a child of his age, his sensual range slightly exceeds the optimum norm, his sleep pattern is regular and properly deep. And as you requested, he has been given a constant sense of universal love.'

'But then why did the school doctor ask me to have his basic prescription changed, Dr Braden? He said that Johnny's prescription was giving him the wrong personality pattern for a school-age child.'

Dr Braden was rather annoyed though of course he would never betray it to the nervous young mother. He knew the sort of failed G.P. who usually occupied a school doctor's position; a faded old fool who knew about as much about psychedelic pediatrics as he did about brain surgery. What he did know was worse than nothing – a smattering of half-assed generalities and pure rubbish that was just enough to convince him that he was an expert. Which entitled him to go around frightening the mothers of other people's patients, no doubt.

'I'm ... ah, certain you misunderstood what the school doctor said, Mrs Lindstrom,' Dr Braden said. 'At least I hope you did, because if you didn't, then the man is mistaken. You see, modern psychedelic pediatrics recognizes that the child needs to have his consciousness focused in different areas at different stages of his development, if he is to grow up to be a healthy, maximized individual. A child of Johnny's age is in a transitional stage. In order to prepare him for schooling, I'll simply have to alter his prescription so as to increase his attention-span, lower his sensory intensity a shade, and increase his interest in abstractions. Then he'll do fine in school, Mrs Lindstrom.'

Dr Braden gave the young woman a moderately-stern admonishing frown. 'You really should have brought Johnny in for a check-up *before* he started school, you know.'

Mrs Lindstrom puffed nervously on her joint while Johnny continued to suck happily on his lollypop. "Well ... I was sort of afraid to, Dr Braden,' she admitted. 'I know it sounds silly, but I was afraid that if you changed his prescription to what the school wanted, you'd stop the paxum. I didn't want that – I think it's more important for Johnny to continue to feel universal love than increasing his attention-span or any of that stuff. You're not going to stop the paxum, are you?'

'Quite the contrary, Mrs Lindstrom,' Dr Braden said. 'I'm going to increase his dose slightly and give him 10mg. of orodalamine daily. He'll submit to the necessary authority of his teachers with a sense of trust and love, rather than out of fear.'

For the first time during the visit, Mrs Lindstrom smiled. 'Then it all really *is* all right, isn't it?' She radiated happiness born of relief.

Dr Braden smiled back at her, basking in the sudden surge of good vibrations. This was his peak-experience in pediatrics: feeling the genuine gratitude of a worried mother whose fears he had thoroughly relieved. This was what being a doctor was all about. She trusted him. She put the consciousness of her child in his hands, trusting that those hands would not falter or fail. He was proud and grateful to be a psychedelic pediatrician. He was maximizing human happiness.

'Yes, Mrs Lindstrom,' he said soothingly, 'everything is going to be all right.'

In the chair in the corner, Johnny Lindstrom sucked on his lollypop, his face transfigured with boyish bliss.

There were moments when Bill Watney got a soul-deep queasy feeling about psychedelic design, and lately he was getting those bad flashes more and more often. He was glad to have caught Spiegelman alone in the designers' lounge; if anyone could do anything for his head, Lennie was it. 'I dunno,' he said, washing down 15 mg. of lebemil with a stiff shot of bourbon, 'I'm really thinking of getting out of this business.'

Leonard Spiegelman lit a Gold with his 14-carat gold lighter – nothing but the best for the best in the business – smiled across the coffee-table at Watney, and said quite genially: 'You're out of your mind, Bill.'

Watney sat hunched slightly forward in his easy chair, studying Spiegelman, the best artist Psychedelics, Inc. had, and envying the older man. Envying not only his talent, but his attitude towards his work. Lennie Spiegelman was not only certain that what he was doing was right, he enjoyed every minute of it. Watney wished he could be like Spiegelman. Spiegelman was happy; he radiated the contented aura of a man who really did have everything he wanted.

Spiegelman opened his arms in a gesture that seemed to make the whole designers' lounge his personal property. 'We're the world's best pampered artists,' he said. 'We come up with two or three viable drug designs a year, and we can live like kings. And we're practising the world's ultimate artform: creating realities. We're the luckiest mothers alive! Why would anyone with your talent want out of psychedelic design?'

Watney found it difficult to put into words, which was ridiculous for a psychedelic designer, whose work it was to describe new possibilities in human consciousness well enough for the biochemists to develop psyche-delics which would transform his specs into styles of reality. It was humiliating to be at a loss for words in front of Lennie Spiegelman, a man he both envied and admired. 'I'm getting bad flashes lately,' he finally said. 'Deep flashes that go through every style of consciousness that I try, flashes that tell me I should be ashamed and disgusted about what I'm doing.'

Oh, oh, Lennie Spiegelman thought, the kid is coming up with his first case of designer's cafard. He's floundering around with that no direction home syndrome and he thinks it's the end of the world. 'I know what's bothering you, Bill,' he said. 'It happens to all of us at one time or another. You feel that designing psychedelic specs is a solipsistic occupation, right? You think there's something morally wrong about designing new styles of consciousness for other people, that we're playing god, that continually altering people's consciousness in ways only we fully understand is a thing that mere mortals have no right to do, like hubris, eh?'

Watney flashed admiration for Spiegelman – his certainty *wasn't* based on a thick ignorance of the existential doubt of their situation. There was hope in that, too. 'How can you understand all that, Lennie,' he said, 'and still dig psychedelic design the way you do?'

'Because it's a load of crap, that's why,' Spiegelman said. 'Look kid, we're artists, commercial artists at that. We design psychedelics, styles of reality; we don't tell anyone what to think. If people like the realities we design for them, they buy the drugs, and if they don't like our art, they don't. People aren't going to buy food that tastes lousy, music that makes their ears hurt, or drugs that put them in bummer realities. *Somebody* is going to design styles of consciousness for the human race, if not artists like us, then a lot of crummy politicians and power-freaks.'

'But what makes us any better than them? Why do we have any more right to play games with the consciousness of the human race than they do?'

The kid is really dense, Spiegelman thought. But then ke smiled, remembering that he had been on the same stupid trip when he was Watney's age. 'Because we're artists, and they're not,' he said. 'We're not out to control people. We get our kicks from carving something beautiful out of the void. All we want to do is enrich people's lives. We're creating new styles of consciousness that we think are improved realities, but we're not shoving them down people's throats. We're just laying out our wares for the public – right doesn't even enter into it. We have a compulsion to practise our art. Right and wrong are arbitrary concepts that vary with the style of consciousness, so how on earth can you talk about the right and wrong of psychedelic design? The only way you can judge is by an aesthetic criterion – are we producing good art or bad?'

'Yeah, but doesn't *that* vary with the style of consciousness too? Who can judge in an absolute sense whether your stuff is artistically pleasing or not?'

'Jesus Christ, Bill, *I* can judge, can't I?' Spiegelman said. 'I know when a set of psychedelic specs is a successful work of art. It either pleases me or it doesn't.'

It finally dawned on Watney that that was precisely what was eating at him.

A psychedelic designer altered his own reality with a wide spectrum of drugs and then designed other psychedelics to alter other people's realities. Where was anyone's anchor?

'But don't you see, Lennie?' he said. 'We don't know what the hell we're doing. We're taking the human race on an evolutionary trip, but we don't know where we're going. We're flying blind.'

Spiegelman took a big drag on his joint. The kid was starting to get to him; he was whining too much. Watney didn't want anything out of line – just certainty! 'You want me to tell you there's a way you can know when a design is right or wrong in some absolute evolutionary framework, right?' he said. 'Well I'm sorry, Bill, there's nothing but us and the void and whatever we carve out of it. We're our own creations, our realities are our own works of art. We're out here all alone.'

Watney was living through one of his flashes of dread, and he saw that Spiegelman's words described its content exactly. 'But that's exactly what's eating at me!' he said. 'Where in hell is our basic reality?'

'There is no basic reality. I thought they taught that in kindergarten these days.'

'But what about the basic state? What about the way our reality was before the art of psychedelic design? What about the consciousness-style that evolved naturally over millions of years? Damn it, that was the basic reality, and we've lost it!'

'The hell it was!' Spiegelman said. 'Our pre-psychedelic consciousness evolved on a mindless random basis. What makes that reality superior to any other? Just because it was first? We may be flying blind, but natural evolution was worse – it was an idiot process without an ounce of consciousness behind it.'

'Goddman it, you're right all the way down the line, Lennie!' Watney cried in anguish. 'But why do you feel so good about it while I feel so rotten? I want to be able to feel the way you do, but I can't.'

'Of course you can, Bill,' Spiegelman said. He abstractly remembered that he had felt like Watney years ago, but there was no existential reality behind it. What more could a man want than a random universe that was anything he could make of it and nothing else? Who wouldn't rather have a style of consciousness created by an artist than one that was the result of a lot of stupid evolutionary accidents?

He says it with such certainty, Watney thought. Christ, how I want him to be right! How I'd like to face the uncertainty of it all, the void, with the courage of Lennie Spiegelman! Spiegelman had been in the business for fifteen years; maybe he *had* finally figured it all out.

'I wish I could believe that,' Watney said.

Spiegelman smiled, remembering what a solemn jerk he had been ten years ago himself. 'Ten years ago, I felt just like you feel now,' he said. 'But I got my head together and now here I am, fat and happy and digging what I'm doing.'

'How, Lennie, for chrissakes, *how?*'

'50 mikes of methalin, 40 mg. of lebemil and 20 mg. of peyotadrene daily,' Spiegelman said. 'It made a new man out of me, and it'll make a new man out of you.'

'How do you feel, man?' Kip said, taking the joint out of his mouth and peering intently into Jonesy's eyes. Jonesy looked really weird – pale, manic, maybe a little crazed. Kip was starting to feel glad that Jonesy hadn't talked him into taking the trip with him.

'Oh wow,' Jonesy croaked, 'I feel strange, I feel *really* strange, and it doesn't feel so good . . . '

The sun was high in the cloudless blue sky; a golden fountain of radiant energy filling Kip's being. The wood-and-bark of the tree against which they sat was an organic reality connecting the skin of his back to the bowels of the earth in an unbroken circuit of protoplasmic electricity. He was a flower of his planet, rooted deep in the rich soil, basking in the cosmic nectar of the sunshine.

But behind Jonesy's eyes was some kind of awful grey vortex. Jonesy looked really bad. Jonesy was definitely floating on the edges of a bummer.

'I don't feel good at all,' Jonesy said. 'Man, you know the ground is covered with all kinds of hard dead things and the grass is filled with mindless insects and the sun is hot, man, I think I'm burning . . . '

'Take it easy, don't freak, you're on a trip, that's all,' Kip said from some asshole superior viewpoint. He just didn't understand, he didn't understand how heavy this trip was, what it felt like to have your head raw and naked out here. Like cut off from every energy flow in the universe – a construction of fragile matter, protoplasmic ooze is all, isolated in an energy-vacuum, existing in relationship to nothing but empty void and horrible mindless matter.

'You don't understand, Kip,' he said. 'This is reality, the way it really is, and man it's horrible, just a great big ugly machine made up of lots of other machines, you're a machine, I'm a machine, it's all mechanical clockwork. We're just lumps of dead matter run by machinery, kept alive by chemical and electric processess.'

Golden sunlight soaked through Kip's skin and turned the core of his being into a miniature stellar phoenix. The wind, through random blades of grass, made love to the bare soles of his feet. What was all this machinery crap? What the hell was Jonesy gibbering about? Man, who would want to put himself in a bummer reality like that?

'You're just on a bummer, Jonesy,' he said. 'Take it easy. You're not seeing the universe the way it really is, as if that meant anything. Reality is all in your head. You're just freaking out behind nothing.'

'That's it, that's exactly it, I'm freaking out behind nothing. Like zero. Like cipher. Like the void. Nothing is where we're *really* at.'

How could he explain it? That reality was really just a lot of empty vacuum that went on to infinity in space and time. The perfect nothingness had minor contaminations of dead matter here and there. A little of this matter had fallen together through a complex series of random accidents to contaminate the universal deadness with trace elements of life, protoplasmic slime, biochemical clockwork. Some of this clockwork was complicated enough to generate thought, consciousness. And that was all there ever was or would ever be anywhere in space and time. Clockwork mechanisms rapidly running down in the cold black wind. Everything that wasn't dead matter already would end up that way sooner or later.

'This is the way it really is,' Jonesy said. 'People used to live in this bummer all the time. It's the way it is, and nothing we can do can change it.'

'I can change it,' Kip said, taking his pillbox out of a pocket. 'Just say the word. Let me know when you've had enough and I'll bring you out of it. Lebemil, peyotadrene, mescamil, you name it.'

'You don't understand, man, it's *real*. That's the trip I'm on, I haven't taken anything at all for twelve hours, remember? It's the natural state, it's reality itself, and man, it's awful. It's a horrible bummer. Christ, why did I have to talk myself into this? I don't want to see the universe this way, who needs it?'

Kip was starting to get pissed off – Jonesy was becoming a real bring-down. Why did he have to pick a beautiful day like this to take his stupid nothing trip?

'Then *take* something,' he said, offering Jonesy the pillbox.

Shakily, Jonesy scooped out a cap of peyotadrene and a 15 mg. tab of lebemil and wolfed them down dry. 'How did people *live* before psychedelics?' he said. 'How could they stand it?'

'Who knows?' Kip said, closing his eyes and staring straight at the sun, diffusing his consciousness into the universe of golden orange light encompassed by his eyelids.

'Maybe they had some way of not thinking about it.'

Mr Black's Poems of Innocence

D.M. THOMAS

This sequence is a poetic exploration of the therapy of operant conditioning in mute schizophrenia, a therapy first revealed to the layman in a prizewinning 1968 radio documentary, *Mr Blake. Mr Black's Poems of Innocence* follows the line of treatment and the terminology of the new therapy, but the case is fictional; Mr Black and his operant conditioner are imaginary characters.

The 'poems' are envisaged as Mr Black's reflections during his long silences or when he is back in the ward.

The eternal gates' terrific porter lifted the northern bar. Thel enter'd in & saw the secrets of the land unknown.

Edited transcript by an operant conditioner of her treatment of Mr Black.

Mr Black was found in a shocked condition, twenty years ago, and consigned to an asylum, where he was diagnosed as a mute schizophrenic. He has spent nearly all his time during those twenty years sitting on his bed without moving or speaking, and paying no attention to nurses or the other patients. At the time my treatment of him began, Mr Black had no words at all.

On first entering the experimental room, Mr Black ignored me completely; he might almost have been a corpse. I worked at gaining his attention by holding up objects, such as a pen or a comb, and persuading him to say their names. The persuasion was by a very elementary form of reward and punishment: if he said anything that remotely approached the right sound, I smiled at him and encouraged him; if he refused to verbalise, I turned away my head sharply and pretended he didn't exist.

Interviewer: Mr Black, I'm going to ask you some questions and I hope you

will answer them. I would like that very much. Would you let me know
   your name?
Mr Black: (*no response*)
Int: Where do you live? What is your address?
Mr Black: (*incoherent*)
Int: How long have you been here, Mr Black?
Mr Black: (*incoherent*)
Int: What's this, Mr Black – in my hand?
Mr Black: (*no response*)
Int: A pen. What's this?
Mr Black: (*no response*)
Int: A comb. What's this, Mr Black?
Mr Black: (*incoherent*)
Int: A handkerchief. Do you like snakes?
Mr Black: (*no response*)
Int: Do you like pain, Mr Black?

Thirty years ago I climbed up into this rooftop, maze of
   chimneys, after
My brother Robert. Grimes was a hard taskmaster. He
   came back drunk
Every night, and beat us. As I got higher and higher,
Scouring the blackness with my brush, I used to dream
Of breaking out of the slates, finding the sky hard with stars
And one small cloud sending down cool rain to wash my
   face free
Of the grime. Or of climbing down into some silken
   chamber
Where a girl like my mother would be sleeping in a wide
   bed,
Her bosom rising and falling and her long yellow curls
   spread out
On the counterpane. But I would always come back to my
   drunken master.
But that day, thirty years ago, I could not climb up or
   down.
This house must have been built on to, many times: a
   whole
Mineworking of twisting chimneys. I passed many small
   corpses,
Chalky bones gripping flu-brushes. In the end I too stuck,

My shoulders wedged between the sooty stone, no light
   anywhere.
I soon gave up struggling, it was pointless to shout. I have
   whiled
Away the years dreaming again the stories I used to read
   over and over
At home, before Grimes caught me. I have grown a skeleton
Dreaming away the dark. Sometimes I think I hear the
   voice
Of the girl in the light, silken chamber. I struggle to shout,
But my mouth is full of black soot.

Int: *During the baseline measure, there was just silence or meaningless noises, what
we term garbage or word-salad. Gradually however he began to show faint signs
of interest, and to follow my hands.*
   Mr Black, do you know what these are?
Mr Black: (*no response*)
Int: Cup, Mr Black. I'd like you to say CUP.
Mr Black: (*garbage*)
Int: (coldly) That was garbage, Mr Black. CUP.
Mr Black: (*garbage*)
Int: CUP! CUP! CUP! Mr Black, CUP.
Mr Black: Ka, Ka.
Int: GOOod! Now CUP.
Mr Black: (*garbage*)
Int: C'mon now, Mr Black. CUP.
Mr Black: Ka, ka.
Int: Good. That was nice, you know that? CUP.
Mr Black: Cu —
Int: GOOod! MARvellous. I liked that, I really did like that. Now try again.
   CUP.
Mr Black: Cup.
Int: GOOod BOOoy! That was VERY GOOD. That was really something.
   Cup.
Mr Black: Ka, ka.
Int: Good. Cup.
Mr Black: (*garbage*)
Int: (coldly) That was garbage, Mr Black. CUP. CUP.

I follow the trail of the lost seekers, Alan Quatermain the
   great hunter,

Stout Curtis and brave good Sir Henry Good; in my hand
The torn yellow parchment bequeathed by the dying
    Portuguese
Seeker, Da Silvestra, to later seekers; crawl with it in hand
Over the shimmering desert fiery gold under a round red
    sun
Filling half the sky and about to explode; suddenly, on the
    horizon.
Out of nothing – Sheba's Breasts, each berg fifteen thousand
    feet
In height, linked by a sheer rock-cliff, swathed in cloud-
    mists
Like a woman asleep, veiled; extinct volcanos, they are gold
In the throbbing sunlight, except that they rise into snow-
    nipples.
Miles to go yet – but there, a dozen yards away, half-sunk
    in a koppie.
As the old Dom's map predicted, unsuspected, the pan
    bad water.
But as I scrabble to it and stoop to suck, it slips away from
    me
Like the lips of a harlot, in loathing, turned aside, spitting
Saying, is it not enough you burrow into my hole
My diamond-mine, my lineaments of scrofulous apathy?
    Across
The desert, I climb the foothills, following the crushed
    twigs
Following the three pairs of footprints still preserved
In the snows after a thousand years and I enter a region
    of ice and silence,
The air thin, difficult to drag your feet;
But at the crest, a cave, and I enter its darkness,
And there, at the end of the cave, seated on a ledge, as
    expected,
Is the body of a man, Da Silvestra, the yellow skin – still
Preserved by the cold after two thousand years – stretched
    tight
Over his bones; in middle life, his features aquiline,
The remains of a woollen pair of hose, a yellow crucifix
    round his neck,
Naked else; a small bone pen at his feet. a wound in his arm

Where he had drawn the ink; now all his words have flowed
Into the winds and mists that swirl around Sheba's nipple.
His mouth hanging open, head slumped, the maker of the
    map has nothing to say.

Int: MR BLACK!! LOOK AT ME!! CUP! Mr Black. CUP!
    (*He had this way of, you know, going dead on you, you might have been a wall
    for all he knew or cared, and when this happened, I'd shout his name, real loud,
    and as though I was mad as hell with him. It was a kind of electric shock, and
    it did seem to work, he did seem to come just a little out of his trance.*)
    CUP! MR BLACK. CUP!
Mr Black: (*garbage*)
Int: NO! Mr Black. NO! NO! NO! Say no, Mr Black.
Mr Black: (*garbage*)
Int: No. No. C'mon now, I thought you said it then. No.
Mr Black: No.
Int: (caressingly) BEAUTIFUL. That was terrific. That was so nice. No.
    No.
Mr Black: No.
Int: GOOod! You make me happy the way you say that ... Do you like
    food?
Mr Black: (*no response*)
Int: Okay, Mr Black, you've been working very hard, you've been really
    trying, I'm going to let you be taken back to the ward now.

It has been restful here; knowing I was in a vice,
I could forget his surliness, and dream of the stars and the
    girl,
Quietly. But now that skin and flesh have dropped away
    from me,
I find that I can move my shoulders down, and there is my
    mother's
Voice calling. I don't want to climb down. My limbs are
    stiffly cramped.
But her nipples call. Her white hands will wash me clean
With a heavy sponge. And I will wriggle into her bed.

Int: What's this I've got between my fingers, Mr Black?
Mr Black: (*no response*)
Int: Cigarette. Say cigarette.
Mr Black: (*garbage*)

Int: CIGARETTE.

Mr Black: (*garbage*)

Int: That was mush, Mr Black, that was garbage. CIGARETTE.

Mr Black: Sa, sa.

Int: GOOod! Now again, Mr Black. Cigarette.

Mr Black: Cigarette.

Int: MARvellous! It really was. I'd like to give you a puff for saying that, Mr
  Black. Once more and you can take it from me. Cigarette. Cigarette

Mr Black: (*garbage*)

Int: CIGARETTE.

Mr Black: (*no response*)

Int: MR BLACK! Look at my hand! MR BLACK!

Mr Black: (*garbage*)

Int: CIGARETTE.

Mr Black: Cigarette.

Int: GOOod BOOoy! Do you want to take it from me, Mr Black?

Behold, in the dark, a man.
A yellow crucifix.
Middle-height, middle-span;
His limbs dry as sticks.

Though natives swear
His body to glory ascended,
The Dom is here;
Here his journey ended.

A wound in his arm
Where the great map spilled;
Now he sits dumb
His voice is stilled.

Forty days he survived
The tortures of the desert;
On snake-flesh he lived,
And wrote with bone his chart.

With what courage he rose!
But himself he could not save;
See how his vision froze
To a ledge in a cave.

Int: It's a bit cool today, Mr Black, do you want a nice drink? Say tea and I'll give you some.
Mr Black: (*garbage*)
Int: Tea, Mr Black, and I'll pour you some.
Mr Black: Tea.
Int: Lovely. Really nice. Tea.
Mr Black: (*garbage*)
Int: No, Mr Black. Tea.
Mr Black: Tea.
Int: GOOod. Tea and you can have some.
Mr Black: Tea.
Int: Good talking. Tea.
Mr Black: Tea.
Int: LOVEly. Terrific. Tea.
Mr Black: (*garbage*)
Int: TEA.
Mr Black: Tea.
Int: GOOD, very good. Tea.
Mr Black: (*garbage*)
Int: (coldly) That was garbage, Mr Black. Tea. Tea, and I'll give you some.

You are more beautiful than in any of the pictures, rising,
Your sweet smiling face framed by the long yellow ringleted
    hair,
Arms stretched out to clasp me to the bosom of your
    nightgown.
You offer me the keys to the gates, all your body's
    openings.
But I cower back into the fireplace, your breasts have
    turned
Into gourds of gold. On your forehead a rose
Is being gnawed by a grey worm. How can I warn you?
My mouth is dry.

Int: MR BLACK!! THIS WAY, MR BLACK!!! . . . That's right. Okay, (*he's not interested in the tea*) let's try some candy. Do you want to say candy and I'll give you some?
Mr Black: (*garbage*)
Int: Candy. Candy.
Mr Black: (*garbage*)

Int: C'mon now, kid. Candy. Say candy.

Mr Black: Ka, ka.

Int: GOOod. Candy.

Mr Black: Ka, ka.

Int: Candy. Candy.

Mr Black: Candy.

Int: (rapturously) TerrRIFic! Good talking. I'd like to give you a square of chocolate for saying it so nicely, Mr Black. Candy. Candy.

Mr Black: (*garbage*)

Int: (coldly) No, Mr Black, that was word-salad. Candy.

Mr Black: Candy.

Int: (rapturously) GOOod. Marvellous. That was a honey. Candy.

Mr Black: Candy.

Int: GOOod! Real nice. You've come a long way today, Mr Black.

The ghosts of Quatermain, Curtis and Good tell me that
    when you reached
The top of the mountain and could climb no further, the
    voice you heard
On the plain could be heard no more, there was only the
    shrieking wind
Around Sheba's barren nipple, grey clouds scudding, letting
    through
Streaks of the dying sun. They tell me you washed
Your sand-raw wounds in the snow. Then you dismissed
Your bearers. Looking down at the other side,
You cried gently. Then found yourself this cave, sat down
    and there
Eased yourself of thirty years' saintliness in a thin stream
Of milk. We see the grey stain on the floor still. There was
No thunder striking you, only a soft down-flurry of snow
    across
The cave-mouth from the peak of the nipple. I reach down
    and break
The string of the crucifix.

Int: *This is Friday, March 3rd, session 5. Mr Black has been doing a lot of vocalising, he's been chatting at quite a high rate. Of course it's mixed up with a lot of garbage. We are looking at a picture of a horse.*

Okay, Mr Black, let's look at the picture. What's this, huh?

Mr Black: (*garbage*)

Int: A horse. Horse. Horse. Horse. Horse. I'd like you to say horse.
Mr Black: (*no response*)
Int: (*I broke off recording there. We didn't get anywhere for, oh, five minutes. Then it started moving.*)
Mr Black: Horse.
Int: GOOD, Mr Black. Terrific. How nice of you to say it to me.
Mr Black: H— h—
Int: Yes, horse. What's this? Horse.
Mr Black: Yes.
Int: OH! GOOod, Mr Black. Yes! Lovely talking. What's this?
Mr Black: (*garbage*)
Int: Point to the horse, Jimmy.

I go down into the secret land that Solomon ruled;
A place of paradisal mills each one a thousand storeys high,
Light, walled in glass, wheel within wheel and without
    wheel visible,
To the amazed eye; they stretch away to the horizon,
The low hills that lead to other mills;
And above the mills of industry where metallic slaves toil,
In a billion glass compartments the Greys are resting,
On the eve of some great battle, for their faces are savage
    and composed;
I see them eat, sleep, make love, with the air of dream
As men do before a battle; a million raise glasses of milk
    to their lips,
A million urinate; I see none born, none dying;
All are in the prime of manhood, womanhood, all hand-
    some, all indistinguishable;
And as I watch the magnificent regiment of the Greys at rest
Before certain annihilation, waiting with a calm despair,
It seems to me that Death has already touched them;
Though below, out of the shining mills, a constant stream
    appears
Of bodily organs; of hearts, lungs, kidneys, genitals, and
    brains.
It is the last, epic stand of the Greys.

Int: MR BLACK!! MR BLACK!! FOLLOW MY FINGER, MR BLACK!
    What do you see, Mr Black? Huh?
Mr Black: Horse.

Int: GOOD BOY! That's good talking. Now what's this in my hand?
Mr Black: Chocolate.
Int: Chocolate, that's nice. You may take it. You named it correctly so you can have it. Now what's this? Brooch. Brooch.
Mr Black: (*garbage*)
Int: Give me the chocolate, Mr Black. What's this?
Mr Black: Brooch.
Int: GOOod! Good talking, Jimmy. Very good. That's a nice chocolate. You may eat it for talking so nicely. Now, Mr Black, would you tell me, what is this? What is this?
Mr Black: (*no response*)
Int: (anger) Back to the ward, back to the ward. You don't know. Out! Out!

Your voice is all caresses; even your scoldings are part of
   your love,
As when I skipped off the pavement or would not drink my
   milk up.
You send me to bed but creep up to kiss me.
You laugh, pulling your nightdress over your head, and I
   long
To reach out and embrace your loins or vanish into that dusky
Grove. But everywhere I touch finds gold not flesh;
Spreads over the serene pacific to the musky indentation,
   spiced,
Trickling down the line of childbirth I printed in you
To the vast jungles of Africa, lakes and cascades and rivers
Shrivelling as the pores close under liquid gold. Your hair
Brushing against me now is metallic, bleeds my face.
The worm's chaps gnaw and you do not seem aware. Your
   laughter,
Golden and metallic, swarms through the rooftops and stirs
All the small skeletons into limb-jerkings. Like insects lying
On their backs, they strive for the word which pleases you.

Int: *It's teatime and I'm going to give him some tea.*
   Mr Black, what's this?
Mr Black: Bread.
Int: You're right, it's bread. I love you talking. What's this, Mr Black?
Mr Black: (*garbage*)
Int: That's chatting, Mr Black, what's this?

Mr Black: Butter.
Int: GOOod! That was good. Yes, butter. What's this?
Mr Black: (*garbage*)
Int: Milk, Mr Black. Say milk and I'll pour you a glass.
Mr Black: (*garbage*)
Int: Nice chatting. Milk.

Grey, behind crystal-walls
The Greys are resting;
Flower of Kukuanaland.
And all, the same arresting
Tomorrow appals.

Awaiting the mighty war
That may never come.
How long must they wait to hear
The cleansing drum,
The cosmic roar?

A million urinate;
A million drink;
A million stare at screens;
A million think;
A million masturbate;
A million cry but keep
Tears hidden by a hand;
In nightmare twitched
By the Greys' last stand
A million million sleep.

God's bravest, combat-steeled;
But how if they never hear
The exultant warcry *Koom!*
The thunder of spear on spear
Tapping against shield?

Int: *So far today we've had an enormous amount of verbalisation, but very few audible words. Also one of his cadaver-like withdrawals in which he just stared down at his hands. But then came a truly amazing sequence of positive responses. We were looking through some more pictures . . .*
     Okay, Mr Black, what's this?
Mr Black: Car.

Int: Car, GOOod. That's nice. And this? Can you say this?

Mr Black: No.

Int: Tape-recorder.

Mr Black: Tape-recorder.

Int: Oh, Mr Black that's a honey. And what's this?

Mr Black: Traffic-lights.

Int: Oh my gosh! (*laughter*) This is terrific, Mr Black. (*I've never had to feed him so fast – about every other time.*)
What's this? – Oh, I'm sorry, I've spilt some on you.

Mr Black: Spilt, yes.

Int: MY! (*laughter*) I can't believe you're talking so well, Mr Black. What's this?

Mr Black: Aeroplane.

Int: What are these?

Mr Black: (*no response*)

Int: What are these, Mr Black?

Mr Black: Skyscrapers.

Int: GOOod. What's this?

Mr Black: (*garbage*)

Int: Can you say typewriter?

Mr Black: Typewriter, yes.

Int: Beautiful. What's this?

Mr Black: Bridge.

Int: Good. Oh you're working terrifically, Mr Black. I can't remember when I had so much fun.
And so it went on, you just couldn't stop him, he just wouldn't be inappropriate! And when he finally flunked out – I think he was tired too – I was actually relieved! I was so tired, he'd really worn me out, but all the same I felt good, I felt that I'd really started to break through.

Sheba, your trillion eyes are glazed and reflect the sun.
There is no warmth, no promise in them except the harlot's
promise.
Yet your eyes shone once with maidenlove in a face that
was fertile
To the farthest low hills loped by the zebra. Now they are
tiers of gold
Sunken in a dust-bowl.

Int: *For the past month, I've been attempting to reinstate his reading and writing behaviour. So far he's learnt how to read one word at a time.*

I'd like you to read this for me, Mr Black. Read this.

Mr Black: (tonelessly) The red balloon.

Int: GOOD. VERY good. The red balloon. I like you reading to me. Read this.

Mr Black: (*garbage*)

Int: That was garbage, Mr Black. I turn away my head when you say that. There was ...

Mr Black: There was ...

Int: GOOD. There was a red balloon.

Mr Black: Balloon, yes.

Int: Good. There was a red balloon. Now tell me what colour was the balloon, Mr Black?

Mr Black: Red, yes.

Int: Very good. Red, yes. You're working beautifully. Right, let's read this, shall we?

Mr Black: There was a red balloon.

Int: TerRIFic. Oh, I liked that. Now, can you say the whole sentence for me again, Mr Black?

Mr Black: (*no response*)

Int: C'mon Jimmy. There was a red balloon.

Sometimes the Greys swarm out onto the streets, form up
    in phalanxes
And look up at the sky. A dusty breeze cuts across the blue
And a shadow falls as the sun is darkly eaten. A soft
    murmur rises
As the red globe is extinguished they remember the stranger
Who was able to darken it at will, and they wait for him
    again
To step down from the sky; but the darkness passes and the
    murmur
Fades as the breeze, the streets are empty.

Int: MR BLACK!! LOOK AT ME, MR BLACK!! Okay, Mr Black. Let's try you with some food.
    New behaviours were starting in Mr Black's life generally, as a consequence of his new verbal behaviour. He walks around, and dresses and undresses himself. I'm actually watching him shave right now – we brought a bowl and a mirror into the experimental room – and I'm giving him encouragement, reinforcing his behaviour with food.
    Now, Mr Black, you're putting on shaving soap, aren't you?

Mr Black: Shaving soap, yes.

Int: That's good. And now you're making a lather.

Mr Black: Making a lather.

Int: VERY good. And this morning we made the toast and the tea together, didn't we? And now what are you using. Mr Black?

Mr Black: Razor, yes.

Int: Oh that's lovely, I'll have to give you some fish for saying that. As soon as you've shaved we'll have some lunch. Do you like fish?

Mr Black: Want some fish, yes.

Int: Oh my gosh, yes! And maybe you'd like some potato and beans?

Mr Black: (*garbage*)

Int: That was garbage. I turn away my head.

There on the ground where the stone has risen are the
    crushed
Bones of old Gagool and near them the poor decaying body
Of Foulata who died peacefully in honest Good's arms for
    the sun
Cannot mate with the darkness nor the white with the black
But O her soul is white. Da Silvestra on the mountain
And Foulata in the depths – what hope is there
That we can survive? No need to mourn the queen and king
When I too am walled in the living grave. Leaving the boxes
    of diamonds
As all seekers have done I heave at the stone-ring
In the floor, and descend, following the draught of air
Into a maze of mine-addits deep in the mountainside, the
    tricklings
Of a stream propelled from nowhere; I too
From nowhere to nowhere through the winding chimneys
    past many a
Trapped skeleton, but at last a pinpoint of light, light only
    to those
In pitch darkness, and I crawl forward forcing my shoulders
    through rock
After rock through earth ever narrower till I am through
    with a heave
The jackal-hole and rolling over and over uncontrollably
Down the mountain-slope. And the dawn bursts to show
Around me and under me, the bones of beasts strewn on
    the hidden snow

Int: *This is the last session. With the aid of cue-cards, we have been working on questions which might be useful to him in the ward. I'm going to cover up the cue-cards and see what happens.*

Mr Black, ask me a question about the month.

Mr Black: The month.

Int: Good. Ask me a question about the month.

Mr Black: (tonelessly) What is the month?

Int: Good. It's August – that's nice. Ask me a question about the time.

Mr Black: What is the time?

Int: Good. It's – it's after eleven. Good. Question me about the day.

Mr Black: (*garbage*)

Int: Question me about the day, Mr Black.

Mr Black: What's the day?

Int: It's Monday. That was very good. Ask me a question about the ward.

Mr Black: What's the ward?

Int: Good. It's Cedar Ward. Ask me a question about the doctor.

Mr Black: (*no response*)

A few slow beasts still crawl
Through the flattened undergrowth,
The jungle carved by the flight
To a fireball's aftermath.

The rest in their myriads crushed
On the snowy mountainside,
Look back at the scene they had left,
And their clamour died.

Famine settled their limbs,
The night shone icy and calm;
The deer lay down by the leopard,
The lion covered the lamb.

Int: *Now we're just going to talk generally for a while.*

Do you like these flowers, Mr Black?

Mr Black: Nice flowers, yes.

Int: Good. They are nice. I picked them myself in the garden this morning. It's late for them but they're so lovely. Is it nice today?

Mr Black: Today.

Int: Is it nice weather today?

Mr Black: Lovely weather, yes.

Int: Good. It's lovely weather, very sunny. What colour is my dress?

Mr Black: (*garbage*)

Int: No, what colour is my dress?

Mr Black: White, nice.

Int: Oh, good. I'll have to give you some candy for doing so well. Oh gosh! it must be very stuffy in here, Mr Black, I'm sorry. What have I just done?

Mr Black: Yawned, yes.

Int: GOOod, I yawned. That's very good.

The treatment was completed, and it only remained to take the final baseline measures.

What is your name?

Mr Black: Black, yes.

Int: Where do you live?

Mr Black: Maple Ward.

Int: How long have you been here?

Mr Black: (*garbage*)

Int: How long have you been here?

Mr Black: Twenty years.

Int: What's this?

Mr Black: Pen.

Int: What's this?

Mr Black: Comb, yes.

Int: What's this?

Mr Black: Handkerchief.

Int: Do you like snakes?

Mr Black: No.

Int: Do you like pain?

Mr Black: (*no response*)

While she sighs in her sleep
His lust devours,
Lip under velvet lip,
The red raw flower.

When she wakes up,
Warm in her rumpled clothes,
She yawns, and has no mirror
To see the rose.

Int: *When I went back to visit him three months later I found that, though there had been some regression and the doctors and nurses reported little difference in* *his behaviour, he could still respond positively. I also learned something that touched me very deeply. About a month after the termination of treatment, one day he just disappeared. He'd just walked out of the gates and kept on walking. I guess deep in his mind he wanted to walk home. He walked all that night. The next day a charge nurse found him and he was brought back. When I heard about this, I didn't know whether to be glad or sorry. He might have got himself killed, of course, he really wasn't safe, and yet I think I was really glad. It showed that Mr Black was alive again, or coming alive, and he'd been dead a long time.*

You tempted me with your loveliness but you withdrew it
    again;
When your legs were stretched wide and your arms, I saw
    that your last
Extremities, arctic and antarctic, were also imprisoned in
    gold.
The last pore shut fast, you could breathe no more. I waited
    for you
To speak but you did not. You have destroyed me with
    absence
– death. Now I walk through you to find you, heal you of
    dumbness;
Or all shall say, without a use this shining woman lived,
Or did she only live to be at death the food of worms? If I
Can find one pore of your body not wholly dead and open
    it,
And plant therein one seed, one flower . . . you will come
    to me again
And speak to me. Through Highgate and Hampstead, to
    Poplar and Bow,
To Islington, all night I walk – home, home.
Dawn breaks over the Surrey Hills. And behind me I see
An angel, smiling, holding out his hands in blessing,
Quickening his steps to catch me up to guide me on my way
To save you, bring you back.

The Soft World Sequence

GEORGE MACBETH

1 the sea

Through the glass floor,
from below,
he could see the girl
in the glass typing-chair,

in the glass skirt,
crossing her flesh legs
over the glass eye
in her groin. Glassily, it stared

at his own eye, and slowly,
the world of glass,
opening, closing,
became soft,

like the lips of an octopus
with eight legs
opening, closing,
in the Indian Ocean.

2 the clouds

The man had been a bit
slow on the uptake, but
when his elbows went through
the light oak,

he saw the point. After his leg, too,
had sunk in
and was shivering
in the middle of the carbon-paper drawer, they began

to realize just how far
it had gone. Not even
the one in the telephone
bothered about the screaming then,

though it did make a hell
of a noise. It was how
to profit from it that occupied
all their minds. After so long

without anyone wondering
how they felt about it all,
none of them was accustomed
to making much of an impact. So

even the one in the floor
let him run his legs through
for a while without
worrying. Of course,

the man did wade in diminishing
circles, evidently
grasping (albeit rather slowly)
just how soft the whole

thing had become. It took him
several minutes, though,
to appreciate the full reason
for the watery coolness.

When he did,
there was more noise. The one in the PAX phone
got quite a headache
in its ear-piece.

Elsewhere I doubt
if they had so much trouble. Just
a fluffy moistness
easing in where

the old edges had been. And then
the slow, steady,
drumming, pita-pata
sound, as the rain started.

3 the earth

Well, it was all, really,
a palpable jelly,
touchable, glaucous,
very good to eat

in its own way, if you liked
that sort of thing. I mean before
the day of the cucumbers.
After that, the hard edges

all became round heads,
and there wasn't much
you could do about it.
Not without risking

a hell of a row,
and maybe getting cut,
or swallowed up
in the ice. Let well alone,

I always say.
Take what comes.
You can't win them all. Not
without being one of them yourself.

Space Hopping with Captain God

JOHN T. SLADEK

Anyone who still believes that a superior being from another star arrived here in the dim, dumb past, to the well-documented amazement of the locals, must read Erich von Daniken's *Chariots of the Gods*. He will probably suffer, as I did, a loss of faith.

From its serialisation title, *Was God an Astronaut?*, one can deduce its smug anthropocentric point of view. Not only did aliens land, they looked like men, acted like men, and used miraculous twentieth-century devices to keep the natives awed. Daniken actually suggests that they planned the Deluge, sired Noah on an earth-gal, and snatched Elijah and Enoch (why not Ambrose Bierce?). Naturally they were worshipped by the simple natives every place they landed; by the Sumerians, the Egyptians, the Jews, the Chinese, the Eskimos, a seventeenth-century mapmaker, and by that funny rustic, Jonathan Swift. Daniken 'proclaims' that they

> *annihilated part of mankind existing at the time and produced a new, perhaps the first, homo sapiens ... It is my aim to try to provide proof of this assertion.*

This he does not do. The *contents* of this book prove nothing, though its *sales* (300,000 in Germany) seem to prove Barnum's famous sucker statistic.

It's a Barnum book, really, a sleazy sideshow crammed with Fortean facts and Ripley rarees, where you'll meet many old favourites like the Great Pyramid, Easter Island, UFOs and ESP.

Beginning with obscure or spurious data, Daniken proceeds by that logical path favoured by all high priests of hokum, where the Barely Possible becomes the Probable and ends up being a Certainty. Do cave drawings show men with thickened limbs and enlarged heads? These can only be SPACESUITS and HELMETS! The things sticking out of their heads (long mistaken by vulgar archaeologists for mere horns) are of course ANTENNAE! The Great Pyramid would have taken 600 years to build by hand (he says) – so they must have quarried the rock with *lasers* and shifted it by *helicopter!*

> *In Helwan there is a piece of cloth, a fabric so fine that it could only be woven today in a special factory with great technical know-how and experience.*

Electric dry batteries, which work on the galvanic principle, are on display in Baghdad Museum.

The chapters on archaeology abound with such *Believe it or so what!* dainties, and I don't doubt a one of them, any more than I doubt that the Deutsches Museum in Munich displays airplanes and bicycles, or that I have one eye.

Now for some mathematics:

Is it a coincidence that the area of the base of the Pyramid [of Cheops] *divided by twice its height gives the celebrated figure of* $\pi = 3.14159$, *discovered by Ludolf?*

I don't know what Ludolf is supposed to have discovered, but this is not coincidence, it is fakery. Notice that the area of the base must be in square units (sq.ft, sq.cm, etc.) and the height must be in linear measure (ft, ins, miles, etc.). Dividing, one gets not π (which is a ratio, and has no dimensions) but some number in linear units. The size of this answer depends entirely on what units one has used in the problem: feet give one answer, inches another, meters another, and so on. By choosing a suitable unit of measurement, one can produce any string of digits one pleases.

And now for literature:

Where did the narrators of The Thousand and One Nights *get their staggering wealth of ideas? How did anyone come to describe a lamp from which a magician spoke when the owner wished?*

Apparently no reader, Daniken thus misquotes the story of Aladdin above as he will the Bible below, to his own purposes. The idea here is that the lamp was some kind of radio, but to get that idea he has to make the story duller and then ask why it was so imaginative; a genie with incredible powers is turned into the voice of a magician.

Moses relates the exact instructions which 'God' gave for building the Ark of the Covenant. [How does Daniken know this?] *The directions are given to the very inch and how and where staves and rings are to be fitted and from what alloy the metals are to be made.*

Anyone who doesn't know his inch from his cubit (forearm) and who thinks that metals are made from alloys has no business trying to make Exodus a radio manual, but Daniken presses on: the Ark was really designed to pick up messages from God in His saucer. The idea is supported by deductions based on the death of Uzzah (in 2 Samuel 6), who put his hand to the Ark to keep it from toppling over and was struck dead for this reflex of little faith. Daniken diagnoses:

Undoubtedly the Ark was electrically charged! If we construct it according to the instructions handed down by Moses, a voltage of several hundred volts is produced.

Well, there is *some* room for doubt, especially since the Ark was only a box of shittim wood, $2\frac{1}{2}$ x $1\frac{1}{2}$ x$1\frac{1}{2}$ forearms in size, gold-plated and fitted with rings at four corners through which pass two carrying staves. Nothing at all is 'produced', and it will not support any voltage. The staves are also of shittim wood also plated with gold, so even if the thing did carry several hundred volts it could not, in turn, be carried. If Uzzah was 'undoubtedly' electrocuted, then Adam and Eve were undoubtedly barred from Eden by an angel with a soldering iron.

Daniken's astronomy is no better: he merely sets out the statistics that look good (there are likely a few planets in our galaxy with intelligent life upon them) and ignores those that don't (the galaxy is very big). Like so many UFOlogists, he insists the problem is only 'Is there life on other planets?'

Since life on other planets associated with our sun has been (for UFO purposes) all but eliminated as a possibility, any space visitors must have come from elsewhere. They would need a near-light-speed drive to get anywhere, and even then the search for earth would take time. The life of a civilisation such as ours (from Cro-Magnon man to?) has been estimated to take about as long as it takes light to cross our galaxy. The astronomers and biologists have more or less agreed:

1. It is almost certain that there are other civilisations in our own galaxy.

2. It is almost certain that we shall never contact them, or find any trace of them, or they us.

But scientists can be wrong (he hammers home this point), and they laughed at Galileo. And I suppose it is just possible that some aliens crossed twenty light years or so of space and searched over a few thousand habitable but uninhabited planets – and just to pick up an Elijah for their zoo. Or maybe they hung around (even less likely) while the Incas built them airfields, while the Egyptians learned a smattering of cryogenics, long enough to give Ali Baba a voice-operated door and Gilgamesh a joy-ride and so on (Daniken mentions these as probabilities). And then they had to leave, with every scrap of evidence of their existence (like the helicopters Ezekiel saw), pausing only to make man in their image. But I don't believe it.

Another possibility is that I'm in their pay or power, that I've been told to say all this to discredit the one man who is on the verge of discovering *the truth*!

Scholia, Seasoned with Crabs, Blish Is

JOHN CLUTE

Stately, anfractuous James Blish comes down from Fabers, bearing a bowl of scholium on which two novels and a best sf of him lie crossed. Lyly's *Geology*, euphuistic sod, is sustained gently behind him by the mild ignorant readership. He holds the bowl aloft and intones:

—The world's my *Ostrea edulis*.

Then closing the preface to his *Best Science Fiction Stories (Revised Edition)* with a sigh, down the dark winding stairs he comes to us with gifts, this grim scholar, fearful Jesuit, reaper of Joyce and biology, Strowger genre switcher (listen for the clunk), misogynist qua texts, apocalypse lover with icy fingers, James Blish who devised the best template series science fiction had ever seen, the Okie stories, and then ruined it, James Blish who now writes the worst, *Star Trek*, and will not stop, James Blish, through whose corpus, as through a moraine, granite and guck interpenetrate cackling beneath the full moon, each new book a spastic *piñata* spewing delirious botched crab-apples forth, inedible cranky mutant gets, but then granite too, the death of God in *Black Easter*, John Amalfi's 'slogging brutal tireless heart', the masked Menippean discourse kicking off *A Case of Conscience*, the Kodiak bear terminating *The Warriors of Day* with a sudden salutary perspective transform, so that in dealing with this most uneven of all major writers of science fiction one never quite knows what to expect next in the dark, quicksand or a bed of nails.

The books on hand – Faber's three, *Best Science Fiction Stories*, *The Day After Judgement*, *And All the Stars a Stage*, a bag sufficiently mixed to be sold only on prescription; plus *Midsummer Century*, a 35,000-word story optimistically bound by Doubleday between hard covers nearly as thick as the text and including a list of Blish's publications nearly as long; and a Penguin release of the superb *Black Easter* from 1968 – all go a long way to increase the confusion in breast and head, and the job of dissevering joy from glop. But there is always a silver lining. Difficulties of gist apprehension, and general fibrillation of the affect, are not in this case intensified by any delirium parataxis from the pen of Donald A. Wollheim as he wields it with his thumb throughout *The Universe Makers*, that inimitable fan's vade-mecum for the sniffing out of security risks ('The New Wave represents a departure from the science fiction directives for mankind') and for the identification of echt-sf on the high road of 'Future Predictions' ('that framework of millions of years to come'), through his expedient refusal to mention James Blish at all. Blish leans to dystopic versions of the future, to rebarbative excursions into moral philosophy, and to apocalypses both frigid and terminal; Wollheim ('Humanity, whatever its faults, is the best darned thing going and will never be pinned to the mat') does not. Perhaps it is for that reason that the raven of DAW has excluded, from his conspectus of the *mind-boggling futures* science fiction is directing us into, any reference to the works of James Blish, inventor of the spindizzy, and flying cities, and consequent models of galactic commerce, and pantropy seeding the spread stars. Certainly it is the case that Mr Wollheim trucks little with moral ambiguities and shades of 20th cent grey (copyright pending), for, as he says, in his own words:

Good lives!
What does it mean when a thirst for novels wherein unmistakable heroes fight against unmistakable villains continues to show itself in fantasy writings . . . ?

It means that there is hope for humanity and hope for youth. For it means that hundreds of thousands – possibly millions – of young intelligent people are not basically cynics and victims of despair. It means that the ancient belief in the rightness of innate Good – that belief which sustained all the armies of prehistory whose battles laid the foundations for all that we call civilization and culture – has not died from the human spirit. Youth recognized it when it came to them in its ancient pure form and rallied to it.

Let the New Wave sneer and snarl and cry that science fiction is dead and its vision of galactic futures dead; let them present their writings of despair filled with shock words and shock concepts; they have been defeated already by the cry *Frodo Lives!*

Some critics – possibly James Blish himself – might discover objections to this remarkable reading of the social consequences of pretending to believe in Frodo buttons, and might interpret the extraordinary popularity of *The Lord of the Rings*, whose author in any case explicitly repudiated any attempt to allegorize his romance, as a sign not of moral rearmament but of its reverse, not 'belief in the rightness of innate Good' but 'shock words and shock concepts' and a growing sense, not solely ecological, that we are the toilet we shit in.

The dejuiced angsty nostalgia for icons that so clearly riddles Frodomania – they might argue – bears a signifying relation to the post-industrial quietism currently infusing modern youth's bosom with repressively-desublimated orexis rot, and the same signification applies to those weenybopper theosophies more recently woven, with dank cabbalistic bootlicking and Art Nouveau cartoons, around the sword and sorcery fantasies of Michael Moorcock, for which he must take some blame, as he does not stop writing them, and has in consequence become a purple sage. In their easy desolateness these fantasies represent – one supposes – a *Star Trek* of the inscape, and in their firm bleached contours and carious irreality they provide decals galore for icon-building; nor, in a world that feels the need for forms of belief, but has generally lost the innocence to believe in the forms of belief, should that accomplishment be counted negligible, just maybe a touch chilling. . . .

Icon-wise, as we shall see, James Blish has a brown thumb, nor is he cheerful, so it is no more surprising to note his failure to build a consistent version of himself for the field to chew on, like Heinlein's, than it is to recollect his exclusion from former Ace kingpin Wollheim's shortlist of future-builders of good faith, which includes guys like Mark S. Geston, and Alexei Panshin, and Dean R. Koontz, and A. Bertram Chandler, and Andre Norton (gal).

Even a selective glance at Blish's oeuvre, none of which ever appeared in Ace Books, demonstrates a formidable yet strangely ill-at-ease range and industry and craft: take *The Warriors of Day* (1951), for instance, or *Jack of Eagles* (1952), both impregnated with pulp but natty; or *Cities in Flight* (1950–1962), inside the avoirdupois of which a template saga begs to be let out, *pace* Spengler, as English readers will at last be able to confirm (or deny) for a small sum early in 1974, when Arrow Books will be publishing the whole sequence in paperback. Speaking of templates (Blish's own term, by the way), Arrow will also be releasing later this year the first three or four volumes of the Dumarest series, E. C. Tubb's fine, modest, rounded, professional quest-for-lost-Earth sequence.

Or take *A Case of Conscience* (1953–1958), the embedded tone- and affect-clarity of whose initial discourse strikes – suggestively – a note of fitness of means to intent lacking elsewhere in the list; or *The Seedling Stars* (stories assembled in 1957), in which pantropy and a sketchy galactic colonization model get too brief a run but live beyond their text.

Or take *VOR* (1949–1958), a misshapen effort, as Damon Knight has shown, a monster story whose peculiarly disgruntled and – as it were – *low-budget* adherence to the sidelines of the action nicely illuminates a seedier aspect of genre sequence construction. One might call it the *metonymy con*, and refer to its frequent appearance in B movies, where budgetary nightmares like car crashes or the end of the world demand avoidance gambits in which a rhetoric of personalized response and simplified gesture will substitute for any attempt at rendering the complex (or expensive) action. It all results in a miniaturized, claustrophobic, sideline, papier-maché world, whose protagonists invariably and very oddly seem half-blinded by flashbulbs, nor are there shadows. A typical shot sequence would be triadic. First (after the quarrel) there would be a quick scared look of outward regard, preferably the hero's, optionally followed by a nerve-shatteringly swift eyeline shot of a Dinky Toy totalling against a twig, and concluded by three lollygagging minutes of con that comprise the heart of the avoidance gambit – an interminable reaction shot synecdoche in which the heroine, leaning against a cardboard tree, nags the protagonist with a shrill, contemptuously 'feminine' monologue until we could all just scream. What do you *mean* Los Angeles is doomed, Harry, what do you *mean* it's the end of the world? Don't be *ridiculous*, Harry, my father, Senator Higginbotham, your father-in-law, a man who has the ear of the President of the United States, he told me there was nothing to worry about, Harry, and *he* wouldn't lie. Harry, I *won't go!* This Hollywood misogyny – which James Blish has indulged in himself more than once, viz. Dee Hazleton – neatly conforms to another conveniently low-budget conceit – which Mr Blish has also made use of, viz. *They Shall Have Stars* – the idea that the audience somehow longs to identify with that generic humour known as the Most Ignorant Participant, who is usually female, and that it therefore welcomes any chance it gets to be told, at stupefying length, facts which, out of the entire cast, she and only she persists in failing to comprehend.

Or take *Titan's* – also listed as *Titans'* – *Daughter* (1952–1961), a book which seems misnamed wherever the apostrophe is placed, as the girl in question, though eight feet tall, and close friend to other, taller, better informed, more important Titans, can claim neither to be the story's protagonist nor the daughter of anyone at all large. More interestingly, however, *Titan's Daughter* is a bumpy, peremptory compendium of narrative dislocations and affect discords, a chilled and chilling demonstration of its author's characteristic impatience with that mimesis of temporal continuity and beingness even sf generic tropes call for, if a novel is intended, and not something else.

Then take *The Star Dwellers* (1961), one of those horrifying juveniles whose protagonist (some kind of cadet) saves Terra, and everyone who lives thereon, through being *liked* by some alien or other sitting in judgment on us all. This one additionally features a saucy teenage girl reporter who, like Good Fellowship in a morality, pops in and out of sight *just as though* she were fulfilling an exemplary function – but the story has no thesis she can illustrate, and the action unfolds as though she were not present. There is a lesson to be learned from this.

Or take *The Night Shapes* (1962), a parody, perhaps not quite sufficiently affectionate, though admirably deadpan, of Haggard Burroughs and Co's melodramatic African wet-dreams of Armed Innocence turned loose to wreak vengeance on all cowardly natives, venomous beasts, craven Arabs and ravishing Princesses whose inner corruption and staple diet, dilled testicle, clues one in to the fact that each and every one of them, natives, beasts, foreigners and self-assertive women, functions in the text as an *earth*, and in this way whitewashes 'Tarzan's' otherwise inadmissable Id. In all of this an uglier form of metonymy holds sway, that form of the con otherwise defined as scapegoating. Philip José Farmer has even more cogently handled the wetdream of the omnipotent Id by making *his* Tarzan *literally* all penis, penis dentata, though it must be admitted that Mr Farmer gives off rather too convincing an appearance of conviction, while Mr Blish certainly does not. I read *The Night Shapes*, incidentally, as a parallel worlds novel, feeling pretty ingenious as I did, and basing my analysis on certain 'errors' that proliferated through the first pages of the text. Lyly, author of *Euphues* (1578), was presented as the author of the 'newly-published *Elements of Geology*', while in this world its author was Sir Charles Lyell, its title *Principles of Geology*, and its date of publication a generation or two prior to the time of the novel, which I took to be around 1904–05. And H. Rider Haggard, nearly fifty in 1904, was referred to as 'young Haggaard,' which also seemed otherworldly enough, even led tentatively to an Afrikaans hypothesis . . . But all in vain. Mr Blish has since indicated (personal conversation, 27 January 1973) that the subtle distortions and hints I had nosed out were nothing more than author's slips, or typos, or printer's errors; the parody was this-worldly. Exegesis bit the dust of consensual London.

Or take any of the books ostensibly on review.

Take the vast *faux-naïf* ungainly array of generic conventions their author lays on and yanks off, or the affect shambles he so often creates with an arbitrary curtain or an icy, stiff-kneed dismissal (like Chris deFord's in *Earthman, Come Home*), or the abiding sense of unease created in the reader by each book's determined avoidance of narrative equipoise, and a unifying conclusion will slowly force itself into view: that we have been traducing intelligent, scholarly, didactic James Blish by considering him a writer of novels at all, nor should that realization read as pejorative.

Blinkered by a procrustean vocabulary, and tactically constrained by a Germanic obsession with anything triune, literary critics have for centuries tended to define all prose fictions as novels, and to derive further generic classifications (like angelic hosts) from that initial act of idiot subsumption, so that we have learned to speak (and think) of realistic novels, and autobiographical novels, and science fiction novels, and fantasy novels, and satirical novels, and utopian novels, and so on, re-enacting the primordial fiat like mad cookycutters, and picking our teeth clean of a lot of mangled Bunyan and Swift and Peacock and Huxley and – right – James Blish as we proceeded, too. That this will no longer do I am not precisely the first to note, nor has the triune hypostasy (lyric – epic – dramatic) only recently become a matter for ribaldry, and so I claim no originality for the impressionistic hints that follow, some of which are based on an attempt to comprehend Northrop Frye, and which are pale suns of that father.

In his *Beyond Genre*, Paul Hernadi discusses Ramon Fernandez's 1926 division of prose fiction into two broad tonalities or aspects. At one pole, the *roman* concerns itself with 'the representation of events as they emerge and develop in time'. Its 'intuitive,' 'synthetic,' 'vital' tonality evokes a '"psychological present" (which has nothing to do with the grammatical tense of a text)'. Clearly, then, the *roman* idiom is instinct with mimesis. At the other pole, the *récit* concerns itself with 'the presentation of past events by a narrator in accordance with the principles of logic and rhetoric'. Its 'logical' and 'analytical' tonality reports a 'conceptualized *temps*', which has nothing to do with tense either, but which gives off a sense of distanced, disjunct pastness. And just as clearly, the *récit* idiom is instinct with exemplification.

Avoiding category errors like the plague (because the *roman-récit* polarity is tonal not formal, and because we have been taught to be neat), we can still see that the traditional novel, as hypostasized by the triune hierophants, is in fact a *roman* – warm, plastic, representational, seamless, lacking any coarse '"holes" in the fabric of time', as Dr Hernadi goes on to say – and that fictions in the *récit* idiom – chilly, didactic, presentational, disjunctive, full of arbitrary lacunae in the quilt of space – will read as deficient *romans*, and assigned to the charnel where Procrustes dumps his legs.

Most of our great novelists have written in the *roman* tradition, it is true, though their fictions bear rather less structural resemblance to each other than one might have guessed from the rubric they bear in common. Fielding, or Richardson, or Smollett, but not Sterne, or Dickens, but not Meredith, can be so read without much discomfort. Nearing our own century, however, the identification of 'novel' and *roman* gets more and more ludicrous, and becomes a formula for the writing of midcult kitsch most serious authors simply fail to heed – cf. Joyce, or Mann, or Proust, but not Maugham, or Faulkner, but not dear Saul Bellow. Still further on, taking a fiction the old vocabulary simply flenses, Nabokov's *Pale Fire* is a 'novel' whose tonal idiom might well be rendered as genuine *récit* pretending to be fake *récit* pretending to be closet *roman*.

And back with James Blish, we're able to dissolve some of the knots and crabbed access he offers to the field through the realization that, as a writer, he is deeply immersed in the *récit* idiom, maugre science fiction's general devotion to a shrill, streamlined mimetic parlance. As his fictions are radically deficient by *roman* canons, their fitness to a less popular idiom seems genuinely redemptive ... Blish's incapacity at shaping a mimesis of time's present tense in the work, his compulsively frigid vetoing of any of his characters' movements towards intersubjectivity or joy, both transform themselves – in this new reading – into valid assays at a different task, the exemplification of dystopic topoi dear to the *récit* mind, like Voltaire's or Swift's, the pointing of a lesson through exemplary catastrophes, exemplary discourse, through exemplary characters and diction and mise en scene – though we're still left with the job of formally defining the fictions through which these dystopias are rendered, because certainly we cannot go on calling them novels.

In the Fourth Essay of his *Anatomy of Criticism*, Northrop Frye divides prose fictions into four categories: the novel, which began in the eighteenth century and continued into ours, though now dead, and from which most *great traditions* select their mash; the romance, whose 'stylized' protagonists 'expand into psychological archetypes', and which 'often radiates a glow of subjective intensity that the novel lacks', so that there should be no doubt where most science fiction slots in; the confession, which includes autobiographies, but also that 'introverted' and 'intellectualized' form of fiction concerned with integrating a life and the thoughts that make it 'worth writing about'; and the Menippean satire or anatomy (or icicle), which James Blish does not always write, but possibly always wants to.

The Menippean satire [says Professor Frye] deals less with people as such than with mental attitudes. Pedants, bigots, cranks ... rapacious and incompetent professional men of all kinds, are handled in terms of their occupational approach to life as distinct from their social behaviour. The Menippean satire thus resembles the confession in its ability to handle abstract ideas and theories, and differs from the novel in its character-ization, which is stylized rather than naturalistic, and presents people as mouthpieces of the ideas they represent ... At its most concentrated [it] presents us with a vision of the world in terms of a single intellectual pattern. The intellectual structure built up from the story makes for violent dislocations in the customary logic of narrative, though the appearance of carelessness that results reflects only the carelessness of the reader or his tendency to judge by a novel-centered conception of fiction.

So – as varyingly for Swift, Thomas Love Peacock, the last things of Wells, for Aldous Huxley, Wyndham Lewis, John Barth, David Stacton, Thomas M. Disch and John T. Sladek – tonal and formal distinctions fuse neatly into a cage for James Blish, whose *récit* mind longs for a cold bath of Menippus to shape its grasp, or so we're claiming. Unfortunately Mr Blish has immersed himself in a field – science fiction – whose generic forms cater to the heated iconicity of the romance, as stripped down for action, and his whole crabby yawing corpus demonstrates the costs of writing against the grain.

A further minatory scouring of the serried cross-grained ranks of his work might, therefore, seem a touch gratuitous, though the cage or model does cast a few broad heuristic shafts of light. Blish's enormous distance, as implied narrator, from the exemplary worlds or dissertations he creates, does come clearer; as does the scholarly brambling of his texts with spinoffs of scholia introduced as their own ends; as does his apparent need to create evolutionary sequences rather than template (exemplary rather than fluvial – not temporal rather than static), which cost *Cities in Flight* its nous, and which segues into a love of the admonitory catastrophe; as does his revealing attempts to subsume disparate texts under post facto rubrics (cf. *After Such Knowledge*); as does his gloom, which is not inhumane, but which is not – a quality Kenneth Rexroth anyway ascribes only to the very greatest flowerings of the novel tradition – magnanimous, either; as does the false innocence that permeates his fictions, as it permeates the works of all *récit* authors, and which abides in the realization that thematically naïve topoi are being required – disingenuously – to illustrate far more than they could possibly *mean* to; and finally the nature of our assent to his successful fictions (like *A Case of Conscience*) does come clearer, for it is an assent to equipoise of assertion not narrative, conveyed through structures in space, not time, and recollected as models, not habitations.

As a Menippean illustration of the hypothesis that black magic literally works, *Black Easter*, one of the newer items, might seem altogether stripped of its skeleton, but in the event the emperor is dressed. Characters and plot are so closely and economically bound to their task of demonstration, and the narrative is so elegantly short, that there is a kind of paronomasia – a kind of 'blessedness' – and a dystopic thesis laves us in the clothes of *fleuve*.

Its sequel, *The Day After Judgement* (1970; 1972 in England), is a disjointed, cack-handed anticlimax, and defrissons the death of God in *Black Easter* by allowing that He might only be on vacation and by putting Satan on His throne pro tem, because Nature abhors a vacuum – which makes it the *real* shaggy God story. In its use of metonymy cons both of character and of narrative it's as miniaturizingly evasive as *VOR;* in its generic chuntering about it's as loopy as *Titan's Daughter;* and in the *Malleus Maleficarum* misogyny it shares with its predecessor it is thoroughly egregious.

And All the Stars a Stage (1960–1972), a grimly jumbled mélange, starts off as a juvenile and closes, to coin a term, as a *senile*. For a while it's a matriarchal dystopia (what else); then it becomes an end of the world story, whose protagonists escape into space, leaving behind them the inevitable panicked mobs; then it's a quest for a new home through the vast reaches of the galaxy story, during which (to validate the title) there is an occasional querulous glimpse of a cardboard star, and during which the heroes visit various strange planets; finally it becomes an arrival at New Jerusalem or kiss the soil children story, rather neat though muffled by lack of space – the new home turns out to be Earth, and the genuinely best thing in the book is its superb closing sentence. Not for the first time in Blish's oeuvre, women composers are calumniated (page 99), and 'simple male pride' (page 43) gets over its dystopia late in the book when Ailiss, once a female dominant (but now a wife), refuses to take over the ship when the clear duty to do so falls upon her; at the last moment her feminine intuition has recognized the natural order of things. 'I will *not*,' she says, possibly in that *dangerously even* tone of voice so characteristic of Doris Day, 'I will *not* be in command over my own husband – not at my age.'

In *Midsummer Century* (1972) a man's mind is accidentally disembodied and cast far into the future where, linked to another discorporate intellect, it gets the chance to observe and comment on a variety of dying Earth dystopias, while time passes. In other words, Blish has structurally disjuncted his protagonist from the exempla of the text, and allied – affianced – him to the functions of the implied narrator, which seems so clarifying a demonstration of the nature of the *récit* perspective that the book might well have been titled *The Eye of Menippus*. Although a clubfooted adventure plot does welsh on this version of a Garden, the storyline eventually wanders back off-stage and the calm, distant, rather melancholy pleasures return, literally embodying, in a sort of pun, what Darko Suvin calls 'cognitive estrangement', a term he seems to intend to use as a monothetic purge of science fiction as a whole, but which seems to work best as a modelling device for the closer description of the Menippean forms of the genre – and not of its dominant romance forms, because cognitive estrangement blights the icon.

And Frodo expires belike.

But our nostalgia (our need) for the steamy, high-pitched, kinetic fatefulness of iconicity persists, for genres work (human perception works) not only through metonymy, the substitution of part for whole, of set for omniscience, but also through the persistence of the image, time's body English. 'Fatefulness,' says Erving Goffman in 'Where the Action Is', 'involves a play of events that can be initiated and realized in a space and time small enough to be fully witnessed.' Icons are torsions in time, which heats them, and gives them pull through the work. Fate is mimed before us, in a matrix co-extensive with vision's. The anatomy shrivels icon to juggle metonymy for the cold eye, hence James Blish draped in icicles; the romance swallows metonymy neat that icons may live, Frodo lives. Pray for light. The hero of romance subsumes metonymy (being rather dumb) and mimes fate's glow, time's fabric's meshing with the ganglia of the icons of our hot breath, and that is meet.

James Blish, *Black Easter* (1968; Penguin, 1972)
James Blish, *The Day After Judgement* (Faber, 1972)
James Blish, *And All the Stars a Stage* (Faber, 1972)
James Blish, *Best Science Fiction Stories of James Blish* (Faber, 1973)
James Blish, *Midsummer Century* (Doubleday, 1972)
Paul Hernadi, *Beyond Genre* (Cornell University Press, 1972)
Northrop Frye, *Anatomy of Criticism* (Princeton University Press, 1957)
Erving Goffman, *Interaction Ritual* (1967; Penguin University Books, 1972)

Sweet Analytics

M. JOHN HARRISON

By the end of the show everything has shaken loose, flaked away: those monstrous insectile bodies, so terrifying when glimpsed briefly in dim underlighting, are after all awkward, callow, made of papier mache and lurex; the antennae of the Scarab Man, fibrillating wildly over his third and final squalling victim, have become mere piano wire, as tawdrily elaborate as his motives (the laboratory scandal, the research grant settled elsewhere, the explanation by some Louis Pasteur in a frock coat and steel-rimmed spectacles of his 'transference'). Boris Karloff has caught fire as we expected, discovered in a shuttered morning room from some other set, kneeling over his dead son and regretting, perhaps, the earlier demonstration of Galvanism in the scorpion's tail which sparked all this demoniac energy of revenge, this terrible, killing creativity. Amid the crackling cheap costumery, the melting fibre glass and the flames that roar like some enormous, vengeful, ironical Primus stove, poor old Faust has bought it again. Even the chambermaid could have told him there are some things we were never meant to know.

Previously, we've had a special fondness for Faust, our test tube clown, and come out of his drama feeling a little sad, if wiser. Now we execrate him. We trusted him, and he gave us DDT; we put up with his absent-mindedness and his cranky white haircut, and he got strontium in the milk; 'glutted now with learning's golden gifts', he invented Lewisite and the unburnt hydrocarbon. We made sure he ate his breakfast, wiped the egg off his tie and managed his bank account: he introduced us to phenacetin, to the MIRV and the core-melt; monosodium glutamate coiled out from under the laboratory door in a creeping poisonous mist. His Magic Food all turned bad, his wings flew *us* a little too near the sun. He had to go.

In a decade – at first apathetic, then coy and willing to be convinced, then tremulous and glad (for did we ever want it all – really?) – we've turned from Einstein to Thoreau, from photo-voltaics to Pre-Raphaelitism, from Doc Smith to Frank Herbert; and finally managed to shed somewhere along the way the Siamese twin horror that's held us rapt for a century and a half: our midnight fear that the scientific, the *power* civilization may fail and leave us back where we were, which is unthinkable – or that it may stay forever, which is worse.

> How I am glutted with conceit of this!
> Shall I make spirits fetch me what I please,
> Resolve me of all ambiguities?
> Perform what desperate enterprise I will?[1]

What a relief to discover that it was really all Faust's fault! He makes a satisfying scapegoat, and a most solid object against which to push: one good hard kick and we're clear of his sordid dream of megawatts and multilevel cross-overs, out of the tangle and the stink and into the simple log cabin by the lake (no matter that you must gut the fish – they're there to be caught!); or floating off downstream from Shalot, where the air is rarified, wrapped up warm with William Morris fabrics, in a barge hand-hewn out of that bemused Ruskinist impulse which led even Oscar Wilde to strip off his coat and 'build a road across a marsh'. If this should fail – and it might well – we have Luddism, recently playing to packed houses as New, Authorized, 'alienation'; and the dour, right wing anarchism of the competent thriller writer, with its body skills, its Outward Bound and its renovated croft in the shadow of the Cuillin ...

All these are symptomatic of a horribly tenacious clutching at significance, the replacement of the actual, the ordinary and the uninvested by great sweeping romantic myths. Rationalism, it would seem, has sold us up a very mucky backwater indeed. Thought turned out to be a straw; we throw each other fat lifebelts of charisma, mysticism and emotion instead. From Jimmy Saville, the Divine Idiot, via the Festival of Light with its Gilbert & Sullivan gullibility, Scientology, a commando of the deluded; from J. R. R. Tolkien, by way of brown rice, to Uri Geller, Madame Blavatsky of the 70s, conducting us – by means of a power he receives from flying saucers – through the seven sacred trances, and so besotting the collective imagination that his disfigured spoons twine themselves round the heart of University College London, while Cambridge nods proudly and possessively on like an emancipated mother hen. In ten years, logic has ceded its place to cheap fantasy and a cheaper superstition. Finally, science fiction really has replaced science fact, and thus become its own subject matter. Ghosts of old Ace Books editors revolve in their grave for joy.

'(The re-enactment of *Morte D'Arthur*) was my last open make-believe before my adolescence, after which time, like everyone else, I lived half the time in fantasy, craftily deceiving both others and myself. This adult make-believe is something we have foolishly ignored ... and in the epoch of Hitler – Siegfried Redivivus – it is not only a mistake but a disaster to ignore those underground motives that cause both war and art ... Man is essentially weak, and he wants power; essentially lonely, he creates familiar daemons,

Impossible Shes ... ' Thus Louis MacNeice[2] the poet, realizing – perhaps too late, like many of the intellectuals of the thirties – that the danger of the time lay not so much with technology or even economics, as in that eerie crepuscular hook-up between questionable fact and ostensible fantasy, between Hollow Earth and Wagner, between the risky ideology of myth and the vast blotting-pad credulity of which we're all capable.

Thirty years on, we're no less desperate for significance. But the washing machine, the prairie farm and the megawatt power station, which looked for a time as if they might provide it, have betrayed us; materialism has tainted reason, and we turn, with the expressed purpose of discovering something 'better' than either, to the solution by myth. This argues not only a superstitious inability to separate Faust's methods, his 'Sweet Analytics' from what is after all *our* abuse of his results, but also a failure of self-confidence which bears all the hallmarks of some dancing epidemic or millenarianistic cult of the Middle Ages. In a sense, we have become the 'rootless poor' again, disorientated and, apparently, disinherited.

We can perhaps discount interest in established non-western religions as a measure of our particular distraction – they have been around as alternatives for some long time and are thus not purpose-built – even their latter-day fractions, the various divine lights and Maharishis have what might be called a traditional basis; most socio-political solutions, too, have deep roots – the Thoreauism now gaining favour, the 'conservationism' which is in fact Conservatism in a new guise; but if we want a really accurate blood pressure of the time, we cannot turn our backs on the vulgar heresies, those clunky, home-made pseudo-sciences and half-religions that have their origins as much in the respectable publishing houses of central London as in the sacred groves of California or the still, cool drawing rooms of votive St Annes-on-Sea (where they believe that NASA is knocking 'holes in the air' at risk of admitting something mortally unpleasant, and simultaneously await the coming of the Master – from Venus, by what transport is unclear).

Nothing advertises so well our fear of impotence in the face of technology as the success of Uri Geller, with his raree-show of purely personal force and his implication that Faust, so apparently secure behind a laboratory door whose lock we haven't the education to pick, may after all have missed the point. The vulgarized anthropology of Erich Von Daniken becomes, in *Chariots of the Gods*, a blueprint for collective inferiority, suggesting a loss of confidence of such an extent that we now prefer to attribute our progress to mere reinvention and our very ability to progress to the result of genetic interference by some spacefaring master-race; and Charles Manson is the very least, if most notorious, of our new Messiahs.

All these myths and myth-figures have two things in common: in the first place they achieve a currency which appears to be out of all proportion to their value – in one way or another they 'sell'; and in the second, they are unoriginal, in the sense that each one borrows for its basis, various well-used but inviting ideas from the science-fictional stockpot – Geller's telekinesis, Von Daniken's visiting aliens, Manson's open use of elements from Heinlein's *Stranger in a Strange Land*.[3] Vendibility and the derivation from fiction coincide perfectly in Scientology, the 'technological' religion invented by a hack. Thus we observe the 'fact' creeping steadily towards the fiction. A movement in the opposite direction completes the dialogue, by way of a vogue for the provision of fictions (and here I use the term to encompass the staged as well as the written) so lavish, so detailed and so long that they provide a complete 'world' for their audience.

Thus we have the World of Tolkien, the World of Michael Moorcock, the Worlds of *Dune* and of *Star Trek*, to mention only a few: most of them supply a thorough physical geography or cosmology (at any rate a complicated, characteristic landscape), with its own maps, its histories and technologies and jargons; each has a multi-element comparative anthropology; and all seem to achieve success in direct proportion to complexity of background and wealth of 'data'. Most important, perhaps, each provides some more or less easily-grasped handle by which to pick up the universe, some combination of (homilectic) philosophy and metaphysic which can be seen as a way of perceiving not simply to world of the fiction but also of reality. All have won a more general audience than one would expect of generic fiction, all bid fair – whatever the original intent of their authors (or 'creators')[4] – to replace in the minds of that audience the World of Disney – funny little distorting mirrors in which we can detect transfigured images of the real.

The next step is replacement or at least augmentation of the world itself. We can see the beginnings of this in the publication of such efforts as *A Guide to Middle Earth*, language primer, Baedecker and *Who's Who* of a country imagined for the amusement of a handful of (mostly dead) dons; or in those enormous gatherings of *Star Trek* devotees, huge flocks of Spock-eared fans, brought together as if in preparation for some unimaginable migration to a sunnier clime. The commentaries and explanatory texts, the societies and conventions, the bibliographies and endless amateur publications, are not simply reminiscent of the crank-cult modus operandi, but might also be viewed by the jaundiced eye as the germs of a well-documented, seriously-conceived attempt to catalogue the physical and cultural phenomena of imaginary realities, the infancy of a natural science of the fictional ...

Will Book Two, Chapters VI–VIII of *The Lord of the Rings* now replace *An Excursion Flora of the British Isles?* – and where we once botanized the chalk downs of Kent or the peaty flush soils of the Cumbrian uplands, will we now discuss the soliology of the Lothorien pre-Alpine woods, whose terminal vegetation is the Mallorn Tree, with its characteristic golden leaves? (What's the matter with real flora? Possibly it's that they demand a real rather than imaginary botany, and for that we must trudge reluctantly back into the cold country of Faust.) In the end, it's no great step from 'Wart Factor 6, Mr Zulu!' to the excesses of the ninth dimension and the personal TL travel offered – whether honestly or cynically and for cash profit makes little difference when the real involvement is on the neophyte's (or sucker's) side – by that Tibetan sage T. Lobsang Rampa.

Plainly, Louis NacNeice's 'underground motives' are surfacing again, drawn into the vacuum created by a technology which has equated reason with material prosperity, materialism in turn with a noticeable erosion of individuality, self-determination and 'quality of life'; in the absence by overt rejection of Faust, they are being catered to, on a considerable scale, as crank-cult and cult-fiction – the one fictionalizing reality while the other struggles to realize fiction – engender a climate of fantasy which not only exacerbates Two Cultures polarization – denying imagination to the scientist and logic to the imaginative – but also furthers their own proliferation.

Just as plainly, no new Nazism prowls the seafront at St Annes: there's no reason to suppose that, left to themselves among the relics of the Master – the weeping pictures, the little dying Belgian dog in whom is reincarnated the soul of some departed guru, the neo-Blakeian daubs and icons – those gentle old flying saucer ladies will ever rediscover the goose-step, or, jackbooted, set fire to the powder keg of bourgeois dissatisfaction. While buttons, and even banners have proclaimed FRODO LIVES no one marching behind them has yet made the critical addition THEREFORE ... In at least one disturbing case, granted, it can be argued that the circuit has been completed – in Mansonism, questionable fact and ostensible fantasy set up a direct relationship, shared an audience, acted in the real world from entirely fantastic premises. Here, though, we may take refuge in the complicating factor of drug abuse, and in the very minuteness of the minority concerned.

Minority has been the way of it so far, and is a protection; and there may be no value at all in reference drawn from an entertainment fad which may already be over the hump and fading. But with crank-cult and cult-fiction pulling large new general audiences, we ought at least to give some thought to the misuse of fantasy – a tool customarily (as far as our industrial culture has been concerned) of escape, of avoidance, suddenly gaining currency as a means of managing the real world. Faust's analytics, his equations and mistakes, however damaging they appear to be, have at least put us on our guard against accepting him as an expediter of easy solutions, a bringer of Utopias: but no similar machinery exists to deal with our own imaginations – and in the age of Frodo Redivivus, gullibility may well be a greater danger than Hubris.

1. Christopher Marlowe, *The Tragical History of Doctor Faustus*.
2. *The Strings Are False*, an unfinished autobiography, Faber & Faber.
3. *The Family*, by Ed Sanders, Hart Davis. See also Charles Platt's article, *Family Literature*, NWQ 5. Platt's call for self-censorship on the part of cult-book authors seems a little naïve in the face of dollar vote and profit motive.
4. In many cases the author's continued presence interferes with interpretation or reinterpretation of his work. It helps if he has the grace to die. Many of Michael Moorcock's audience, for instance, are convinced of his demise, attribute his continuing prolific output to the discovery of MSS unpublished in his lifetime, and show a disturbingly energetic resistance to proofs of the contrary.
5. Efforts such as *The Third Eye* are an amusement in themselves, and well worth struggling through for the accidental humour; but for those wishing a quick resumé there is nothing better than John Sladek's *The New Apocrypha* (Hart-Davis McGibbon) – a comprehensive guide to strange sciences and occult beliefs.

A Literature of Acceptance

JAMES COLVIN

It has never seemed coincidental to me that sf appears to flourish at times of stress in the West; for better or worse it has been, through much of its existence, primarily a literature of paranoia. The last 'boom' came at the time of the Korean War and McCarthyism; the present one exists side by side with the Vietnam War and race riots. Flying saucer sightings (always a lovely sign of national paranoia) were multitude in the early fifties; flying saucer sightings are proliferating again in the US as the Vietnam War escalates. The TV series *The Invaders* enjoyed an enormous popularity when it came out in the US last year and the film *War of the Worlds* (with, consciously or unconsciously, the Martians clearly equated with the Russians) had a similar popularity in the fifties.

Whatever the economic, social and psychological reasons for the wars, witch-hunts and riots, there does seem to be a resemblance in atmosphere to that of the late eighteenth and early nineteenth centuries – a time of revolutions and wars accompanying or resulting from the full impact on people's lives of the Industrial Revolution. The popular fiction that flourished then was the Gothic horror novel and the Gothic historical romance. The former reflected the buried fears of the time, while the latter offered an escape from the object of those fears (essentially the new industries and their workers). Like all great paranoid fiction, the best of it had a crude power of its own, as had some of the pulp fantasy and sf of the thirties and forties (Lovecraft, R. E. Howard, Hubbard and van Vogt spring to mind). Where Gothic fiction offered 'remedies' for the ills it felt, it was in a return to a better, simpler age of chivalry, a benevolent agricultural feudal society where every man (and woman) had his place and was content with his lot, for 'order' prevailed. There is no need to detail why this society never did exist outside the pages of Arthurian legend. Similarly, in science fiction, authors often looked forward to a world of equal simplicity, basically an agricultural feudal society (the result of planetary colonisation or an atomic war) where men were men and women were women and the 'individual' could live wild and easy (the *Astounding* school of the forties and fifties – Heinlein, van Vogt and, to a certain degree, Blish and Asimov), and sometimes they assumed that such a world could be created by the application of technology, with peasant-robots and engineer-barons.

To me there are distinct likenesses between Scott, Radcliffe and Lewis and Ayn Rand, Heinlein and Tolkien – all offer escape into a simpler world, most offer simple ideas of how to create such a heaven on earth. It might strengthen my case to mention that the three authors are all objects of cult worship amongst the West Coast opters out, and this popularity I find almost inevitable. The saving grace of a writer like Asimov in his hey-day was that he at least saw the problem as being more complicated and the solutions as necessarily more sophisticated. But it was the later school that grew up around *Galaxy* – Bester, Pohl and Kornbluth, Budrys, Sheckley *et al.* – which began to engage itself more fully with attempting to isolate the causes of its society's ills and produce a fiction far less reactive than that which had preceded it. Even in the best of these, however, one finds a certain note of hysterical paranoia, a tendency to go for fashionable answers, a nostalgia that harked back to the 'golden age' of America's agricultural period, a certain tendency to indulge in little witch-hunts of their own while condemning others. Yet they often came closer to discovering the causes of their discomfort while elsewhere McCarthy screamed of Commie plots and Packard and McLuhan yelled that the admen were out to destroy our minds.

What is actually happening, of course, is that the West (the USA in particular) is feeling the effects of a new industrial revolution, possibly even harder to take than the last, as society changes from an economy based on trading and processing of natural resources to meet actual needs into a 'consumer' economy based on created demand. There is no stopping it, either, as we now realise. The economic structure is far too complex in the West to be easily dismantled by simple acts of revolution or changes of government. This is the future for the next hundred years at least, unless an economic crisis occurs that brings down the structure and lets it fall into the hands of the present-day Right (which at present consists, as in pre-Hitler Germany, of a number of disaffected minorities, some activist, some passive, from Birchers to Flower Children) which would only need such a crisis to become a coherent political force. Foreign wars and the space race are at the moment preserving this economy. It is a sad fact that modern society is between the Scylla of Vietnam escalation and the Charybdis of a new depression and a rise of the Right. We are all of us conscious of some such dilemma, but most of us are by now aware that it cannot be resolved simply and that no amount of clock-rolling, whether backward or forward, is going to help. Before we begin to investigate it, we must accept the existence of the situation. This, it seems to me, is what authors are now beginning to do.

My feeling is that just as a mood of pragmatism followed the mood of paranoia in the 19th century (reflected in art as well as in politics) so we are entering a more pragmatic mood, and just as the Gothic literature of fear and reaction developed techniques and subject matter that were used to great effect by serious writers (there would be no *Wuthering Heights*, possibly no *Bleak House*, without *The Old English Baron* and *The Mysteries of Udolfo*) so science fiction has developed – or is developing – techniques and subject matter that are beginning to be used to great effect by serious writers. The interesting thing is that many of the most serious writers are emerging from the field itself, and not all of them are of the younger generation, either. Writers like Leiber, Budrys and Sheckley seem on the brink of producing their best work, writers like Aldiss and Ballard are beginning already to produce extremely rewarding fiction. Then we have the so-called 'new wave' writers – Moorcock, Disch, Sladek, Jones, Spinrad, Sallis, Carol Emshwiller, Platt and many more who are in their individual ways experimenting like mad with the rich vein of material and possible techniques that have emerged from sf. And elsewhere the great artists of paranoia – Burroughs, Pynchon and even Mailer – whose intellectual strength and considerable talents have enabled them, in their noble madness, to home in on the real issues at stake in modern society. Great days are ahead.

Meanwhile, escapist sf and fantasy flourishes in profusion and represents, in the USA and parts of the Continent, at least, the most popular vein still. Serious, engaged sf has yet to convince its largest potential audience of its credentials. The work of Tolkien and Heinlein and Ayn Rand (crypto-Fascist fiction if ever there was) is still more popular than the work of Ballard, Burroughs and the others. As we learn to accept the facts of a so-called 'artificial' economy, however, the reversal of this situation seems in sight and a truly popular but uncompromising literature may come about – our new Dickens may soon emerge.

It is an ironic fact that today the old Left and the new Right both seem to have much in common. Both are refusing to accept the facts of our economic and social life and it is left principally for painters and writers to try to bring them to light. The most interesting of these writers are producing what might almost be called a literature of acceptance, delighting in the changes and possibilities of modern society while still concerned with the need to find a new set of morals and ethical principles that will make that society a just one. They are well past the stage of reaction. However, it must sometimes be difficult for a reader used to the old didactic, almost journalistic, approach of good sf of the 'fifties to recognise the considerable merits of the new 'subjective' school, one of whose most important exponents and greatest talents is J. G. Ballard. There is no whit less concern and sense of engagement in Ballard than there was in Wells (still the greatest of the didactic school). Far from dealing in straightforward philosophical ideas à la Kafka and Hesse, Ballard is involved with the detailed physical and psychological reality of the immediate present and near future. If he leaves things out of his stories, it is for well-considered reasons (I'm reminded of the New York film critic discussing Kafka's *The Trial* who condemned it 'because you never do find out what the hell he's accused of') and, certainly in his later work, if he puts things in it is for good reason, too. Ballard is perhaps the most disciplined of all the writers I have mentioned. In his new collection of short stories, *The Overloaded Man* (Panther), we have, unfortunately, a poor representation of some of his early work – some of it clumsily written and consisting principally of raw subject matter that is worked in only the simplest and most obvious ways. This is certainly true of the first story, 'Now: Zero', about a man with the power to wish people to death, and is scarcely less true of some of the others (the famous 'Track 12' about the man who drowns in a kiss). There is a powerful talent here, of course, and as horror stories the collection succeeds excellently (far surpassing Bradbury in this respect), but most of these stories lack the purpose and involvement and intellectual toughness of Ballard's current work and will doubtless disappoint some readers who have come to him via his trilogy and his recent stories in *New Worlds* ('The Atrocity Exhibition', etc.). The most worthwhile item in this collection – which, I hasten to add, is considerably better than almost anything else to hand this month – is Ballard's essay 'The Coming of the Unconscious' which was first published in *New Worlds* and makes explicit to the interested reader many of Ballard's concerns as a writer (though the article itself is about Surrealism) as does his later piece 'Notes From Nowhere', which was published in *New Worlds* 167 (October, '66) and contains the statement '*Au revoir*, jewelled alligators and white hotels, hallucinatory forests, farewell'.

It was pleasant to receive a new edition of *Tiger, Tiger* by Alfred Bester (Penguin) since this is the greatest of the baroque science fiction tales and represents (as perhaps 'Melmoth the Wanderer' represented for the Gothic) the ultimate expression of the 'they're all against me' school of sf, with a clean, honest prose, marvellously wild invention, a beautifully constructed plot (even better than 'The Count of Monte Cristo') and an almost naïve idealism that is lacking in much later work that seeks to imitate it, but that has the burning power of faith in its own convictions.

Kit Reed is of that school of writers, sober, sophisticated and concerned, who emerged in the fifties around *Galaxy* and *Fantasy and Science Fiction*. Her stories in this first collection of hers to be published here (*Mister da V. and Other Stories*, Faber) display clever craftmanship and cool intelligence and are eminently readable. Perhaps 'Judas Bomb', one of her best-known stories, is my favourite – about a society run by teenage gangs. The rationale of this story is pretty convincing, but not nearly as convincing as the prediction itself, for by 2000, if the present population curve continues, this society will almost certainly be run by teenage gangs of some description. It is odd how often good sf stories have hit on a sound instinctive prediction but have somehow failed to hit upon the actual causes of the events they predict. No matter.

The Seedling Stars by James Blish (Faber) is the collection of stories about 'seeding' or colonising the planets with people physically modified for different environments. The first written (and last in the book) 'Surface Tension' remains the best. Blish has always been surprised by its great appeal to his readers. It is about tiny people under the water battling against all sorts of horrors and problems in their efforts to reach the surface and explore it. This book is far better than those who have only read Blish's interminable Cities in Flight stories might think him capable of producing. Here he seems to be mining an inventive vein much closer, as it were, to his heart.

The last book I have before me is sadly the most disappointing in that it was written by a relative newcomer who does not seem ready yet to begin fulfilling his early promise. Perhaps he is over-producing and should slow down. The writer is Roger Zelazny, the book is *Lord of Light* (Doubleday) and it is Zelazny's first hardbound publication in the US. It seems a shame, therefore, that this will be his introduction to a number of critics who, not knowing his earlier novels (*This Immortal* and *The Dream Master*), will not know that, in fact, Zelazny can be a disciplined and thoughtful writer. This stuff is self-indulgent, infantile, self-conscious, escapist, derivative fantasy fiction that lacks even the saving grace of Tolkien's relatively clean style. The book is pretty near unreadable, is based on Indian mythology, has a style derived, apparently, from Sanskrit, is patronising in tone (so that one cannot even think of it as a good children's book as one can, with an effort, think of *Lord of the Rings*), is arid in idea and inspiration, and is altogether a very embarrassing book indeed. If science fiction has shifted itself from the ghetto, this kind of sf has turned itself into a gateau. I can only hope that Zelazny (who I hear is planning a series of nine in this vein) will pull himself together before he wastes any more of his undoubted talents on this sort of stuff.

If there is a split in the sf ranks, as some people have suggested lately, it is not between the generations but between those writers who have become tired and self-indulgent purveyors of cheap opium and those who are still trying to tackle real issues (no matter how ineptly). The sooner everyone realises that fresh subject matter and techniques have to be found if they are to do their job properly, the better for all of us. The fancy journalism of Kurt Vonnegut (whose best novel, *God Bless You, Mr Rosewater* has just appeared in paperback from Panther) is much more palatable than fancy word-for-word's sake escapism, but is still only a poor substitute for the real thing – style and technique that derive naturally from the ideas and subject matter of the author and which produce work that stands totally on its own terms as *fiction*. Didacticism, however entertainingly done, often defeats true literary invention. But perhaps the day of the didactic, too, is nearly done in sf.

Next year should see a fine crop of new books appearing in Britain and the USA, among them Disch's *Camp Concentration*, Spinrad's *Bug Jack Barron*, Aldiss's *Report on Probability A*, an as yet untitled Ballard book, Sladek's *The Reproductive System* and several more. All of them extremely individual works of fiction, all serious, all committed, all highly inventive and all indicating very definitely that the best is yet to come and that the new sf is producing not only quality and quantity, but a wide variety as well.

Alphabets of Unreason
J.G. BALLARD

The psychopath never dates. Hitler's contemporaries – Baldwin, Chamberlain, Herbert Hoover – seem pathetically fusty figures, with their frock coats and wing collars, closer to the world of Edison, Carnegie and the hansom cab than to the first fully evolved modern societies over which they presided, areas of national consciousness formed by mass-produced newspapers and consumer goods, advertising and tele-communications. By comparison Hitler is completely up-to-date, and would be equally at home in the sixties (and probably even more so in the seventies) as in the twenties. The whole apparatus of the Nazi super-state, its nightmare uniforms and propaganda, seems weirdly turned-on, providing just that element of manifest insanity to which we all respond in the H-Bomb or Viet Nam – perhaps one reason why the American and Russian space programmes have failed to catch our imaginations is that this quality of explicit psychopathology is missing.

Certainly, Nazi society seems strangely prophetic of our own – the same maximising of violence and sensation, the same alphabets of unreason and the fictionalising of experience. Goebbels in his diaries remarks that he and the Nazi leaders had merely done in the realm of reality what Dostoevski had done in fiction. Interestingly, both Goebbels and Mussolini had written novels, in the days before they were able to get to grips with their real subject matter – one wonders if they would have bothered now, with the fiction waiting to be manipulated all around them.

Hitler's 'novel', *Mein Kampf* (Hutchinson) was written in 1924, nearly a decade before he came to power, but is a remarkably accurate prospectus of his intentions, not so much in terms of finite political and social aims as of the precise psychology he intended to impose on the German people and its European vassals. For this reason alone it is one of the most important books of the 20th century, and well worth re-printing, despite the grisly pleasures its anti-semitic ravings will give to the present generation of racists.

How far does Hitler the man come through the pages of this book? In the newsreels Hitler tends to appear in two roles – one, the demagogic orator, ranting away in a state apparently close to neurotic hysteria, and two, a benevolent and slightly eccentric *kapellmeister* sentimentally reviewing his SS bodyguard, or beaming down at a picked chorus of blond-haired German infants. Both these strands are present in *Mein Kampf* – the hectoring, rhetorical style, shaking with hate and violence, interspersed with passages of deep sentimentality as the author rhapsodises to himself about the mystical beauty of the German landscape and its noble, simple-hearted peoples.

Apart from its autobiographical sections, the discovery by a small Austrian boy of his 'Germanism', *Mein Kampf* contains three principal elements, the foundation stones, walls and pediment of a remarkably strong paranoid structure. First, there are Hitler's views on history and race, a quasi-biological system which underpins the whole basis of his political thought and explains almost every action he ever committed. Second, there are his views on the strict practicalities of politics and the seizure of power, methods of political organisation and propaganda. Third, there are his views on the political future of the united Germanies, its expansionist foreign policy and general attitude to the world around it.

The overall tone of *Mein Kampf* can be seen from Hitler's original title for the testament: *A Four and a Half Years' Struggle Against Lies, Stupidity and Cowardice: A Reckoning with the Destroyers of the Nazi Party Movement*. It was the publisher, Max Amann, who suggested the shorter and far less revealing *Mein Kampf*, and what a sigh he must have breathed when Hitler agreed. Hitler's own title would have been far too much of a giveaway, reminding the readers of the real sources of Hitler's anti-semitic and racialist notions.

Reading Hitler's paranoid rantings against the Jews, one is constantly struck by the biological rather than political basis of his entire thought and personality. His revulsion against the Jews was physical, like his reaction against any peoples, such as the Slavs and Negroes, whose physique, posture, morphology and pigmentation alerted some screaming switchboard of insecurity within his own mind.

What is interesting is the language in which he chose to describe these obsessions – primarily faecal, one assumes, from his endless preoccupation with 'cleanliness'. Rather than use economic, social or political arguments against the Jews, Hitler concentrated almost solely on this inflated biological rhetoric. By dispensing with any need to rationalise his prejudices, he was able to tap an area of far deeper unease and uncertainty, and one moreover which his followers would never care to expose too fully to the light of day. In the unanswerable logic of psychopathology, the Jews became the scapegoats for all the terrors of toilet-training and weaning. The constant repetition of the words 'filth', 'vileness', 'abscess', 'hostile', 'shudder', endlessly reinforce these long-repressed feelings of guilt and desire.

In passing, it is curious to notice that Hitler's biological interpretations of history have a number of striking resemblances to those of Desmond Morris. In both writers one finds the same reliance on the analogy of the lower mammals, on a few basic formulas of behaviour such as 'struggle', 'competition', 'defence of territory'. There is the same simple schematic view of social relationships, the same highly generalised assertions about human behaviour that are presented as proven facts. Hitler talks without definition of 'lower races' in the same way that Morris refers to 'primitive societies' and 'simple communities'. Both are writing for half-educated people whose ideas about biology and history come from popular newspaper and encyclopaedia articles, and whose interest in these subjects is a barely transparent cover for uneasy fantasies about their own bodies and emotions.

In this preface, the translator of *Mein Kampf* describes it as written in the style of a self-educated modern South German with a talent for oratory. In this respect Hitler was one of the rightful inheritors of the 20th century – the epitome of the half-educated man. Wandering about the streets of Vienna shortly before the first World War, his head full of vague artistic yearnings and clap-trap picked up from popular magazines, whom does he most closely resemble? Above all, Leopold Bloom, his ostensible arch-enemy, wandering around Joyce's Dublin at about the same time, his head filled with the same clap-trap and the same yearnings. Both are the children of the reference library and the self-improvement manual, of mass newspapers creating a new vocabulary of violence and sensation. Hitler was the half-educated psychopath inheriting the lavish communications systems of the 20th century. Forty years after his first abortive seizure of power he was followed by another unhappy misfit, Lee Harvey Oswald, in whose Historic Diary we see the same attempt by the half-educated to grapple with the information overflow that threatened to drown him.

Language Mechanisms

a review of the work of Eduardo Paolozzi

CHRISTOPHER FINCH

It is a commonplace that a painter or sculptor in the 1960s finds himself in competition with a whole range of technically sophisticated media and with a massive diffusion of information and imagery. One course open to him is to opt out of this competition and to produce something which exists wholly on its own fine-art terms; something which has an independent and stable existence. Alternatively he can expose himself to the media bombardment, explore the patterns of syntax which operate within it, investigate the possibilities of cultural control or communication systems, etc.

In 1952 Eduardo Paolozzi projected, at the ICA, a programme of imagery taken from the rapidly expanding worlds of Admass and the New Technology. Publicity material, popular illustrations and circuit diagrams – seen away from their usual context and on a greatly enlarged scale – suggested areas of visual delight unsuspected at that time by the majority of his audience. For almost a decade, however, this visual delight remained latent within his own work and only in the early 'sixties did he strike upon an idiom which allowed it to become articulate.

His first sculptures within this new idiom were Towers cast from engineering templates and machine parts (*Wittgenstein at Casino/The World divides itself into Facts:* 1963). Towards the end of '63 and through the next year he produced pieces welded together from standard machine castings (*Crash/Artificial Sun*) and then, in 1965, highly polished pieces welded from castings of his own design (*Akapotik Rose/Marok-Marok-Miosa*). Some of the Towers and also some of the more recent pieces have been painted; and since 1965 there has been a parallel series of sculptures made from rolled and chromed steel (*Foto/Jazmin/Twisprac*).

These sculptures have become increasingly simple in appearance but all function in the same way. There is no question of Paolozzi's main aim being to create a single *gestalt* image (as is the case with much recent American sculpture). His pieces function, rather, as servomechanisms. According to McLuhan the artist is the only person in a position to grasp the Present as a whole. If the artist can use this privileged position to devise a basic system of syntax, he can provide us with mechanisms that will translate his personal grasp into a far more comprehensive grasp of the constantly evolving situation. Paolozzi – in his sculpture and in his other activities – has provided a series of prototypes for this new kind of cultural device.

Language Games

All of Paolozzi's products are essentially language mechanisms. The recurring references to Ludwig Wittgenstein in his work are by no means gratuitous: Paolozzi is involved in a field of activity directly related to Wittgenstein's theory of language games. In common with other artists of his generation Paolozzi has devised (or recognised) new patterns of syntax that enable him to bring together elements drawn from the vocabularies of many different language systems which, at one time, seemed mutually exclusive. His sculptures concentrate these elements and patterns into a single icon. It is in his para-literary activities that we can more easily distinguish the mechanics of this process.

For several years Paolozzi has experimented with the programmed or random reorganisation of words and images, using a collage method reminiscent of William Burroughs and of dadaists such as Tristan Tzara. In 1962 he produced a book called *Metafisikal Translations* in which words and images were released from the normal restrictions of sequence and syntax (sequence and syntax still exist here but are constantly shifting; the reader is at liberty to scan the material in any way that he likes). A novel – *KEX* – has recently been published by the Copley Foundation. In this case Paolozzi simply selected the material and handed it to the editor (Richard Hamilton) to assemble as he thought best.

On a slightly different plane is the series of Wittgenstein prints – *As is When* – published in 1965. Paolozzi is moved as much by Wittgenstein's visits to the cinema as by his thoughts on reality but, in structure, the collage from which each print was screened is a faithful reflection of Wittgenstein's method. The series is in fact a sample of language games comparable with those that Wittgenstein himself put forward; Paolozzi totally accepts the philosopher's emphasis on linguistics as reality. ('A *picture* held us captive,' wrote Wittgenstein. 'And we could not get outside it for it lay in our language and language seemed to repeat it to us inexorably.')

The Media Landscape

The most ambitious of Paolozzi's works in this idiom is Moonstrips Empire

News, the first volume of which has been recently published by Editions Alecto. Moonstrips is a perspex box containing one hundred loose sheets each of which is screen-printed with text and/or images. The fact that the sheets are loose in the box means that its owner functions as an editor or performer, able to choose the sequence in which the material is scanned and thus form new syntactical links (though all possibilities are pre-determined by the elaborate pattern of choice and chance which constitutes the artist's programme).

Texts and images are montaged from a variety of sources:

Film stills/molecular diagrams/language primers/architectural schema/ Disney characters/weaving patterns indexes/space hardware/pulp fiction/car stylings, etc.

Moonstrips is, then, an excursion into the media landscape.

Programmes

In this new situation the emphasis shifts to the artist as programmer. In the case of both Moonstrips and the recent sculpture most of the responsibility for the physical realisation of the work is delegated to craft specialists. The sculpture is created not in a studio but at an engineering works (art is produced here alongside crane bearings and aircraft components). Once the artist has devised his programme, specialists are contracted to carry it out. Castings are ordered from one firm of specialists, assembled by another skilled worker one hundred miles away and the completed structure is passed on to someone else to be polished or painted as the case may be. In other pieces sheets of metal are bent, under the artist's supervision, on an industrial roller, welded together on the spot, then sent some distance to the chromer.

Similarly, with Moonstrips, the basic programme is pasted-up by Paolozzi, then it is handed over to an expert to be screened with colour translations and other adjustments. Not all of these adjustments are necessarily specified by the artist but, where they are not the outcome of a first-hand decision, they are implicit within the overall concept. For all this to be carried out successfully the artist must, of course, have a thorough grasp of the techniques involved. There is no abdication of responsibility; simply a redeployment of skills.

Energy Levels

To Paolozzi the anonymous beauty of technology offers a model for art. There is no point, however, to competing with technology; accept its methods – and economics if necessary – but compete and everything is lost. In his sculptures Paolozzi simulates the elegance of technology but translates it into another context where it does not have to compete with its functional antecedents (to lay a work of art open to direct comparison with a gas-turbine engine would be absurd). Paolozzi takes the imagery and methods of technology but energises them within a totally different language structure.

Imagery of any kind can only function at certain levels of energy. Paolozzi is using material which has previously been energised in other contexts – which has functioned as part of an already existing kinetic system, whether narrative, analytical or structural. Once detached from this context it is reduced to its ground state – the lowest stable energy level. Paolozzi's commitment is to create a new environment or system which will return the imagery to a pitch of energy equivalent to that which it enjoyed in its original context. Since he is concerned with reflecting the world as it is, and not with solving some specific problem, it is inevitable that all narrative or logical bias should be dropped. Literary or scientific induction is abandoned in favour of a picture of the world structured according to a system which we can all recognise even though it remains unspecified.

Paolozzi's imagery is energised within the context of language as reality; and we are not talking, here, of some ideal language but of something nearer to Rimbaud's Alchemy of the Word – though Alchemy of the Word itself becomes inadequate. J. L. Borges refers, in *The Mirror of Enigmas*, to Machen's hypotheses, 'that the outer world – forms, temperatures, the moon – is a language that we humans have forgotten or which we can scarcely distinguish. ... ' At all times it has been the business of the artist to present the elements of this language in such a way as to give us some hope of cracking the code. Within the framework of the 'sixties, it is with this that Paolozzi is concerned.

The Languages of Science
DAVID HARVEY

'A theory,' said the English philosopher Ramsey, 'is a language for discussing the facts the theory is said to explain.' This view of a theory has important implications. Explanation depends upon theory. If theory is a language then it follows that the explanations we offer for events occurring in the real world around us must depend upon the nature and character of the languages which we can develop to represent them. If scientific understanding is to progress, we must necessarily invent vaster, more comprehensive and more logically coherent languages to facilitate that progress. In inventing such new languages the scientist is not reversing the intellectual process which led fundamental sensations and percepts to be represented by speech and written word. He is, rather, pressing that intellectual process to its ultimate conclusion. The sign and the symbol no longer represent anything specific – they are abstract relata and thereby freed from subjective and emotive interpretation. As Cassirer wrote in *The Philosophy of Symbolic Form*, 'the word of language differs from the sensuous intuitive image precisely in that it is no longer weighted down, so to speak, with a sensuous matter of its own'. Scientific concepts are even more abstract, 'freeing the sign from all its restrictive sensuous conditions ... the sign tears itself free from the sphere of things, in order to become a purely relational and ordinal sign'.

The process of abstraction is continuously evident in linguistic systems. Even so there is some ground for differentiating between natural languages (such as English, French, Japanese, etc.) and the so-called 'artificial' languages of symbolic logic, set theory, and the various branches of mathematics. Laymen frequently suppose, erroneously, that the latter group of languages exhibit the power of total objectivity. Such languages, it is true, exhibit a consistency and logical coherence uncharacteristic of the natural languages which are plagued by ambiguity. But artificial languages vary a great deal in their capacity to convey certain kinds of information. Indeed there are many languages which can only be applied for very specific purposes.

It is generally held, of course, that the various natural languages vary in their capacity to convey information. Spanish is sometimes regarded as the language of violent passion, French the language of rhetoric and English the language of empiricism. At times analysts have suggested that the characteristics of the language affect the way of life and limit the field of experience: are the English incapable of grand passion simply because theirs is the language of empiricism? It is perhaps no accident that English philosophy is predominantly analytical and French philosophy predominantly existential. But the ambiguity of natural languages allows a far greater degree of flexibility in the use of the language. The languages of science, on the other hand, by reducing this ambiguity reduce the flexibility of application of the language.

As science has progressed and the number of artificial languages multiplied, so scientists, philosophers and logicians have become more and more concerned with establishing the properties of the languages they are using. Whitehead and Russell, in their famous *Principia Mathematica*, succeeded in demonstrating the relationship between different types of symbolic system and, in particular, demonstrated the relationship between various branches of mathematics and symbolic logic in general.

Each artificial language expresses something special. At one time it was thought that one and only one artificial language could be regarded as the 'true' language of research, and indeed one of the aims of science was to show and demonstrate which language was the most correct. Thus Euclidean geometry was regarded in the early nineteenth century as the only artificial language for discussing spatial form, and it was assumed that the intuitive sense of space could be reduced to this single symbolic system. But there were a number of logical difficulties to such an assertion.

In an attempt to resolve these difficulties Lobachevski (probably more famous to laymen by way of Tom Lehrer than from his extraordinary mathematical accomplishment) and Bolyai simultaneously discovered a new kind of geometry which is just as good as Euclid's. Later Riemann discovered a third, and it now emerges that there are an infinity of geometric systems which can be invented if needs be. Each system in itself may be considered as a language and each language, it turns out, is appropriate for different kinds of analysis. Euclid is the appropriate language for discussing Newton's views of space, Riemann's geometry is the appropriate language for discussing Einstein's view. Suddenly, in the mid-nineteenth century, geometry came to be regarded as a family of languages for discussing spatial form.

The history of geometry demonstrates an interesting phenomenon. It suggests that within the scientific community a particular language may emerge as the dominant form of communication, and it also suggests that science itself, by inventing a particularly powerful language, may inhibit its own development simply by placing too much store by that language. Too many languages, on the other hand, lead only to a breakdown in communication. A language, after all, is designed to communicate. If every scientist possessed his own 'language' then the purpose of symbolic abstraction would be defeated. This is the tension that leads science to periods of conservatism followed by explosive new developments as new languages are learnt and explored. The particular set of artificial languages which are 'in power' at any particular time serve to mould our view of the world and limit our potential for understanding. They do so simply because they determine the nature and form of our theories about reality.

This brings us to the function of such languages, for it is here that we must ultimately judge the utility of any particular language. How does a new language add to our understanding of the nature of the sense perception data which we obtain from the real world? A language functions as a model of real world structure. Suppose, for example, we have a generalised abstract relationship of the following form:

If $A \rightarrow B$; $B \rightarrow C$; then $A \rightarrow C$.

This is a simple linguistic rule which states how new propositions may be formulated from an existing set. The rule states that relations between elements possess the property of transitivity. We can now map into this system a particular set of real world events. We may take a sequence of the following type: failure of the monsoon causes failure in the rice harvest; failure in the rice harvest causes famine; therefore failure in the monsoon causes famine. The linguistic rule seems perfectly appropriate. Now consider a sequence of the following type: John likes brandy more than whisky; John likes whisky more than marijuana; therefore John likes brandy more than marijuana. Again, the conclusion seems logical enough. But when we examine the way in which people in fact order their preferences, we find that the inference is not valid. It proves to be valid only when the choice has to be made at the same instant in time and if the preference can be measured on a stable, one-dimensional preference scale. But people's preferences are multi-dimensional. The language which contains this rule is not, therefore, appropriate to the particular data set we are examining. Further, the behavioural scientist is sometimes guilty of cowing the subject of investigation into a conformity of behaviour which does not in fact exist. Imagine an argument between John who stoutly maintains his preference of marijuana over brandy in spite of the market researcher's claim that this is illogical in view of John's other preferences!

In applying a particular linguistic rule, therefore, we need to be certain that the rule represents something which is true of the data. At this point we find that the linguistic systems of science can frequently constrain our vision to the extent that we spend inordinate amounts of time trying to stuff a particular behaviour pattern into a mould entirely unsuited to it.

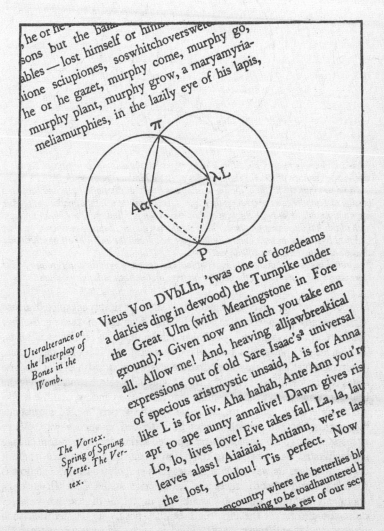

Artists and writers frequently create new languages or modify the old in order to convey rather different sensations and perceptions. James Joyce in Finnegan's Wake, and Anthony Burgess in The Clockwork Orange, created new linguistic styles for such specific purposes.

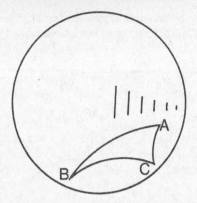

Non-Euclidean geometries are difficult to represent but the accompanying diagram gives a simple interpretation of some of the properties of Lobachevskian geometry.

Imagine a man the height of the bar starting out from the centre of a circle and becoming smaller and smaller as he approaches the edges of that circle. He will take smaller and smaller steps and he will never reach the edge of the universe – it is infinite but bounded. A universe such as this has interesting properties. Thus the shortest distance between two points becomes a curved line and a triangle looks like the figure ABC – and the angles of a Lobachevskian triangle add up to less than 180 degrees.

Einstein suggested that the universe is in fact best described by Riemann's geometry – but there is growing evidence that the way we perceive that universe is Lobachevskian.

Most of the revolutionary movements in science are simply a result of the new wine bursting open the old bottles. The language of cause-and-effect dominated the thought of J. S. Mill and the nineteenth-century positivists. The language is powerful – perhaps too powerful. But it is only appropriate to certain situations. It assumes discrete states and it assumes that discrete states can be identified. If I state that the window breaks because I threw the brick, it seems reasonable to assume that I, and the window, and the brick, are discrete units. But there are some systems which involve continuous movements and flow which cannot be described in such a way. Water evaporates from open surfaces, is transported and under temperature change is precipitated either back into the ocean or on the land surface where it deviously makes its way back to the sea or is evaporated again. The flow is continuous and smooth, there are no discrete states. Chicken and egg arguments simply cannot be examined in terms of the language of cause-and-effect. Yet the nineteenth-century positivists insisted that such systems could, and must, be examined in terms of such a language. No wonder that many (although note not all) of the inferences made with the help of such a language were misleading and often downright mischievous.

It is a curious fact that the language of science, of which we, as laymen, are frequently not explicitly aware, penetrates and permeates our thinking. But as with most transferences of this kind there is a time lag of significant proportions. It is curious to note, for example, the pervasive influence of the second law of thermodynamics upon our thinking. This law simply states that energy tends to dissipate itself and that a particular system tends to assume a state of increasing disorder (or entropy). The notion of inevitable equilibrium and a smoothing out of all differences has been peculiarly pervasive in our social thinking and even though many an arts student cannot, according to Snow, state the law precisely, its influence is extraordinarily dominant. Only certain types of system can be successfuly analysed by means of this model. Not only does the model require that the system be closed, but it also requires that the elements contained in the system are non-homeostatic (i.e., they are not in any way self-organising). But there are all kinds of systems which are in fact self-reproducing and self-organising. Scientific knowledge itself appears to be one of them. Economic activity is another. Yet for many years it was assumed that the natural laws of economics would lead to an evening-up in economic development throughout the world. Perhaps one of the most significant of all practical discoveries of the economist in the past twenty years has been the elementary fact that the rich regions grow rich while the poor regions grow relatively poorer, and that this is probably more the natural law of economic growth than an inevitable evening-up process. Only now, via regional planning and aid to under-developed countries, is some recognition of this basic fact implicit in political decision making.

The significance of this self-organising process in human affairs has been most cogently analysed by George Kingsley Zipf in his book on *Human Behaviour and the Principle of Least Effort*. Zipf noted the tendency among humans to seek out a least effort solution to any problem confronting him. Cultural form, sexual behaviour, economic behaviour, could all be analysed by referring to this basic proposition. And the end result of such a proposition, curiously enough, is a society which is so completely organised that it only succeeds in stifling itself. Zipf predicted, for example, that migration would tend to make big cities bigger and the smaller cities relatively smaller. The nineteenth century saw in most of western Europe the depopulation of the countryside. The twentieth century has seen the beginnings of small town depopulation to feed the growth of the large metropolitan areas. Population distribution is not developing according to the second law of thermodynamics. Far from it. We are witnessing a self-organising system at work which may well stifle activity by over-organisation.

Our image of the world is probably more conditioned by the language of science than we care to think. These languages are specially created tools suitable for particular kinds of function and analysis. Perhaps the greatest problem of communication which our society currently faces is to create an awareness of the power, function and dangers of such artificial languages. They give us what control we do possess over the happenings in the real world around us. But they can mislead on occasion. Science cannot advance without such languages. But without a full and complete understanding of the properties of these languages there can be no guarantee against false inference and false prediction.

The Circle of the
White Horse

FRANCIS ARNOLD

The newcomer to the *White Horse Tavern* may well wonder why there should
be so much excited interest in the group of such ordinary-looking people
relaxing in the saloon bar on a Thursday evening. He, or she, has heard
perhaps that 'science-fiction personalities' meet there and discuss their
favourite subject. He notices the little piles of books and magazines that
accumulate on the tables, and witnesses some of the friendly bartering and
bargaining that goes on. If he too is interested in science-fiction he will
probably want to know more about all this, and know too how long it has been
going on, and how it started in the first place.

What a distance this group has travelled, from the days when it was a stolid,
formal Association with Secretary and Treasurer and governing body, to the
free-and-easy fellowship of to-day! What a distance, and what a journey – a
journey in time of fifteen earth-shattering years replete with disaster and
achievement and concluding perhaps with the promise of triumph to come.
This is the story that the newcomer will hear, in fragments of conversation,
as he settles into the Circle of the *White Horse*.

In January of the now-distant year 1937 six young men went to Leeds as
guests of the local Chapter of the Science-Fiction League, a body of
enthusiasts originating in America and organised by a magazine publisher.
These young men – E. J. Carnell, W. H. Gillings and A. C. Clarke of London,
L. Johnson and E. F. Russell of Liverpool, with M. K. Hanson of Nuneaton
– were drawn together by mutual interest in a form of literature: that flood
of dramatic and exhilarating visions of the future known by the simple, rather
unsatisfactory, name of 'science-fiction'. They were well read in the novels
of H. G. Wells, Olaf Stapledon and other prophets, and they steadily acquired
the American fiction magazines which followed the Wellsian tradition. They
believed that this literature was something better than the cut-and-dried
fiction of the day, that it had a unique high quality of its own, even an
idealism, and a purpose. Their ambition – we might even call it an aspiration
– was to forward that purpose.

At Leeds they helped found the Science-Fiction Association, as they called
it, which later moved to London, with E. J. Carnell as Treasurer and another
Londoner, G. Ken Chapman, as Secretary. Branches were established in

London, Leeds, Liverpool and Manchester. They invited membership through the correspondence columns of their magazines, writing letters all over the country and all over the world. They accepted small subscriptions, and in return produced small mimeographed sheets of literary news. Branch meetings were held weekly, and national meetings, called conventions, were arranged annually.

Despite all this activity, the Science-Fiction Association achieved little. Its programme was 'to forward the aims and objects of science-fiction in this country', and its members, full of ardour and excitability, made drastic demands and counter-demands upon each other. Nobody, unfortunately, had a clue as to what the 'aims and objects of science-fiction' were.

One thing desired by all, however, was a British science-fiction magazine. No spirit of transatlantic rivalry inspired this wish, for the American publishers, knowing that science and science-fiction are international forces, had done their best to offer stories with an international flavour, and in doing so had proved very hospitable to British contributors. Nevertheless, British readers felt that a home-produced magazine was needed alongside the very welcome imports.

Not only the readers but the writers wanted it. During years of economic depression, while British magazines were ceasing publication, British authors turned increasingly to the American market, and in the science-fiction field particularly many writers made reputations in the United States while remaining unknown in their own country. Thus there was a double demand for the magazine, and the need seemed to be met when Walter Gillings's experimental *Tales of Wonder* began quarterly appearances in 1938.

There were no luxurious haunts or club-rooms for members of the Association. The Londoners met in the Lyons tea-shops of Holborn, wandering from one to another and talking science-fiction until it was time to go home. Then two young men from the British Interplanetary Society, Arthur Clarke and William F. Temple, set up home in a large bachelor flat along Gray's Inn Road and kept open house for their friends every Friday. Here, in an atmosphere of books and astronomical pictures, the London Branch grew into a real fellowship of readers, writers and students of the future.

But for men and women of 1938-39 the immediate future held one sole appalling phenomenon: the Second World War, and all its abominations. *Tales of Wonder* was discontinued, the Association broke up, its members scattered to the Forces and to the far corners of the earth along with everyone else. Whenever they could they read whatever science-fiction they could get, and some of them even continued to write it. Mimeographed news-sheets still circulated and kept ex-members in touch; the *Futurian War Digest*, produced by Michael Rosenblum of Leeds, appeared steadily for years. When on leave and visiting London, members often called on the present writer in his book-filled flat off Baker Street, which became, in its way, a minor echo of Gray's Inn Road.

Time hurried on, the war drew to its dreadful close, and towards the end I made an encounter which was to have a lasting effect on the progress of the group. At a literary circle which met for a while at a club in Soho I became acquainted with an adventurous author-cum-publisher, one Stephen D. Frances, to whom I talked enthusiastically of science-fiction. Twelve months later he invited me to prepare a collection of my own stories for Pendulum Publications, his company; and then, out of the blue, proposed that I edit his new science-fiction magazine. Hastily demurring, for I had no qualifications, I suddenly recollected that my friend John Carnell had left the Army only two days before and possessed a most valuable property, in the form of some typescript stories for an abandoned magazine to be called *New Worlds*. And so, one grey afternoon in January 1946, we met at Charing Cross and hurried down the slushy Strand to the Pendulum offices in Lincoln's Inn, where, amid much argument, excitement, misunderstanding and enthusiasm, the new science-fiction magazine was born.

Meantime, with the war well behind us, demobilisation was setting in fast. One by one ex-members of the SFA came back to rejoin old friends in old haunts. The Gray's Inn Road establishment was in other hands and its neighbouring *Red Bull Tavern* had been bombed, so they gathered round the three promoters of *New Worlds* in the *Shamrock*, in Fetter Lane, until their growing numbers forced them to cross the road to the greater spaces of the *White Horse*.

As the weeks wore on and men grew accustomed to peace-time life again, as they thawed out and recovered the sense of old acquaintance, talk flowed, laughter echoed and the old-time cheerfulness crept back. It was a stimulating group, that first post-war clutter of authors and artists. They included men who had already made reputations in the American magazines, John Beynon, A. Bertram Chandler, William F. Temple, and others. In time there appeared other young men whose names have become known to our present-day readers: Peter Phillips, E. C. Tubb, Sydney Bounds, Don Doughty, Peter Hawkins, John Christopher, Bob Clothier and Alan Hunter.

The six-year interlude had made one startling difference to the new London circle: there was no desire at all to revive the Science-Fiction Association. That body had been good, in its time, and in its three years of life it had created many friendships that might never have come about. But as an active group it had involved much tedious and unrewarding work for one or two people with no great benefit to the majority. For the future the Circle determined to remain as they had become, an informal, unorganised literary discussion group whence everybody came together to meet the boys and talk shop.

There was plenty to talk about. The scientific imaginings of twenty years ago had assumed forceful reality in the shape of radar, television, jet-engines, atomic energy, high-altitude rockets and ultra-sonic aircraft. A new generation of young readers was emerging with an appetite for these modern phenomena, and the writing fraternity of the *White Horse* was ready to cater for them and for the older generation too. The most enterprising of these was Arthur C. Clarke, one-time host of Gray's Inn Road who came out of the RAF determined to put the British Interplanetary Society on the map. With a stream of newspaper articles, magazine stories, broadcast talks and books, culminating in his best-selling *The Exploration of Space* in 1951, he did more than any other man to make the nation interplanetary-minded, as it is, perhaps, to-day.

On his heels came the other resident of Gray's Inn Road, William F. Temple. After steadily building a reputation as a short-story writer of merit, Temple too soared to success with his novel *The Four-sided Triangle* of 1949, which so far has been published in six countries and translated into three languages. He followed this with a detective novel, also successful, and has kept up a steady output of short stories as well.

The most stylish and distinguished author of the group, John Wyndham, brought years of magazine writing to a climax with his outstanding story *The Day of the Triffids*, 1951, a novel which wrung astonished praise from experienced reviewers, some of whom were ready to hail the advent of a second H. G. Wells.

But long before these successes the literary men of the group had faced discouraging prospects. In its early days *New Worlds* had proved a winner, but soon commerce as a whole was sinking into the ice-age of Austerity, and Pendulum Publications was feeling the pinch. Before the firm closed down in 1947 a third issue of *New Worlds* appeared and confirmed the magazine's success.

The irony of the situation was appreciated, but not enjoyed, by the promoters. They talked it over, week after week, at the bar of the *White Horse* until at last, in humour rather than hope, someone suggested that the group form its own company and publish the magazine themselves. The idea was all the more startling because none of those present had thought about going into business on their own; and whilst all of them were respectably settled in life, none of them were plutocrats. Nevertheless, a handful pooled their resources and in 1948 Nova Publications emerged as the proprietors of *New Worlds*.

There were difficulties galore – with paper, with printers, with trade distributors, with authors, with artists, and difficulties of inexperience too. Despite all this, the promoters knew they had one overwhelming advantage: a public that was interested in their goods, and ready to buy them. One after another difficulties were overcome, with impatient good-humour and the capacity to learn by experience. By 1951 *New Worlds* was an established periodical, selling steadily, and in its first five years it had discovered twenty-four new authors and six new artists – a striking achievement.

Meantime the Circle of the *White Horse* had grown out of all knowledge. An impetus was given by the advent of a new landlord, Lou Mordecai, a retired sailor with pronounced literary leanings and a fund of good stories. In the genial presence of their host the Circle members grew more than ever expansive, and eager to greet the newcomers who were appearing in a steady trickle. The 'London Circle' had become known to science-fiction readers all over the country, and a recent glance at the Visitors' Book of the *White Horse* shows callers from (in order of appearance) Newport (Mon), Stoke-on-Trent, Rye, Trumpington, Glasgow, Gillingham, Spalding, Inverness, Cardiff, Leicester, Loughborough, the BAOR, Stirling, Dereham, Nottingham, Wymondham, Entwistle, Weston-super-Mare, Oxford and Farnborough. A contrast, this, to the time when a dozen or so young men would gather in the rooms of Gray's Inn Road; now an average of forty or fifty men and women came together every week in the saloon bar to talk science-fiction. Yes, women too to-day, and in growing numbers. The reason was given us by a leading journalist, Mrs Joni Murray, Editor of *Heiress*, who remarked that thousands of young women like herself had done scientific work on radar, aircraft engines and so on in the Forces, and had acquired a taste for science, and with it, for science-fiction.

The Circle was also becoming known outside the clannish world of science-fiction readers. Arthur Clarke's broadcast talks on rockets had brought a welcome BBC visitor, John Keir Cross, author of *The Other Passenger*, who dropped in from time to time when duties permitted. Occasional newspaper men from neighbouring Fleet Street called and made interested enquiries. Most notable of these were two young journalists from Kemsley Press, Miss Joyce Emerson and Mr Skelton Robinson, whose evening of interviews with Circle members brought a friendly article in the magazine *GO*. Our contacts with the Press brought some interesting and surprising revelations. The success of books like Wyndham's *Day of the*

Triffids, Clarke's *The Exploration of Space*, Bradbury's *The Silver Locusts* and others which commanded widespread attention, showed that the legion of science-fiction readers was far larger than we formerly supposed. To clinch the supposition, the appearance of such films as 'Destination Moon,' 'When Worlds Collide' and 'The Day the Earth Stood Still' showed that many reviewers had been reading science-fiction since they were so high, and though they usually scoffed at it in public they belonged too to the great literary 'underground movement', and could now admit it openly!

The Festival Year of 1951 saw the crowning achievement of the *White Horse* circle as a social group when the great international Festival Convention was held at Whitsun. Yes, 'international' now, for the Circle was known the world over. Let us glance again at the Visitors' Book and see whence the visitors came: Minnesota, Vancouver, Wellington (NZ), New York City, Maine, Couchella (Calif.), Sydney (NSW), Wassenaar (Holland), Haarlem (Holland), Dayton (Ohio), Melbourne, Toronto, Wallingford (Penn.), Los Angeles, Haifa and Chicago – all drawn by the potency of science-fiction to this port-of-call whence they could meet friends and talk things over. It was a happy state of affairs for the organisers. Men who had been to the pre-war conventions remembered how fifty or sixty young men met and chatted in a Saturday afternoon meeting. Now they greeted upwards of two hundred people including visitors from eight countries, and enjoyed two days each twelve hours long of continuous discussion and hospitality.

Guests of honour at this memorable gathering were Forrest J. Ackerman, the most famous science-fiction publicist in America, and his wife Wendayne, an acknowledged expert in 'Dianetics – the new science of Mental Healing'. It was Forrest J. who accepted, on behalf of the recipients, the International Fantasy Awards for the best science-fiction novel and the best technical book of the year. The idea of bestowing such an Award had been the inspiration of somebody at the *White Horse* only a few weeks previously and a Committee was set up on the spot, so that there was only time to make replicas for display at the Convention.

Soon after the Convention the *White Horse* group had the pleasure of welcoming L. Sprague de Camp, one of the three or four leading American authors in the field, who gave us a glorious hour or two of dissertation. There was a fleeting glimpse of another brilliant American writer, Poul Anderson, and his brother John, who dropped in while on a tour of Britain and Europe. In the autumn, Mr Harry Pease, of the 20th Century Fox Film Corporation, kindly arranged a special showing of 'The Day the Earth Stood Still' for a large *White Horse* party. A few weeks later Miss Dolly Gwynne, of the Chepstow Theatre in Notting Hill Gate, came to tell us of the remarkable interplanetary play, *6000 Years to Sirius* by Peter Tremlett, which was to be produced at her theatre, and was later much admired by *White Horse* theatre-goers. With this rush of visits and return visits an exciting year concluded. Newcomers to the Circle of the *White Horse* in the last weeks of 1951 were to find themselves in a group which had seen its much-loved literature, once derided as the most ridiculous of sensational trash, establish itself in books, plays, films, broadcasts and television as an intellectual force that had to be reckoned with. Well might they look into the future, as they usually did, with confidence, hope, and expectation.

NEW WORLDS

An Index

The first eight issues of *New Worlds* appeared somewhat spasmodically. In 1951 it became a regular quarterly, then a bi-monthly (in 1952) and eventually (in 1954) a monthly. It ran as a monthly until 1964 when, with the change of publisher and editor, it became a bi-monthly again for a short time, then a monthly again (1965), then a quarterly (1971) until the present, when it is back on a deliberately irregular schedule. Many of the issues listed between 1951 and 1964 lacked interior illustrations, book reviews or even distinctive covers, but contained regular science articles. In the case of pseudonyms we have occasionally given the real name of the author rather than the pseudonym. This index is therefore deliberately idiosyncratic and might afford the reader some interest. Thanks to Mike Ashley for his help in preparing this list.

1

1946 (no month)
Vol. 1 No. 1

Cover and interior illustrations by R.A. Wilkin. *(9¼ x 7¼". 64 pages. Pendulum Publications. Subtitled 'Fiction of the Future' on the cover and 'A Fiction Magazine of the Future' on the contents page. This issue was withdrawn and the cover replaced with one by Victor Cassari. The Cassari cover was also used on the second issue.)*

Fiction

The Mill of the Gods	Maurice G. Hugi
Solar Assignment	Mark Denholm
Knowledge Without Learning	K. Thomas
Sweet Mystery of Life	John Russell Fearn

The Three Pylons — William F. Temple
White Mouse — Thornton Ayre

Feature

Editorial — E.J. Carnell

Illustrations by Wilkin

2

1946 (no month)
Vol. 1 No. 2
Cover by Cassari (see Vol. 1 No. 1)

Fiction

The Living Lies — John Beynon (Wyndham)
Space Ship 13 — Patrick S. Selby
Vicious Circle — Polton Cross
Lunar Concession — Thornton Ayre
Foreign Body — John Brody
The Micro Man — Alden Lorraine
Green Spheres — W.P. Cockcroft

Features

Editorial — E.J. Carnell
Ahead of Reality — L.J. Johnson
Pacificon — F.J. Ackerman

Illustrations by Wilkin

3

1947 (no month)
Vol. 1 No. 3
Cover by Slack

Fiction

Features

Illustrations by Dennis and Slack

4

1949 (no month)
Vol. 2 No. 4
(8½ x 5½". 88 pages. *Nova Publications*)
Cover by Dennis

Fiction

Features

Illustrations by White and Dennis

5

1949 (no month)
Vol. 2 No. 5
Cover by Clothier
(96 pages)

Fiction

Cassandra	John K. Aiken
The Forgotten Enemy	Arthur C. Clarke
Unknown Quantity	Peter Phillips
Too Efficient	S.J. Bounds
Necessity	F.G. Rayer
Time to Rest	John Wyndham
Pool of Infinity	W. Moore

Features

Editorial	E.J. Carnell
Book Review	

Illustrations by Clothier and Turner

6

Spring 1950
Vol. 2 No. 6
Cover by Clothier

Fiction

Phoenix Nest	John K. Aiken
Adoption	Don J. Doughty
Castaway	George Whitely
Adaptability	F.G. Rayer
Jet Landing	Francis Ashton
Coefficient X	A. Bertram Chandler

11

Autumn 1951
Vol. 4 No. 11
Cover by Bull

12

Winter 1951
Vol. 4 No. 12
Cover by Clothier

Fiction

Time Was	F.G. Rayer
Question Mark	Gregory Francis
Liaison Service	Sydney J. Bounds
When Aliens Meet	J.T. M'Intosh
No Heritage	George Longdon
Entrance Exam	E.C. Tubb

Features

Digital Computer	Arthur F. Roberts
Editorial	
Book Reviews	

Illustrations by Clothier, Hunter and Quinn

13

January 1952
Vol. 5 No. 13
Cover by Quinn

Fiction

Pest	A. Bertram Chandler
Alien Analysis	Dan Morgan
Without Bugles	E.C. Tubb
A Matter of Salvage	Sydney J. Bounds
Operation Exodus	Lan Wright

Features

Illustrations by Clothier, Hunter and Quinn

14

March 1952
Vol. 5 No. 14
Cover by Clothier

Fiction

Features

Illustrations by Clothier, Quinn and Hunter

15

May 1952
Vol. 5 No. 15
Cover by Quinn

Fiction

Features

Illustrations by Quinn, Clothier and Hunter

16

July 1952
Vol. 6 No. 16
Cover by Clothier

Fiction

Feature

Editorial

Illustrations by Quinn, Clothier and Hunter

17

September 1952
Vol. 6 No. 17
Cover by Quinn

Fiction

Features

Editorial
Book Reviews

Illustrations by Quinn, Clothier and Hunter

18

November 1952
Vol. 6 No. 18
Cover by Bull

Fiction

Features

Illustrations by Bull, Quinn, Clothier and Hunter

19

January 1953
Vol. 7 No. 19
Cover by Quinn

Fiction

Features

Illustrations by Quinn, Clothier and Hunter

20

March 1953
Vol. 7 No. 20
Cover by Clothier

21

June 1953
Vol. 7 No. 21
Cover by Quinn

22

1953/54 (no month)
Vol. 8 No. 22
Cover by Kinnear

Fiction

Takeoff (Part 1)	Cyril Kornbluth
Museum Piece	John Christopher
Only an Echo	Alan Barclay
Relay Race	J.T. M'Intosh
Opposite Numbers	John Wyndham
The Sentinel	Arthur C. Clarke

Features

Eclipse	Maurice Goldsmith
Editorial	
Book Reviews	

Illustrations by Quinn and Hunter

23

May 1954
Vol. 8 No. 23
Cover by Quinn
(*Beginning of regular monthly publication*)

Fiction

Takeoff (2)	Cyril Kornbluth
Zoological Specimen	A. Bertram Chandler
The Gamble	Jonathan F. Burke
Space Capsule	E.R. James

Features

Illustrations by Quinn, Hunter and Smith

24

June 1954
Vol. 8 No. 24
Cover by Quinn

Fiction

Features

Illustrations by Quinn, Hutchings and Hunter

25

July 1954
Vol. 9 No. 25
Cover by Quinn

Fiction

Features

Illustrations by Quinn and Clothier

26

August 1954
Vol. 9 No. 26
Cover by Quinn

Fiction

Features

Illustrations by Quinn and Lewis

27

September 1954
Vol. 9 No. 27
Cover by Quinn

Fiction

Wild Talent (2)	Wilson Tucker
Suicide Mission	James White
Come Away Home	Francis G. Rayer
A Pound of Cure	Lester del Rey
Strangers in Town	Lan Wright
The Perfect Secretary	J.F. Burke

Features

The 1954 Fantasy Award	Leslie Flood
Editorial	
Book Reviews	

Illustrations by Quinn and Hunter

28

October 1954
Vol. 10 No. 28
Cover by Quinn

Fiction

Wild Talent (3)	Wilson Tucker
Homecoming	E.C. Tubb
Dominoes	Cyril Kornbluth
Regulations	Richard Varne
Portrait of a Spaceman	S.J. Bounds
Occupation	E.W. Ludwig

31

32

Fiction

Features

Illustrations by Quinn, Hunter and Hutchings

33

March 1955
Vol. 11 No. 33
Cover by Quinn

Fiction

Features

Illustrations by Quinn, Hunter, Hutchings and Osborne

34

April 1955
Vol. 12 No. 34
Cover by Bradshaw

Fiction

Star Ship (Part 1)	E.C. Tubb
The Other Door	Arthur Coster
The Real McCoy	Alan Barclay
Visitors' Book	John Brunner
Forgetfulness	Phillip Martyn
No Place for Tears	R.H. Godfrey
Asylum	Kenneth Bulmer

Features

Food of the Future	John Newman
Film Review	J. Carnell
Book Reviews	L. Flood

Illustrations by Bradshaw, Quinn, Woodward, Hunter and Lewis

35

May 1955
Vol. 12 No. 35
Cover by Quinn

Fiction

Star Ship (2)	E.C. Tubb
Outrider	James White
Compassion Circuit	John Wyndham
Ferryman	Richard Rowland
Survival Ship	Judith Merril
Samson	Alan Guthrie

Features

Invisible Astronomy   John Newman
Editorial
Book Reviews   L. Flood

Illustrations by Quinn and Osborne

36

June 1955
Vol. 12 No. 36
Cover by Quinn

Fiction

Star Ship (3)   E.C. Tubb
Bluebird World   J.T. M'Intosh
Man of Parts   H.L. Gold
Highwayman Green   E.R. James
Our Kind of Knowledge   Brian W. Aldiss

Features

A Tenth Planet   Roy Malcolm
Editorial

Illustrations by Woodward, Quinn and Hunter

37

July 1955
Vol. 13 No. 37
Cover by Quinn

Fiction

Features

Illustrations by Quinn, Hunter, Woodward and Hutchings

38

August 1955
Vol. 13 No. 38
Cover by Quinn

Fiction

Features

Illustrations by Quinn

39

September 1955
Vol. 13 No. 39
Cover by Quinn

Fiction

The Time Masters (Part 1)	Wilson Tucker
The Single Ship	Alan Barclay
Any More at Home Like You	Chad Oliver
Life Agency	Dan Morgan

Features

P's and Q's	John Newman
The 1955 Fantasy Award	Leslie Flood
Editorial	

Illustrations by Quinn and Hutchings

40

October 1955
Vol. 14 No. 40
Cover by Bradshaw

Fiction

The Time Masters (2)	Wilson Tucker
The Con Game	Lan Wright
Stormhead	Francis G. Rayer
Rock 83	Alan Barclay
Little Girl Lost	E.C. Tubb

Features

41

Fiction

Features

42

Fiction

Lawyer at Large	E.C. Tubb
Puzzle for Spacemen	John Brunner
Panel Game	Brian W. Aldiss
The Jakundi Moduli	F.G. Rayer
Prime Essential	Frank Weight
Getaway	Michael Harrison

Features

Solar Interference	John Newman
Editorial	
Book Reviews	L. Flood

Illustrations by Quinn and Lewis

43

January 1956
Vol. 15 No. 43
Cover by Quinn

Fiction

Host Age	John Brunner
Red Alert	James White
The Hot Potato	Alan Barclay
The Pensioners	Alan Guthrie
Magic Touch	Duncan Lamont

Features

The Mighty Midgets	John Newman
Editorial	
Book Reviews	L. Flood

Illustrations by Quinn and White

44

February 1956
Vol. 15 No. 44
Cover by Bradshaw

Fiction

Features

Illustrations by Quinn and Hunter

45

March 1956
Vol. 15 No. 45
Cover by Terry

Fiction

Fiction

Features

Illustrations by Quinn, Lewis, Hunter and Hutchings

48

June 1956
Vol. 16 No. 48
Cover by Terry

Fiction

Features

Illustrations by Quinn and Taylor

49

July 1956
Vol. 17 No. 49
Cover by Quinn

Fiction

Features

Illustrations by Quinn and Taylor

50

August 1956
Vol. 17 No. 50
Cover by Terry

Fiction

Features

Illustrations by Quinn and Hutchings

51

September 1956
Vol. 17 No. 51
Cover by Quinn

Fiction

Features

Illustrations by Quinn and Hutchings

52

October 1956
Vol. 18 No. 52
Cover by Terry

Fiction

Features

Illustrations by Quinn, Hutchings and Taylor

53

November 1956
Vol. 18 No. 53
Cover by Terry

Fiction

Features

Illustrations by Quinn and Eddie

54

December 1956
Vol. 18 No. 54
Cover by Quinn

Fiction

Features

Illustrations by Quinn, Hutchings and Lewis

55

January 1957
Vol. 19 No. 55
Cover by Terry
(First J.G. Ballard story)

Fiction

Features

Illustrations by Quinn and Lewis

56

February 1957
Vol. 19 No. 56
Cover by Terry

Fiction

Features

Illustrations by Lewis, Jackson and Eddie

57

March 1957
Vol. 19 No. 57
Cover by Terry

Fiction

Features

Illustrations by Lewis and Eddie

58

April 1957
Vol. 20 No. 58
Cover by Terry

Fiction

Features

Illustrations by Lewis and Jackson

59

May 1957
Vol. 20 No. 59
Cover by Elton

Fiction

Features

Illustrations by Lewis and Eddie

60

June 1957
Vol. 20 No. 60
Cover by Terry

Fiction

Features

Illustrations by Harry

61

July 1957
Vol. 21 No. 61
Cover by Lewis

Fiction

Features

Illustrations by Jackson

62

August 1957
Vol. 21 No. 62
Cover by Terry
(Decision to drop interior illustrators)

Fiction

The Uninhibited (Part 1)	Dan Morgan
The Book of Power	A.B. Chandler
The Underlings	J. Kippax
Manhunter	John Boland
Buried Talent	P.E. High
According to Hoyle	Paul McClelland
Native Law	K. Bulmer

Features

Antarctica	K. Johns
Editorial	

63

September 1957
Vol. 21 No. 63
Cover by Terry

Fiction

The Uninhibited (2)	Dan Morgan
Mission 100	K. Bulmer
Sister Under the Skin	A.B. Chandler
Made on Mars	E.R. James
Watcher on Sargan IV	P. Hawkins

Features

Power in the Sky	K. Johns
Editorial	

64

October 1957
Vol. 22 No. 64
Cover by Lewis

Fiction

Features

65

November 1957
Vol. 22 No. 65
Cover by Lewis

Fiction

Features

66

67

68

February 1958
Vol. 23. No. 68
Cover by Terry

Fiction

Threshold of Eternity (3)	John Brunner
Requiem for a Harvey	E.C. Tubb
The Unwanted	Dan Morgan
The Unreluctant Tread	Kenneth Bulmer
The Fortieth of December	Robert Presslie

Features

Life at Last	Kenneth Johns
Editorial	
Book Reviews	L. Flood

69

March 1958
Vol. 23. No. 69
Cover by Lewis

Fiction

Wasp (Part 1)	Eric Frank Russell
Secret Weapon	John Boland
Captain Bedlam	Harry Harrison
Next of Kin	Robert Presslie
Painters of Narve	F.G. Rayer
The Lonely One	Robert Silverberg

Features

Outward Bound (1)	K. Johns
Editorial	

70

April 1958
Vol. 24 No. 70
Cover by Lewis

Fiction

Wasp (2)	E.F. Russell
For All the Night (1st Troon story)	John Wyndham
The House of Lights	Donald Malcolm
The Macauley Circuit	Robert Silverberg
Track 12	J.G. Ballard

Features

Low Gravity	D.J. Francis
Editorial	

71

May 1958
Vol. 24 No. 71
Cover by Lewis

Fiction

Wasp (3)	E.F. Russell
The Wanton Jade	E.C. Tubb
Routine Observations	E.R. James
Tableau	James White
Companion	John W. Ashton
In the Box	B. Chandler

Features

The Sunspot Cycle	K. Johns
Editorial	

72

June 1958
Vol. 24 No. 72
Cover by Lewis

Fiction

Idiot's Delight (Troon 2)	John Wyndham
The Star Game	Dan Morgan
Absolutely Inflexible	Robert Silverberg
Ringside Seat	John Brody
The Wayward Ship	S.J. Bounds
One for the Road	R. Presslie

Features

Outward Bound (2)	K. Johns
Editorial	

73

July 1958
Vol. 25 No. 73
Cover by Lewis

Fiction

Segregation	B.W. Aldiss
Thin Gnat-Voices (Troon 3)	John Wyndham
Outside	S.J. Bounds
Keepers of the House	L. del Rey
Tower for One	John Kippax
The Shadow People	Arthur Sellings

Features

Life at Last	K. Johns
Guest Editorial	Leslie Flood

74

August 1958
Vol. 25 No. 74
Cover by Lewis

Fiction

The Ideal Captain	James White
Stability	L. del Rey
The Mules	S.J. Bounds
Slice of Life	C.M. Knox
Space Command	K. Bulmer
Death on the Wheel	C. Jackson

Features

The Challenge of the Sea	K. Johns
Editorial	

75

September 1958
Vol. 25 No. 75
Cover by Lewis

Fiction

Equator (Part 1)	Brian W. Aldiss
Space is a Province of Brazil (Troon 4)	John Wyndham
Morgan's Galatea	C.C. Reed
Trainee for Mars	H. Harrison
Life Hutch	Harlan Ellison

Features

Outward Bound (3)	K. Johns
Editorial	

76

October 1958
Vol. 26 No. 76
Cover by Lewis

Fiction

Equator (2)   B.W. Aldiss
Dreamboat   Bertram Chandler
The Guardian   P.E. High
The Different Complexion   W.F. Temple
Deny the Slake   Richard Wilson

Features

The Solacon   Ron Bennett
Book Reviews   L. Flood

77

November 1958
Vol. 26 No. 77
Cover by Lewis

Fiction

Trouble with Emily   James White
Life Plan   Colin Kapp
Sendoff   R. Presslie
Carrion Country   B.W. Aldiss
The Dusty Death   John Kippax
Flatiron   Arthur Sellings
Who's There?   Arthur C. Clarke

Features

Life with Coriolis   D.J. Francis
Editorial

78

December 1958
Vol. 26 No. 78
Cover by Lewis

Fiction
A Man Called Destiny (Part 1)   Lan Wright
Signora Porfiria   John W. Ashton
Another Word for Man   Robert Presslie
Incentive   Brian W. Aldiss
The Still Waters   Lester del Rey

Features

Year 102 A.F.   Roger Critchley
Editorial

79

January 1959
Vol. 27 No. 79
Cover by Lewis

Fiction

A Man Called Destiny (2)   Lan Wright
Insecurity Risk   Dan Morgan
The Unbeaten Track   Brian W. Aldiss
In Gratitude   Robert Silverberg
The Right Ingredients   George Whitely
For the Colour of his Hair   Arthur Sellings

Features

Outward Bound (4)   K. Johns
Editorial

80

February 1959
Vol. 27 No. 80
Cover by Edwards

Fiction

A Man Called Destiny (3)	Lan Wright
Earthman's Burden	R. Silverberg
The Towers of San Ampa	B.W. Aldiss
Friday	John Kippax
The Stuff of Dreams	D. Malcolm

Features

The Meson Story	K. Johns
Editorial	

81

March 1959
Vol. 27 No. 81
Cover by Lewis

Fiction

Count-Down (Part 1)	Charles Eric Maine
Dogfight	James White
The Trouble I See	John Brunner
Squeeze Box	P.E. High
Chance Encounter	B. Chandler

Features

The Ages of Ice	K. Johns
Editorial	

82

April 1959
Vol. 28 No. 82
Cover by Lewis

Fiction

Count-Down (2)	C.E. Maine
Survival Problem	C. Kapp
The Silver Moons	Alan Barclay
The Other One	Brian W. Aldiss
Confession is Good	R. Presslie

Features

Cetex	K. Johns
Editorial	

83

May 1959
Vol. 28 No. 83
Cover by Lewis

Fiction

Count-Down (3)	C.E. Maine
I See You	H. Harrison
Project – Stall	P.E. High
The Outstretched Hand	A. Sellings
Searchpoint	F.G. Rayer

Features

Biologically Speaking	K. Johns
Survey Report 1958	John Carnell

84

June 1959
Vol. 28 No. 84
Cover by Lewis

Fiction

Visitor at Large	James White
Idiot Stick	Damon Knight
Calling Mr Francis	Colin Kapp
Strange Menhir	E. Henley
Sands Our Abode	F.G. Rayer
The Gentle Approach	K. Bulmer

Features

Editorial	
Book Reviews	L. Flood

85

July 1959
Vol. 29 No. 85
Cover by Lewis

Fiction

The Patient Dark (Part 1)	K. Bulmer
Joker's Trick	Lan Wright
Sprinkler System	E.R. James
Malnutrition	Robert Silverberg
Round Trip	John Brunner

Features

Moon Bright	K. Johns
Editorial	

86

August/September 1959
Vol. 29 No. 86
Cover by Lewis

Fiction

The Patient Dark (2)	K. Bulmer
The Birdcage	P. Hawkins
Complex	D. Malcolm
Beyond Realism	E.R. James
Pseudo Path	P.E. High

Feature

Editorial

87

October 1959
Vol. 29 No. 87
Cover by Lewis

Fiction

The Patient Dark (3)	K. Bulmer
The High Road	James White
Continuity Man	G. Longdon
The Railways up on Cannis	C. Kapp

Features

Outward Bound (5)	K. Johns
Editorial	

88

November 1959
Vol. 39 No. 88
Cover by Lewis

Fiction

Grapeliner   James White
The Waiting Grounds   J.G. Ballard
Almost Obsolete   Donald Malcolm
I Like You   G. Longdon
Aberration   Roy Robinson and J.A. Sones

Feature

Editorial

89

December 1959
Vol. 30 No. 89
Cover by Lewis
(First Moorcock story – with J. Bayley)

Fiction

Time Out of Joint (Part 1)   Philip K. Dick
Breaking Point   Colin Kapp
Appropriation   Robert Silverberg
Peace on Earth   Michael Moorcock and Barrington
                                   Bayley
Nearly Extinct   Alan Barclay

Features

Outward Bound (6)   K. Johns
Editorial

90

January 1960
Vol. 30 No. 90
Cover by Lewis

Fiction

Time Out of Joint (2)	P. K. Dick
O'Mara's Orphan	James White
Under an English Heaven	B.W. Aldiss
Mumbo-Jumbo Man	Philip E. High

Feature

Editorial

91

February 1960
Vol. 31 No. 91
Cover by Lewis

Fiction

Time Out of Joint (3)	P.K. Dick
Enigma	Colin Kapp
The Destiny Show	Derek Lane
Survival Demands	E.C. Tubb
Static Trouble	F.G. Rayer
The Shrine	Alan Guthrie

Feature

Editorial

92

March 1960
Vol. 31 No. 92
Cover by Lewis

Fiction

X for Exploitation (Part 1)	Brian W. Aldiss
The Third World	David Porter
Zone of Terror	J.G. Ballard
Profession, Spaceman	K. Bulmer
Badman	John Brunner
Bill of Sale	Wynne N. Whiteford
The Pathfinders	D. Malcolm

Features

Editorial	
Book Reviews	L. Flood

93

April 1960
Vol. 31 No. 93
Cover by Jarr

Fiction

X for Exploitation (2)	B.W. Aldiss
The Fourth Power	John Brunner
The Jarnos Affair	Lan Wright
Man of War	E.C. Tubb

Features

Outward Bound (7)	K. Johns
Editorial	

94

May 1960
Vol. 32 No. 94
Cover by Jarr

Fiction

X for Exploitation (3)	B.W. Aldiss
The Bright Ones	J. Phillifent
The Winds of Truth	D. Malcolm
Ozymandias	R. Silverberg
Lost Thing Found	B. Chandler

Features

The Deeps	K. Johns
Editorial	
Book Reviews	L. Flood

95

June 1960
Vol. 32 No. 95
Cover by Jarr

Fiction

Outpatient	James White
Chronopolis	J.G. Ballard
Creatures, Incorporated	Larry Maddock
Soldiers Running	B.W. Aldiss
Pursuit Missile	P.E. High

Features

Belts of Van Allen	K. Johns
Editorial	

96

July 1960
Vol. 32 No. 96
Cover by Lewis

Fiction

The Fatal Fire (Part 1)	K. Bulmer
Moment of Decision	W.N. Whiteford
The Realists	Richard Graham
Wingys and the Zuzzers	R.J. Tilley
Homing Tantalus	G. Whitley
Nuclear Justice	Lance Horne

Features

Outward Bound (8)	K. Johns
Editorial	

97

August 1960
Vol. 33 No. 97
Cover by Jarr

Fiction

The Fatal Fire (2)	K. Bulmer
Still Time	David Porter
The Funnel	Harold Parsons
Alien for Hire	Larry Maddock
No Return	G. Whitley

Features

Space Today	K. Johns
Editorial	
Book Reviews	L. Flood

98

September 1960
Vol. 33 No. 98
Cover by Lewis

Fiction

The Fatal Fire (3)	K. Bulmer
Theory	J. Rackham
The Doorway	W.N. Whiteford
Test Case	D. Malcolm
The Best Possible World	Richard Wilson

Features

Limitless Life	K. Johns
Editorial	

99

October 1960
Vol. 33 No. 99
Cover by Jarr

Fiction

The Apprentice	James White
The Exposing Eye	Colin Kapp
Memories are Important	E.C. Tubb
Red Dominoes	W.T. Webb
The Voices of Time	J.G. Ballard

Features

Anyone at Home?	K. Johns
Editorial	
Guest Editorial	Sam Moskowitz
Book Reviews	L. Flood

100

November 1960
Vol. 34 No. 100
Cover by Lewis
(Special 100th issue with specially written Aldiss story)

Fiction

Sitting Duck	William F. Temple
The Glass of Iargo	Colin Kapp
The Emptiness of Space	John Wyndham
Unfinished Symphony	John Hynam
Old Hundredth	Brian W. Aldiss
Prerogative	John Brunner
Greater than Infinity	E.C. Tubb
Countercharm	James White

Features

The Science Fiction Ethic	J.T. Phillifent
A Trench ... And Two Holes	E.F. Russell
Editorial	
Film Review	Arthur Sellings

Illustrations by Thomson

101

December 1960
Vol. 34 No. 101
Cover by Lewis

Fiction

Trial Run	John Rackham
Greenie Gunner	K. Bulmer
The Bell of Ethicona	C. Kapp
Reason	R.J. Tilley
When in Doubt	Larry Maddock

Features

Time and Dr Mossbauer   K. Johns
Editorial
Book Reviews   L. Flood

Illustrations by Thomson

102

January 1961
Vol. 34 No. 102
Cover by Jordan

Fiction

Venus Plus X (Part 1)   Theodore Sturgeon
The Edge of Oblivion   Peter Hawkins
Hiatus   K. Bulmer
The Spirit is Willing   R. Graham
Stopover Earth   Dan Morgan
Starting Course   Arthur Sellings

Features

Radio Space   K. Johns
Editorial
Book Reviews   John Carnell

103

February 1961
Vol. 35 No. 103
Cover by Lewis

Fiction

Feature

104

March 1961
Vol. 35 No. 104
Cover by Lewis

Fiction

Features

105

April 1961
Vol. 35 No. 105
Cover by Jordan

Fiction

Venus Plus X (4)	Theordore Sturgeon
The Scapegoat	Alan Barclay
The Ark	M. Lucas
The Other Face	D. Malcolm
Button Pusher	Bill Spencer
Time of Arrival	David Rome

Features

Space Rescue	K. Johns
Editorial	
Book Reviews	L. Flood

106

May 1961
Vol. 36 No. 106
Cover by Lewis

Fiction

Blink	John Rackham
This Wonderful Birthday	John Ashcroft
The Jackson Killer	P.E. High
Haircrack	Alan Barclay
Deep End	J.G. Ballard

Features

Space Bullets	K. Johns
Guest Editorial	David Kyle

107

June 1961
Vol. 36 No. 107
Cover by Lewis

Fiction

Put Down This Earth (Part 1)	John Brunner
Morpheus	R. Hoskins
Jackpot	E.C. Tubb
Delete the Variable	Philip Heath
Mantrap	Kathleen James

Features

Editorial	
Book Reviews	J. Carnell

108

July 1961
Vol. 36 No. 108
Cover by Lewis

Fiction

Put Down This Earth (2)	John Brunner
Trinity	David Rome
The Overloaded Man	J.G. Ballard
Junior Partner	D.D. Stewart
The Trouble with Honey	J. Rackham

Feature

Editorial

109

August 1961
Vol. 37 No. 109
Cover by Jordan

Fiction

Put Down This Earth (3)	John Brunner
Goodbye, Dr Gabriel	John Rackham
Company Store	Robert Silverberg
The Ship of Heaven	Mike Davies

Features

Bigger Birds	K. Johns
Editorial	
Book Reviews	L. Flood

110

September 1961
Vol. 37 No. 110
Cover by Quinn
(*First Ballard novel, later* The Wind from Nowhere)

Fiction

Storm-Wind (Part 1)	J.G. Ballard
Resident Physician	James White
Nelson Expects	John Kippax
Change of Heart	G. Whitley
The Fortress of True	David Rome

Features

Stress	D.E. Ellis
Editorial	
Book Reviews	L. Flood

111

October 1961
Vol. 37 No. 111
Cover by Lewis

Fiction

Storm-Wind (2)	J.G. Ballard
For the Love of Pete	Colin Kapp
The End of the Line	Lan Wright
Cold Blood	George Langalaan
Conviction	Lee Harding

Feature

Guest Editorial	Arthur Sellings

112

November 1961
Vol. 38 No. 112
Cover by Quinn

Fiction

The Golden Age (Part 1)	Rupert Clinton
Echo	Lee Harding
Billenium	J.G. Ballard
All Laced Up	G. Whitley
The Martian Hunters	P.E. High

Features

Guest Editorial	John Phillifent
Book Reviews	L. Flood

113

December 1961
Vol. 38 No. 113
Cover by Lewis

Fiction

The Golden Age (2)	Rupert Clinton
Black Knowledge	P. Hawkins
The Gentle Assassin	J.G. Ballard
Survival Course	P.E. High
Protected Species	David Rome

Features

Gravity	K. Johns
Guest Editorial	Brian Aldiss
Book Reviews	John Carnell

114

January 1962
Vol. 38 No. 114
Cover by Quinn

Fiction

Basis for Negotiation	Brian W. Aldiss
Field Hospital (Part 1)	James White
Little Horror	Bill Spencer
Psi Squad	P.E. High

Features

Guest Editorial	John Brunner
Film Review	J. Carnell

115

February 1962
Vol. 39 No. 115
Cover by Lewis

Fiction

Field Hospital (2)	James White
The Pioneer	B.N. Ball
Late	Lee Harding
The Engineer	Joseph Green
Conversation Piece	B.W. Aldiss
The Bundenberg Touch	H.L. Draper

Features

Guest Editorial	W.F. Temple
Film Review	John Carnell
Book Reviews	L. Flood

116

March 1962
Vol. 39 No. 116
Cover by Quinn

Fiction

Field Hospital (3)	James White
Flame in the Flux Field	K. Bulmer
Stimulus	John Brunner
Probability Factor	P.E. High

Features

Editorial	
Book Reviews	L. Flood

117

April 1962
Vol. 39 No. 117
Cover by Lewis

Fiction

The Dawson Diaries (Part 1)	John Rackham
Dragonfly	Lee Harding
The Seventh Man	Kathleen James
Initiation Rites	Joseph Green
Play Planet	Alan Burns

Feature

Guest Editorial	Philip E. High

118

May 1962
Vol. 40 No. 118
Cover by Enrique

Fiction

The Dawson Diaries (2)	John Rackham
Terminal	Lee Harding
Think of a Number	Steve Hall
Dictator Fait	P.E. High
The Analyser	Bill Spencer

Features

Guest Editorial	J.G. Ballard
Book Reviews	L. Flood

119

June 1962
Vol. 40 No. 119
Cover by Lewis

Fiction

Features

120

July 1962
Vol. 40 No. 120
Photographic Cover

Fiction

Features

121

August 1962
Vol. 41 No. 121
Photographic Cover

Fiction

Minor Operation (3)	B.W. Aldiss
The Colonist	Joseph Green
One Foot in the Door	Robert Presslie
Variant	F.G. Rayer
Thousand Deep	E.R. James

Feature

Guest Editorial   Robert Silverberg

122

September 1962
Vol. 41 No. 122
Photographic Cover

Fiction

Crack of Doom (Part 1)	John Brunner
Moonbeam	David Rome
The Streets of Ashkalon	Harry Harrison
Pandora's Box	Steve Hall
Serpent in Paradise	Morris Nagel
Craving for Blackness	Robert Ray

Feature

Guest Editorial   John Baxter

125

December 1962
Vol. 42 No. 125
Photographic Cover

Fiction

Lambda One	Colin Kapp
Mood Indigo	Russ Markham
Meaning	David Rome
Capsid	F.G. Rayer
Operation Survival	Paul Corey
Transmitter Problem	Joseph Green

Features

Guest Editorial	Lan Wright
Book Reviews	L. Flood

126

January 1963
Vol. 42 No. 126
Photographic Cover

Fiction

Dawn's Left Hand (Part 1)	Lan Wright
Ecdysiac	R. Presslie
Big Tin God	P.E. High
Burden of Proof	David Jay
The Statue	R.W. Mackelworth
The Subliminal Man	J.G. Ballard

Features

Guest Editorial	David Rome
Book Reviews	L. Flood

127

February 1963
Vol. 43 No. 127
Photographic Cover

Fiction

Dawn's Left Hand (2)	Lan Wright
Twice Bitten	D. Malcolm
Live Test	Peter Vaughan
Pet Name for a World	George Locke
Till Life Us Do Part	R. Presslie

Features

Guest Editorial	James White
Survey Report 1962	John Carnell

128

March 1963
Vol. 43 No. 128
Photographic Cover

Fiction

Dawn's Left Hand (3)	Lan Wright
Inductive Reaction	Russ Markham
Aqueduct	F.G. Rayer
Eviction	John Baxter
Bottomless Pit	P.E. High
Too Good to Be True	Walter Gillings

Feature

Guest Editorial	D. Malcolm

129

April 1963
Vol. 43 No. 129
Photographic Cover

Fiction

Window on the Moon (Part 1)	E.C. Tubb
Adaptation	Roy Robinson
Dossier	John Rackham
Quest	Lee Harding
Compensation	James Inglis

Features

Guest Editorial	Michael Moorcock
Book Reviews	L. Flood

130

May 1963
Vol. 44 No. 130
Typographical Cover

Fiction

Window on the Moon (2)	E.C. Tubb
The Under-Privileged	Brian W. Aldiss
Confession	John Rackham
The Jay Walkers	Russ Markham
I, The Judge	R.W. Mackelworth

Features

Guest Editorial	Lee Harding
Book Reviews	L. Flood

131

June 1963
Vol. 44 No. 131
Photographic Cover

Fiction

Window on the Moon (3)	E.C. Tubb
The Old Man in the Mountain	Joseph Green
End-Game	J.G. Ballard
Occupation Force	David Rome
Dipso Facto	Robert Presslie

Features

Day of the Triffids (review)	John Carnell
Guest Editorial	John Ashcroft

132

July 1963
Vol. 44 No. 132
Typographical Cover

Fiction

Refuge	Joseph Green
The Last Salamander	John Rackham
The Nothing	Bill Spencer
Pattern of Risk	R.W. Mackelworth
Point of No Return	P.E. High
Flux	Michael Moorcock and Barrington Bayley

Features

Guest Editorial	E.C. Tubb
Book Reviews	L. Flood
First International SF Film Festival	J. Carnell

133

August 1963
Vol. 45 No. 133
Cover by Quinn *(standard design)*

Fiction

To Conquer Chaos (Part 1)	John Brunner
The Shtarman	John Ashcroft
Natural Defence	Barrington Bayley
The Lonely City	Lee Harding
Disposal Unit Man	David Alexander
Foreign Body	David Rome

Features

Guest Editorial	Robert Presslie
Book Reviews	L. Flood

134

September 1963
Vol. 45 No. 134
Cover by Quinn *(standard design)*

Fiction

To Conquer Chaos (2)	John Brunner
Lack of Experience	John Garfield
Not by Mind Alone	Michael Moorcock
Deep Freeze	John Rackham
The Rotten Borough	R.W. Mackelworth
The Game	James Inglis

Features

Guest Editorial	Dr I.F. Clarke
Trieste Film Festival Report	J. Carnell

135

October 1963
Vol. 45 No. 135
Cover by Quinn *(standard design)*
(First story by Hilary Bailey)

Fiction

To Conquer Chaos (3)	John Brunner
Man-Hunt	John Rackham
Breakdown	Hilary Bailey
Forty Years On	E.R. James
Project 13013	Bill Spencer
Yutzy Brown	Mino Puggioni

Features

Guest Editorial	G.H. Doherty
Book Reviews	L. Flood

136

November 1963
Vol. 46 No. 136
Cover by Quinn *(standard design)*

Fiction

The Dark Mind (Part 1)	Colin Kapp
Crux	John Rackham
The Postlethwaite Effect	B.N. Ball
Interlude	John Baxter
Return Visit	B.J. Bayley
No Ending	David Busby

Features

Guest Editorial	John Ashton

137

December 1963
Vol. 46 No. 137
Cover by Quinn (*standard design*)

Fiction

The Dark Mind (2)	Colin Kapp
Relative Genius	P.E. High
The Cliff Hangers	R.W. Mackelworth
When I Come Back	Jonathan Burke
No Brother of Mine	R. Presslie
Tee Vee Man	R.A. Hargreaves

Features

Guest Editorial	Roberta Rambelli
Book Reviews	L. Flood

138

January 1964
Vol. 46 No. 138
Typographical Cover

Fiction

The Dark Mind (3)	Colin Kapp
Dilemma with Three Horns	D. Malcolm
The Last Generation	Ernest Hill
The Countenance	B.J. Bayley
Toys	John Baxter

Features

Guest Editorial	John Brunner
Book Reviews	John Carnell

139

January 1964
Vol. 46 No. 138
Typographical Cover

Fiction

Open Prison (Part 1)	James White
Counter-Feat	Brian W. Aldiss
One-Way Strait	Brian W. Aldiss
The Unexpected Martyr	R.W. Mackelworth
The Time Dweller	Michael Moorcock
Die and Grow Rich	John Rackham

Features

Guest Editorial	L.H. Barnes
Book Reviews	L. Flood

140

March 1964
Vol. 47 No. 140
Typographical Cover

Fiction

Open Prison (2)	James White
The Terminal Beach	J.G. Ballard
The Traps of Time	John Baxter
Unfinished Business	Clifford C. Reed
The Unremembered	Edward Mackin
Jetway 75	William Spencer

Features

Editorial	
Book Reviews	L. Flood

141

April 1964
Vol. 47 No. 141
Typographical Cover
(*Farewell editorial by John Carnell*)

Fiction

Open Prison (3)	James White
Beyond the Reach of Storms	Donald Malcolm
Megapolitan Underground	William Spencer
Now is the Time	Steve Hall
Farewell, Dear Brother	Barrington Bayley

Features

Survey Report 1963	John Carnell
Postmortem	Letters about *NW* (including Moorcock)
Book Reviews	L. Flood

142

May-June 1964
Vol. 48 No. 142
Cover by Cawthorn
(*First Moorcock-edited issue*)

Fiction

Equinox (Part 1)	J.G. Ballard
Never Let Go of My Hand	Brian W. Aldiss
The Last Lonely Man	John Brunner
The Star Virus	B.J. Bayley

Feature

Myth Maker of the 20th Century	J.G. Ballard

143

144

Features

Illustrations by Cawthorn, Gilmore, Graham, Thomson

145

November-December 1964
Vol. 48 No. 145
Cover by Tilley

Fiction

Features

Illustrations by Cawthorn, Gilmore, Thomson

146

January 1965
Vol. 48. No. 146
Cover by Tilley

Fiction

Features

Illustrations by Gilmore and Cawthorn

147

February 1965
Vol. 48 No. 147
Cover by Jakubowicz

Fiction

Features

Biological Electricity	Science feature
Can Spacemen Live with Their Illusions?	Science feature
The Cosmic Satirist	James Colvin
Did Elric Die in Vain?	Alan Forrest
Hardly SF	Hilary Bailey

Illustrations by Gilmore, Cawthorne, Thomson

148

March 1965
Vol. 48 No. 148
Cover artist unknown

Fiction

All the King's Men	B.J. Bayley
Sunjammer	Arthur C. Clarke
First Dawn	Donald Malcolm
Dune Limbo	J.G. Ballard
Escape from Evening	Michael Moorcock
The Uncivil War	R.J. Tilley

Features

Film Review	Alan Dodd
Book Review	Langdon Jones
Letters	

Illustrations by Gilmore and Thomson

149

April 1965
Vol. 48 No. 149
Cover by Tilley

Fiction

The Life Buyer (Part 1)   E.C. Tubb
The Changing Shape of Charlie
   Snuff   R.W. Mackleworth
In One Sad Day   George Collyn
Death of an Earthman   Gordon Walters
Third Party   Dan Morgan
What Next?   Edward Mackin
The Flowers of the Valley   Keith Roberts
Reactionary   B.J. Bayley

Features

Book Reviews   Langdon Jones
Letters

Illustrations by Gilmore

150

May 1965
Vol. 48 No. 150
Cover by Tilley
(*Special 150th issue*)

Fiction

Time Trap   Charles Harness
The Small Betraying Detail   Brian W. Aldiss
Nobody Axed You   John Brunner
Prisoner of the Coral Deep   J.G. Ballard
Alfred's Ark   Jack Vance
The Life Buyer (2)   E.C. Tubb

Features

151

June 1965
Vol. 49 No. 151
Cover artist unknown

Fiction

Features

Illustrations by Cawthorn, Douthwaite, Thomson

152

July 1965
Vol. 49 No. 152
Cover probably by Tilley
(*First Platt story*)

Fiction

Lone Zone   Charles Platt
The Leveller   Langdon Jones
The Silent Ship   E.C. Williams
A Funny Thing Happened   Dikk Richardson
A Light in the Sky   Richard Gordon
Supercity   Brian W. Aldiss
The Night of the Gyul   Colin R. Fry

Features

Roger Corman and Edgar Allan Poe   Al Good
Tomorrow in Retrospect   George Collyn
Shorter Reviews   James Colvin and
                                           Langdon Jones

Illustrations by Cawthorn and Gilmore

153

August 1965
Vol. 49 No. 153
Cover artist unknown

Fiction

Bill, The Galactic Hero (Part 1)   Harry Harrison
The Source   Brian W. Aldiss
And Worlds Renewed   George Collyn
The Pulse of Time   W.T. Webb
By the Same Door   Mack Reynolds

154

155

October 1965
Vol. 49 No. 154
Cover artist unknown

Fiction

Features

Illustrations by Cawthorn

156

November 1965
Vol. 49 No. 156
Cover artist unknown

Fiction

Features

Fiction

Features

Illustrations by Kearn and Cawthorn

159

February 1966
Vol. 49 No. 159
Cover artist unknown

Fiction

Features

Illustrations by Cawthorn

160

March 1966
Vol. 49 No. 160
Cover artist unknown
(*Increase of price and pages – 160*)

Fiction

The Evil that Men Do (Part 1)	John Brunner
The Great Clock	Langdon Jones
From ONE	Bill Butler
Psychosmosis	David I. Masson
The Post-Mortem People	Peter Tate
The Disaster Story	Charles Platt
For a Breath I Tarry	Roger Zelazny
Phase Three (Cornelius)	Michael Moorcock

Features

Visions of Hell	J.G. Ballard
Mainly Paperbacks	James Colvin
Rose Among Weeds	Langdon Jones

Illustrations by Douthwaite and Cawthorn

161

April 1966
Vol. 49 No. 161
Cover artist unknown

Fiction

The Assassination Weapon	J.G. Ballard
Skirmish	John Baxter
No Guarantee	Gordon Walters
House of Dust	Norman Brown
The Ruins	James Colvin

162

May 1966
Vol. 49 No. 162
Cover artist unknown
(First Butterworth story)

163

June 1966
Vol. 50 No. 163
Cover by Roberts

Fiction

Features

Illustrations by Cawthorn, Douthwaite, Yates, Gilmore

164

July 1966
Vol. 50 No. 163
Cover artist unknown

Fiction

Features

165

August 1966
Vol. 50 No. 165
Cover by Roberts
(Charles Platt becomes designer)

Fiction

Features

166

September 1966
Vol. 50 No. 166
Cover by Roberts

Fiction

Features

Illustrations by Cawthorn

167

October 1966
Vol. 50 No. 167
Cover by Roberts

Fiction

Features

168

November 1966
Vol. 50 No. 168
Cover by Roberts
(First Sladek story)

Fiction

Features

169

December 1966
Vol. 50 No. 169
Cover by Price-Sims

Fiction

Feature

Illustrations by Cawthorn and Young

170

January 1967
Vol. 50 No. 170
Cover by Jones

Fiction

Features

Illustrations by Cawthorn and Young

171

March 1967
Vol. 50 No. 171
Cover artist unknown
(128-page issue)

Fiction

Illustration by Young

172

April 1967 *(Mis-dated for March)*
Vol. 50 No. 172
Cover artist unknown

Fiction

Features

Illustration by Cawthorn

173

July 1967
Vol. 51 No. 173
Cover by Escher
(*First large-format issue*)

Fiction

Camp Concentration (Part 1)	Thomas M. Disch
The Death Module	J.G. Ballard
1937 A.D.!	John T. Sladek
The Heat Death of the Universe	Pamela Zoline
Not So Certain	David Masson
In the House of the Dead	Roger Zelazny

Poetry

The Soft World Sequence	George MacBeth

Features

Sleep, Dreams and Computers	Dr Christopher Evans
Expressing the Abstract	Charles Platt
The Lessons of the Future	Thomas M. Disch
The Hiroshima Man	Brian W. Aldiss

Illustrations by Zoline, Douthwaite, Young, Cawthorn, etc.

174

August 1967
Vol. 51 No. 173
Cover by Paolozzi

Fiction

Camp Concentration (2)	Thomas M. Disch
The Green Wall Said	Gene Wolfe

175

September 1967
Vol. 51 No. 175
Cover by Phillips

176

October 1967
Vol. 51 No. 176
Cover by Hamilton
(21st Anniversary issue)

Fiction

An Age (Part 1)	Brian W. Aldiss
Solipsist	Bob Parkinson
Camp Concentration (conclusion)	Thomas M. Disch
The City Dwellers	Charles Platt
The Baked Bean Factory	Michael Butterworth
The Last Inn on the Road	Roger Zelazny

Features

The Language of Science	Dr David Harvey
A Fine Pop Art Continuum	Christopher Finch
The Inconstant Alpha	Dr Chris Evans
The Rise of the Decline	Thomas M. Disch
A Reverie of Bone	Langdon Jones

Illustrations by Young, Zoline, Lambourne, Platt, Peake

177

November 1967
Vol. 51 No. 177
Cover by Young

Fiction

An Age (2)	Brian W. Aldiss
Stand on Zanzibar (extracts)	John Brunner
Wine on an Empty Stomach	George Collyn

179

February 1968
Vol. 51 No. 179
Cover from *Barbarella*

Fiction

Bug Jack Barron (2)	Norman Spinrad
The Serpent of Kundalim	Brian Aldiss
The Square Root of Brain	Fritz Leiber
A Single Rose	Jon DeCles
In Seclusion	Harvey Jacobs

Features

Barbarella and the Anxious Frenchman	Michael Moorcock
Under the Sea with Hubert Humphrey	Hubert Humphrey
Atrocities of the Loves-Slaves of Equanimity	John Sladek

Illustrations by Rose, Cawthorn, Platt, etc.

180

March 1968
Vol. 51 No. 180
Cover by Young
(*The largely undistributed 'banned' issue*)

Fiction

The Eye of the Lens	Langdon Jones
Lib	Carol Emshwiller
Bug Jack Barron (3)	Norman Spinrad

181

April 1968
Vol. 52 No. 181
Cover by Dwoskin

182

July 1968
Vol. 52 No. 182
Cover by Moorcock (design Dwoskin)

Fiction

Scream	Giles Gordon
Drake Man Route	Brian W. Aldiss
Bug Jack Barron (5)	Norman Spinrad
Plastitutes	John Sladek
Methapyrilene Hydrochloride Sometimes Helps	Carol Emshwiller
The Circular Railway	John Calder
A Landscape of Shallows	Christopher Finch
Definitions	Bob Marsden

Poetry

Instructions for Visiting Earth	Christopher Logue
Two Voices	D.M. Thomas

Feature

Dr Moreau versus the Utopianists (1)	Brian Aldiss

Illustrations by Dean, Cuff, Gordon, Epps, Imrie, Vasseur, Cawthorn

183

October 1968
Vol. 52 No. 183
Cover by Dean

Fiction

Features

184

November 1968
Vol. 52 No. 184
Cover by Nasemann
(*Special 'New Writers' Issue. First M. John Harrison story*)

Fiction

185

December 1968
Vol. 52 No. 185
Cover by Nasemann
(*This issue largely pulped by distributors*)

186

January 1969
Vol. 52 No. 186
Cover by Nasemann
(*First A4 size issue: Moorcock publisher*)

Fiction

The Tank Trapeze	Michael Moorcock
Anxietal Register B	John T. Sladek
Epilogue for an Office Picnic	Harvey Jacobs
The Summer Cannibals	J.G. Ballard
Spiderweb	John Clute
Juan Fortune	Opal Nations
Ouspenski's Astrobahn	Brian W. Aldiss

Poetry

Hospital of Transplanted Hearts	D.M. Thomas

Criticism

The 1000 Wounds and Flowers	J.G. Ballard
John Cage's 'Silence'	Langdon Jones
Predictive Parameters	John Brunner
The Patsy	William Barclay
Buying Brutish	James Cawthorn
On 'Quicksand'	Thomas M. Disch
The Anthology Bag	Joyce Churchill

Illustrations by Dean, Nasemann, Platt, Jones, Haberfield

187

February 1969
Vol. 52 No. 187
Cover by Nasemann

Fiction

Poetry

Features

Illustrations by Nasemann, Platt, Peake, Prigann, etc.

188

March 1969
Vol. 52 No. 188
Cover by Nasemann

Fiction

189

Fiction

Poetry

Features

Illustrations by Dean, Nasemann, etc.

192

July 1969
Vol. 53. No. 192
Cover by Dean
(*Last of the 64-page issues*)

Fiction

Feature

193

194

Fiction

Poetry

Features

Illustrations by Dean, Peake, Nasemann, Platt

195

November 1969
Vol. 53 No. 195
Cover by Bayley

Fiction

196

December 1969
Vol. 53 No. 196
Cover by Lanyon

197

January 1970
Vol. 53 No. 197
Cover by Platt
(*Special '1980' issue*)

Fiction

Concentrate 3   Michael Butterworth
The Suicide Machines   Graham Charnock
Sending the Very Best   Ed Bryant
The Glass Teat   Harlan Ellison
The Nature of the Catastrophe   Michael Moorcock
The Nostalgia Story   M. John Harrison
Coitus 80   J.G. Ballard
198–, A Tale of Tomorrow   John Sladek
The Wind in the Snottygobble
   Tree (3)   Jack Trevor Story

Poetry

Two Poems, Six Letters   R. Glyn Jones
Baby Watson (1936-1980)   Hilary Bailey
Four Crosswords of Graded   Thomas M. Disch
   Difficulty

Features

The Secret of Holman Hunt   Brian W. Aldiss
What is the Nature of the Bead
   Game   Dr John Clark
Big Brother is Twenty-One   Joyce Churchill

Reviews

The Wireless School   M. John Harrison
Gonorrhoea and Logorrhoea   John Clute

Illustrations by Nasemann, Platt, Jones, Bayley, Hunter, Cawthorn, Zoline,
Cornwall

198

February 1970
Vol. 53 No. 198
Cover by Cornwall

Fiction

Journey Across a Crater	J.G. Ballard
Soul Fast	Gwyneth Cravens
6B 4C DD1 22	Michael Butterworth
The Bait Principle	M. John Harrison
The Wind in the Snottygobble Tree (conclusion)	Jack Trevor Story

Poetry

Apocrypha	D.M. Thomas
A Spot in the Oxidised Desert	Paul Green
A vid	James Sallis

Feature

Japan	Ian Watson

Illustrations by Bayley, Watson, Stephenson, Cornwall, Platt

199

March 1970
Vol. 53 No. 199
Cover by Platt

Fiction

The Sex Machine	Ian Watson
Agatha Blue	Hilary Bailey
Princess Margaret's Facelift	J.G. Ballard
Cinnabar Balloon Tautology	Bob Franklin

200

April 1970
Vol. 54 No. 200
Cover by Lanyon
(*Last monthly issue on general sale and Special 200th Issue*)

201

February/January 1971
Vol. 54 No. 201
Cover by Dietterlin
(*Special 'Good Taste Subscription Only' issue. Last in large format.*)

202

September 1971
Vol. 55 No. 202
Cover artist unknown
(*Simultaneous UK/US edition as* NWQ 1. *Contained some reprints from earlier issues.*)

Fiction

Angouleme	Thomas M. Disch
Journey across a Crater	J.G. Ballard
The Lamia and Lord Cromis	M. John Harrison
The Day We Embarked for Cythera	Brian W. Aldiss
Pemberly's Start-Afresh Calliope	
or, The New Proteus	John Sladek
The God House	Keith Roberts
Prisoners of Paradise	David Redd
The Short, Happy Wife of Mansard	
Eliot	John Sladek
A Place and a Time to Die	J.G. Ballard
Exit from City 5	B.J. Bayley

Features

A Literature of Comfort	M. John Harrison
The Authors	

Illustrations by Peake, Dean, Roberts, Jones, Vickers

203

December 1971
Vol. 55 No. 203
Cover artist unknown
(*Simultaneous UK/US edition as* NWQ 2. *Contained some reprints from earlier issues*)

Fiction

Monkey and Pru and Sal	Keith Roberts
No Direction Home	Norman Spinrad
The Meek	William Woodrow
The Causeway	M. John Harrison
The Four-Colour Problem	B.J. Bayley
Fifth Person Singular	Peter Tate
Listen, Love	George Zebrowski and Jack Dann
Feathers from the Wings of an Angel	Thomas M. Disch
Monitor Found in Orbit	Michael G. Coney
Pandora's Bust	Richard A. (later Rachel) Pollack
The Key of the Door	Arthur Sellings

Features

Visions of Hell	J.G. Ballard
Keeping Perspective	Michael Moorcock
By Tennyson Out of Disney	M. John Harrison

Illustrations by Roberts, Dean, Murrell, Jones.

204

March 1972
Vol. 55 No. 204
Cover artist unknown
(*Simultaneous UK/US edition as* NWQ 3. *No reprints*)

Fiction

The Machine in Shaft Ten	M. John Harrison
I Lose Medea	Keith Roberts
As for Our Fatal Continuity ...	Brian Aldiss
Julio 204	Pamela Sargent
The Wonderful World of Griswald Tractors	Thomas M. Disch
And Dug the Dog a Tomb	Laurence James
The Grain Kings	Keith Roberts

205

June 1972
Vol. 55 No. 205
Cover artist unknown
(*Simultaneous UK/US edition as* NWQ 4)

Fiction

Features

206

1973 (no month)
Cover by Roberts
(*Published in UK only as* NW5. *Breakdown of quarterly schedule*)

Fiction

The Crack	Emma Tennant
Some Rooms	Merle Kessler
Name (Please Print):	John Sladek
The Mammoth Hunters	David Redd
The Cake Chronicle	Michael Ahern
Me and my Antronoscope	Barrington Bayley
There Are No Banisters	Jack M. Dann
The Disinheriting Party	John Clute
Bill Gets Hep to God	John Sladek
Smack Run	Marta Bergstresser
The Only Man on Earth	Laurence James
The Trustie Tree	Keith Roberts
Flatland	John Sladek

Poetry

Sonoran Poems	D.M. Thomas
Walking Backwards	Philip Lopate
Ode to a Time Flower	Robert Calvert
The Assassination of the Mayor	Thomas M. Disch

Features

The Future on a Chipped Plate	Brian W. Aldiss
Family Literature	Charles Platt
Motivation Chart	Charles Platt
The Stars and Beyond on the Fabulous Anti-Syntax Drive	M. John Harrison
Shucksma	John Clute
The Authors	

Illustrations by Dean, Skellern, Cawthorn, Judith Clute, Roberts

207

Published 1973 (no month) as *NW6*
Published January 1974 in US as *No. 5*
Cover artist unknown
(*Jointly edited with Charles Platt*)

Fiction

Poetry

Features

No illustrations

208

1974 (no month)
Vol. 58 No. 208
NW 7 (UK)
NW 6 (USA)
Cover artist unknown
(*Edited by Hilary Bailey and Charles Platt*)

Fiction

Poetry

Features

Illustrations by Cawthorn, Cross, Zoline, Judith Clute, Sladek, Phyllida Peake

209

1975 (no month)
Vol. 58 No. 209
NW 8 (Not published in US)
Cover artist unknown
(*Hilary Bailey editor*)

Fiction

Poetry

Features

Mal Dean   Michael Moorcock
I Say Begone! Apotropaic Narcosis,
   I'm Going to Read the Damned
   Thing, Ha Ha   John Clute
Coming to Life   M. John Harrison

Illustrations by Dean, Jones, Rickards, Cawthorn, Francis

210

1975 (no month)
Vol. 58 No. 210
NW 9 (Not published in US)
Cover artist unknown

Fiction

The Ministry of Children   Keith Roberts
Ancient Shadows   Michael Moorcock
Daddy's Girl   Joanna Russ
The Hammer of Evil   John Sladek
Patagonia's Delicious Filling
   Station   Brian W. Aldiss
Maestro   Giles Gordon
The Illusionist   Giles Gordon
Narrative of Masks   Charles Partington
The Journal of Bodley Clive   Matthew Paris

Features

Sweet Analytics   M. John Harrison
Trope Exposure   John Clute

Illustrations by Roberts, Cawthorn, Clute, Jones

211

1976 (no month)
Vol. 58 No. 211
NW 10 (not published in US)
Cover artist unknown
(*Last paperback issue in this series*)

Fiction

Constant Fire	Michael Moorcock
The Boy	Bruce McAllister
As American As . . .	William Nabors
Christmas Story	Michael Butterworth
The Cabinet of Oliver Naylor	Barrington Bayley
Before She Started Packing, Strawberry	Chris Young
Kong	Adrian Eckersley
The Diary of the Translater	Geoff Ryman
A Tear in the Camera	Robert Meadley
Time Machine	Anna Ostrowska
In Love with Centaur and Roses	Peter Jobling
Mirror, Mirror on the Wall	Keith Roberts

Poetry

A Lazy Outpost	W.J. Watkins
The Naked and Transparent Man Gives Thanks	Robert Calvert

Features

The Eternal Invalid (parody)	Thomas M. Disch
A Date with the Hydra	Robert Meadley
Arthur C. Clarke's Clone	John Clute

212

Spring 1978
Vol. 60 No. 212
Cover by Moorcock (collage)
(*Mainly reprints by* NW *editorial team from* FRENDZ *newspaper, 1971*)

213

Summer 1978
Vol. 60 No. 213 (*beginning of irregular publication*)
Cover: Empire, Leicester Square, programme
(*Published by the* NW *Group*)

(This issue, the first of a new kind, contained a great deal of primarily visual material and the contents is a trifle difficult to list and to give credit, since much of it was the work of a group.

The printer, Charles Partington, had a great deal to do with making the issue possible; it was produced after he had offered to print it free. Distribution was limited to specialist shops and mail order.)

214

Autumn 1978
Vol. 60 No. 214
Cover (*Zenith the Albino in Novya Miri*) by Platt

Graphics by Judith Clute, Britton, Platt, Trevillion, Riches, Toomey, Arnold, Preston and others

*(This was not printed because the feminist typesetters refused to let it go through on moral and political grounds)

Appendix

Fan magazines

Novae Terrae was an amateur magazine edited by Maurice K. Hanson, with Arthur C. Clarke and William F. Temple as assistant editors. An official journal of the Science Fiction Association, it was first published in 1936 and lasted until February 1939, when it was replaced by *New Worlds*. The new editor was Ted Carnell (now known to the public as John or E.J. Carnell), with G. Ken Chapman (now an sf bookseller) as assistant editor. Associate editors were Hanson, Clarke, Frank Edward Arnold and Harold Kay. The first issue contained work by these writers as well as John Russell Fearn, J.F. Burke, Sam Moskowitz and others. *Novae Terrae* and *New Worlds*, though amateur magazines, were nevertheless considered to be the voice of new, young writers much given to criticism of the state of sf (particularly of the need to introduce more human interest) and of the poor quality of magazines. Both contained the early work – short stories, commentaries and so on – of most of the British sf writers who came to prominence after the war: John Beynon (Harris/Wyndham), Eric Frank Russell, and Dave McIlwain (Charles Eric Maine). There were also letters and other contributions from writers involved in US fanzines.

Publishers

New Worlds ceased publication in this form in August 1939. Plans to turn it into a professional sf magazine were shelved, and were not revived until after Arnold joined Pendulum Publications, editing several books and anthologies for them in 1945 and 1946. The first collection which Carnell edited for Pendulum was *Jin and Jitters*, an anthology of fantasy stories. When *New Worlds* was launched in April 1946 (as a substitute for the other titles) Carnell remained editor. When Pendulum collapsed, Carnell retained his rights to the title and a fan consortium formed Nova Publications which ran the magazine on a fairly irregular basis (quarterly and bi-monthly) until 1954 when Maclarens, a firm specialising in trade magazines, took Nova Publications over as a subsidiary. For the next ten years *New Worlds* appeared regularly from Maclarens, until 1964 when Roberts and Vinter took the magazine over and Carnell resigned as editor, recommending Michael Moorcock in his place. Roberts and Vinter published the magazine regularly until 1967 when a company formed by David Warburton and Michael Moorcock published it. In 1968 Stonehart were publishers for a brief period until Michael Moorcock became sole publisher. The paperback volumes were published by Sphere Books and Corgi Books respectively (Berkley and Avon in the US).

Sisters

Science Fantasy was first published in Summer 1950 (with Walter Gillings as editor) and eventually came to publish much of the best-known early work of J.G. Ballard, Brian W. Aldiss (whose first published story appeared there in 1954), Michael Moorcock, John Brunner and Thomas Burnett Swann. From 1951 it was edited by Carnell. The last issue edited by Carnell was No. 64 (April 1964) and contained the last episode of Moorcock's *Stormbringer* as well as *The Deep Fix* by 'James Colvin' (Carnell's choice of pseudonym taken from the *Railway Guide*) and the final article in a series called 'Aspects of Fantasy', wherein Moorcock bemoaned the collapse of the Nova magazines at a time when they were developing so many good writers. No. 65 (June-July) was bi-monthly, alternating with *New Worlds*, and edited by Kyril Bonfiglioli until August 1966 when Harry Harrison became editor. Keith Roberts as Associate Editor had a great deal to do with shaping the editorial policies of *Science Fantasy* and of contributing some of the best fiction published there during this phase. Both magazines became monthlies in 1965 as their circulations improved. Bonfiglioli changed the title to *SF Impulse* with the March 1966 issue and it ran under that title until it was absorbed into the March 1967 issue of *New Worlds*. Kyril Bonfiglioli is the author of several excellent comic thrillers, including *Something Nasty in the Woodshed* and *Don't Point that Thing at Me*.

Science Fiction Adventures was first published in January 1959 as the UK edition of the US magazine started in 1953 and originally edited by Lester del Ray, then by Larry Shaw. It specialised in long novellas, many of which completely contradicted its title, and ran until May 1963, although the original US magazine had long-since collapsed. Among many other excellent and innovative stories, it ran J.G. Ballard's *The Drowned World* (No. 24). It was edited by John Carnell throughout its British publication period.

Developments

Whilst running the Nova Magazines, John Carnell became an agent for (at one time) most of the well-known British and American sf writers. The E.J. Carnell Literary Agency was continued after his death by his long-time friend and associate Leslie Flood, one of the founders of Nova Publications and a regular contributor of reviews to *New Worlds*. Leslie Flood's shop in Sicilian Avenue was for many years the main source of good science fiction in England, as well as a meeting place for most of the people involved in sf during the 1950s and 1960s.

Nova Publications also published a *Nova Science Fiction Novels* series beginning with John Beynon's (John Beynon Harris/Wyndham) *Stowaway to Mars* and Malcolm Jameson's *Bullard of the Space Patrol* (both books were essentially juveniles) in 1953. Later books (remarkable for their design which, at the time, was much in advance of any paperback sf) included *The City in the Sea* by Wilson Tucker, *The Weapon Shops of Isher* by A.E. van Vogt, *The Dreaming Jewels* by Theodore Sturgeon and *Jack of Eagles* by James Blish. The series failed through inadequate distribution. All the books were bought on the editorial decision of John Carnell who also advised other publishers on sf. Later he advised Tony Richardson, then an editor at Penguin, on a good many of the Penguin sf titles, although it had been Brian Aldiss with his *Penguin SF* series who had had much to do with the improvement of the science fiction image during the mid-sixties. Carnell was a strong publicist of British sf and had been since before the war when his fan-magazine editorials had annoyed the old-guard of the day. He came to be regarded in the United States as the chief representative of a specifically British school and, as an agent, succeeded in publishing many British writers (including J.G. Ballard, Michael Moorcock and James White) there for the first time.

During the mid-sixties, Michael Moorcock started an sf list for Compact Books (then the publishers of *New Worlds*). The series included a number of Moorcock's own early sf titles published for the first time (*The Deep Fix, The Fireclown, The Sundered Worlds, The Twilight Man*) and included the first book publication of Charles Harness's *The Rose*, Thomas M. Disch's *102 H-Bombs*, John Brunner's *No Other Gods But Me*, Kenneth Bulmer's *The Demons* and Dan Morgan's *The Richest Corpse in Show Business*. The series also included paperback editions of Arthur Sellings' *Time Trap*, Judith Merril's *Shadow on the Hearth* (revised), Kenneth Harker's *The Symmetrians* and L. Sprague de Camp's *A Planet Called Krishna* and *The Floating Continent*. As advisor to publishers during this period, Moorcock helped to publish the work of new writers – Disch, Zelazny, Delany, Russ, Sladek, Spinrad, Jones, Sallis among others – in book form. As well, he publicised the work of Americans such as Philip K. Dick who at that time were scarcely known to the British public. Similarly, Charles Platt, as an editor in the US, promoted the work of British authors including J.G. Ballard, M. John Harrison, Hilary Bailey and Barrington Bayley, as well as the work of young Americans (such as Ed Bryant and James Sallis) associated with *New Worlds*. Anthologies by various of these writers – Bryant, Sallis, Sprinrad and (notably) Thomas M. Disch – displayed literary preferences first found in *New Worlds*. Another great publicist for British writers in the US was Judith Merril. An anthology by Judith Merril with the euphoric (and horrifying) title of *England Swings SF* was published in the US in the late sixties and contained work primarily drawn from *New Worlds* and *SF Impulse*. Miss Merril also tended to draw her inspiration from what she termed the British 'new thing' in her last *Years Best SF* volumes. These definitions – 'new wave' and so on – were given to *New Worlds* writers by US publicists in the 60s and 70s but the term (as usual) was never used by the writers and editors themselves (except ironically or in retrospect). Harlan Ellison also drew inspiration for his seminal *Dangerous Visions* original anthologies from what was happening in Britain and Terry Carr was similarly inspired to produce his *Ace SF Special* series, which published the best work of many now-popular writers such as Joanna Russ and Ursula K. Le Guin.

The aims and ideas of the various American publicists were never quite the same as those of their British counterparts. The US 'new wave' tended to concentrate on 'tabu-breaking' in terms of the commercial magazine policies of the day and as such was part of the general movement in the US towards liberalism. The British *New Worlds* writers tended to concentrate on specific kinds of literary development, producing a laconic, richly textured fiction which had something in common with developments in poetry during the late nineteenth and early twentieth centuries but possessed rather more sophisticated subject matter. It can be seen as a romantic reaction to the classical and realistic tendencies of imaginative fiction as discovered in writers as different, say, as Heinlein, Clarke or Wyndham – as well as a general reaction against the moribund naturalistic novel.

Anthologies

A variety of anthologies drawn from (or chiefly from) *New Worlds* edited by John Carnell or Michael Moorcock have appeared over the years. A series of *Best SF Stories from New Worlds* (Nos 1-8) was published by Panther Books between 1967 and 1974 and are now out of print. These were edited by

Michael Moorcock and drew largely on material published in the Moorcock-edited magazine. While it has not been thought worth listing all anthology contents, it has seemed worthwhile to list two drawn from the Carnell period, one drawn from both periods, and one which was not directly drawn from *New Worlds* but which was an 'off-shoot' original anthology edited by *NW* Associate Editor Langdon Jones.

THE BEST FROM NEW WORLDS
First published by Boardman Books, 1955
Edited by John Carnell

Contents

Introduction	John Wyndham
Foreword	John Carnell
The Hard Way	Alan Barclay
Crossfire	James White
Jetsam	A. Bertram Chandler
Rockets Aren't Human	E.C. Tubb
Ship from the Stars	Peter Hawkins
Robots Don't Bleed	J.W. Groves
The Broken Record	J.T. M'Intosh
Unknown Quantity	Peter Phillips

LAMBDA ONE AND OTHER STORIES
First published by Penguin Books, 1965
Edited by John Carnell

Contents

Introduction	John Carnell
Lambda One	Colin Kapp
Tee Vee Man	H.A. Hargreaves
Beyond the Reach of Storms	Donald Malcolm
Quest	Lee Harding
All Laced Up	George Whitley
Routine Exercise	Philip E. High
Flux	Michael Moorcock
The Last Salamander	John Rackham

THE BEST OF NEW WORLDS
First published by Compact Books, 1965
Edited by Michael Moorcock

Contents

Introduction	Michael Moorcock
The Pit My Parish	Brian W. Aldiss
Tableau	James White
Another Word for Man	Robert Presslie
I See You	Harry Harrison
The Outstretched Hand	Arthur Sellings
The Railways Up on Cannis	Colin Kapp
The Time Dweller	Michael Moorcock
The Terminal Beach	J.G. Ballard
The Traps of Time	John Baxter
The Last Lonely Man	John Brunner
The Fall of Frenchy Steiner	Hilary Bailey
New Experience	E.C. Tubb
I Remember, Anita ...	Langdon Jones
The Mountain	James Colvin
All The King's Men	B.J. Bayley

THE NEW SF
First published by Hutchinson, 1969
Edited by Langdon Jones

Contents

Preface	Michael Moorcock
Fourteen Stations on the Northern Line	Giles Gordon
The Peking Junction	Michael Moorcock
Fast Car Wash	George MacBeth
The Anxiety in the Eyes of the Cricket	James Sallis
The New Science Fiction	J.G. Ballard and George MacBeth
So Far from Prague	Brian W. Aldiss
Direction	Charles Platt
Postatomic	Michael Butterworth

For Thomas Tompion	Michael Moorcock
A Science Fiction Story for Joni Mitchell	Maxim Jakubowski
The Communicants	John Sladek
Seeking a Suitable Donor	D.M. Thomas
The Holland of the Mind	Pamela Zoline
Quincunx	Thomas M. Disch

New Writings in SF, edited by John Carnell and published in paperback by Corgi Books, was a direct continuation of John Carnell's editorial policies in *New Worlds*. These ran for 21 numbers until John Carnell died suddenly, aged 60, in 1972. The series was taken over by Kenneth Bulmer who has edited it very much in the Carnell tradition.

Foreign editions of *New Worlds* and of the *New Worlds* anthologies have appeared in many languages (notably the rather strange Japanese '*NW*' which borrowed heavily from *New Worlds* without acknowledgement) including French, Spanish, German, Portuguese, Italian, Danish, Japanese, Czech and Hungarian.

The Savoy Book, edited by David Britton and Michael Butterworth and containing work by M. John Harrison, Heathcote Williams, Harlan Ellison and a number of other writers and artists associated with *New Worlds*, is a conscious attempt on the part of the editors to carry on the 'tradition' of the Moorcock-edited magazine.